"Kill the Harlot!"

Shouting in a frenzy of blood lust, the crowd seized the half-naked girl. Rahab, an Armorite woman, had dared to love a Hebrew warrior.

Wounded in a dozen places, Rahab cried in agony the name of her beloved—Joshua—who was marshaling the forces of Israel in the surrounding hills.

THE SCARLET CORD
was originally published by
Doubleday & Company, Inc.

Other books by Frank G. Slaughter

Air Surgeon
Battle Surgeon
Buccaneer Surgeon
The Curse of Jezebel
David: Warrior and King
Daybreak
The Deadly Lady of Madagascar
Doctors' Wives
East Side General
Epidemic!
Fort Everglades
God's Warrior
The Golden Ones
The Healer
In a Dark Garden
The Land and the Promise
Lorena
A Savage Place
Spencer Brade, M.D.
Storm Haven
Surgeon, U.S.A.
Sword and Scalpel
That None Should Die
Tomorrow's Miracle
A Touch of Glory

Published by Pocket Books

Frank G. Slaughter

The Scarlet Cord

PUBLISHED BY POCKET BOOKS NEW YORK

THE SCARLET CORD

Doubleday edition published February, 1956

Pocket Book edition published July, 1957

5th printing............July, 1970

This *Pocket Book* edition includes every word
contained in the original, higher-priced edition. It is printed
from brand-new plates made from completely reset, clear, easy-to-read
type. *Pocket Book* editions are published by Pocket Books, a division
of Simon & Schuster, Inc., 630 Fifth Avenue, New York, N.Y. 10020.
Trademarks registered in the United States and other countries.

L

Acknowledgment

The author wishes to acknowledge his indebtedness to *The Story of Civilization* by Will Durant (Simon and Schuster) for the text of the Song of Ikhnaton and other poems of ancient Egypt that appear in this novel. He is also indebted to *Daily Life in Bible Times* by Albert Edward Bailey (Charles Scribner's Sons) for the details of Baal worship appearing in the text and the description of the water tunnel of Megiddo. To the other hundreds of references consulted in the writing of this novel, he owes most of the details given concerning the fascinating civilizations existing circa 1250 B.C., as well as to the Old Testament, from which came the original story of Joshua, Salmon, Caleb, and Rahab, the harlot of Jericho.

—FRANK G. SLAUGHTER

Jacksonville, Florida
May 20, 1955

Behold, when we come into the land, you shall bind this scarlet cord in the window through which you let us down. . . .

If any one goes out of the doors of your house into the street, his blood shall be upon his head, and we shall be guiltless; but if a hand is laid upon any one who is with you in the house, his blood shall be on our head.

Joshua 2:18–19

Contents

The
Scarlet
Cord

Book One

~~~~~~

*And Sihon would not suffer Israel to pass through
his border . . . And Israel smote him with the edge
of the sword, and possessed his land . . .*

NUMBERS 21:23–24

~~~~~~

One

ALL DAY LONG the young woman standing in the
mouth of the cave had watched the battle raging upon the
plain and along the small valleys and ravines opening into it.
The cave was located halfway up the mountain, its mouth
just above a sparkling spring that gushed from the rocks and
painted a swath of green where its waters tumbled down the
steep slope. From the broad ledge before the cave's mouth
she could watch every exciting detail of the bitter conflict
raging about the foot of the mountain.

Upon the summit of this mountain—called Nebo by the
Amorites, in whose land it towered above plain and lesser
hills—was a temple to the great god Baal. The rude structure
of stone was served by a half dozen wild-eyed priests who
gashed themselves with knives of flint and bronze in the
orgies of Baal worship during the ritual feasts of autumn and
spring and on the occasions when the high priest from the
great temple in the city of Heshbon to the north visited the
lesser domiciles of his god.

Being only the home of a lesser deity—variously called Yah,
Yahu, and by some simply El—the cave on the slope of
Mount Nebo saw few worshipers, however. None had come
this day while Rahab, keeper of the Cave of Yah, watched
upon the hillside.

In truth, the men of King Sihon's domain had little time

1

for gods today, save to gasp out a prayer for help as they fought with the fierce invaders from the south called Habiru, who justified this outright invasion of the Amorite lands with the astounding claim that their god had given them this whole region, plus the land of Canaan across the river, for their own.

Small wonder, then, that Sihon, King of the Amorites, had treated the Habiru emissaries with contempt when they had arrogantly demanded passage through his kingdom. He had cut off one hand of each according to the Egyptian custom, and sent them howling back to the goatskin tents from which they had come.

The Amorites were a peaceful people, established for generations upon the fertile land along the east bank of the river called Jord—which means "to flow down." The river was well named indeed, for on its way southward from the lakes in the shadow of snow-capped Mount Hermon to the sea that knows no life, the stream tumbled many thousands of cubits.

Naturally the Amorites had not looked favorably upon the motley aggregation of ragged, wild-eyed nomads from the south. They were clad in goatskin tunics with rough skin sandals on their feet—if they were not barefoot—and armed with spears, bows and arrows, slings for throwing stones, and rough skin shields reinforced with strips of bronze. It was obviously absurd for such a people to take the battlefield against the Egyptian-trained troops of Sihon of Heshbon, whose chariots were armed with murderously sharp scythe blades, capable of shearing off a man's legs at full gallop without checking. Nor could the rough arms of the invaders expect to oppose shields of metal and officers' swords forged of bronze by artisans taught their skill by the Hittite smiths to the north.

A few Egyptian mercenaries were also among the troops of Sihon, giant black-skinned Nubians and hawk-faced Sherdans. The generals of Pharaoh, who ruled this part of the world from his palace at Thebes on the Nile, a full month's journey distant, saw to it that a hard core of their own troops always formed a nucleus for the armies of each of the subject kings. Actually, this precaution was as much an insurance that the kings themselves would remain loyal, as to protect them against invasion from without.

2

A great rebellion of vassal kings throughout Canaan and Syria had occurred not many years before, at the climax of the Pharaoh Ikhnaton's ill-fated attempt to make all Egypt worship one god. It had been put down by the great General Harmhab in a lightning campaign through Canaan and Syria, and most of the subject kings had taken the bloody lesson to heart. They were reasonably loyal now, although always ready to bilk their Egyptian master whenever the occasion arose.

As Rahab had seen demonstrated today, King Sihon had badly underestimated the caliber of the invaders. On the plain below, where the Amorites had expected to fight, their Egyptian chariots would indeed have been murderous, the scythes cutting down the invaders like the grain of the field. Had the battle gone as planned, it would have lasted only a little while.

The Habiru, however, seemed to be familiar with this kind of fighting. They had deployed on the plain in battle formation at the beginning of the conflict, but the appearance of the chariots had seemed to terrify them. Without even engaging the Amorites, they had broken into headlong flight toward the maze of valleys and gullies through which dozens of small creeks tumbled down to the River Jord. There, it developed, the rest of the Habiru warriors had been waiting. Falling upon the chariots with the high-pitched keening cry that seemed to be their war chant, the invaders had smashed them in the narrow defiles where the clumsy vehicles were at a disadvantage. Only when the chariots were out of commission did the invaders pour down upon the plain to attack the footmen of Sihon.

Even then the advantage had been with the Amorites, the ragged men from the desert country to the south being still outnumbered, at least two to one. But they seemed to be fired by a fanatic zeal which quickly reversed the odds. Throughout most of the day—as Rahab watched from her vantage point before the Cave of Yah—the tide of battle had been going against the Amorites. Now the center of fighting had moved northward as Sihon's troops retreated, almost as far as the gates of Heshbon itself, visible in the distance with its white walls and buildings shining in the afternoon sunlight.

3

Again and again Rahab had seen a tall man with a compact sinewy body and a leonine mane of black hair leading the Habiru into battle. He stood out even in the midst of the fighting, laying about him with the short sword he carried, or stabbing with a long-handled bronze-pointed spear, obviously inspiring his comrades to redoubled efforts by the very fire of his own zeal.

It had been easy for the girl to follow the Habiru captain's progress during the ever-changing pattern of the fighting below as the day wore on. Wherever the thickest of the battle was, there she could distinguish his tall body in its short goatskin tunic, bronze-studded shield, and copper helmet.

She had not seen him for over an hour, though, and was beginning to wonder if something had happened to him. No young woman could have failed to be impressed by the sturdy handsomeness of the Habiru captain, for he would have stood out as a natural leader anywhere, even among the men of King Og of Bashan to the north, said to be a giant whose bed was twice as long as the height of an average man.

Slender, graceful, and quick, with mobile features, a generous mouth, and warm brown eyes, Rahab possessed a quiet loveliness, in keeping with the character of the deity she served. Yah was the god of wisdom, kindness, and brotherly love among the Amorites. And since the people of the outlying villages were for the most part farmers and shepherds, they found more satisfaction in such a god than in the warlike Baal who dwelt in the temple of Heshbon—except in times of danger such as this, when a man naturally looked to a deity of violence and bloodshed.

Earlier in the day, while the battle had raged back and forth on the plain and in the minor gorges and valleys opening into it, Rahab had been concerned lest the Habiru attack her own village of Medeba, which lay about a mile beyond the foot of the mountain, beside another spring. But the invaders seemed intent upon destroying the armies of King Sihon, although according to the custom of victorious armies the world over, unrestrained pillaging would certainly come later.

Once Rahab had even started down the mountain toward Medeba, hoping to bring her father, Chazan, back to the Cave of Yah for safety until the fighting was over. But a

4

surge of the battle had swirled between her and the town before she could reach it, and she had been forced to turn back to the refuge of the god for sanctuary. Now, as she watched the defeat of the Amorites, her lovely features were drawn with concern for her father and her friends in Medeba.

Rahab was a lovely picture as she stood in the afternoon sunlight against the rocks before the mouth of the cave. The sun made a coppery golden aureole of her hair and highlighted the planes of her face, with its high cheekbones and slender high-bridged nose, heritages of beauty from a hundred generations of a people who had come to this fertile land from the valley of the Tigris and Euphrates long ago, under the patriarch called Abram.

Many of the descendants of Abram had been carried into Egypt when the Hyksos invaders from the north had swept into that most ancient of lands generations before, to wrest control from the weakest in a long dynasty of Pharaohs. It was even rumored among the Amorites—where many descendants of Abram dwelt in peace—that these new invaders, known as Habiru to the dwellers upon the eastern side of the Jord Valley, were likewise descendants of this same Abram. It was also told—although few believed the story—that the newcomers had escaped from the slave drivers of Pharaoh and made their way across the great desert wilderness areas of Sin and Paran into the region of the great smoking mountain, even as far as Ezion-geber at the head of the Gulf of Aqabah. Thence it was reported they had traveled east of the Salt Sea and the King's Highway leading to the great cities of Ashtaroth and Damascus, which lay north of the domain of King Sihon.

Such a thing hardly seemed likely to Rahab, however, as she watched the fierceness of these same Habiru in war. For the descendants of Abram who lived with the Amorites—as well as among the other peoples of Canaan and in the lands west of the River Jord and the Salt Sea—were for the most part like her father and herself, artisans, scribes, or shepherds, devoted to more gentle pursuits than those of war. And robber bands—particularly a group called the Sa Gaz from the desert lands to the east—were always harassing the peace-loving Amorites and their neighbors to the south, the Moabites and the Edomites.

5

Educated in the Akkadian school for scribes at Byblos—there was one of these schools in almost every large city in this area, for Egypt demanded many scribes to keep the multitudinous records required by the overseers of Pharaoh—Rahab's father, Chazan, had served at Heshbon for many years, keeping records for the Egyptian taxgatherers and recording the expenses of the mercenaries garrisoned there by the armies of Egypt. He had moved to the village of Medeba near the foot of Mount Nebo only a few years ago, preferring the simple life of an Amorite village to that of the capital city.

In Medeba, Chazan had bought a house which served also as an inn for travelers along the King's Highway. And here he performed—far more happily than he had ever kept the intricate records of the Egyptian taxgatherers—the functions of a village scribe. On sheets of papyrus when he could get them from Egypt, or on tablets of clay that were later baked to the hardness of brick in the village kiln, he had inscribed the few legal documents required by the people of such a village.

Most of all, Chazan and his daughter had been happy to be near a sanctuary devoted to the worship of their god Yah. According to a tradition dating back centuries before, Yah had been brought by Abram from the great city of Ur Kasdim, whose glories were said to outshine all, save only those of Egypt itself.

At her father's feet, Rahab had learned to write the intricate Akkadian script that served as a common legal language throughout the domains of Egypt. And since her father dealt with the Egyptians and knew their language, she had naturally learned that tongue also.

Most of all, however, Rahab loved to spend her time fashioning exquisite little statuettes of clay and baking them in the kiln. These she would paint with bright colors she had learned to mix herself from the pigments of plants and colored earths and from the purple shellfish brought sometimes by traders from Tyre and Sidon and from Byblos, on the coast of the Great Sea.

In Byblos, it was said, skilled weavers had learned to fashion cloth so light and thin as to be practically transparent. The caravan drivers who often stopped at the inn on their way to and from the cities of Egypt along the King's Highway swore that Egyptian women of high degree often dressed in garments of such cloth, exposing their whole bodies to the gaze of men, without even a narrow strip wound about their loins, such as Amorite women wore under even their heaviest dresses. These tales Rahab could hardly believe, however, since it was indecent and a mockery for a woman to expose her body and stir the lusts of men.

Already Rahab knew something about the passions of men. Of all the young women of Medeba, she was by far the most beautiful. And since her father kept an inn, she came more in contact with strangers than did the others. Rather than parry the clumsy advances of the travelers and listen to their frank comments on her loveliness and the desire it stirred within them, she preferred to spend much of her time, when the caravans stopped to trade at Medeba, in the Cave of Yah upon the side of Mount Nebo.

In the cave she kept clay and paints and could model to her heart's content, letting her fancies roam and her thoughts give themselves expression in the soft clay beneath her fingers. Often she stayed there for days at a time, sleeping on a couch in the cave and cooking her food over the fire she kept burning for any who might wish to sacrifice. And since it was known to be the sanctuary of a god, she had no fear of being molested.

Even while she had been watching the battle on the plains below today, Rahab's fingers had worked with the clay as they often did, almost without volition. Now, with the noises of the fighting dying away to the north, she glanced down at the board on which she had been modeling, and a sudden warmth arose in her breast, sending a flush to her cheeks and a bright light to her dark brown eyes. Quite unconsciously her busy fingers had modeled in miniature the tall, handsome captain of the Habiru whose progress through today's battle she had been watching so eagerly, proving how much he had captured her thoughts and her attention.

A noise on the slope below the mouth of the cave suddenly brought Rahab's attention back to the present. Alarmed by the thought that some of the Habiru soldiers might be hunting stragglers on the mountainside, she sprang to her feet and hid behind a rock at the mouth of the cave, from which she still had a full view of the tree-girt slope below. It was late for anyone to be making a sacrifice to Yah now; people were concerned today with affairs more within the premise of Baal, with battle and bloodshed, plunder and lust. Yah's virtues would be needed badly tomorrow, when the victors impressed their will upon the vanquished.

The sound of men's voices came to Rahab's ears now, although she could not see them yet. Prudence dictated the wisdom of not revealing her presence, however, until she was sure of the newcomers' identity, so she stayed behind the rock.

While she watched, Rahab heard a man curse and grunt, as if bearing a heavy burden. Shortly two Habiru soldiers came into view, carrying a third upon a rude litter fashioned from two goatskins stretched between poles. Behind them stumbled a slender man who limped a little. Over his shoulder he carried a goatskin bag, and a small bottle of earthenware hung from his belt, evidently for carrying wine or water.

The man on the litter was wounded; a large circular stain was slowly spreading across his back, soaking his goatskin tunic. But Rahab recognized him nevertheless—it was the captain she had been watching throughout the battle, the handsome man who had been in the thick of the fighting and whose heroic figure in miniature she had modeled from clay.

Two

FORGETTING that to these people she was an Amorite, and therefore an enemy, Rahab left the cave and ran down the hillside toward the spring before which the litter-bearers had laid down their burden. The slender man with the goatskin bag was kneeling beside his wounded comrade, but when one of the soldiers gave a grunt of surprise at seeing a lovely girl emerge from the cave, he jumped to his feet and snapped a command. Instantly the soldiers lifted their weapons and faced toward the slope down which Rahab was running. At their threatening manner she stopped, suddenly afraid.

8

"From whence did you come, girl?" the slender man demanded. His eyes were wary and his wiry body tense. What surprised her most, however, was the fact that the tongue he spoke was understandable to her, being quite similar to that spoken by the people in this region who claimed descent from the patriarch Abram.

"I was in the cave up there," Rahab explained, pointing toward the mouth of the Cave of Yah above them. "It is the sanctuary of a god."

"Are you alone?"

"Yes. I wait upon those who worship Yah."

A puzzled look came into the wiry man's eyes. "What did you say was the name of this god?"

"Yah——"

He looked down at the wounded man and back at Rahab. "If this is the place of a god, you must have fire inside the cave."

"Yes. I keep one burning for the sacrifice."

"Is the cave roomy and dry?"

"Yes." She realized now what was in his mind. "But you cannot use it."

"Why not?"

"Yah is not a god of war. He teaches wisdom and kindness and understanding."

"My friend is wounded," the slender man said crisply. "Wisdom tells me he must be treated at once. And kindness says a warm, dry cave is better for a wounded man than the open. If your god is as understanding as you say he is, he will welcome us."

Without waiting for her to answer, he turned to the litter-bearers and barked a command. He carried no golden whip of authority, as did the officers in the Amorite army, but the men obeyed him without question. Picking up the litter, they carried it up the slope and into the cave.

Rahab followed them inside and saw the slender man look around him with a quick, appraising glance. A smile softened his features for a moment when he saw the row of figurines on a rocky shelf and a frieze depicting the story of Yah and his works, which she had painted on a flat section of rock making up one wall of the cave.

"This will do very well," he approved, and went to steady

9

the litter while the bearers placed the wounded man on the low couch covered with skins where Rahab slept when she spent the night in the cave. With the same brisk air of assurance and command he directed one of the soldiers to stand guard outside the opening of the cave and sent the other to bring water from the spring. He nodded with approval again when he saw the cooking pots and the small supply of staple foods that Rahab kept in the cave.

"What is your name?" he asked crisply.

"I am called Rahab. My home is in Medeba."

"My name is Salmon," he told her. "And this is Joshua, captain of a hundred in our army. He is badly wounded."

"I have been watching him most of the day," Rahab admitted, blushing a little. "He is indeed a mighty warrior."

"None is greater in all of Israel. What is this?" He picked up the board on which was the tiny clay figure of Joshua which she had modeled as she watched the battle surge back and forth on the plain before her.

"I did that this morning," she explained, blushing.

"I have seen none better, even in Egypt," he said. "You are an artist!"

Rahab flushed with pleasure at the compliment. "Your friend will need a leech," she said. "I could go to Medeba for help."

"And bring your friends back to kill us?" Salmon demanded sharply. "King Sihon would give a hundred men to destroy the one who lies before you. Build up the fire," he ordered as he knelt beside the couch. "I am a physician."

"But Yah——"

"If he is a god of kindness, as you say," he told her crisply, "he will be glad to have his sacred fire used to save the life of a man. Build it up quickly, girl."

Rahab put fresh wood on the fire upon the stone altar— the smoke rose by way of a narrow shaft leading up through the roof to the rocky mountainside above the cave's mouth. Salmon busied himself cutting away Joshua's bloodstained clothing, using a bronze knife with a thinner and sharper blade than she had ever seen before.

The wound came into view as the physician cut away the tunic, a jagged furrow across the muscles of the shoulder and back, exposing a rib in its depths. Projecting from the lower

10

corner was the broken shaft of an arrow, the head apparently firmly embedded in the wounded man's body. It was a horrible wound, all matted with blood. Rahab felt herself grow a little faint at the sight of it and turned quickly away.

"Will he die?" she asked tremulously.

"Heroes are made of tough metal." Salmon did not look up. "The wound is deep, but it will heal in time, even with the ribs exposed. I must first remove the arrowhead embedded in the bone of his back and cleanse the wound with fire."

"With fire?" she gasped.

"Your people poison their arrows with the juices of putrid meat. The poisons must be killed with fire."

The soldier who had gone for water had left his spear in the cave. Picking it up, Salmon carefully examined the point, a long blade of bronze with flat sides.

"This should do," he said as if to himself. Wiping the spear on his tunic, he handed it to Rahab. "Heat the spearhead until it glows," he directed.

Obediently she placed the head of the weapon in the center of the now briskly burning flames.

"Do you have any wine?" Salmon asked.

"A little."

"Bring it to me. Joshua will need it before this is over."

Rahab brought the wine in a jug of fired clay. When the physician knelt to lift his friend's head, she saw that his movements were skilled and gentle, in spite of his brusqueness of speech and manner.

"Joshua," he called. "Wake up. Here is wine."

The wounded man slowly opened his eyes. "Am I dying, Salmon?" he asked.

Salmon smiled, and all the harshness went out of his face. Surprised by the change, Rahab almost dropped the wine jar. "I will not let the Amorites boast of slaying the champion of Israel this day," the physician said. "With my skill and this young woman's wine, you will be healed before it is time to fight again."

"The battle goes well then?"

"The forces of Sihon flee, and the hosts of Israel pursue them. A cowardly bowman of this young woman's people

11

shot from ambush and struck you, but he will wound no others."

"Is it cowardly to protect our country from invaders?" Rahab cried indignantly. "I saw your friend kill at least ten Amorites today."

"Better say a hundred," Salmon agreed matter-of-factly as he held the wine jug to the wounded man's lips. "But Joshua fought in the open and did not shoot men in the back from hiding places among the rocks."

The Habiru captain drank deeply and lay back, his face white from pain and loss of blood. "The Amorites are brave men, Salmon," he said. "They had the right to wound me if they could. My sword tasted enough of their blood this day, as the girl says." He turned his head to look at Rahab, and his eyes widened.

And well they might, for she made a picture of extraordinary beauty in the light from the dancing flames of the fire on the stone altar. The day was warm, and she had put aside the cloak she wore as an outer garment. Her robe of soft light cloth was draped to leave one lovely arm and shoulder bare and reveal the virginal whiteness of her skin. The rest of her body was completely covered down to her slender ankles, and her feet were encased in graceful sandals of leather bound with thongs and tooled with an intricate beadwork. But modest though it was, and in excellent taste, her robe did not hide the grace and loveliness of her slender figure.

"By the altars of Baal!" Joshua said admiringly. "You are exceedingly fair, young woman. I have seen none such among the Amorites."

"I am not an Amorite," Rahab said quickly, blushing a little under the frankly appraising stare of the handsome Habiru in the bloodstained tunic. But she was not offended; no woman would be when told she was beautiful by such a handsome man.

"You cannot deceive us with lies, girl," Salmon warned. "The bleeding stumps of our ambassadors, who asked only the right of passage along the King's Highway, cry out the crimes of your people."

"I really am not an Amorite," Rahab protested. "We have dwelt in this land for many generations, but my people came

12

long ago from Ur Kasdim in the valley between the great rivers."

"Did they follow one whose name was Abram?" Joshua asked quickly.

"Why, yes. How did you know?"

"You must be the same people as we are, of the tribes who did not go down into Egypt."

"Drink again," Salmon ordered, holding the wine bottle to Joshua's lips. "You will need it before I am through."

Joshua drank obediently. To Rahab it seemed strange that such a great warrior obeyed one so obviously inferior to him in physical prowess. Salmon was almost slight of build, although wiry and obviously strong. His features were cleanly but delicately cut, his forehead high and his head narrow, somewhat like an Egyptian. He had the same jutting nose as the other Habiru whom Rahab had seen, however, although to a lesser degree. And when he moved about the cave, everything he did seemed purposeful and practiced, as if he knew exactly what he was doing at all times.

"If the girl is one of us, Salmon," said Joshua, "there must be others in this region. Surely they will want to help us, since our forefathers were the same."

"You have only her word that she is of our own people," Salmon reminded him. "The words of women are a deceit and a mockery. Who should know that better than the son of Nun?"

The two were speaking in their own tongue, but Rahab had already discovered that she knew many of the words, so she understood what they were saying. "I speak truth," she cried indignantly. "Why should I lie to you?"

"I don't know," Salmon said matter-of-factly. "But be sure I will find out if you are. Look to the spear, Rahab. Does it glow yet from the flames?"

She lifted the spearhead from the fire for him to examine. It was smoking, but the metal was not yet red.

"Leave it in the fire a little longer," he directed. "We will use that cloth hanging there for a bandage." He nodded toward the back of the cave, where a fine cloth woven by Rahab's own hands hung before the inner sanctum of the god. "Mine have been used up."

"Not that one," Rahab cried. "It hides the holy place of

13

Yah." Hers was a wise and understanding god, but even the most tolerant of deities, she was sure, would be offended at such a sacrilege.

"An image?" Salmon asked.

"Yah will have no images. It is forbidden by his teachings."

"How do you know these things, girl?" Joshua asked. "Are they written down?"

"They have been told from father to son since the time of Abram," Rahab explained. "My father says they are written in the hearts of those who love Yah."

"Your father must be a learned man."

"None is more learned in Medeba than Chazan," Rahab said proudly. "Or wiser."

"Have you anything else I can use for bandaging the wound?" Salmon inquired.

"Only a strip of linen I was going to make into a head-dress," she said a little reluctantly. It was a fine piece of cloth from Egypt that she had bought only a few days before from a caravan traveling along the King's Highway.

"Hair like yours should not be covered," the wiry man said, startling her with the compliment. "Give it to me and I will repay you from my share of the plunder from King Sihon's palace."

Rahab brought the piece of linen from where she had hidden it in a crevice among the rocks. It was white and soft in texture.

"It is indeed a fine fabric," Salmon approved, drawing the cloth between slender and sensitive fingers. "Fit to bind the wounds of him who will one day be leader of all Israel."

"I am but one among the captains of a hundred, Salmon," Joshua corrected, but Rahab saw that he was pleased by the physician's words. "Do not place me higher than I am."

"I but gave you a title you deserve. Tomorrow you will lead a thousand, and the next day ten thousand."

Joshua smiled at Rahab. The wine he had drunk was already beginning to glaze his eyes a little. "All physicians are braggarts," he told her. "The pain they cause others makes them feel powerful."

"Would that I had berries from the poppy plant to crush in the wine and relieve the pain," Salmon said. "Perhaps we will find that and the other drugs I need in King Sihon's palace at Heshbon." He opened his goatskin bag and began to lay out upon a flat stone the medicaments he carried inside it. They were pitifully few in number, as were the instruments of his trade.

In addition to the few drugs, he brought out a second bronze knife like the one he had used to slit Joshua's goatskin tunic. Beside it he placed a heavier knife of bronze with a toothed edge and a fairly long handle. Noticing Rahab's glance on the strange tool, Salmon said matter-of-factly, "The large one is for cutting bone. I had it from a merchant of Babylon in return for curing him of a fever."

Rahab shuddered, but she found that she was already becoming accustomed to the sight of blood, perhaps because of the calm way Salmon approached sickness and injury. In fact, it almost seemed as if he believed such things came from definite causes instead of—as everyone well knew—from the displeasure of the gods. On the flat rock beside the knives he placed another tool, a long-handled instrument with a flattened end that had been ground to a fairly sharp edge.

"Look to the spear point in the flames," he told Rahab. "It should be glowing by now." The handle of the weapon had already begun to smoke where the metal was thrust into the cleft at its end. And the thongs of goat hide that bound the head to the shaft were charring from the heat of the metal tip. Half the blade glowed a cherry red from the flames, she saw as she lifted it up by the handle. Salmon glanced at it and nodded approvingly.

"Set your teeth upon this, Joshua." He handed the Israelite captain a piece of goatskin. "I will work as fast as I can, but unless the poisons of the Amorite arrows are all burned away, Israel will be without a leader."

Joshua gripped the goatskin between strong white teeth. Sweat popped out on his forehead as Salmon touched the shaft of the arrow projecting from his back and began to move it gently, trying to loosen the head. When he applied more pressure to the shaft, the wood broke where it had been attached to the metal head of the arrow itself.

With a muttered curse Salmon reached for the long instrument. Slipping the narrow end deftly into the wound beside the arrowhead, he began to work it down beside the broken weapon. He moved the tool gently, using it as a lever to work

15

the arrowhead loose, but Joshua groaned with pain and bit into the goatskin gag.

Rahab was sure now that Salmon would never be able to move the arrowhead, for it seemed to be embedded firmly into the bone of Joshua's back. The physician appeared to have no intention of giving up, however, although sweat was already pouring off him in rivulets.

"Keep the spearhead in the flames, Rahab," he directed without taking his eyes from the wound. "This is taking longer than I expected."

"By the gods of Egypt!" Joshua groaned. "Get on with it, Salmon."

"I should have it soon." Just then a loud cracking sound broke the tense stillness inside the cave.

"The arrowhead moved!" Salmon cried exultantly. "Hold on a little longer, Joshua. It will soon be over."

"Else I will be dead!" Joshua gasped. "Would that I had left you to die that day in the desert, Salmon."

"Then you would perish of worse tortures than this," the physician retorted. "The poison of putrid flesh works slowly." He was working swiftly with the long bronze tool as he spoke, using it to pry at the arrowhead very much as a man levers a rock from the ground with the sharpened end of a long sapling.

The cracking sound came again. This time Rahab could see the arrowhead move, and with a cry of triumph Salmon seized it and drew it from the depth of the wound. Blood welled up in its wake, and Rahab felt the walls of the cave suddenly begin to sway about her. Salmon, however, paid no attention to her. He was studying the arrowhead intently, examining the point particularly, to see if any part of it had broken off.

"It is all here!" he cried, dropping the bronze point. "Hand me the spearhead, Rahab."

She obeyed but turned her eyes away, knowing she would faint if she watched any longer. Leaning against the wall for support, she heard a grunt from Salmon as he plunged the glowing bronze head of the spear into the depths of the wound.

Three

THE horrible bubbling and frying of blood and flesh made a great roaring in Rahab's ears. As if it were in a dream, she saw Salmon drop the spearhead.

"Hold this linen pad against the wound," he told her, "while I bandage it into place."

Rahab had been holding herself rigid to keep from fainting, and when she did not move at once, he took her hand with an oddly gentle movement and placed it upon the pad of linen that was once to have been her headdress. She saw the wound now, and the blackened surface with flesh seared and nearly all bleeding controlled startled her, so much had it changed in the past few moments.

"Hold the pad tightly," Salmon directed. "You cannot hurt him now."

"Is he—is he dead?"

Salmon laughed. "Even strong men faint from pain, especially when they are full of wine. He will sleep awhile, and the agony of the burning will be less when he awakens. Tomorrow I will see if I can find some of the trees from which a healing balm is made; I hear this part of the world is famous for it."

"I know where they are," she said. "Are the poisons all killed?"

"Let us hope so." He was cutting Joshua's bloodstained tunic into strips as he spoke, working with rapid, sure movements. These he fashioned into a long bandage which he wound about the Habiru captain's massive chest to hold the pad of soft linen against the wound.

When he had finished, Salmon surveyed his handiwork with some satisfaction. "I could have done a better job in Egypt with proper materials," he said, "but this will do for the present." He looked directly at her for the first time since he had started to treat the wound, and with a quick movement picked up the wine jug from the floor.

"Drink some of this," he ordered. "You are as white as the

17

snow on the mountains in winter. It will put the sun in your cheeks again."

The wine burned going down, but almost immediately Rahab felt a pleasant warmth spreading through her body. "You did very well," Salmon complimented her. "I don't suppose you have seen much fighting and bloodshed before."

Rahab shook her head. "Our land was peaceful until——" She stopped, not wanting to say flatly that the Amorites had been at peace until the coming of the Habiru. "Until today," she finished a little lamely.

"Today you saw a real battle," he agreed. "No one can stand against the hosts of Israel."

"If King Sihon is beaten, will you stay in our country?"

"We may stay for a while now," he told her. "Our people have been hungry a long time. But had your King granted us passage, as we asked, no battle would have been fought. Our god has promised us the land of Canaan across the River Jord, but we had no quarrel with the Amorites."

"The cities of Canaan are strong fortresses! And the walls of Jericho are even thicker than those of Heshbon."

"The priests tell us that Yahweh will destroy the kings of Canaan in the same way that he gave us the victory over your King Sihon this day."

"You must have a new weapon!" she said. "One that gives you victory even when you are outnumbered."

"Our weapon is as old as man," Salmon said cryptically. "But lately he seems to have forgotten how to use it." He folded one of the skins that had made up part of the litter and placed it under Joshua's head. "He should sleep for a while; the rest will do him good. He fought as ten men today."

The physician picked up the board with the tiny clay figure of Joshua on it. The tall, commanding body, the leonine head, the helmet of leather and copper—all of it was there, a tiny replica of Joshua in battle, even to the grace of his movements arrested at the moment her fingers had shaped the clay.

"You have a great gift, Rahab," he said almost humbly. "Perhaps an even greater gift than beauty, although few will be able to appreciate it."

"I suppose I modeled him because he stood out so much

above the others on the battlefield," she explained, half in apology.

"Joshua stands out everywhere. In all of Israel no one is stronger." He turned abruptly away. "I am going to send one of the soldiers down to the plain for supplies and to tell our people that Joshua will live. Do you want me to send a message to your family that you are safe?"

Rahab's face brightened; she knew her father would be worried. "My father's name is Chazan," she said. "He keeps an inn in Medeba beside the north gate and is also the town scribe."

"I will order in Joshua's name that your people shall not be harmed," Salmon promised, and went to send the soldier away.

"I was wondering why you spoke so well," he said when he came back into the cave. "But being the daughter of a scribe, you will naturally have had some teaching."

"I speak the tongue of Egypt too," she said proudly. "And I can write upon papyrus, and also in tablets of clay." She hesitated a moment, then went on.

"Are you going to stay here long?"

"Until Joshua's wound has begun to heal. A warm, dry cave like this is far better than a goatskin tent with the wind howling through it and blowing sand into his wound. I told the soldier to bring some food, but he will not get back before morning."

"I have some goat cheese and dates," Rahab offered. "And a little olive oil and some bread."

Salmon's face brightened. "Joshua will sleep until morning, but the soldier and I have not eaten since morning."

"I saw some berries ripening when I came up the mountain yesterday," she added. "I could gather them before dark."

He gave her a speculative look, and she knew he was trying to decide whether or not to trust her. "I promise not to run away," she assured him.

He smiled, and once again she was startled by the change in his face. "Gather the berries, by all means, daughter of Chazan. Meanwhile, I will see what I can knock down with a sling."

It was almost dark when Rahab came back up the moun-

19

tainside carrying a basket filled with luscious ripe berries. A cheerful glow and a savory smell came from inside the cave. When she reached its mouth she saw that Salmon had spitted a brace of plump fowls on a pair of sticks. Suspended over the coals, they were already beginning to simmer and drop grease upon the fire. Joshua was still asleep.

"We will dine well tonight, young lady," Salmon said jovially when he saw her basket. "I was lucky enough to knock down these birds within sight of the cave."

They ate on a flat rock in front of the cave. To Rahab's surprise, the soldier on guard sat down with them. On the few occasions when soldiers of the Amorite army had visited her father's inn, the officers had been haughty and far above breaking bread with a common soldier. They were all hungry, so the meal was eaten in silence as they pulled the birds apart with their fingers and tore the meat from the bones with strong teeth.

Joshua roused before they finished, but Salmon gave him the rest of the wine and he was soon asleep once more.

"Truly your god Yah is a generous host, Rahab." Salmon tossed a handful of bones down the mountainside and leaned back contentedly against the rock at the cave's mouth. The low ground below them was already blanketed in darkness. A little to the east a large group of fires glowed like some new constellation. To the south a smaller number of lights were grouped together, and much farther east and north could be seen the fires of a larger city.

"The large lights a long way off there must be at Heshbon," Salmon said. "Those large ones to the right of it look like the encampment of Israel, so the smaller group would be your village of Medeba?"

"I think so," Rahab agreed. "You can see the roofs of the houses from here when the sun is shining."

"It is a fertile land, especially in the valley where your village lies. Have you lived here always?"

"Oh no. My father was trained as a scribe at Byblos before I was born. I lived most of my life in Heshbon, where he kept the records for the Egyptian taxgatherers. We came to Medeba only a few years ago."

"Were you a priestess of the god you call Yah in Heshbon?"

"Yah is the god of our family and a few more of us in Medeba who are descendants of Abram," she explained. "I chose this cave as his dwelling place and keep it as a shrine for anyone who wishes to worship here."

"I should think a pretty young woman like you would be more interested in getting yourself a husband."

Rahab was not offended by the irony in his tone. It was strange, she thought now, how instinctively she trusted this slender, wiry man with the quick skilled movements, even though he often spoke sharply to her. In fact, it almost seemed as if they had been friends for a long time instead of having known each other just for a few hours.

As if he were reading her thoughts, Salmon said, "We are very much alike, I suspect, Rahab. Your fingers are skilled in making figures of clay, while mine heal wounds. Even in bloodshed and plunder I sometimes manage to see beauty and set it down in verse." He smiled wryly. "Few listen to the songs of the physician Salmon who sings only of peace and beauty, though. They are all concerned with war and bloodshed, like my friend Joshua."

"But you *are* friends," Rahab pointed out. "Even though you are different from each other as day and night."

"You mean because he is strong and handsome while I am lean like the curs of your village?" Salmon asked mockingly.

She shook her head. "I watched while you removed the arrowhead and dressed his wound. Your hands are even more skilled than a warrior's—and more important, I think."

"Physicians are never heroes," he reminded her.

"Why did you choose to be a leech then?"

"Perhaps because it is better than hauling blocks of stone all day and feeling the whip of an overseer upon your back."

"I—I don't understand."

"I was a slave in Egypt until about three years ago," he explained. "But I was quick and seemed to have been born with a skill for treating the sick, so my master sent me to the temple schools at Thebes, knowing that a slave trained in the art of healing would bring a higher price in the market. When my studies were finished I was sold to a contractor who furnished slaves to haul stones for the tombs of Pharaoh. Then one day I killed an overseer who was flogging another slave to death and had to run away into the desert. A

21

shipmaster bound for Ezion-geber hid me on his galley, expecting to sell me to a Babylonian caravan master. They prize physicians from Egypt very highly in that land."

"How did you escape?"

"At Ezion-geber they told me a band of Israelite slaves had escaped from Egypt and were traveling toward Canaan, so I slipped away into the wilderness one night to seek them. I was wandering without food or water, half dead among the sands, when Joshua found me and took me to his camp. If you had gone for days without water as I did and given up all hope, you would realize the obligation I feel toward Joshua."

"Anyone could see that there is a strong bond between you," she agreed.

"What more could you owe another than the debt of your life?"

"You repaid that debt today," she reminded him. "If you had not removed the arrowhead and cleansed the wound with fire, your friend would surely have died."

"I had to save Joshua at all costs," he said soberly. "You see, Rahab, he is cut from the stuff that heroes are made of, heroes and kings."

"I didn't know you Habiru had a king."

"We don't—yet," he admitted. "At the moment we are only a loose band of nomad tribes in flight from slavery in Egypt. But if our destiny is to be fulfilled, we must have a great leader. It may even take a king to fire a band of wandering tribes into becoming a great nation."

Rahab looked at Joshua. Even as he lay asleep there was something almost majestic about him. "He fought today as a king should fight," she said softly. "No wonder you want him to be one."

Salmon smiled. "You are a sorceress, young lady. I have never told these things to anyone before." His eyebrows lifted. "Truly, with your beauty, all men will be like the clay you mold."

"You think me beautiful?" she asked, pleased.

"Come now, Rahab." The cynicism was back in his voice and in his manner, like a garment put on when he wished to hide the real self she had been allowed to glimpse for only a few moments. "Surely the travelers in your father's inn have

22

told you many times how beautiful you are. I doubt not that many men have desired you."

A hot flush of embarrassment and anger flooded Rahab's cheeks. "I have lain with no man, if that is what you are hinting at!" she said angrily.

"I do not question your virtue, Rahab." The jeering note had left his voice as quickly as it had come. "But only that any man could look upon your beauty and not desire you. Believe me, the fact that you are virtuous will make them want you even more, for virginity in a beautiful young woman is rarely to be found in Egypt any more—or in the camp of Israel, for that matter." He looked at her keenly. "With both loveliness and a quick mind, you might even find yourself one day the consort of a king."

Months later she would remember those words and wonder if, with his other talents, Salmon might not also be a soothsayer.

Four

RAHAB slept at the back of the cave in order to be nearby if Joshua wakened, while Salmon alternated with the soldier in keeping watch outside. No one troubled them during the night, however. The remnants of the Amorite army had either retreated inside the walls of Heshbon or were hiding in the wild mountain country forming the eastern shore of the landlocked body of water called the "Salt Sea" because its water was so salty and bitter that nothing could live in it.

It was daylight again before Joshua awakened from his wine-drugged sleep. Rahab went to the couch on which he lay and saw that his eyes were burning with fever and that his skin was hot and dry. He asked for wine but there was none, so she gave him water. The fever made him hungry, too, so she brought the remainder of the fowls left from the night before and fed him some of the meat.

From where she sat feeding Joshua, Rahab could see Salmon lying across the mouth of the cave, asleep. He was unarmed, but the knife he had used to cut Joshua's tunic lay

23

beside him. He looked oddly boyish and young, his body graceful as a child's in its relaxed, sprawling slenderness. Even from that distance Rahab could see that Salmon's right ankle was puffed and discolored, and she remembered now that he had been limping as he had followed the improvised litter on which Joshua had been carried up the mountainside. Yet he had said nothing at all about his own discomfort, although she was sure he must have been in almost constant pain.

Joshua finished eating and closed his eyes, but when Rahab started to move away, he reached out and took her wrist. "Stay here, girl," he told her. "My body is afire with thirst."

She gave him another drink from the jug and poured some water into a basin of fired clay. They had not used the entire strip of linen cloth last night for the bandage, and as she went to get it to use for bathing Joshua's face she saw his fever-hot gaze following her. At the frank admiration in his eyes—tinged also with desire—she could not suppress the sudden warmth that welled up deep in her body, quickening the beat of her heart and her breathing and setting her cheeks afire. It was a disquieting sensation, this response to his admiring gaze. And yet it was exciting and pleasant too.

Men had looked upon her with desire many times before, as Salmon had suggested. More than once she had left the inn when it was filled with travelers and come to the cave in the mountainside to escape their attentions. But never before had she been close to a man whose sheer virility stirred an answering response in her own body. Suddenly afraid of this thing that was happening to her in spite of herself, Rahab started to move away, but Joshua's fingers tightened at once upon her wrist. And somehow all capacity to resist seemed to go out of her as he drew her closer to him.

"Why does your heart beat so quickly, beautiful one?" he whispered. "The pulse in your throat is like a frightened dove." His eyes were glowing like the fires upon the altar of Yah when she kindled them to burn a sacrifice. And her own body was beginning to burn with a flame she had never known before, threatening to destroy her strength to resist him.

"Please let me go," she begged in a whisper. "No man has treated me thus before."

24

"Would you stay if we were betrothed?" he asked.

Rahab could not still the sudden wild surge of her heart. To become betrothed, according to the custom of the Amorites, was the same as being wed, save for the formal contract of marriage. The pride and excitement she had felt as she had watched the strong and handsome warrior in battle yesterday; her relief at learning he had not been killed as she had feared; the vibrant force of his attraction for her, which she had felt even across the distance separating them when she was on the mountain and he on the battlefield—all swept in from her memory and set her natural resistance to this dangerous emotion tottering.

When Joshua's arm went about her waist, she let herself be drawn closer to him until her soft breast was pressed against the massive sinews of his chest. Her senses were swimming in the wild throbbing of her heart, and she was sure now that she must faint away.

Suddenly a sharp challenge came from outside the cave where the sentry watched in the misty light of dawn. The sound broke the spell that had claimed Rahab, and as she moved quickly away from the couch she saw Salmon sit up and seize the knife that had been beside him. In the same lithe movement he was erect, staring down the mountainside, where the morning mist still wreathed the trees in ghostly raiment.

"What is it?" Rahab asked. She moved quickly to the mouth of the cave, welcoming the excuse to get away from Joshua.

"I don't know." Salmon put out his hand to keep her from going outside. His body was tense and alert.

Down the slope Rahab saw something move, but before she could make out what it was she saw the tension go out of Salmon's body.

"Caleb!" he cried. Thrusting the knife into the sheath that hung from his belt, he started down the slope to meet the newcomers.

Rahab saw a stocky man with grizzled hair and beard approaching the spring now, at the head of a dozen Habiru soldiers. He wore a goatskin tunic like Joshua's and a helmet reinforced with copper. On his left arm was a shield strengthened with plates of beaten bronze, and he was armed with a

25

spear and the long dagger that seemed to distinguish the
Habiru captains from the common soldiers. The men behind
them carried—in addition to their arms—a variety of bottles
and baskets. One bore a freshly skinned kid over his shoulder.

"How is it with Joshua?" the newcomer called to Salmon.
"When last I saw him he had been stricken down by one of
the cursed poisoned arrows of Sihon's troops."

"I removed the arrowhead yesterday and cleansed the
wound with fire." Salmon seized the older man's arm in a
gesture of friendly welcome. "The fires in his body burn
brightly, but the fever will help drive off the poison that remains."

"Praises be to the gods that you were nearby when he fell,
Salmon," Caleb said fervently. He gave Rahab a quick, appraising glance from eyes that were keen, yet not hostile.

"I am Rahab, sir," she said quietly, "daughter of Chazan,
the innkeeper and scribe of Medeba. Our forefathers came
here from Ur Kasdim."

"So?" Caleb's eyebrows rose with surprise. "We may be of
the same people then."

"Is my family safe?" Rahab asked quickly.

"Safe and well, as Joshua ordered." Caleb entered the cave
and stood looking down at his wounded brother-in-arms.
"How is it with you, son of Nun?" he inquired.

The wounded man grimaced. "How could I be with a hole
in my back burned out by a fiend of a physician who calls
himself my friend? What of the battle, Caleb?"

"Sihon's forces are broken and have been driven from the
field. We crushed his chariot wheels as you ordered, but to
me it seemed a foolish thing."

"With no chariots, the Amorites are unequal to us. Riding
on wheels has ill fitted them to fight on foot."

"We could have used the chariots and horses ourselves,"
Caleb grunted. "On the plains, the scythe blades can cut
down troops on foot like wheat before the harvest."

"We of Israel are not Egyptians to fight on wheels," Joshua
said contemptuously. "We fight in the hills, where wheels are
useless."

"The champions of Israel need not quarrel over the way to

fight," Salmon interposed. "Both have proved their right on the field of battle to be named captains of a thousand."

"I bring news of such a commission for both of us," Caleb said. "Though why such a stubborn mule should be captain of a thousand I cannot see."

"Did you hear him, Joshua?" Salmon cried. "The elders could not deny you what is rightfully yours any longer."

"He earned it yesterday," Caleb admitted. "The field of battle is stained with Amorite blood let by the hand of the son of Nun."

"And you, Caleb?" Salmon continued. "We are all happy for you too."

Joshua grinned. "Even I agree, Caleb, my brother-in-arms. In all of Israel none is braver, although you are overly inclined to take up foreign ways of fighting."

Caleb laughed, his broad, compact body shaking with merriment. "Verily, the letting of blood has taken some of the sting out of the Hornet of God, Salmon," he observed. "Perhaps he should be wounded more often.

"I brought a freshly slain kid," Caleb continued, "and herbs to prepare it, with fruits and bread and wine. We will have a feast to celebrate the naming of the son of Nun as captain of a thousand." He turned to Rahab. "Can you cook, girl? Or shall we leave that to Salmon? He has many skills besides that of physician."

"Bid your men bring the kid," Rahab assured him. "I will prepare it for roasting."

While Rahab rubbed spices and condiments into the tender flesh of the baby goat, the soldiers built a fire outside the cave over which to roast it. Caleb walked around the cave, studying the drawings Rahab had made on the stones and the exquisite figurines standing here and there in niches among the rocks. He paused finally before the stone altar and the cloth that hid the inner place of the god.

"This looks like a shrine of some sort," he observed.

"It belongs to the god Yah," Rahab confirmed.

"Yah." Caleb's bushy eyebrows lifted. "Is he sometimes called Yahu?"

"Yes. Many call him by that name now."

"And sometimes El?"

"The Amorites have a god called El," Rahab told him. "My father thinks he is the same as the one we call Yah."

"I heard my father tell in Egypt how El led our people out of Ur Kasdim," Caleb said. "He was the god of the patriarch Abram, so we must worship him under different names."

"Many of us here on the east side of the River Jord are descended from Abram," Rahab told him.

"And on the west bank in the land of Canaan?" Caleb asked quickly. "Do many dwell there?"

"I know nothing of that, sir," she said. "But my father came from Byblos on the shores of the great sea. He might know whether any of the descendants of Abram dwell in those lands."

"I will talk to Chazan this very day," Caleb said. "Do you think the worshipers of Yah among the Amorites would fight with us against King Og of Bashan and the Canaanite peoples?"

"We are not soldiers, sir," she protested. "Most of our people are scribes or artisans. And Yah is not a god of war."

"What is he then?" Joshua demanded.

"The god of wisdom and understanding," Rahab exclaimed. "And of brotherly love among all who follow him."

"By the beard of Pharaoh!" Caleb exclaimed. "This god must have two faces then. He leads us to war."

Salmon spoke for the first time during this interchange. "Perhaps he has only one face, Caleb," he said quietly. "We of Israel may have made him something he is not."

"Yahweh is the god of the storm—and of battle and conquest," Joshua broke in impatiently from the couch. "His altar is the battlefield, and the sacrifice he loves best is the blood of a conquered enemy."

"I see nothing godly in slitting other men's throats," Salmon said sarcastically. "Perhaps the Pharaoh Ikhnaton was right when he decreed only one god for Egypt, the sun."

"You are a fine physician, Salmon," Caleb growled, "but poor stuff for a warrior. You forget that Ikhnaton almost gave Egypt away and lost his own life as a result."

"There is more to bravery than stabbing people with spears and swords," Salmon said angrily. "A skilled physician is worth ten warriors any day."

28

"No one doubts your courage," Caleb said soothingly. "We all saw you dressing the wounded yesterday, with Amorite arrows buzzing about your head like hornets. But wars are for glory and power, and a man needs the approval of a god to stir him on to mighty deeds of valor."

"What say you, daughter of Chazan?" Joshua inquired.

He seemed not to doubt for a moment that Rahab would agree with him. And somehow she could not find now the same words to defend the gentle god she served that had come so easily to her lips a short time before.

"The god you serve gave you victory over the Amorites— yet you say he is the same as mine," she said slowly. "Perhaps, as the noble Caleb says, Yah does have two faces."

Salmon's laugh was brittle, like clay molded too thin and fired too long. "The god of woman is man; why should she worship another? Enough of gods—and women. I will set the kid to roasting, else we will all go hungry this day."

Five

THE feast of thanksgiving for Joshua's escape from death lasted through the day. When darkness approached, Salmon ordered the cave cleared so that Joshua might get some rest. After Caleb and the Habiru soldiers had gone— leaving an ample supply of food at the cave—he called Rahab to help him dress Joshua's wound for the night. She had pointed out to him the trees whose sap formed the balm famous in these parts for its healing properties, and they had collected a liberal supply of the fragrant balsam.

Having first fortified Joshua against the pain of the dressing with copious drafts of wine, Salmon had him lie on his face and removed the bandages as gently as he could. Yesterday they had not paused to bathe the wounded man's skin. Rahab did this now, sponging away dried blood and the discharges from the wound with warm water.

When suddenly she began to laugh, Salmon looked up from where he was preparing the balsam for dressing the

29

wound. "What are you laughing at?" he asked a little curtly. She knew he had not yet forgiven her entirely for taking Joshua's side that morning in the argument over the relative virtues of Yah and Yahweh.

"Look!" Rahab pointed to an area over each of Joshua's shoulder blades. "The champion of Israel has dimples on his shoulders, just like a woman."

Salmon came closer and studied Joshua's back. Over each of his shoulder blades there was indeed a tiny pit, exactly like a dimple in a woman's cheek.

"The son of Nun has been hiding something from us," he agreed with a smile.

"The marks are signs of strength," Joshua growled. "My father bore them and his father's father before him."

"I have heard of such marks being handed down in some families from generation to generation," Salmon agreed. "At the Temple of Thoth in Thebes, where I studied the art of healing, the priests keep a record of such things."

Joshua's wound was an angry, raw surface, the flesh charred in places from the heat of the gleaming spear point with which Salmon had burned away the poisons of the arrowhead. Rahab shuddered when she looked at it, but the physician seemed entirely satisfied. "The skin is hardly red around the wound," he pointed out, running his fingers lightly along the edge. "And it is not hard, as it would be if the arrow poisons had not all been burned away. We did a good job, Rahab."

"All of Israel sings the praises of Salmon the physician," Joshua said sarcastically. "If they did not, he would do it for himself."

"Someone must preserve heroes for the plaudits of the crowd," Salmon retorted. Placing a cloth on which he had spread the balsam over the wound, he bandaged it snugly in place with long strips that Caleb had brought. Joshua was tired from the day, and the wine he had drunk made him sleepy. By the time Rahab and Salmon had finished making him comfortable for the night, the Israelite captain was snoring.

Salmon went outside the cave while Rahab finished tidying it up. When she came out, night was already beginning to throw its dark mantle over the plains below, although here on the heights the sun still shone above the tops of the distant mountains. The fertile fields clustered at the foot of Mount Nebo were a dark green carpet in the twilight, for the *malquosh*, the spring rains, had been heavy. Even in battle the Israelites always avoided trampling down crops as much as possible, for a crop failure meant suffering and famine for conqueror and conquered alike.

Salmon was sitting at the edge of the escarpment that formed a broad ledge before the cave. "You must be tired," he said, making room for Rahab beside him. "There are dark shadows beneath your eyes."

She was absurdly pleased by his noticing her that closely. "Joshua's wound is doing well, isn't it?" she asked. "You were not just saying that to keep him from worrying?"

"Joshua is a soldier and accustomed to facing death. I would not keep the truth from him even if it were bad. The wound heals well; he will live to slay many more in battle."

"Why are you so bitter about war, Salmon? Fighting is a part of the duty of men."

"To protect their homes and families, yes. But I know of no right by which one man can seize the home of another and kill him if he resists."

"Joshua said your god had given the land of Canaan to you."

He looked at her keenly. "You seem much taken with the son of Nun."

"Why do you say that?"

"Your eyes have betrayed you all day. And I do not sleep as soundly as I seem."

"Oh!" Suddenly ashamed, she started to move away, but he took her hand and would not let her go.

"You have no reason to be ashamed of falling in love with Joshua, Rahab. It takes a strong woman indeed to see a hero through any eyes save those of romantic infatuation."

"I—I don't know what you mean."

"You will—in time. I hope it doesn't come too late."

"Why do you always talk in riddles?" she cried.

Salmon grinned. "We that you call Habiru are a peculiar people. You know our story, don't you?"

"Only a little of it."

"We do not know just why Abram and his family left such

31

a fertile country as that around Ur Kasdim," he began. "I have always suspected it was because they would not bow their necks to the heel of a ruler not of their own people. In the land of Canaan across the Jord they began to multiply and would soon have taken the country for themselves. Then a savage people called the Hyksos swept down from the north and carried many of them into Egypt. When the Pharaohs drove out the Hyksos, the Israelites remained as slaves. From time to time some managed to escape under great leaders and seek the old homes of our people in the land of Canaan."

"Is that why you believe Canaan belongs to you?"

He nodded. "The others were smaller bands than we are. They could not conquer, so they joined the descendants of Abram still living in Canaan, people like you and your family. Many were skilled workers in stone and metal, so the Canaanites let them remain. There are whole cities in Canaan now controlled by descendants of our people who escaped from Egypt many years ago."

"You seem to know much of Canaan."

"Several years ago Caleb and Joshua went into it from the south and spied out the land," he explained. "It was then that they found me. We could have invaded it from the south, but we were too weak to launch an attack across the desert sand, so we chose to follow the King's Highway around the east side of the Salt Sea and the River Jord."

"When will you attack the cities of Canaan?"

Salmon shrugged. "That is for the elders to decide. To me this land we have conquered from King Sihon seems more fertile and promising than the rough mountainous country to the west. Our flocks and our herds would do well here, and our children would know something else besides famine and bloodshed and hunger. Were it left to my judgment, I would settle the people here, choose Joshua for a king, and set about making Israel into a strong and prosperous nation."

"Don't the others agree with you?"

"You heard them talking this morning. Joshua thinks only of war. He sees the cities of Canaan falling like ripe plums before our armies and dreams of the riches they contain. But I cannot keep from wondering how we can become truly great when our young men will lie dead upon the battlefield

32

and the wombs of the young women cry for strong seed that is no more."

Rahab could not help being moved by his obvious sincerity. "Surely the mothers would listen if you told them how war means killing the very flower of your nation," she suggested.

Salmon shook his head. "If you knew what it is to be a slave, Rahab, you would understand how the need to become even richer and more powerful than those who are your masters is like a fever eating at your soul. It even made the priests turn Yahweh into a god of battle."

"Then he was really once like Yah?"

"I am sure the god Abram brought from Ur was the same as the one you call Yah," he agreed. "But people no longer want a kind and tolerant god, for then they must try to be like him to win his favor. Ikhnaton discovered that in Egypt——"

"I heard you speak of him," Rahab interrupted. "But I don't know the story."

"A young Pharaoh called Amenhotep IV rebelled against the worship of Ammon when he came to the throne of Egypt," he told her. "The priests were fat and corrupt; they kept young women in the temple as brides of the god and used them for their own purposes. And since the priests owned much of the land, most of the people were enslaved too. Amenhotep revolted against the worship of Ammon and decreed but one god for Egypt, a deity called Aton, whose dwelling was in the sun. He changed his own name to Ikhnaton and wrote some of the most beautiful poems ever sung by man."

A wry smile softened Salmon's lean face and warmed his dark eyes. "Perhaps I like Aton because in my weaker moments I too am a poet," he admitted, "just as you are an artist."

"It is nothing to be ashamed of," Rahab said spiritedly.

"Not to you and me," he agreed. "But warriors like Joshua and Caleb compare the songs of poets to the wailing of lovesick fools, so I keep mine to myself."

"I would like to hear them," Rahab said impulsively.

Salmon shook his head. "Mine are but poor things, unworthy of being repeated. But when I see the bodies of our

young men lying dead on the battlefield and am no longer
sure of myself or the destiny of my people, I remember the
song of Ikhnaton to the sun-god, and it brings me a measure
of peace."

"Please sing it for me," Rahab begged.

He began to sing in a low vibrant voice, but not loud
enough to wake up the sleeping Joshua:

> *"Thy dawning is beautiful in the horizon of the sky,*
> *O, living Aton, beginning of life.*
> *When thou risest in the eastern horizon,*
> *Thou fillest every land with thy beauty.*

> *"Bright is the earth when thou risest on the horizon.*
> *When thou shinest as Aton by day,*
> *Thou drivest away the darkness.*
> *When thou sendest forth thy rays . . .*
> *All cattle rest upon their pasturage,*
> *The trees and the plants flourish,*
> *The birds flutter in their marshes,*
> *Their wings uplifted in adoration to thee.*
> *All the sheep dance upon their feet,*
> *All winged things fly,*
> *They live when thou hast shone upon them.*

> *"How excellent are thy designs,*
> *O Lord of Eternity!*
> *There is a Nile in the sky for the strangers,*
> *And for the cattle of every country that go upon their*
> *   feet.*
> *Thy rays nourish every garden;*
> *When thou riseth they live,*
> *They grow by thee.*
> *Thou makest the seasons*
> *In order to create all thy works:*
> *Winter to bring them coolness,*
> *And heat that they may taste thee.*

> *"Dawning, glittering, going afar and returning.*
> *Thou makest millions of forms*
> *Through thyself alone; cities, towns and tribes,*

Highways and rivers.
All eyes see thee before them,
For thou art Aton, of the day over the earth . . ."

"It is beautiful, Salmon," Rahab cried, her eyes shining. "I never heard anything so lovely."

"Perhaps because Ikhnaton had the courage to speak what he felt."

"I feel the same way about Yah."

His smile was like a warm mantle spread about her shoulders. "Someday you can lead me to your god," he said. "I seem in danger of losing mine in the thunder of war, the cries of the wounded and the dying, and the whips of the overseers upon the backs of those who dare not strike back."

Six

JOSHUA was still feverish the next morning and, being accustomed to action, naturally fretted at the necessary inactivity while his wounds healed. Directly after the morning meal Salmon went down the mountain to the Israelite camp to visit the sick and wounded there, promising to return by nightfall with fresh supplies.

Rahab was acutely conscious of Joshua's eyes upon her as she moved about the cave. Again and again he made obvious excuses to bring her near him, and when she gave him wine or food, he often took her hand and made her stay beside him. Nor was she unconscious of Joshua's presence and her own response to his touch. If this was love, she told herself, it was an exciting and thrilling game, with an element of danger, too, that often left her a little breathless.

Two soldiers were on guard outside the cave, but they might as well have been in the camp of the Israelites as far as their presence affected the tense little drama of rising passion going on inside the cave. Again and again Rahab managed to remove herself from Joshua's embrace before he could seize her firmly, but as the day went on and the game of cat

35

and mouse became more and more tense, she found herself wishing Salmon would return early.

It was midafternoon when a hail from down the slope indicated the physician had come back from his mission. She was touched and surprised to learn that he had visited her home, talked with her father, and had even brought her fresh clothing. He also carried meat for the evening meal and fresh cheese and more wine. Salmon's observing eyes did not miss Rahab's bright cheeks or the telltale warmth in her eyes brought about by her romantic tilting with Joshua during the day. There was no time for him to talk with her, however, for Joshua demanded at once to know the news of the Israelite camp.

"The elders were discussing what course to follow when I left," Salmon told him.

"What is there to confer about?" Joshua snorted. "We must move against King Og of Bashan at once."

"It will take time to drive the Amorites from Heshbon and the other fortified cities," Salmon pointed out. "And several of the tribes are already talking about remaining in the Amorite lands."

Joshua pushed himself up on the couch. "Bind up these cursed wounds so I can go down to the camp at once," he shouted. "The men of Bashan are quaking in their cities after our victory over Sihon. If we stop now, they will have time to count our numbers and see that we are fewer than they."

"You cannot leave fortified cities behind you uncaptured," Salmon reminded him. "The Amorite soldiers who escaped could still attack from the rear and cut us to pieces while we were fighting King Og."

"Then tell Caleb to get about the business of taking Heshbon. The men must not be allowed to rest."

"Lest they have time to wonder why there is need for more war?" Salmon asked sarcastically.

"Else they have time to grow soft in their hearts and their bellies," Joshua snapped. "A hungry soldier fights for his food and his life. A fat one thinks only of how soon he can get back to camp and the harlots who follow the armies."

Salmon shrugged. "Obviously you are in no condition to go down to the camp, so quiet yourself. Caleb is arguing for

36

continuing the fight, holding out the lure of great plunder from the towns of Bashan. The people of Israel are as greedy as anyone else, so no doubt he and his arguments will prevail."

"Curse you for troubling me with old wives' tales then!" Joshua raged. "When I can leave this couch I will have you flogged in the sight of the people."

"You are not king yet," Salmon reminded him complacently as he began to arrange the contents of a bag of medicines and other supplies on a rocky shelf just inside the cave. First he took out a pot of the balsam he had used to dress Joshua's wound. Beside it he placed a small wooden box of purgative pills compounded of honey, wormwood, and onion. For mild headaches there was a jar of frankincense, cumin, U'an berries, and the fat from a goose, boiled together and used to rub on the temples. And when the pain was severe, a still more effective remedy consisted of a preparation of coriander, wormwood, juniper, honey, and berries from the poppy plant.

"I had the good fortune to meet a caravan bound from Egypt to Babylon," Salmon explained. "In fact, your father directed me to it, Rahab. They had a good supply of medicines, so I bought most of them." He grinned as he held up a jar. "This might even help you, Joshua. I notice that your hair is growing a little thin on top."

Joshua cursed him, but Salmon continued maliciously. "It was prepared for a queen of Egypt and contains equal parts of the heel of an Abyssinian greyhound, date blossoms, and asses' hoofs boiled in oil. The merchant swore that it is guaranteed to grow hair."

Joshua snorted indignantly, and Rahab could not help smiling, although she was careful not to let him see her.

"Here is a tonic you may need soon in your old age, too," Salmon continued gleefully. "It is compounded of figs, Syrian plums, grapes, frankincense, cumin, wine, beer, yeast, and the grease of a goose. They say it will warm any man's loins and make him feel young again."

"Wine and red meat are the only tonics for warriors," Joshua growled. "Save your medicines for old women and fat merchants."

"At least I would be better paid if I did," Salmon retorted.

"These things were all purchased from my own small share of the spoils from King Sihon's defeat." He turned to Rahab. "And I did not forget you either, beautiful one. Here is a pot of antimony paste to whiten your cheeks, though I prefer them pink as they are now. And a case to hold your cosmetics."

Rahab cried out with pleasure at the latter gift. It had been cleverly made by Egyptian artisans of two scallop shells from the broad gulf formed by the mouth of the Tigris and Euphrates rivers. Held together with tiny hinges of gold and polished until it shone, the shell case contained a small paint stick for applying carmine to the lips and cheeks and painting the nipples of the breasts when the sheer transparent tunics favored by Egyptian women were worn. There was kohl, too, for applying shadow to the eyelids and a paste made from a powdered black mineral for darkening the eyebrows and eyelashes.

"Thank you, Salmon," Rahab said happily as she rubbed the paint stick in carmine and applied it to her lips, heightening their already vivid color. "Nobody ever gave me anything like this before."

"Caleb needed a scribe to keep records on the division of the spoils," the physician continued. "I arranged for your father to take the position. From now on you are one of us."

Rahab glanced quickly at Joshua to note his reaction to this news. It would make her even more acceptable to his people, in case he should wish to bring her to the Israelite camp as his wife. But Joshua was still fuming about the action of the elders in considering a cessation of fighting after their great victory over the forces of Sihon and did not seem to have heard.

"Caleb should be training the men," he fretted. "They will grow soft like women if they are allowed to eat well and grow fat with nothing to do."

"Sihon had a store of wine under royal seal in every village, part of the tax he required the people to pay," Salmon told him. "The men broke into the stores and now half of them are drunk day and night."

"Wine is good for soldiers," said Joshua.

"Is it good for our people to take up the custom of the Amorites? On the outskirts of the camp today I saw a golden calf taken from a temple of Baal. Some were already worshiping it."

"You are overly concerned with gods, Salmon," Joshua said complacently. "Yahweh will triumph over the others once the battle is joined again. Meanwhile it does not hurt to have the Amorite gods favorable to us."

Salmon remained at the cave most of the next day while his patient fumed, both because of his own inactivity and because Rahab avoided him, lest the physician notice Joshua's not too furtive attempts to caress her. It was not a pleasant day for anyone, but when they dressed the wound that afternoon, even Rahab's untutored eyes could see that healing was progressing more than satisfactorily. And the sick man's fever had definitely begun to subside.

"This balm of Gilead is truly miracle-working," Salmon approved. "I must collect more of it before we go into battle again."

"When can I go down to the camp?" Joshua demanded. He was sitting up on the couch now, propped against the wall of the cave, with a padded goatskin to protect his tender back from the stone.

"Why hurry?" Salmon asked. "I told you Caleb would convince them we should go on fighting." Word had come that afternoon when the guards were changed that the elders who ruled the Israelites had agreed to continue with the military campaign against King Og of Bashan, whose territories lay to the north. But they had also added the provision that this attack should not be launched until Heshbon, the Amorite capital, had been taken.

"Besides," Salmon continued, "Caleb needs time to train the stone throwers in hitting moving targets."

"What are you talking about?" Joshua asked suspiciously.

"One expert thrower with a sling could knock the driver out of a chariot and allow it to be captured without damage," Salmon pointed out. "When I reminded Caleb of that, he started men training immediately in throwing stones at moving targets."

"I want no chariots," Joshua shouted, but Salmon interrupted the tirade before it could begin.

"Stop roaring like a wounded bull," the physician ordered. "The Amorites say the warriors of Og have sworn not to make

39

the mistake the forces of Sihon did by following our men into the hills where we can cut them to pieces."

"We will not fight upon the plain," Joshua snapped.

"You will be attacking them," Salmon reminded him. "They will choose where to fight, not you. And I hear rumors that the men of Bashan carry heavy shields of a new metal that can turn arrowheads and splinter a bronze spear point."

"What do you propose then?" Joshua demanded sarcastically. "That we give up and go no farther?"

"No, obviously you cannot leave a strong force like that of King Og unconquered and ready to attack you whenever they wished."

"I suppose you have a plan for overcoming them then?" Joshua said caustically. "With chariots, no doubt."

Salmon nodded cheerfully. "First we will capture the chariots of the Amorites by knocking out the drivers with stones thrown from slings. Then the vehicles can spearhead our attack and protect our soldiers as they advance."

Joshua started to retort, but a thoughtful look came over his face instead. "I have a better idea," he said. "Chariots move rapidly, so we will place an expert spear thrower beside the driver in each one, with a number of spears. As the chariots move close to the enemy, we can throw spears over their heads where their shields will not protect them."

"Suppose they raise the shields above their heads?"

"Then our bowmen will slay them with arrows driven in at close range as they advance behind the chariots."

"It might work," Salmon agreed. "If——"

"It is bound to work," Joshua said emphatically. "You are just envious because I thought of it first."

Salmon shrugged. "I am no soldier, Joshua. But were I in King Og's place, I could easily defeat this plan of yours."

"How?"

"By sending a picked band of men ahead of my troops, carrying long saplings and protected by arrows shot over their heads by bowmen. When the chariots came they would thrust the poles between the spokes of the wheels and break them. Then your chariots would collapse on the field and be of no use to you."

"The enemy will not think of that," Joshua said confidently.

40

"Maybe you are right." Salmon grinned. "The men of Bashan are probably soldiers like the Israelites, not thinkers."

Joshua snorted and called for more wine. While Rahab was bringing it, Salmon picked up a small package of instruments he had brought back with him. "I will be outside at the spring sharpening my tools," he told her. "Don't let him drink all the wine or there will be none for tomorrow."

When Rahab came down to the spring with the water jar to fill it for cooking the evening meal, she found Salmon busy sharpening his instruments on a flat rock. He looked up at her and grinned. "Don't let Joshua think too hard," he advised. "It always gives him a headache."

She filled the jar and set it beside the spring but did not immediately go back to the cave. "Why are you not a captain like Joshua and Caleb?" she asked.

"What!" He looked at her as if he thought she had lost her senses. "I am no soldier, girl."

"But you devised the stratagem for luring the Amorite chariots into the hills, didn't you?"

"Any fool could have thought of that."

"And you saw at once what was wrong with using the chariots for a quick attack with spears thrown over the heads of the enemy."

Abruptly he picked up the instrument he had been sharpening, a short heavy blade of bronze with a sharp edge. "If I had not left Egypt in such a hurry, I would have stolen one of these," he said, changing the subject. "Fortunately I was able to buy one today from the caravan."

"What is it?"

"A special knife for drilling the skull. In Egypt it is used by a priest-physician who calls himself the 'royal skull opener.'"

Rahab shivered. "Why would anyone want to do that?"

"In Egypt, skull opening is used chiefly for getting rid of the aged and the weak," he explained. "But as long as a thousand years ago physicians knew that the control of the legs lies within the brain. Today battles are fought with chariots, and men's skulls are often broken by the hooves of horses. If pieces of bone are driven down upon the brain, their bodies are paralyzed and they die."

41

"Can you cure them with that?" Rahab asked in amazement.

"Not so often as I would like," Salmon admitted, "but enough to be worth trying. This heavy knife is used to scrape a hole through the bone beside the broken place. And this"—he held up the slender bar of bronze with the narrow flattened end that he had used to pry the arrowhead from Joshua's back—"this you slide beneath the broken part to pry it up so that it no longer presses upon the brain."

"Is there anything you do not know, Salmon?" Rahab asked impulsively.

He frowned. "What do you mean?"

"You said you could use these tools to save the lives of men who were as good as dead. And just now you were telling Joshua how to fight a battle."

He looked at her for a long moment. When he spoke his voice was almost sad. "When it comes to the secrets of a woman's heart, Rahab, I am as a babe who knows nothing."

"What do you wish to know?"

"Why her heart beats quickly when the eyes of one man are upon her and not those of another. Why one man's desire brings soft color to her cheeks and a sparkle to her eyes, while the love of another does not."

Rahab was so startled by this oblique avowal of love that she caught her breath in a gasp. Not wanting to hurt him, she used a tactic women have known since the world began and changed the subject. "Tell me how you would win over the troops of King Og," she said a little breathlessly.

He shrugged. "My main purpose would be to gain victory with as little loss of men as possible. In this case, I would use chariots to break the ranks of Bashan so their shields would be less important."

"Joshua did not think of that."

"He probably would—eventually. Joshua is no fool, Rahab," he said earnestly. "At the moment he is concentrating upon one way of fighting and has trained our men for it. And it is a good way, for it brought us victory. Sometimes Joshua and I chaff each other, but you have seen him fight, so you know that none in Israel is half his equal." He grinned suddenly. "And don't mistake me for a wise man, young woman. There are others who can think far better than I."

"I don't believe it."

"What have I done to deserve such a confidence from you?"

"You brought me presents."

"Was that so much?"

"No other man ever did except my father, unless they hoped to—unless they desired me."

"You mean I am the only one who thought of what he could give to you rather than what you might give to him?"

"Why—yes," she admitted, startled that he had been able to put her thought into exact words when she could not.

"Then they are fools," he said. "The love a man bears a woman should be as much because he wants to make her happy as because of the pleasure she may give him."

"You must have loved someone very much to know that," Rahab said softly.

"A slave has no time for love," he said a little gruffly. "I have been too busy healing the wounds of Israel since Joshua and Caleb found me in the desert to be troubled by anything else."

"These are things women know instinctively in their hearts, Salmon. Women—and perhaps poets."

He gave her a long look before he turned his attention back to the stone and the surgeon's tool whose edge he was sharpening. "My feelings are no different from other men's, Rahab. I love as others love. And even though I know in my heart that I am a fool, I still dare to hope for a miracle."

"I—I don't know what you mean," she stammered.

"You must know that no man could look upon you and not feel differently afterward," he said bluntly.

"You mean and not lust after me?" Her voice hardened a little. "I have known enough of that in my father's inn. It is one reason why I spend so much time in the Cave of Yah."

He raised his head from the sharpening stone and looked directly into her eyes. Nor did she look away, for nothing in his gaze made her either afraid or ashamed. "When I look upon your beauty, Rahab," he said gently, "my body yearns for yours. But I would still love you, even though I knew our bodies could never be united."

43

Seven

JOSHUA improved rapidly during the next few days and was soon able to be up and around the cave. Once or twice, when he watched Salmon and Rahab together, both of them slender and graceful as they worked side by side at the spring or over the cooking fire, Joshua frowned. Afterward he was particularly attentive to Rahab, and, as for the girl, she went about with shining eyes and often sang at her work.

As the days passed, Rahab found herself beginning to understand better the relationship between Joshua and the physician. As Salmon had told her, it was more than just the tie between one man and another to whom he owes his life. There was also a deep bond of genuine affection between the two men. Salmon overlooked few opportunities to bait Joshua about his love of battle and his obvious belief that the highest calling of man was in the taking up of arms. Nor did Joshua fail to remind the physician of his own status as a non-fighter. But Rahab could see that deep inside them each had a profound respect for the other.

As Joshua improved he went about the courting of Rahab with the same thoroughness and determination that he would have given to the prosecution of a battle. And she would have been made of stone not to respond to it. The Israelite leader was not only handsome, he radiated a sense of power and certainty in his own abilities that she found it difficult to resist. In fact, she soon did not really try.

The touch of his hand upon her body through the thin stuff of her robe as she moved about the cave was enough to set her breathing quickly. And occasionally, when they were alone together while Salmon was hunting on the mountainside or tending the sick who flocked daily now to the foot of Mount Nebo for treatment, Joshua would take Rahab in his arms hungrily. Then she felt again the same wild clamor of her senses that she had experienced the first morning here in the cave. And both of them knew without any avowal that whenever he asked the gift of her body she would not refuse.

44

Even Salmon considered them betrothed now, and as her love for Joshua grew stronger, Rahab found herself looking forward eagerly to the day when she would become his bride.

Good-naturedly yielding to Rahab's insistence upon formality, Joshua had promised to visit Chazan as soon as he was able to leave the cave, bearing the *mohar*, as the marriage price was called. If his eagerness for the wedding did not quite parallel Rahab's, this, too, was understandable, for he was much older than she, although still in the prime of life. He acquiesced in Rahab's plans for the marriage rites, however. And, as a young girl naturally would, she wished to make them as elaborate as possible. Going about the cave in her duties as homemaker, Rahab visualized over and over again the scene of the wedding.

First would come the procession, with Joshua in full military gear marching through the streets of Medeba to her father's house to claim his bride. The minor details of the bride price would, of course, have been decided upon already and the agreed-upon amount paid to her father.

Custom demanded that Chazan give Rahab most of the price as her dowry, to be put away in case Joshua died or—a thought she did not let enter her mind—divorced her. Divorce was simple, however. For sufficient cause, mainly unfruitfulness, a husband could put his wife away merely by announcing in the public square of the village that he no longer claimed her as his own.

Those in the wedding procession would be garlanded with flowers, while Joshua, as the bridegroom, would wear a crown of bright-colored blossoms. As the party of the bridegroom approached her father's house, the young people would be dancing and singing in the streets so that everyone, including the ever-present demons, would know this was a wedding and not a funeral. The young men with Joshua would also flourish their weapons to frighten away any evil spirits that might seek to cause trouble.

After the procession reached the house of Chazan and Joshua had claimed Rahab as his bride, there would come the wedding feast. With this would be much drinking of wine, singing, and dancing, for it was a time of rejoicing, almost as much so as the celebration of the festival of the harvest in a good crop year. One of the young men would play a harp,

45

perhaps a large one with many strings. Others would strum smaller instruments with three or four strings stretched across a piece of sandalwood bedecked with two horns by which the player carried it.

The shepherd boys who looked after the village flocks always brought their flutes for wedding celebrations and reed pipes that made merry tunes for dancing. The girls would shake sistrums in rhythm with the playing of the harps and the thin high wailing of the flutes and reeds. Others would thump upon timbrels, bowl-shaped drums that gave the music a throbbing note and encouraged the dancers to new efforts while they sang such songs as:

> Turn, turn, O Rahab the beautiful,
> Turn, turn, that we may gaze upon thee.
> Ah, gaze on the beautiful one
> In the Mahanaim dance.
> How beautiful are your steps in sandals,
> How beautiful are your feet,
> O rapturous maiden.

The music, feasting, and dancing at such functions always continued until far into the night. And finally, as a climax to the festivities, people would stand outside the house beating timbrels and shaking sistrums while the bridegroom carried his bride to the upper room and the nuptial couch prepared there.

Here Rahab's thoughts had always stopped, for no bride of innocence would even imagine the joy of the nuptial couch. Yet from her brief experience in the arms of Joshua, she already knew that her body would respond to his love-making like a harp to the touch of a skilled musician or a poem of love to the voice of the singer of songs.

Late in the afternoon a messenger came from the camp of the Israelites asking that Salmon come down at once and attend some desperately wounded men. There had been a skirmish near the city of Heshbon, and the Amorite troops, sallying suddenly from their fortress city, had cut an Israelite patrol to pieces.

"I will probably not be back before morning," he told

Rahab and Joshua as he was leaving. "But you are well guarded, and there is plenty of food and wine."

With Salmon away, Rahab felt strangely lonely as she busied herself preparing the evening meal. It was dark already, and she was alone in the cave with Joshua, for the soldier on guard remained at the spring, farther down the mountainside. When she went to serve the food, Joshua insisted that she spread out the viands before them and share the meal.

"A woman should not eat with men," Rahab protested.

"A wife shares the wedding feast with her husband, and we are betrothed," Joshua reminded her. "When Salmon lets me go down to the camp in a day or two, I will take your father the *mohar* from my share of the spoils. Then it will be official."

"The price will be high," she warned him with a smile, seating herself on the couch beside him and pouring a cup of wine for each of them. "My father values me highly."

"And rightly so," he agreed. "With my share of the plunder from King Sihon's palace in Heshbon and the coffers of Og of Bashan, you will be the wife of a rich man, Rahab." Joshua took a hunk of roast goat meat and bit into it with strong teeth. Tearing loose a great piece, he crammed it into his mouth with his fingers, washing the meat down with a great draught of wine. He was an enthusiastic trencherman, if not a very delicate one.

Rahab ate more daintily, but she too used her fingers, for there were no eating utensils, save a knife to cut the meat into chunks.

"Sit closer, Rahab," Joshua commanded, putting his arm about her waist and drawing her near him. "And drink some wine; a feast is nothing without wine."

"What will your people say when you take a wife outside the camp of Israel?" she asked.

"They will welcome the wife of Joshua, son of Nun and captain of a thousand. Else I will knock a few heads together."

"Do you think they may not want to receive me?"

He shrugged. "The young women and the mothers of young daughters will hate you for your beauty and because you are marrying me. But in time they will accept you."

47

"We are of the same people," Rahab protested. "Our father was Abram, the patriarch."

"But you are marrying a leader of Israel and a rich man," he reminded her, drawing her still closer to him. "They will envy you your position in the camp because you are my wife."

"Salmon believes you will one day be a king of Israel," Rahab said happily, "and that I will be your queen."

Joshua laughed. "Salmon is overly ambitious for me. First I must carve out a kingdom for the children of Israel in the land of Canaan. Then there will be time enough to talk of kings."

"But you have thought about it, haven't you?"

"Any man would become a king if he could." Joshua was in an expansive mood now, the wine having stirred his blood.

"What would *you* do if you ruled Israel?" she asked.

He took her chin in his hands and kissed her lips, setting her limbs to trembling. Her blood was afire—partly from the wine she had drunk, it was true, but largely from the sheer animal vitality of his body pressed so close against hers.

"You worry about things that do not concern a woman, Rahab," he said genially. "A king fights for power and wealth. He is respected and envied by his people and by other kings because he is strong—and rich."

"Wouldn't you be concerned with the good of the people you rule?"

"You sound like Salmon," Joshua said, a little irritated by her questioning. "Dreamers and poets are not expected to be practical, Rahab. A king should rule his people with a strong hand. If he is wealthy and prosperous, they should be content that he brings glory to the nation. Here"—he poured another cup of wine—"drink more wine. It will drive such thoughts from your head."

"What would you have your wife do while you were winning more power and wealth?" Rahab asked when she put down the cup.

"She must busy herself pleasing her husband, as all good wives should, and bear strong sons to comfort me in my old age. She must prepare my food and see that there is cool wine to refresh me when I come home from the battlefield or the chase. She must carry water for me to wash myself at the

48

end of the day and give me pleasure upon my couch at night."

"A slave or a concubine could do all those things," Rahab protested.

"You shall have slaves," he promised, missing her meaning altogether. "And when you are a queen, people will wait to do your every wish. What more could you want, girl?" He swept her into his arms and across his breast, so that her head was pressed against his massive shoulder.

"I say it again, Rahab, you think too much. Worry will take away the softness of your lips." Here he kissed her roughly until she clung to him, out of breath. "It will make you grow thin and your loins will lose their plumpness and their beauty in the sight of your husband." His hands upon her body, caressing her warm flesh, set the blood to pounding in her ears like the throbbing beat of timbrels, driving out all other thoughts and sweeping away all her reserve.

It made no difference now that his answers to her questions were not the ones that Salmon—who also loved her—would have given. Nothing made any difference save that her body cried out for his and that his mouth upon hers seemed to draw the very strength from her, until she thirsted for his caressing hands even though they hurt her in the urgency of his own now thoroughly aroused desire.

If the men outside heard her single cry of pain, they were soldiers and trained not to interfere except upon the orders of an officer. The fire in the cave had died out, leaving a faint rosy glow to illumine the darkness, so only the little statuettes on the rocky shelves of the cave witnessed their union. And, being inanimate, they could know nothing of the soaring ecstasy that only man and his mate, of all living things, experience in the embrace of love.

Sometime during the night Rahab awakened, half smothered by the weight of Joshua's arm across her body. Slipping from beneath it, she moved quietly to the mouth of the cave and sat with her back against the rocky wall, looking out on the countryside below. Only the occasional gleam of a camp-fire betrayed the location of the Israelite army at the foot of the mountain. Farther away, both Medeba and the walled city of Heshbon were hidden under the enveloping mantle of the night.

Above Rahab's head the star-girt canopy of the sky was ablaze with light. And the moon, riding high, seemed indeed the very dwelling place of Yah that she believed it to be. Remembering the precious moments she had spent in the arms of her lover and betrothed husband, their ardor spent and their passions assuaged in the mystical union that gives conception to another human, Rahab had no regrets. Before the altar of Yah she and Joshua had become one. And since they both served the same god, nothing could be wrong in their union.

Deep within her body, where Joshua's seed was even now mingling with hers, Rahab imagined she could already feel a quickening of new life. He would be strong, this child of hers, she knew. His body would be like Joshua's, his sinews as massive as those of his father sleeping on the couch in the faint moonlight that seeped into the cave.

The thought that her child might one day be a king—as Salmon had said—was exciting, too. But most of all she prayed to Yah that he would be strong, not only in his body but also in his spirit, strong enough to become a true leader of men and lead them in the ways of peace and love, one for another.

Eight

JOSHUA grumbled a little at being left alone after Rahab hurried him through the morning meal so that she could go down to Medeba to tell her father of the betrothal and arrange for the formal wedding. He gave her his purse with the *mohar*, or bride price, however, and, leaving him plentifully supplied with wine and fruit, Rahab took a basket and hurried down the winding path leading to the village below.

It was a fresh spring morning, and the whole world seemed to be rejoicing with her. The sun shone brightly and the birds

of the village were the shops, open-fronted structures where each merchant sat on a raised platform with his goods piled behind him beneath the shelter of the roof. His position there had a twofold purpose, allowing him to call out his wares to the passers-by and at the same time watch the door to see that no one carried out anything without paying.

Behind each open-fronted shop was a wall and a door leading to a small enclosed garden. Around this court were the sleeping rooms, likewise built of sun-baked brick daubed with mud. There were no windows in the walls, but rushes were laid on each flat roof, and in hot weather the family slept on the rooftop, where the cool night breeze from the deep valley of the River Jord could caress tired and sweating bodies.

This was Rahab's village; she knew most of its people by name. Her first stop this morning was at the shop of the charcoal seller, Joel, with its brazier of hot coals glowing beside the owner so that any who had allowed their fires to die out during the night could buy one to light them again.

"*Shalom,* Joel," she said happily. "How are Rebecca and the boy?"

"They are well by the grace of the great god Baal who giveth life," the charcoal seller said, but he did not smile upon her as usual. "Do you wish to buy coals, daughter of Chazan?"

"I stopped to greet you," Rahab said, surprised by his unfriendly tone. "And to tell you——"

"You have greeted me," he interrupted. "Now be on your way."

Hearing voices outside, the charcoal seller's wife Rebecca came from the court at the back of the shop. At the sight of Rahab she drew herself up sharply, a picture of outraged virtue. "Begone, harlot!" she snapped. "Defile us not with your presence."

"I am no harlot," Rahab cried indignantly. "You both know me well." She lifted the purse she carried. "This purse contains the bride price I am carrying to my father now, and soon I will be married to Joshua, captain of a thousand among the Habiru. I came to tell you and Joel first, Rebecca, because you are my best friends."

At the sight of the well-filled purse Rebecca's eyes narrowed and a cunning light shone in them, but her manner did not change.

"No harlot has friends in Medeba," she snapped.

"Why do you call me that—that name?"

"As soon as the cursed Habiru came, did you not fly to them? And have you not defiled the cave of the god Yah with your lechery?"

"I only helped to care for a wounded man," Rahab protested. "Just as I helped nurse your child when he was sick last year."

Rebecca laughed, a short, brittle sound like a curse. "While the Habiru kill our husbands and brothers in battle, you lie with them for their gold and to have your father chosen as their scribe."

"That's a lie!" Rahab cried indignantly. "My father was chosen as scribe while I was at the Cave of Yah—by Salmon, the physician."

"Go back to the cave of your stupid god then!" Rebecca screamed. "Go back to your Habiru lovers, slut!"

As always in a village such as this, the sound of raised voices brought people from every side. All of them had been her friends until a few days ago; Rahab had expected them to rejoice with her in her good fortune. But when she looked about her, she saw only hostility in their eyes.

A group of men who had been loitering around the well, waiting to be hired, joined the women now and began making rude remarks. Encouraged by them, one of the women spat upon Rahab and leaped in to rake at her face with sharp, grimy nails.

When Rahab raised her arm to protect herself, the woman's fingers caught the girl's robe at the shoulder, snapping the pin that held it and tearing it apart. As the torn garment fell from her shoulder, Rahab was forced to seize it with one hand to keep her upper body from being exposed.

"Harlot!" the woman screamed shrilly. "Traitor!"

"The men of Israel mean no harm to the Amorite people," Rahab pleaded. "They only fought because King Sihon refused them passage. The Habiru are descended from Abram, as I am and many of you."

"You lie!" Rebecca cried. "They are runaway slaves and robbers, the scum of Egypt come to take our homes from us."

"Are the Habiru men better lovers than those of Medeba?" one of the men asked with a leer, and was rewarded by a roar of laughter from his fellows. "Or do they pay you more?"

"I am to be married to Joshua, captain of a thousand," Rahab tried to explain again. "This morning I came back to invite all of you to the wedding feast."

"Go to the Habiru camp and invite the other harlots to your wedding," Rebecca shouted. "We want none of it."

One of the women moved closer now and slapped Rahab's face. And as she tried to protect herself, another seized her robe at the back and ripped it to the waist. Hiding her body from the leering gaze of the men as best she could with an arm across her breast, Rahab began to back away, seeking to escape from the jeering, hooting crowd. But they ringed her in with a solid wall of hostile faces, while a barrage of vile insults and a shower of spittle buffeted her.

Determined that Rahab should not escape with the purse, Rebecca made her move now. "Will we let this harlot go unpunished for bringing shame upon our city?" she demanded of the crowd.

"Let her be stoned for her adultery!" the woman who had spat upon Rahab cried. "It is the will of the gods!"

"Stone her!" The men took up the cry at once.

"Kill the harlot!" the women screamed.

Half naked and shaking with terror, Rahab looked desperately about her for help from any source but found none. In their orgy of self-righteousness the crowd did not even notice that the slave caravan Rahab had seen on the road was passing the gate, a sight that would ordinarily have brought the men, at least, to line the walls and comment upon the charms of the slave girls.

Shouting and jeering now in a frenzy of blood lust, the crowd seized Rahab and began to draw her toward the gate. Foremost among them was Rebecca, who managed, in the crush of the crowd, to jerk the purse containing the bride price from the thong by which it hung from the terrified girl's belt.

Eager hands shoved Rahab into the niche in the wall outside the gate that served as a place of execution. There was one such in every town, its walls stained by blood spattered from the bodies of victims of the stones. Half conscious,

Rahab was left alone for a moment and, realizing that she was no longer being cuffed and pummeled by the crowd, she raised her head and looked about her. But the momentary respite, she saw at once, was only to give the crowd time to select the stones for the next episode in this brutal drama.

They went about the job methodically, picking up small stones and stuffing them into their robes. By using small missiles first, the agony of the victim would be prolonged, gratifying to the full the blood lust of the crowd.

A jeering shout went up as the first stone missed its mark, but the second throw was more skillful. It struck Rahab on the temple as she staggered along the wall, instinctively seeking some loophole by which she might yet escape the certain death that awaited her. Weakened as she was, Rahab was driven to her knees by the blow, but a blind impulse toward self-preservation kept her going on somehow. Blood trickled down her face from a cut laid open by the stone. When the crowd saw it, their baying suddenly took on a deeper animal-like quality, the growl of the pack closing in for the kill.

A hail of stones filled the air now. More than half missed their mark, else Rahab would have been beaten to death at the first onslaught. Buffeted in a dozen places about her head and body, she went down, but the instinct to live kept her crawling even now, tearing her finger ends against the gravel until the blood came and making it harder for the throwers to hit her body.

The cut on Rahab's temple was opened wider by the barrage of stones, and blood flowed down into her eyes, blinding her so that she could see only through a red haze. "Joshua!" she cried at the height of her agony. "Joshua, save me."

"She calls to the Habiru," Rebecca cried. "Kill her! Kill her!"

But Rahab was already beyond hearing, for even as Rebecca spoke a large stone struck her temple, mercifully dropping her into a bottomless void where she felt no more pain.

Book Two

THE HORNET OF GOD

And I sent the hornet before you, which drave them out from before you . . .

JOSHUA 24:12

One

TWO of the Israelite soldiers wounded during the fight outside the city of Heshbon had been in serious danger. Salmon did not feel safe in leaving them until the day after Rahab had come down the mountain so happily, only to be stoned by those she had counted as her friends. And since he had been in the Israelite camp all the while, he knew nothing of the tragedy that had taken place in Medeba.

Joshua was pacing angrily up and down outside the cave when Salmon came up the slope. "Where is Rahab?" he demanded peremptorily.

"I left her here with you."

"She went down to the village yesterday morning to make arrangements for our wedding. And took a purse for the bride price with her."

"You have not heard from her since?"

"How could I?" Joshua demanded testily. "I have not left the cave."

"Why didn't you send the guard to look for her?"

"And make a fool of myself?" Joshua shrugged. "She must be down there at Medeba prattling to her friends of what she will wear at the wedding. Women think of nothing else."

"You should know Rahab better than that," Salmon said curtly. "Why did she decide so suddenly to arrange the wedding?"

"Perhaps she wanted it before I go into battle again—so she can be a rich widow if I am killed."

"There would be plenty of time after you are able to go down to the camp."

"She may have thought she was with child then."

Salmon stiffened at the words. It was true that he had urged Rahab into this union, with his talk of Joshua's role as a possible king of Israel and hers as queen. But at the realization that Joshua had already claimed Rahab, he could not control a stab of pain like a knife plunged into his heart.

"By the gods, I will punish her for neglecting me!" Joshua raged. "I had to eat cold meat for the morning meal. And the wine gave out last night."

"A little hardship will be good for your soul," Salmon told him shortly. "I am worried more about Rahab than whether or not you eat cold meat."

"I told you she's prattling with the women of Medeba about marrying and clothes. They forget all about time, but I will change that after we are married."

Salmon looked at the Israelite champion thoughtfully. "Why are you marrying Rahab, Joshua?"

"Why does any man take a woman to wife? So she can warm his bed at night, cook his food, raise his children, and make others envy him with her beauty."

"Rahab is marrying you because she loves you."

Joshua shrugged. "I am a soldier, not a poet, Salmon. And I have seen nearly forty years. Love is for the young."

"Why did you lie with her then, if you don't love her?"

Joshua flushed with annoyance. "Who I marry or why is no concern of yours, Salmon, but I will tell you this much. When he weds, a man wants to be sure no others have been before him."

"Did you have to seduce her to know that?" Salmon demanded angrily.

"Don't talk like a priest," Joshua snapped. "How else would I know she was a virgin?"

"You don't even understand what I am talking about," Salmon said in disgust.

"Then don't talk like a fool. How badly did Sihon's troops maul us before Heshbon?"

"It was only a skirmish. One of our patrols went too near

58

the walls. The enemy sallied forth and cut them to pieces."

"Did they learn anything important?"

"Only that the Amorites are foolish enough to leave the walls if they think they can destroy a small force. That should tell you how to capture Heshbon, though."

Joshua nodded. "We will bring up our troops by night and hide them in the hills around the city. Then we will draw the Amorites out of Heshbon and fall upon them in small bands until their forces are whittled down and we can take the city."

"If they are fools enough to come out a second time."

"Then we will assault the walls."

"And kill a thousand men?"

"One day you will go too far, Salmon." Joshua flushed angrily. "I am captain of a thousand, remember, not you."

"What will your thousand be worth to Israel when all of them are dead?"

"What would you do then?"

"Any fool can thrust with a sword or a spear," Salmon told him. "The wise leader wins wars in his tent before they begin."

"Speak your wisdom then, O learned one," Joshua said caustically.

"Draw out the Amorites just before dawn by launching an attack against Heshbon with a small force," Salmon told him. "If you make it look like a full retreat, they will follow our men into the hills, where we can fall upon them with a larger force and take them alive. Then dress our own warriors in the enemy's clothing and let them carry his weapons. An Amorite force leaves the walls, and what the guards will take for the same force in the darkness returns—to hold open the gates until our main body of troops can storm the city and capture it."

"By the gods of Israel, that is a fine plan," Joshua exclaimed, his anger at Salmon gone as quickly as it had come. "I will lead those who hold the gate. We must go down to the camp now and plan it with Caleb."

"What about Rahab?"

"You can go to Medeba and tell her we have left the cave. She will be somewhere in the town planning the wedding. And tell her I forgive her for not coming back," Joshua added

59

magnanimously. "She is still young and I can teach her later the proper behavior for a wife."

At the edge of the Israelite camp Joshua went to find Caleb, being anxious to confer at once and plan the battle for Heshbon according to the strategy Salmon had outlined. Salmon went on to Medeba alone to search for Rahab.

The town was quiet when he entered it, although had he looked he would have seen fresh bloodstains on the rocks outside the walls. The usual knot of men lounged beside the well with the excuse that they were waiting to be hired. Several ancients sat in the sun at one side of the curb, jabbering at each other about the weather, the latest scandal, and the hundreds of topics that delight the ears of the old. A group of women chattered as they washed clothes in the rock-lined pool to one side of the well.

Salmon approached this group, since they would be likely to know about Rahab if she had come as far as Medeba. Anything of interest in these towns, he knew, was discussed by the women at their washing before it happened, and Rahab's coming marriage to Joshua would be the most important thing to happen in Medeba for a long time.

"I seek a young woman called Rahab," he said courteously to one of the women. "Can any of you tell me where her father's inn is located?"

The woman looked away quickly, too quickly, he thought. "We know nothing of Rahab," she mumbled.

"She is known to have come here yesterday," he said. "Surely one of you must have seen her."

There was no answer. Salmon looked inquiringly from one to the other of the groups around the well, but as his eyes met each surly gaze in turn, the villager looked away.

"Are you sure you know nothing about her?" he repeated.

"We know she is a harlot and that she gave herself to the Habiru so her father could be their scribe," one of the women snapped. It was Rebecca, the wife of Joel, ringleader in the crowd that had stoned Rahab.

"When did you decide Rahab was a harlot?" Salmon asked quietly, sure now that he had stumbled upon a clue.

"Yesterday, when she came here to boast——"

"Then you lied!" he said quickly. "You did see Rahab."

"You did not ask me," Rebecca said virtuously. "But we only lied to hide the shame of Medeba that one of our daughters chose to be a harlot."

"Rahab is no harlot," Salmon said curtly. "You know that as well as I do. What have you done with her?"

"See." Rebecca clucked virtuously and looked around at the other women. "She has turned even the head of the physician."

"Enough of this," he said. "Where is Rahab? And no more lies, mind you."

"Rahab did come here yesterday," Rebecca admitted. "She strutted through the town boasting how she made the Habiru captain give her money for lying with him."

Salmon was sure the woman was lying, but he hoped, by letting her talk, to gain some inkling of what had really happened.

"What did she do then?" he asked.

"A caravan with women for the slave markets of Egypt was passing the city on the King's Highway," Rebecca continued. "Before any of us could stop her, Rahab went to the leader. We heard her bargaining with him to take her along."

If any part of this was true, it was astounding news indeed. "Why would she do such a thing?" he asked. "Her father lives here."

Rebecca shrugged. "I have heard Rahab say many times that she did not intend to spend her life in a little village like Medeba. With the money she got from the Habiru captain she could set herself up as a harlot in Egypt. With her beauty she will no doubt become rich and famous."

The tale had just enough seeming truth in it to give the appearance of fact, but Salmon still could not believe it. Yet when he questioned the others, they all told the same story, having seen at once the advisability of sticking together in their accounts of what had happened here yesterday. And since he could not find any evidence to disprove their story, however unbelievable it was to him, he finally had no course left save to go back to the Israelite camp.

Two

JOSHUA was in deep conference with Caleb, discussing the strategy to be used against Heshbon, when Salmon returned. The plan was the one Salmon had devised, although Joshua had not announced it as other than his own. Salmon, however, was not concerned with military campaigns today. He was sure the people of Medeba had lied about Rahab, but he could not as yet put his finger on the flaw in their story.

When he recounted to Joshua what he had been told, the Israelite captain's face flushed. "By the beard of Pharaoh!" he snapped. "She fooled me with her air of innocence. And stole the bride price as well."

"Rahab was a virgin before you lay with her," Salmon said angrily. "You said so yourself."

"A girl as clever as that could fool any man. I remember now that she came to me easily enough, once we were alone."

"She expected to marry you," Salmon said. "After all, you were betrothed."

Caleb, who had been listening, now spoke. "You are skilled in healing the sick and clever at devising military strategy, Salmon," he said, "but apparently you are a mere babe in arms where women are concerned. The girl took Joshua's money and went to Egypt, where harlots are well paid. It is as simple as that."

"I still don't believe it," Salmon said stubbornly.

"She fooled me, Salmon," Joshua admitted. "And I have had some experience with women. You need not feel badly that she took you in too."

"Give me a hundred men and I will follow the caravan along the King's Highway," Salmon suggested. "It cannot have gone very far in two days of travel. Then we will see what is the truth in this affair."

"That would not be wise," Caleb objected.

"The responsibility will be mine," Salmon insisted. "No one else will be blamed for my action."

"The borders of Moab are only a day's journey south of Medeba along the King's Highway," Caleb pointed out. "They must have crossed it hours ago."

"We came a long way around to keep from fighting the Moabites," Joshua agreed. "We can't afford to have them prodding spears into our backs just when we are ready to attack Heshbon and move against King Og of Bashan."

Reluctantly Salmon agreed, for there was no arguing against their logic. With the remains of a once powerful enemy still safe within the walled city of Heshbon, no one with the best interests of Israel at heart could wish to incite a strong force like the Moabites to attack from the rear. The success of the final moves against King Sihon and later against the men of Bashan depended largely upon the certainty that Moab and Edom to the south would remain neutral. And as Caleb had pointed out, the Israelites had journeyed many painful miles outside the straightest route along the King's Highway through these countries in order to be certain of their neutrality.

Leaving the tent where Joshua and Caleb pored over their plan of battle, Salmon sought out Rahab's father, at his work. He found the scribe sitting cross-legged on the floor of a large goatskin tent that served as the military headquarters for the camp of Israel. He was a plump man with a round face, greying hair, and wise and kindly eyes.

"Greetings, O physician," Chazan said warmly. "It is said in the camp that but for your skill the men wounded before Heshbon would all be dead."

"Yahweh favored my puny efforts in their behalf," Salmon admitted, taking a seat on the ground beside the scribe.

Chazan's kit of writing materials was slung from his waist, and a papyrus roll—purchased from the same Babylonian caravan from which Salmon had bought medicines and new instruments—was spread out before him. Made from the cellular pith of the papyrus plants that grew so vigorously in the lowlands along the Nile, the parchment-like material was one of Egypt's most valuable exports.

The making of papyrus had been a fine art along the Nile for over a thousand years, as had been that of writing upon it. Stalks of the tall reeds, often reaching the height of twenty or more feet, were first cut into strips and placed side by side

63

in a horizontal row to whatever width was desired. Across these was placed another row of similar strips with a paste made of vegetable gum to cement the layers together. When pressed skillfully until dry and then pumiced, a smooth, flexible sheet resulted that could be rolled up for almost any length with a wooden rod in the center for support.

Some of these papyrus rolls containing accounts of military expeditions and other important records were more than a hundred paces in length. Literary works were even illumined with colored pictures by experts in that art. And the recent substitution of an alphabet for the ancient and cumbrous method of picture writing had increased tremendously the efficiency of the scribes.

Everywhere, now, men were beginning to learn the value of keeping detailed records of taxes, business transactions, and even the manifold activities of everyday life. Without such accounts a man might be forced to pay a debt over and over, or even be sold into slavery for a deed he did not commit, merely because he possessed the same name as a known criminal and could not prove his own identity and activities by means of a written record.

Beside Chazan lay his palette, a rectangular wooden case with a central groove into which the reed pens of his trade could be stored. As many as ten of the pens with their fine points were held in place by a piece of wood glued across the groove in such a manner that the top of the box could slide in and out over the pens without injuring the points.

At one end of the box were six small hollows for holding ink or paints. Only two of them were filled now, one with red ink to mark disbursements on the long papyrus roll on which Chazan was working, the other to indicate the value of trophies, tributes, spoils of war, and gold from ransoms. A strict record had to be kept since each of the fighting men shared in the loot obtained by the military victories, with the captains drawing larger shares according to the number of soldiers they led.

Chazan had been writing with ink made from a mixture of colored earths and vegetable dyes, stirred up with gum and water. The ingredients were in a small goatskin bag beside him, with the little earthenware pots in which the ink was skillfully blended to the right color.

64

"I hope you bring a message from Rahab," the scribe said. "One of the men who was guarding the Cave of Yah told me he heard her and Joshua discussing a wedding. I have been expecting to hear from her."

"I——" Salmon stopped, reluctant to disclose the bad tidings he brought, but Chazan did not seem to notice his hesitancy.

"My daughter and I are indeed honored that so great a captain as Joshua would take her to wife," he continued. "I could not wish a better marriage for her."

Salmon took a deep breath. "Rahab has disappeared, Chazan."

"Disappeared!" A drop of black ink fell from the point of the reed pen in the scribe's fingers and formed a circular blob on the spotless surface of the papyrus roll. "What do you mean, Salmon?"

"Rahab came down to Medeba from the Cave of Yah yesterday morning," the physician explained. "She was carrying a purse from Joshua containing the bride price."

Chazan's face brightened. "Then she is probably at our old home, the inn, preparing for the wedding."

"The women at Medeba tell me Rahab left there yesterday morning with a caravan of women slaves bound for Egypt."

In his agitation Chazan started up from the mat, tossing pens in every direction and dropping the papyrus roll to the floor. "She did not go willingly," he cried. "Rahab would not do such a thing."

"The women of Medeba swear she bargained for her passage with the leader of the caravan," Salmon told him, "paying for it from the purse she carried."

"They have taken the money and hidden Rahab away somewhere. She may already be dead."

"Of course that is what happened." Salmon got to his feet quickly. "I was a fool to believe them even for a moment. We must search the town at once."

"I know Medeba like the palm of my hand," Chazan said. "If Rahab is there we will find her."

Reluctantly Joshua agreed to let Salmon have a patrol of soldiers to conduct the search of Medeba. He obviously did not believe they would find any evidence of Rahab's presence, however, having accepted already the women's story

65

that she had gone to Egypt, where the trade of a harlot was vastly more profitable than in a small town.

And indeed, after hours spent searching every house in Medeba, Salmon was almost prepared to admit wearily that Rebecca might have been telling the truth. They found no sign of Rahab, nor any evidence that she had been slain and her body hidden away as Chazan had feared. All the people they questioned who admitted to having seen the girl at all told the same story; namely, that she had left with the caravan of the flesh peddler, and of her own accord.

Sadly Chazan and Salmon returned to the camp of Israel. If Rahab had indeed gone to Egypt, Salmon knew, the chances of their ever meeting her again were remote. For among the teeming millions of that fertile land along the Nile she could drop out of sight as easily as if she had fallen into a bottomless pit.

Three

RAHAB had awakened sometime in the afternoon to a throbbing agony all over her body. She had no idea where she was or what had happened after she had lost consciousness during the stoning. In fact, what surprised her most was the fact, finally inescapable as consciousness returned, that she was actually alive.

When finally she became conscious enough to recognize her surroundings, Rahab realized that she was lying with her body trussed across the back of an ass like a sack of grain. She could hear women's voices around her as the patient animal plodded along, but beyond that she could not go.

Finally the animal carrying Rahab stopped. Rough hands loosened the ropes that held her across its back and carried her a short distance, placing her on the ground. Every movement brought pain, but she managed to turn her head enough to see that she was lying on a plot of grass beside a stream that tumbled from a spring at the edge of a clearing.

All about her people were busy setting up camp for the

night. Several men—slaves by their dress and manner—were removing the packs from some of the asses and tethering the animals out to graze on the rich grass beside the small stream. Others were raising tents, and behind her Rahab could hear the chatter of women's voices.

"What a bag of bones that one is," one of the women said in a Canaanite dialect. "Abda should have let them kill her with the stones."

The words filled out a chain of memory in Rahab's mind. She recalled now that she had seen a caravan with many women in it moving along the highway between Heshbon and Medeba when she'd come down the mountainside that morning. And she remembered, too, that it had been in the act of passing the gates of Medeba as the crowd was dragging her outside the walls to be stoned.

The people of the caravan must have saved her life and carried her away with them, she realized now. But she still could not understand how they would have been able to accomplish such a feat in the face of the crowd's blood lust. Nor could she find much room for rejoicing, even in the fact that she was alive.

From the stories she had heard caravan drivers at her father's inn tell about the slave markets of Egypt, Rahab had no illusions about why the leader of the caravan would have saved her life or what her ultimate fate would be. The brothels of Memphis and the other cities along the Nile needed a constant supply of young and pretty girls, and the flesh merchants of the slave caravans made a tidy profit through supplying that demand.

A dark-haired young woman with merry eyes and a rather opulent body knelt on the grass beside Rahab and held a bottle to the injured girl's lips. "Drink," she commanded. "Abda's wine is not the best, but at least he is free with it."

Rahab drank gratefully. The wine was sour, but it warmed her body a little and eased some of her pain. "Where are we?" she asked.

"In Moab. The caravan crossed the River Arnon a little while ago; this brook runs into it."

"How did I get with you?"

"We were passing your town just as they were stoning you," the girl explained. "Abda has a keen eye and saw how

67

pretty you are, so he intervened and offered them gold for you before they could kill you."

Rahab managed to smile wryly. "I could not have brought a very high price."

"You didn't," the other girl assured her cheerfully. "But at least you are still alive."

"I—I thank you for that."

"Thank Abda, not me. My name is Tamar. I am a slave just as you are."

"I am called Rahab." She hesitated, then voiced the thought that was uppermost in her mind. "What will—the one you call Abda do with me?"

"Sell you in the slave markets of Egypt like the rest of us —at a fat profit, of course. Abda is not a bad fellow, though. Most of us came willingly; in Egypt men know how to appreciate a girl's beauty."

"But you will still be slaves."

Tamar shrugged. "Among my people a woman is the slave of her husband anyway. She cooks his food, makes his clothes, lies with him when he desires her, and bears his children. In Egypt they tell me the concubines even have slaves of their own." Her eyes narrowed a little. "Why did they stone you in Medeba, Rahab?"

"They said I was a harlot."

"Were you?"

"Of course not," Rahab cried with whatever indignation she could muster from her small reserve of strength.

"There are worse things than being a harlot," Tamar said matter-of-factly. "Did you lie with a man you were not married to then?"

It seemed almost a sacrilege to tell another of the rapture she'd found in Joshua's arms. And yet Rahab sensed that Tamar was offering to be her friend and might be offended if she lied. "Only once," she admitted. "With my betrothed."

Tamar shrugged. "If they stoned every woman who lay with her betrothed husband—or with some not betrothed— most of us would be dead."

"Joshua is captain of a thousand Habiru warriors," Rahab explained proudly. "As soon as he finds out what has happened, he will come after me."

Tamar's eyes widened. "We heard of this Joshua when we

68

came through the land of King Og. The men of Bashan have sworn to destroy him. Tell me," she continued on a confidential note. "What is it like to lie with a Habiru? I'll wager they are no milksops."

"Joshua is very strong," Rahab said proudly. "His hands upon your body take away all your strength, just as he sweeps the enemy from his path in battle."

Tamar shivered. "Would that I had found a man like that for a husband. I might not have minded cooking his food and mending his clothes, or even bearing his children, although childbearing makes a woman's body unsightly in the eyes of other men."

"Why did you leave Canaan, Tamar?"

Tamar laughed. "I am what the people of Medeba claimed you were, Rahab, a harlot."

"But you seem——" Rahab stopped, not wanting to hurt the other girl's feelings.

"I see Abda looking this way," Tamar said quickly. "Soon he will come to see what sort of a bargain he got for his gold."

"Will he——"

Tamar understood her thought. "Abda is a eunuch," she explained. "With him, beautiful women are only merchandise." She gave Rahab a keen glance. "You are innocent-enough looking with your white skin and red hair. Did you speak the truth just now when you said you had lain with a man only once?"

"By the wisdom of Yah, I swear it was the truth," Rahab assured her.

"I don't doubt you, and perhaps Abda will not either, if you do as I say. Anyone can tell you are innocent and gently bred from your speech and manner."

"What do you want me to do?"

"Tell Abda you are a virgin and that the people of Medeba stoned you because you became betrothed to the Habiru captain."

"Why should that make any difference?"

"Virgins bring high prices in the slave markets of Egypt, and only princes can afford them," Tamar explained. "If Abda believes you, he will give you special treatment."

"But it would still be deceiving him. And I do owe him my life."

"Did he ask you whether you wished to be a slave?" Tamar demanded. "Be sure he lost nothing in the transaction. Even for a harlot named Tamar he had to pay more than he did for you."

"Couldn't he tell?"

"Perhaps. Abda has dealt in woman flesh for a long time, and they have few secrets from him. He will not insist upon being too certain, though, just so he can claim you are a virgin. As for whoever buys you, I will tell you ways of deceiving any man so he will think you as innocent as a babe."

"I will not need to deceive anyone," Rahab assured her. "Joshua is sure to rescue me by tomorrow at least."

"The people who sold you will lie to him," Tamar warned. "And even if your Joshua tried to follow you, the Moabites would kill him when he crossed the River Arnon into their territory."

"I hadn't thought of that," Rahab admitted. Then her face brightened. "Salmon will think of a way, then."

"So?" Tamar's eyebrows lifted expressively. "Now there are two of them."

Rahab laughed. "Salmon is a physician and a very dear friend. He is very clever."

"Here is Abda," Tamar warned her in a low voice. "Be careful what you tell him."

The slave merchant was a mountain of fat. His hair was thin and silky like a woman's, and his hands, for all their pudginess, had an almost feminine delicacy about them. His face was round and his jowls hung down over his neck.

"So, young woman," he said pleasantly, "I see that you have decided to live." Abda's eyes, almost hidden in his plump cheeks, were shrewd, but Rahab was sure at first glance that he was kind, in spite of his occupation.

"Tamar told me how you saved me from the stones, sir," she said gratefully. "I owe you my life."

"You see, Tamar," the eunuch said approvingly, "I knew this girl was gently bred the moment I saw her, even through the bruises. Listen to her speech."

"Truly you have the eye of a hawk, Abda the mountainous," Tamar said impudently. "Or a buzzard."

The slaver laughed until his mountainous belly shook. "You are a joy to my soul, O shrew of Canaan. Your tongue is sharp like the teeth of a jackal. I will be loath to sell you when we get to Egypt."

"Promise to sell me only to a brothel for rich men," Tamar said, "and I will tell you something to gladden that money-bag you call your heart."

"It shall be done. What is this good news you have for me?"

"I have been looking over this girl's body to see if her wounds are grave. She is virgin."

Abda's eyes gleamed. "Are you sure?"

"As sure as that I am not."

Abda guffawed again, holding his sides. "Nothing could be more certain than that," he agreed. Then his mirth subsided and his shrewd eyes turned to Rahab once more.

"How can this be, girl?" he asked. "The women of Medeba said they stoned you because you were a harlot and had brought disgrace on them."

"Does she look like a harlot?" Tamar demanded indignantly before Rahab could answer. "The merest glance tells you they lied."

Before Rahab realized what Tamar was doing, she had stripped down the rags that covered Rahab, exposing her body to the waist. "Look at her breasts," Tamar said. "They are as firm as pomegranates and the nipples are like red cherries."

Abda pursed his lips thoughtfully. Strangely enough, Rahab felt no more shamed by his appraising glance than she would have by that of another woman.

"And look at her belly," Tamar went on, stripping off the rest of Rahab's garments. "See how milk-white it is, even under the bruises. The thighs are like slender saplings guarding a flower of exquisite beauty."

The slave merchant rubbed his beardless chin while Rahab covered herself again with her rags. "The women still called her a harlot," he observed. "And people are not stoned without reason."

"I had just become betrothed to the Habiru captain Joshua," Rahab explained. "They stoned me so they could divide the bride price I carried."

71

At the mention of Joshua, Abda's eyes gleamed suddenly, as if a new thought had come to him. "How is it that you were betrothed to the Habiru captain if you are an Amorite?" he asked. "The Israelites are very strict about marriage between their men and women of other nations."

"My family is of the same descent as the Israelites," Rahab explained. "We are all descendants of Abram, who came into this country many centuries ago from Ur Kasdim. We even worship the same god, except that we call him Yah and they call him Yahweh."

"Then you are really an Israelite too." For some reason Abda appeared to be very pleased with the thought.

"We do not call ourselves by that name," Rahab explained, "but we are of the same stock."

The slave merchant rubbed his hands together with obvious satisfaction. "Truly we did find a pearl of great price outside Medeba today, Tamar," he admitted. "But do not think to fool Abda, the seller of women, with this talk of being virgin." He turned to Rahab. "How many times had you lain with your Habiru captain?"

Rahab crimsoned with embarrassment. "Only once," she mumbled.

"Good! With the arts that Tamar here shall teach you, it will be easy to fool a purchaser into believing you are still virgin. Egyptians favor Israelite women very highly," Abda continued. "They think them the most beautiful of all, including their own, and pay high prices at the slave market."

"Am I still to be sold?" Rahab asked.

Abda looked at her in astonishment. "Why else would I save you from the stones, girl? When I saw that you were young and beautiful I knew you would bring a high price in Memphis."

"But my betrothed is a leader of Israel," Rahab protested. "He will pay you a good price if you take me back to him."

Abda shrugged. "The Israelites are a nomad people with few riches. They do not buy slaves."

"Joshua is captain of a thousand, and his share of the spoils from conquering King Sihon will be great."

"The Habiru have not yet taken Heshbon, girl, and this lover of yours would not dare to cross into Moab, even for you. Believe me, Rahab, I am doing you a great favor in taking you to Egypt," he added kindly. "Some concubines have become as powerful as queens."

"I don't want to be a concubine," Rahab wailed. "I only want to wed Joshua." Then a thought came to her. "Joshua will soon be the King of Israel and then I will be a queen. I could arrange for you to buy Israelite women and make a profit selling them in Egypt."

Abda laughed, his great belly shaking again. "Truly you are as droll as you are beautiful, Rahab. The Habiru are only nomads and ex-slaves, robbers of caravans and plunderers of those weaker or more foolish than themselves. What good would it do them to have a king when they have no kingdom?"

"They will have one when Joshua conquers King Og of Bashan."

Abda's eyes widened. "These Habiru are greater fools than I thought, to think of attacking Bashan. King Og is a giant; his men will make your lover look like a child. No, Rahab," he said kindly. "Do as I tell you, and you will have a great future in Egypt. One day you will thank Abda, the slave merchant, for taking you there."

Four

WHATEVER her morals, Tamar was a good nurse. And Abda, for all that he trafficked in human flesh, took good care of his valuable merchandise. After bathing Rahab's bruised and battered body with warm water, Tamar found a clean robe and combed her hair. The cut on her temple was above the hairline and would leave no scar. In fact, it had already closed itself with clotted blood and did not even require a bandage.

Rahab felt much better the following morning, after a good night's sleep in the goatskin tent she shared with Tamar. Abda gave her a mule to ride, as the other women did, and the caravan continued along the King's Highway through the fertile land of Moab.

Travelers had used this caravan trail between Babylon and the cities of the Nile for at least a thousand years, so the stopping places were well defined and the trail worn smooth by thousands of feet, both human and animal. And although every hour carried her farther away from Joshua, Rahab was still sure in her heart that he would somehow manage to follow and rescue her before she could be sold as a slave in Egypt.

Through the high plains of Moab paralleling the eastern shore of the Salt Sea in its cup-shaped depression far below them, across the Brook Zered marking the southern border of the kingdom, and into the vast wastes of Edom, the caravan moved at a steady pace. Rahab looked behind as often as she did ahead, but as the days passed with no sign of Joshua, her hopes slowly faded. The people of Moab had refused him passage along the King's Highway, as Tamar had said, she told herself. Or the women of Medeba could have lied, sending him northward in a fruitless search for her. The real truth, that he had simply accepted their accusations that she was a harlot, did not occur to her, for Joshua himself knew it to be a lie. As the long days wore on, however, hope slowly faded and she had no choice now save to resign herself to whatever fate awaited her in Egypt.

Ten days after leaving Medeba, they were at Ezion-geber, the city at the head of the Gulf of Aqabah, from which many-oared galleys traveled regularly back and forth to Egypt. From here they could have reached Memphis entirely by water, but Abda turned his mules westward instead, across the peninsula between the sea called Red and the Gulf of Aqabah, which formed an arm of it.

Through the scorching wilderness country the caravan hurried during the daylight hours. Stops and watering places were far apart and throats grew parched and dry. Water had to be used sparingly and tempers became short, but the caravan plodded on. Occasionally Abda had to take the whip to one of the girls whose complaints incited the others, but for the most part they all accepted the discomforts, as did Rahab, with good grace.

Then came a day when they reached a canal leading to a broad gulf stretching southward. Here, at the boundary of Egypt proper, a fort guarded the frontier. Traffic on the road was heavy, for this was also the highway to the turquoise and copper mines in the Wilderness of Sin farther down the eastern shore of the gulf, in sight of the great smoking mountain called Horeb. Abda paid the charges for entrance into Egypt and hurried his caravan through the barrier, into the fabled land of the Pharaohs.

Now the pattern of the countryside changed sharply, for they were in the great delta of the Nile. Along the streams that formed a dense network through the lower valley of the great river, wide stands of papyrus reeds grew in the shallow, brackish waters. The countryside was dotted with villages, each surrounded by fields assigned to its inhabitants and dependent upon the life-giving river with its annual rise and fall to bring new life each year.

It was summer now, and the lands were still flooded, but here and there higher bits of ground were covered only by shallow water in which planting could be done. Men dotted these fields, rowing about in light papyrus-stalk boats that could float in a hand's thickness of water. As they scattered seed broadcast over the muddy earth, other men drove herds of cattle over the fields so their hoofs would tread the seed into the ground.

Cannily, the villagers had learned to conserve their labor. Instead of leading the cattle, one man at the head of the herd led a calf on a tether handled from one of the papyrus-reed boats. The mother naturally followed her bawling offspring, and the rest of the herd plodded along behind her.

In the more elevated spots men were at work turning up the soil by means of plows. Each plow was drawn by a cow across whose horns was fastened a bar of wood attached to a long pole which, in turn, dragged the plow through the ground. In some places where the water had already receded, men were busy at the long well sweeps that could be seen everywhere along the banks of the streams and the canals. Through them water was lifted from the lower levels of the streams after the yearly inundation had receded and poured into a network of ditches to irrigate the fields. Everywhere as they rode through the countryside they saw the teeming population of Egypt busily at work upon the endless task of keeping themselves alive.

As they approached their immediate destination, the city

of Memphis—or Mennufer, as it was often called in Egypt—
Rahab became more and more concerned about her immediate future. Abda was kind and she enjoyed being with the other girls, particularly Tamar, who had become her fast friend. And although many of them plied a trade that, with her gentle upbringing, naturally filled Rahab with loathing, she soon discovered that most of them had the same hopes, fears, and ambitions, the same desire for the security of a home, a husband, and children that formed the driving force in every normal woman's life.

"You have not laughed today, Rahab," Tamar said one evening as they lay in their tent with the flap open to catch the breeze that sprang up in this steamy flat land along the Nile with the coming of night. "What is wrong?"

"I have been wondering who will buy me in Egypt."

Tamar laughed. "Trouble yourself no more then. Abda tells me he gets the best prices in the foreign quarter of Memphis, where the officials from the other cities of the empire live." The fat eunuch was passing the tent just then and Tamar called to him, "Come and tell Rahab about the foreign quarter of Memphis, Abda. She is worrying lest she be bought by a poor man."

"I don't mind being poor," Rahab protested as Abda joined them. "But I would like a good master."

"I will set a high price upon you, Rahab," the eunuch assured her. "High enough so that only a prince of Syria or an ambassador can afford to buy you."

"Why would a prince of Syria be in Memphis?"

"Egypt is now burdened with a weak Pharaoh," Abda told them. "He prefers his gardens, his palaces, and his women to war and affairs of state. As a result, barbarians like the Habiru have attacked the cities of kings subject to Egypt and have gone unpunished. Unless this is stopped, those who have not been attacked will soon tire of collecting taxes for Egypt and decide to keep them only for themselves."

"Why don't the Syrians and the Canaanites stay at home and defend themselves?" Rahab asked.

"It is important for them to know whether or not this worm of a Pharaoh will finally turn and loose the chariots of Egypt upon invaders, as Harmhab, the great warrior prince, did when the kings strayed during the rule of Ikhnaton."

"Salmon, the physician, told me of Ikhnaton," Rahab interrupted. "He was a great man who worshiped only one god, as I do."

"Ikhnaton was a weakling idealist who destroyed the wealth of Egypt," Abda corrected. "Only the strong win in this world, Rahab. With your beauty you will attract many men. Choose the right ones as steppingstones and you may one day be a queen."

"Joshua would have made me a queen," Rahab said proudly.

Abda laughed, holding his belly. "The Israelites will be kings of a herd of goats or occasionally of a city, but nothing more. Your Habiru lover and his men are making a loud noise on the east bank of the River Jord, where the bonds with Egypt are weak, but he will think twice before crossing the river into Canaan. Meanwhile the ambassadors from Canaan and Syria idle away their time in Memphis, waiting for Pharaoh to decide what he will do." His eyes twinkled merrily. "And how better can a rich man occupy himself in a warm climate than with a beautiful female slave?"

Five

JOSHUA AND CALEB put Salmon's stratagem into effect in the attack upon Heshbon with marked success. The forces of King Sihon, hoping to repeat their victory of a few days before and cut the Israelites to pieces again, surged forth from the gates in the half darkness of early dawn against the small group that launched the initial attack against the walls of the city. But the Israelite band, retreating in good order to the shelter of a small hill hiding them from the view of the city, lured the Amorites into ambush. The fighting was brief but not very bloody, for the Israelite warriors had strict orders to capture the Amorites with their gear intact.

Joshua himself led the group that quickly donned the gear of the Amorite soldiers. This consisted of the short skirts of white linen favored by the Egyptians, extending almost to the knees, with a tunic of a heavier material over it. On their heads they wore the rounded caps of beaten copper or bronze favored also by Egyptian soldiers, and leathern sandals were laced about their calves with narrow thongs.

For weapons, each of the Amorites had carried a long spear with a point of bronze or flint, sharpened on a stone until it could penetrate a man's body at one thrust. A short bronze or flint knife was also thrust beneath the girdle that bound the tunic at the waist. The rounded shield of cowhide over thin wood was reinforced with plates of copper or bronze, and on his back each warrior carried a bow and a quiver of arrows. From the girdles of some—the doughtiest fighters—also hung a battle-ax of flint or a heavy war club of hardwood, a murderous weapon in the hands of a strong fighter at close range.

Quickly the Israelites stripped the gear from the captive Amorite soldiers, then killed each mercifully with a blow from a heavy club. Wearing Amorite garb and carrying Amorite weapons, the party that returned triumphantly to the city of Heshbon less than an hour later even carried the heads of some of the victims impaled upon their spear points, as further evidence of another victory.

The mists of early morning made identification difficult, and no move was made to shut the gate when they marched up the ramp leading to it. The returning party was a few paces away when a man on the walls recognized one of the heads carried high on the spear point of an Israelite soldier as a brother-in-arms. The warning came too late, however. At the first outcry Joshua and the Israelite warriors surged through the gate, stabbing and hacking at the surprised guards.

The resistance of the Amorite guards lasted only a few moments, most of them being killed where they stood, with hardly a chance to lift their weapons. With the gate secured, Joshua lifted the great ram's horn or *shophar*, the trumpet of Israel, which he carried upon his back, and blew three loud blasts, the agreed-upon signal for the advance upon the city by the main Israelite army hidden behind the hill.

The defenders of Heshbon rallied as soon as they realized how small a party held the gates, and they launched an attack to retake it and shut out the main body of the Israelites.

Outnumbered for the moment at least ten to one, Joshua and his men fought valiantly, their leader, as usual, the mightiest of all. Stabbing, hacking, bludgeoning, Joshua stood his ground like a rock, and his warriors, taking heart from his courage, rallied behind him. The pile of dead before them in the gateway rose higher and higher, while the stone floor under their feet became slippery with blood.

Then a great shout sounded as Caleb leaped into position beside Joshua. A horde of screaming Israelite warriors poured after him up the ramp, and the defenders were forced to retreat in a state of disorder into the city itself.

Of King Sihon's men, only the mercenaries fought to the end. Stalwart Nubians, dark-skinned Sherdans, and men from the roving bands of desert nomads called "Sa Gaz" by the Amorites and the Canaanites—they knew they could expect no mercy from the Israelites.

In Egypt, mercenaries like these often guarded the slave gangs that labored for long hours in the hot sun, dragging huge blocks of stone from desert quarries to the site of the great tombs which the Pharaohs were constantly building. And since this very Israelite band had not so long ago been a part of the slave population of Egypt, their memory concerning the cruelty of the slave guards was still vivid.

Less than two hours after Joshua secured the gate, Sihon was dead and his palace and the public buildings of the city teemed with Israelite soldiers, seeking loot and women to rape. To the screams of the latter no one paid any attention, however, such things being considered the just rewards of soldiers attacking a city.

The loot was another matter. By strict order everything of value went into a common pile in the open square of the city. With Chazan and the other scribes keeping record, the booty was then scrupulously divided.

The portion belonging to Yahweh was taken out first. This the priests added to the chests containing the wealth of the god, captured during previous battles. Next came the allotment of the captains, apportioned according to the number of men they commanded. In the case of Joshua and Caleb, this amounted to a considerable sum. Lesser officers received their shares next, and so on down through the ranks to the common soldiers.

Last of all was the portion reserved for those unable to fight, the old, the widows, and the children of warriors. No one was left out, for Sihon's treasure was large and Heshbon a wealthy city. Amorite men who were not killed and women who survived the orgy of rape were roped together as slaves; some would be sold and their prices divided as scrupulously as the loot; others would become hewers of wood and drawers of water, human pack animals for the Israelites.

One group among the conquered was exempt from slavery, however: those who, upon questioning, were found to be descendants of Abram and who also served the god called Yah in this land. These were turned loose and allowed to go unharmed, to settle in the villages of what had been the kingdom of Sihon or, as most of them promptly did, escape across the borders of the surrounding countries and over the River Jord to the cities of Canaan.

Salmon had suggested this device, moved, however, by more than just the wish to spare people who might be of the same blood line as the Israelites, if traditions current among both groups were to be believed. What he hoped for—and what shortly happened—was that these "children of Abram," as the Israelites called them, would promptly spread abroad lurid tales about the invulnerability of the Israelites as well as about the fact that they made no quarrel with those who could claim descent from Abram.

By this shrewd maneuver Salmon sought to create, in every city that the Israelites expected to attack, a group of people who would look forward to its fall. As a result, they could be counted upon to help the invaders in many ways, from protecting spies to outright weakening of the defenses from within. Knowing that the Israelites—who were invincible anyway, according to the stories of the refugees—would spare them in the inevitable sack of the kingdom and city, these "children of Abram" would have no thought of loyalty save to the invaders.

Heshbon was the first large city to fall into the hands of the Israelite band. Being an important stop on the caravan routes between Egypt and the cities of Babylon, it had been in constant touch with the great commercial centers on the shores of the Great Sea, such as Tyre, Sidon, and Byblos. The invaders naturally found here a greater degree of magnificence and luxury than they had ever known before.

A veritable treasure-trove fell to the eager hands of the conquerors, rich jewelry from Egypt, exquisite scarabs, amulets of gold, and containers of the delicate blue-tinted bone glass for which Egyptian craftsmen were famous. There were also rings and chains, precious stones in settings of delicate gold filigree, and the even scarcer "white metal," silver. Rich fabrics filled the closets of the palace, many of them the gauzy thin products from the looms of the Canaanite weavers, so prized by women in the cities of the Nile. In all the world, no weavers were as skilled in their art as those of Canaan.

Cauldrons of copper from the forges of the metalsmiths on the coast of the Great Sea hung over the fires of the cooking yard, with all manner of pots and pans and utensils of the same metal. Fly flappers of gold decked the palaces of the nobility, bowls, cups, rings, ladles, tripods for holding pots over the coals, bronze dishes, and pottery. There were even pieces of the ivory furniture fashioned patiently by the skilled craftsmen of the Nile.

Everywhere in the stricken city new treasures constantly were being turned up, until the cries of wonder from the fascinated Israelites and the voices of the counters and dividers dictating to the scribes began to drown out even the screams of the women.

Salmon prowled Heshbon alone, but he did not seek loot of the kind favored by the others. In the house of a physician he searched for new drugs and instruments. A store of dried poppy plants brought a smile of approval because of their propensity for relieving the pain of the sick and wounded. But finding nothing else of value to a physician, he turned his attention next to the armory of King Sihon.

Rumors had been spreading before the battle that Sihon possessed chariots with wheels made of iron, the black metal of the Hittites that was slowly replacing bronze as the material for weapons. But the vehicles of the Amorites turned out to be made of wood, like those of Egypt, with strips of leather lashed to the frames of the wheels as a covering to keep the wood from wearing out so quickly on the rocky ground.

Like the Egyptian chariots, the wheels of the Amorite

vehicles were at the back part of the chariot itself, thus throwing a heavy load on the horses and making it difficult for them to maneuver quickly. If they possessed any advantage over the war carriages of Egypt, Salmon decided, it was because they could be easily taken apart, lashed to the backs of pack animals, and carried over rough terrain to distant battle-fields.

None of the other weapons of the Amorites was much of an improvement over those of the Israelites, except the battle-axes. These, Salmon recognized, could be important weapons for close-range fighting, as the cleft skull of many a corpse in the pile before the gate eloquently testified. Salmon's particular military interest, however, was in stratagems through which one army could defeat another by the swift movement of relatively small bodies of men, instead of by wholesale slaughter, where the deciding factors were the relative numbers engaged and their strength to stab and smite the enemy.

In one chest of the armory he found something that did excite his interest. It was a set of delicate chains of a dark metal made up of thousands of small links so interlaced that each was attached to at least four others and sometimes more. The whole had been fashioned as the outer layer of a sort of quilted tunic that could be pulled over the upper part of a man's body as a garment.

Salmon's quick mind saw at once the value of this device, and he sought out Joshua and Caleb with his discovery. They were standing in the square at the center of Heshbon, supervising the allotment of the spoils. Joshua laughed when he saw what the physician bore in his hands.

"You should have laden yourself with gold, Salmon," he said jovially. "Knowing you would not think of it, I set apart the share of a captain of a hundred for you."

"Don't sneer at what I carry," Salmon advised him. "It could be more valuable to you than all the gold in that pile."

Joshua frowned. "Sometimes your jests do not make sense. Is this one of them?"

Caleb, however, had a better opinion of Salmon's ability. He knew that but for the physician's gift for strategy much of their success might not have been accomplished. "What is it you have there, Salmon?" he asked curiously.

"A fabric made of chains, to be worn in battle."

"How could a man leap about in battle with so much weight on his body?" Joshua demanded. "The enemy would cut him down before he could strike one good blow."

"Not without a sword that could slash through this metal," Salmon said. "And I doubt if you have any such in Israel."

"Yahweh gives strength to my arm when he fights at my side," Joshua boasted. "You saw how we held the gates of Heshbon this day? No man could stand against us."

"Even the favorite of Yahweh can be slain," Salmon reminded him dryly. "I seem to remember digging an arrow out of your back not many days hence."

Joshua shrugged. "That thing you carry does not look tough enough to stop a knife."

Caleb had been examining the tunic of interlaced chains. "Before we left Egypt I heard of a new metal that is used by the Hittites," he said. "Is this the same, Salmon?"

"I believe so, although I have never seen it myself."

"Sir"—a Sherdan mercenary among the prisoners spoke—"I can tell you about this garment. It is made of a new metal from the country of the Hittites. I have seen it ward off even a spear thrust, and flint weapons are turned by it as if they had struck a rock."

"By the gods of Egypt!" Joshua exclaimed. "This is a great thing if it be true."

"Will you wear this tunic and let us test weapons against it?" Salmon asked the prisoner.

The man hesitated, and Caleb added, "If the chains turn our arms, you will go free."

"Give it to me," the Sherdan said promptly.

While they waited for him to don the strange garment, Joshua said chaffingly to Salmon, "I will wager the value of a gold neckchain that the arrow pierces yonder tunic at the first shot."

"Taken," Salmon said promptly.

Although covering the mercenary's upper body and hanging a little below his loins, the tunic still looked like small protection against a weapon in battle. Salmon found himself wondering wryly whether he had not let his eagerness betray him into making a fool of himself.

"Choose an arrowhead of flint," Caleb ordered one of the

bowmen standing close by. "Aim for his body, and see that you do not miss."

The bowman stepped back a little way, fitted an arrow to his bow, and let fly. Sparks flew where the arrowhead struck the metal, but it only splintered and the shaft fell to the ground, useless.

Joshua grunted with surprise. "Try your spear," he directed another soldier. "Strike him a glancing blow."

The soldier rushed upon the man wearing the strange tunic made of chains. The force of the spear's impact knocked the prisoner to the ground, but the blade of the spear point was only blunted by the blow. As for the chains, a long scratch appeared on the tunic and some links were cut through, but the man was only partially stunned by the attack. When Salmon examined him, a large reddened area showed on his chest where the blow of the spear had driven the metal against his skin. But there was no wound.

"A spear thrust such as that could pierce a copper shield," Caleb said in amazement. "Yet his skin is unbroken. Does an evil spirit protect him?"

"Nothing more evil than the looseness of the links, I suspect," Salmon explained. "The force of the blow must be taken up before the weapon can penetrate. Only a direct thrust could deliver a mortal wound to a man protected by such as this."

"If you paused to aim a direct thrust in the heat of battle," Caleb observed, "you would never aim another."

"We have not tested this thing against a knife of bronze," Joshua interposed. "I will deliver the stroke myself. If your coat of chains can turn my weapon, Salmon, I will admit its value."

"You have lost the wager already," Salmon reminded him. "It was only for an arrow shot."

While the others stood back, Joshua stabbed at the prisoner, driving his knife against the links of metal. The Sherdan, being a trained warrior, instinctively rolled with the thrust, and the blade struck him a glancing blow. A stunned look came over Joshua's face as the knife, a favorite with which he had fought many battles, split lengthwise and the blade dropped from the ivory handle in which it was embedded.

A shout of wonder went up from the watching soldiers.

Joshua shook his head like a man who cannot believe the evidence of his own eyes. "Take a searching party, Salmon," he ordered gruffly. "Turn up the very stones of Sihon's armory in search of more of the Hittite metal. This garment is yours by right of discovery, but I would have one for all the officers."

"I will try to find out what smith forged it," Salmon promised while the mercenary was removing the tunic. "Perhaps he can make more." He took the metal-studded garment and went to where Joshua was standing. "A physician has no need for weapons or armor, but the leader of Israel must be preserved. Wear this in battle, Joshua, and save me the job of drawing spear points from your tough hide."

Joshua looked at Salmon for a long moment with a strange expression on his face. Finally he took the tunic almost reverently in his hands. "Truly our god sent you to discover this in Sihon's armory," he said finally. "It must be the will of Yahweh that I should be protected by it in battle." Turning, he strode away, carrying the garment over his arm.

"By the Baal of Heshbon!" Caleb snorted. "The son of Nun takes much credit to himself. There are other leaders of a thousand in Israel besides him." He wheeled upon Salmon angrily. "And you!" he snapped. "When will you claim the credit that is due you? It is your genius for planning, not the strength of Joshua's sword, that wins battles for Israel."

"Nay, Caleb," Salmon objected mildly. "What man can kill an enemy or storm a wall merely by thinking?"

"I know your purpose," Caleb said angrily. "You would make Joshua King."

"Could you find a better one in Israel?"

"I would rather have you as King than that boasting hero yonder."

"Heroes are the stuff that kings are made of, Caleb," Salmon said seriously. "The people will follow Joshua without looking twice to see whether or not he is worthy. It may really be, as he says, that Yahweh has chosen him already."

Caleb shook his head slowly. "Were you to turn your talents to war, Salmon, you could be the greatest general in Egypt or anywhere else."

"But I am not a warrior."

"I am. Stand behind me and we will make this nation great

85

together, greater than even the Hittites and the Horites, perhaps as great as Egypt itself."

"I owe my life to Joshua, and so do you, Caleb," Salmon reminded him. "More than once you have told me how he saved you in battle. We two must stand behind him, whatever happens."

"And have him lord it over us with his talk of being the anointed of Yahweh?"

"He who would make a king," Salmon said with a wry smile, "must, I suspect, first put his own neck beneath the royal foot. Come, let us find another tunic of metal so the broad sinews of Caleb will not be lost to Israel by the spear thrusts of the men of Bashan."

Six

AS THEY RODE toward the city of Memphis in the bright morning sunlight, Tamar's mule, as usual, walked beside Rahab's. "After tomorrow we will be scattered over Memphis," the older girl said. "Are you sure you remember all I told you, Rahab?"

"I remember. But it hardly seems right to deceive——"

"Deceiving men is women's business," Tamar assured her crisply. "When the one who buys you takes you to his house, insist upon warm water for bathing and perfumed oil to rub on your body. When he dines before taking you to his couch, be sure his wine cup is filled as often as it is emptied. Take little yourself, though," she warned. "Else the wine will heat your blood and make you ardent. Then you might forget and let him discover he was not the first."

"Tamar," Rahab said, embarrassed. "Must we——"

"Yes, we must," Tamar said positively. "You are not like the rest of us, Rahab. Make the man who buys you think he has purchased a pearl beyond price, and he will treat you kindly lest you be angry with him and become as other women who want only his money. Make him believe he cannot live without you. And if you give him a son, he might

86

even make your child his heir. Then you will have a favored position in the household, almost like a wife, and he cannot sell you because his friends would speak ill of him for selling the mother of his child."

"All that I know, but——"

"What happens to you depends upon how well you deceive him in the first embrace. Resist him at first, but not too strongly. If he is an older man his ardor may suddenly wane and he will be angry at you for revealing his impotence. And be sure to cry out at first as if you are in great pain. It is expected of a virgin."

"Tamar, you make it all sound so—so ordinary."

Tamar shrugged. "Men set great store upon this business of lying with a woman, but to me it is generally a very overrated thing. Since they do value our favors so highly, though, we must not dispel their illusions."

"Tamar," Rahab cried in sudden panic, "I can't go through with it. Lying with a man I do not love is a—a sin."

"You have no choice."

"I could run away. Salmon did when he was a slave in Egypt."

"Do you know what happens to a woman without a husband or protector in a city like Memphis?" Tamar asked sharply.

"No."

"She is raped by any man who can catch her, and no one will defend her against him. As beautiful as you are, Abda is certain to ask a high price for you. That means you will be bought by a rich man and live in luxury. But if you are not obedient to your master, he will flog you and sell you. Then what have you gained? Your skin will be marked from the lash, and only the worst of the brothels will buy you to lie with soldiers and sailors from the Nile boats or porters from the docks."

"But I love Joshua," Rahab wailed. "I want only him."

"Do as I tell you and you may be able to buy your freedom later," Tamar advised. "Then if you still wish, you can seek out this Habiru lover of yours."

"He might not want me then."

"If you take care not to let your beauty be marred, any man will pant with desire at the sight of you," Tamar assured her. "Beauty like yours is not seen every day, even in Egypt, so you will surely get a fine master at the very beginning and come to love him——"

"No! I could not."

"A woman can love any man who is kind to her, Rahab; such an affection is even better than the hot fire of young love. You will understand how that can be when you have known many men."

"I hope I never know them," Rahab said bitterly.

"You may be fortunate enough to be loved by your first master," Tamar said. "But it is better to be ready for whatever happens."

"I will ask Yah to send me back to Joshua."

Tamar shrugged. "Choose an Egyptian god. Or better sacrifice to Ashtarth; she has temples everywhere. I suspect this god of yours is too weak to have much power in Egypt."

Disturbed as she was at the prospect of being sold to a stranger as a slave or concubine, Rahab could not help admiring the beauty of the city called both Mennufer and Memphis. Most startling of all to the traveler approaching the great metropolis on the west bank of the Nile was the long line of huge stone pyramids stretching for miles along the western hills. In their grandeur, shining in the afternoon sunlight, the tombs of the Pharaohs dwarfed the city itself, although the sprawling population center contained nearly two million people within its confines, guarded by the famous fortress of the "White Wall."

Built mainly of sun-baked brick and wood, the city extended—it seemed to Rahab—for miles and miles along the banks of the Nile. She was sure she had never seen so many people in her whole life.

Even the magnificence of Memphis could not blind Rahab to her own fears, however, and as they moved through the streets toward the house in the foreign quarter where Abda made his headquarters, her spirits grew lower and lower. In such a great city as this, Rahab was sure now, she would never have a chance to escape and return to Joshua. Nor could he, even if he came seeking her, have any hope of finding her here. It did seem sensible, as Tamar had advised, to try to please the first man who bought her and thus find what measure of security she could, even though a slave.

The house to which the caravan made its way just before dark was in the foreign quarter of Memphis, a section inhabited, Abda told them, largely by representatives of the various cities, states, and minor kingdoms that were vassal subjects to Pharaoh. Although the residence of the Egyptian ruler was now farther upriver at Thebes, Memphis had been the old capital, and much of the business with foreigners was still transacted here.

The house stood in one corner of a large garden planted with dark green trees, figs, pomegranates, and an arbor covered with vines. Actually it was the most famous brothel in the entire city, patronized largely by rich foreigners of the district. These counted among their number princes of Syria and ambassadors from the city-states of Canaan and surrounding lands. In fact, the titled representatives of kings who looked to Egypt for protection were Abda's best customers.

The slave merchant did not sell his lovely chattels at the common auction blocks spaced here and there in Memphis, however. The women he gathered on his semi-annual trips to Babylon and the lands along the fertile crescent of the Tigris and Euphrates to the east and the valley of the River Jord to the west were selected with care and sold in a similar manner. In the luxurious surroundings that Abda cannily provided as a setting, the girls could be inspected leisurely by a prospective purchaser. As a result, they brought far higher prices than they would have on the auction block. Not only was Abda's profit greater, therefore, but the fact that he sold usually to rich men made it much easier for him to find merchandise of a high quality.

The courtyard was surrounded by a wall of brown brick before whose doors stood two giant Nubians with naked spears, a warning that only men of consequence should seek to cross the portals. And since it was already evening, the establishment was beginning to awaken for its night of pleasure.

From the kitchens occupying one side of the rambling house of brick and stone came the aroma of exotic foods, for the eunuch had the good sense to employ cooks skilled in preparing foreign dishes that his patrons could not find elsewhere. Wine jugs half filled the central fountain of the courtyard, being cooled against the thirsts of the night. And from the great main room came the sound of a lute being strummed while a girl musician sang a lilting melody in a soft pleasing voice.

The girls of the caravan were not to pass the inspection of the patrons tonight, however. Instead, they were hurried through a back entrance to another part of the house, where comfortable beds were provided for them. Only after a good night's sleep had relieved the fatigue of the journey did the routine of preparing them for inspection begin, a process that consumed most of the day.

First the stains of travel were removed by bathing with hot water and scented soap, a luxury which many of them had never enjoyed before. Next, by repeated rubbings with perfumed oils, their bodies were cleansed of the odors of sweat from the mules upon which they had ridden for several weeks. Appetites, too, must be assuaged, since it was not ladylike to be ravenously hungry in the presence of the nobility who patronized an establishment like this. And then there was the excitement of being fitted with new clothing, having the hair dressed properly, eyebrows plucked, and body hair removed, since to Egyptians that, too, was offensive.

Rahab was young and, being a woman, could not help being pleased by the bath of warm, scented water in a pool lined with glazed tiles of blue and yellow. The weariness of her body evaporated under the skilled hands of a coal-black slave girl who rubbed her with pleasantly scented oils. Her hair had been washed carefully during the bath, and since it was long and lustrous, Abda had decided that she would not wear a wig as most Egyptian women did. When it was dry she let it hang almost to her waist, with a chaplet of golden filigree about her temples.

For an undergarment, the slave brought Rahab a girdle of soft linen, wide enough only to swathe her loins. Over this she put on a single garment of fine linen, fitting so closely that every sweet line of her lovely body was fully revealed, although modestly covered nevertheless. Compared to the robe of heavy cloth that she had been wearing, the Egyptian dress felt almost as if she wore nothing at all. As she observed herself in a mirror of polished metal with a handle of carved ivory, she could not help being pleased by the way the Egyptian style of dress enhanced her naturally graceful loveliness.

Next the slave brought a jar of rouge to adorn Rahab's cheeks and showed her how to rub it on gently so as to achieve just the right tint for a blushing maiden. From a pot of dark paint, eyebrows and eyelids were next darkened to make the eyes appear more brilliant. And for a cosmetic there was stibium—the oil of antimony, called *mesd'emt* in Egypt —with which her cheeks and neck were carefully whitened.

Finally, when the toilette was almost finished, the slave brought a small white box of the perfume called *kyphi*. Made from musk, myrrh, broom, frankincense, buck's-horn, and other exotic plants mixed together in an ointment, it was rubbed behind her ears and along the crevices of her body. In another box were pellets of the same perfume mixed with honey. When chewed, these made the breath sweet.

Abda came into the room where Rahab was being dressed just as the preparations were finished. He surveyed her with admiring eyes, making her turn and move about so he could be certain that the cut of her dress shrewdly brought out the lovely lines of her body. Then he showed her how to walk so as best to please a possible buyer, mincing about daintily until Rahab could not help laughing.

"Be careful," the eunuch warned. "It is good to be merry, but do not make the paint run, at least not until you have drunk wine and your body is warmed to ardor by it."

The word "ardor" drove the laughter from Rahab's lips. The preparations for the night had taken up most of the time since their arrival and she had been allowed little opportunity to think. Now her fears began suddenly to crowd in upon her. Tonight, if Abda's hope of a sale to the first prospective customer was realized, she would almost certainly become the property of a man she had never seen, forced to share his couch and let him do his will with her. And suddenly panic-stricken at the thought, she fell upon her knees and buried her face in the ample folds of Abda's rich robe.

"Don't sell me, Abda," she begged. "Take me back with you in the next caravan, and Joshua will pay you more than you would get for me here."

The eunuch soothed her with his hand upon her shining head as he might have a frightened child. "I do not work for

91

myself, Rahab," he explained. "My employer is a prince of Egypt who owns several establishments such as this in various parts of the country. He leaves me to my own devices so long as the profit he receives is great. But if I did not sell such a pearl as you at a high price, he would have me flogged and set me to hauling stone for the tombs."

"What are you going to do with me?" Rahab wailed.

Abda clapped his hands for the slave. "A little more *mesd'-emt* for her cheeks," he directed. "Put a heavier layer of carmine upon her lips and darken the shadow on her eyelids a little." With a pudgy hand he lifted Rahab's right breast through the thin linen fabric until it was exposed above the edge of her gown, which had been cut low to bare the right shoulder and arm. "Good," he said. "You have put just the right tint of rouge on the nipples, I see. These things are what make rich men rush to buy the girls from Abda's caravans.

"Ah, yes," he continued, returning his attention to Rahab as casually as if he were inspecting a vase or a painting. "Of course I cannot guarantee that my plan will go into effect, Rahab, but as soon as we reached Memphis I sent out inquiries in the foreign quarter here, seeking to find some nobleman from your part of the country who might be interested in buying you. Then when he returns to his own land and takes you with him, you will dwell near your family."

"Did you find anyone?" Rahab asked almost fearfully.

"I think so. The man I selected is a widower. He will be looking for gracious beauty in a woman instead of the fire young men seek, not knowing that such may only mean a bad temper. I saw him for only a few moments this afternoon, but I hear that Prince Hazor is——"

"Prince Hazor!" Rahab cried. "The son of the King of Jericho?"

"The same. You have heard of him, I see."

"Only from travelers. Medeba is not far from Jericho."

"That is why I thought of you as soon as I learned Prince Hazor had come to Egypt to seek aid from Pharaoh."

"Why would he seek aid? The walls of Jericho are thick and strong."

"His city stands full in the path of your Habiru friends if they decide to invade the land of Canaan," Abda explained.

"It is said in the city that Prince Hazor has tried to persuade Pharaoh to send troops to Jericho and stop the Habiru before they can threaten the other cities."

"Has he succeeded?" Rahab asked quickly. If Egyptian troops fought against Joshua, it could be very bad for the Israelites.

"The rumor in the wineshops is that Hazor saw Pharaoh at Thebes. Certain it is that one of the wiliest captains in Egypt, a man named Kanofer, has been assigned to equip a band of mercenaries and take them to Jericho. But Pharaoh's vizier has sent no gold to pay them, so Prince Hazor remains in Memphis."

"You have gone to much trouble on my behalf," Rahab said impulsively. "Why, Abda?"

The slave merchant grinned. "I will be amply repaid, never fear. Prince Hazor is rich, and possessing a jewel such as you will no doubt make him look with favor upon Abda, the slave merchant, when next I seek merchandise in Canaan."

While the slave repaired the dark shadow about Rahab's eyes, rubbed more of the antimony paste on her cheeks, and heightened the tint of carmine on her lips, she considered what Abda had said. And the more she thought of it, the more it did seem that this must be part of a pattern cut by a divine will working in her behalf.

Had not Abda and his caravan been passing Medeba at just the right moment, she would surely have been stoned to death. And now, when she had been sure she would be lost amid the two million inhabitants of Memphis, Abda and the Prince of Jericho had been brought together to ensure her return to the land that she loved. Surely, since he had done so much already, Yah would see that she was eventually reunited with Joshua.

"No more tears?" Abda took her chin between his pudgy fingers. "I thought you would be happy with my arrangements. You see, my dear, even a dealer in human flesh has his good side."

A slave entered the room just then. "A nobleman of Canaan and a captain of Egypt are asking for the noble Abda," he reported.

"Come, Rahab," Abda said heartily. "We will see whether the Prince of Jericho knows real beauty when he sees it."

93

Seven

THE SACK OF HESHBON raised the spirits of the victorious Israelites even higher than had their initial victory, and no one was more sanguinary than Joshua. Had the decision been his alone, he would have marched his troops northward at once against King Og of Bashan. But the elders in the council that ruled what was still a nomad band decreed a period of waiting before another campaign began.

Dependent for so long upon the meager diet of the desert nomads, the people did indeed need time to gorge themselves on the stores, granaries, and flocks of Heshbon and the Amorite people. Outvoted, then, Joshua agreed to the delay, but Salmon knew he was concerned—with considerable reason—lest the people begin to covet this fertile land and decide to settle down to more sedentary pursuits than warfare and raiding before the program of conquest that he had planned was completed.

When the wounded had been treated, Salmon went searching again in Sihon's armory and storerooms for new weapons and tools not possessed by the Israelites. Particularly valuable when the Israelites took up once again the growing of grain and fruit would be plows and hoes of bronze, as well as other tools of the same metal.

The women welcomed tweezers to keep their bodies free of hair, as the Egyptians did, and knives and shears for cutting cloth. The artisans prized saws for working wood and axes and adzes for shaping it, plus chisels and spinning drills for making wooden joints. And to the masons, tools for working stone were welcome, although most of the construction here was of sun-dried brick or wood.

Salmon was familiar with all these things from his period of slavery in Egypt, for, as a skilled leech, he had visited all parts of the city of Tanis near the Nile mouth, where he had lived and cared for the slaves of his master. He was looking particularly now for more of the strange hard metal from which the chain mesh of Joshua's armored tunic had been made.

94

He had heard that the Hittite people to the northwest, on the shores of the Great Sea, had been using this metal for several hundred years. A few instruments and tools of it had come to Egypt, but the Hittites guarded jealously the secret of smelting and working this metal, knowing that once their monopoly of it was broken a powerful advantage in war and commerce would be lost to them.

Salmon found another of the armored tunics for Caleb, but little more of the Hittite metal. From the mercenary whose life he had saved by letting him demonstrate the effectiveness of the armor, however, he learned that the soldiers of Bashan, reputed to be giants with the strength of two men, were also protected in battle by large shields made apparently of this same metal. And knowing how important this information was, he arranged with Caleb to present it to the council of the captains that met every few days to plan the next military campaign.

Joshua opened the meeting and described the tactic he proposed of using chariots to make a rapid foray while spears were hurled over the heads of the enemy. Finally he turned to Salmon. "I hear you have news of interest concerning the troops of Bashan," he said.

"I talked with a Sherdan who at one time was with the forces of Og," Salmon told the group. "He says that they do fight as we have heard, in the Babylonian fashion, with their troops massed close together in a front or square, protected by large shields."

"Then a rain of spears from above will easily demoralize them," Joshua interrupted triumphantly.

"Perhaps. But their shields are of the Hittite metal, and you know how the tunics you and Caleb wear turn our best weapons."

"Are you sure of this, Salmon?" Caleb asked soberly. "Of their having the new metal, I mean?"

"The Sherdan who reported it would have no reason to lie."

"Shields will not help them when our spears and arrows rain death from above upon the men inside the square," Joshua insisted. "They will have to break ranks, and then we can charge through and destroy them."

"Suppose they are expecting weapons from the air and protect themselves?" Caleb said.

"How can they?" Joshua asked.

"By putting extra men inside the square to hold their shields aloft and protect the archers and others behind the massed ranks when they attack."

"Who will fight then?" Joshua demanded belligerently.

"Even if only half of them fight," Caleb pointed out, "they could still crush us with a wave of men bearing shields of the Hittite metal, like a rock rolling down a hill crushes ants."

"Are we to give up then?" Joshua demanded angrily. "That means keeping forever armed and on watch at the borders lest forces of Og attack us."

"We might make treaties with them, as we did with the men of Moab and Edom," one of the captains suggested.

Joshua shook his head. "The people of the lands to the south of us are of a similar stock to ourselves. Most of our forefathers were kinsmen, but the Amorites and the men of Bashan are from the north and not to be trusted."

"What Joshua says is true," Salmon agreed. "Many of our own people do inhabit the territory south of us. And even though they denied us passage, I do not believe they will attack so long as we leave them alone. We must conquer Bashan if we are to occupy this part of the world in peace."

"I agree with Joshua and Salmon," Caleb said. "Og and his men must be smashed—but how?"

Many of the captains turned to Salmon, so accustomed were they to looking to him in matters of strategy. Joshua's lips tightened at the unconscious gesture, and a flush of annoyance stained his neck. "How else shall we conquer save with the courage of our hearts and the valor of our arms?" he demanded. "Some of you hesitated to go against the Amorites, yet Yahweh delivered them into our hands. If we do not falter, he will bring the forces of Og to our feet too."

Knowing the Israelite leader as he did, Salmon understood the reason for the handsome warrior's vexation. "The son of Nun is right," he said placatingly. "Our god has taken the battlefield with us each time we have fought. Surely he will be on our side when we attack Bashan."

"I am glad *you* approve of our going against Bashan, Salmon," Joshua said sarcastically.

"I may not be a warrior, Joshua," Salmon said quietly, "but I have always followed you into battle. Do you plan to draw out the forces of Og first with a small sortie, so you can decide just what strategy to use against them?"

"Did we not do that in the case of Heshbon?"

"In the case of Heshbon," Caleb observed dryly, "our small sortie was cut to pieces. Is this to be the fate of those who prick the hide of King Og?"

"Joshua's plan to use chariots for a lightning attack should prevent that," Salmon interposed quickly. "The men who launch the first attack can move in, throw the spears, and move away while you captains study the enemy's defense."

"I will agree to that," Caleb said, and the other captains chimed in. Joshua was the last to speak. "I will lead the party," he said. "Then no man can say that the son of Nun sends his men into battle without leading them himself."

The conference turned next to the job of assigning duties and setting a date for the feeling-out attack upon the domain of King Og. Twenty chariots had been discovered in Heshbon with more than enough horses in Sihon's stables to draw them. Joshua took ten of these and a large number of spears, intending to put into effect his daring plan of racing close to the troops of the enemy and raining down spears upon them from above before they could strike back. If the enemy raised their shields above their heads to ward off the deadly spears, as Caleb had suggested they might do, he planned to loose a hail of arrows at close range from the weapons of bowmen behind the chariots.

The expedition left Heshbon two days later and met a company of King Og's guard near the border on the fourth day of their march. The engagement was fought on a small plain where Og's men chose to stand and deny passage to the invaders.

Moving close behind the bowmen with his goatskin bag of medicines and instruments slung over his shoulder, Salmon could see most of what took place. He was able to determine that the men of Bashan, although taller and larger than the Amorites, were not the giants they had been reported to be. And he confirmed the story of the wounded Sherdan that they bore large shields reinforced with the Hittite metal.

The skirmish—for it was little more than that—lasted less

than an hour before the Israelite forces, badly cut up by the enemy, retreated into the hills. The soldiers of Bashan refused to follow them, however, apparently having heard of the tactics whereby the Israelites had been able to cut the Amorites to pieces. Last of all came Joshua, riding in a chariot, his face dark with weariness and anger and his body covered with dust.

"Your strategy of using chariots failed, Salmon," he announced as he stepped from the vehicle and dropped to the ground.

Salmon controlled his resentment at having the plan of battle attributed to him now that it was a failure, although the actual method had been Joshua's. "In what way did it fail?" he asked as he gave Joshua a drink of wine from the stores brought up by the slaves for treating the sick.

"Just as I said it would happen, their bowmen could not find us with their arrows because we were in motion. But they had men posted throughout their ranks, holding shields over the heads of the bowmen, so our spears took little effect. Each time we went at them we were driven off."

Salmon finished extracting a broken spear point from the thigh of one of the chariot drivers and bound up the wound. "What are you going to do now?"

"Go back to the camp and report our failure," Joshua said in disgust. "The wives of the dead will wail and the old ones will talk of giving up the battle, at least until their bellies and purses grow lean again."

As Joshua had predicted, there was much wailing in Israel over the minor defeat they had experienced. Some of the elders stroked their beards and gave the opinion that Yahweh had spoken out in this way against further wars. But the more sober minds among them could see the danger of their position, with the strong forces of Bashan to the north, the wild, rolling deserts and mountain country to the east, and the armed neutrality of the Moabites directly to the south.

Nor could they be sure of Canaan to the west, with its strong walled cities. Some of the children of Abram from Canaan, who had joined them following the release of the worshipers of Yah in Heshbon, reported that the son of the King of Jericho had gone to Egypt to try to persuade Pharaoh to send troops for the defense of that city. Although no one knew whether Pharaoh would agree or whether Egyptian troops would cross the River Jord if he did, none of the Israelites wanted the seasoned mercenaries employed to keep order in the empire launched against them.

A desperate sort of urgency governed the situation of the children of Israel then, despite their great victory over the Amorites. If they were going to crush King Og of Bashan, it must be soon. Then with the east side of the Jord in their hands, Israel could present itself as a peaceful people, having no quarrel with anyone, and thus perhaps escape punishment by Egyptian troops if they did come.

Although Joshua had condemned the chariots as useless, he ordered them repaired and put in good condition against some possible use, should a stratagem for utilizing them again be devised. And the wheeled vehicles did prove of great service in at least one activity, the task of hauling wood from the forests for building cooking fires.

Salmon was watching one of these loads being driven into the city, the horses laboring under the weight of the piled-up faggots, when a startling idea came to him. He went at once in search of Caleb and Joshua and found them playing at a draughts game called *senit* which was very popular in Egypt.

A beautiful game box made of cedar inlaid with blue *faïence* had been among the treasures of Sihon's palace. The top and bottom of the box were in the form of squared lay-outs or boards, *senit* on one side and the game of *tshau* or robbers on the other. A drawer in the end of the box held the exquisitely carved ivory pieces, squares for one player and cones for another. All of them were now on the board, and the game was at a tense stage, with a heavy wager on the outcome.

"You find the warriors of Israel reduced to playing old men's games, Salmon," Joshua said wryly as he picked up the four carved wands that were tossed on the floor like dice in playing the game. The positions in which they fell, whether crossed or pointed, determined the moves on the board.

"Toss them well," Caleb warned, "or all your gold will be mine."

"What good is gold to a fighter"—Joshua threw the wands —"save to buy wine when the battle is over?"

99

"Or the favors of women," Caleb said slyly.

Joshua flushed with annoyance and tossed the wands so they bounced sharply. He had taken a great deal of joking from his fellow soldiers, for everyone except Salmon and Chazan believed Rahab had left Medeba of her own accord, with Joshua's money, for a career as a harlot in Egypt.

"Hah!" The throw gave Joshua the advantage and put him on a key square of the board. His good humor restored, he moved one of his pieces to the new place and tossed the wands again. Once more the turn fell in his favor, and he was able to move two of his pieces through those of Caleb and back to the starting point, putting him well ahead.

"The object of the game," he explained jovially as he tossed the wands, "is to drive through your opponent and then turn upon him, just as in war."

"Yahweh favors the son of Nun," Joshua shouted when the turn came once more in his favor. "It is a good omen."

An idea burst like a shooting star in Salmon's mind. "Do you win this game by driving through your opponent's pieces with yours and coming back?" he asked quickly.

"You are learning quickly," Joshua approved.

"Why are you so excited, Salmon?" Caleb said, looking up from the board. "It is only a game."

"If you like it so much I will gladly teach the game to you and take your gold," Joshua offered with a grin.

"Suppose you were able to drive through the massed shields of King Og's men," Salmon said quickly, "and turn back, as you do in this game, to fight them from inside their ranks—would you be able to overcome them?"

"It would be easy," Joshua said promptly. "The weight of the shields makes them clumsy. But who can beat down such a wall? Our bronze spear heads splintered upon the Hittite metal."

"The Babylonians used battering-rams a thousand years ago to knock down city walls," Salmon pointed out. "The same tactic would work here."

"The enemy would mow down the men carrying the logs forward," Joshua objected. "You must have lost your senses even to suggest such a thing, Salmon."

"The rams I plan to use will be borne on chariots," Salmon

explained. "They will move so fast that neither spears nor arrows can stop them."

"By Rameses!" Caleb stood up suddenly, overturning the *senit* board. "It might be done at that."

"We have twenty chariots," Salmon said. "A heavy ram can be hung between each pair, making ten in all. If the rams are driven right into the wall of shields, the logs will batter the shield-bearers down and open holes in their ranks. Then our men can rush in behind the rams and cut the enemy to pieces."

"Even the weight of a man in a chariot makes it heavy on the horses and hard to maneuver," Joshua objected. "They would have to bear the weight of both the log and the driver."

"If we move the wheels forward beneath the chariots," Salmon explained, "most of the weight will be borne upon them. The rest can be carried by a bar extending between the teams." His agile mind was racing now. "We can even fix the logs so they will slide forward when we are ready to attack. Then the enemy will not know what is happening until the battering-rams strike."

Joshua's face showed his doubts, and his next words told them why. "Wars are won by men fighting with weapons," he objected, "not by horses and wheels."

"The only purpose in using rams is to knock down the wall of men bearing the shields," Salmon explained. "You would not hesitate to batter down the walls of a city in order to get inside it. The fighting will still be done by soldiers with spears and battle-axes."

Joshua's doubts were waning too, reassured by the fact that the glory of the battle would still come to him and his foot soldiers. "How soon could you build these rams?" he asked.

"I will need workers in wood and men who can heat and bend metal," Salmon said thoughtfully. "The main task will be to move the chariot wheels forward and secure them."

"Two days?"

"A week," Salmon temporized.

Joshua threw up his hands impatiently. "Five days are long enough and more. Take as many men as you need, but get to work at once. Meanwhile Caleb and I will be training

101

our warriors to rush in behind the rams and take the enemy from the rear." He flexed his mighty arms. "I am not called the Hornet of God for nothing. This time Yahweh will fight beside me and give us victory."

"Caleb, the son of an ass, will plod along behind," the older captain snorted, "to see that no one shoots an arrow into the backside of the son of Nun. Let us pray that the sting of the hornet will be at least half as strong as the loudness of his buzzing."

Eight

SALMON conscripted immediately all the men who were skilled in working with wood and the few who had some experience in handling metal. With forges and bellows of asses' skins from the loot of Heshbon, even unskilled smiths such as they were could heat bronze to a red glow. Fortunately this was all that was necessary in order to work it with hammers upon blocks of obsidian, the hard rock quarried from the wild country to the south where the famous smoking mountain stood, believed by the Israelites to be the earthly domain of their warlike god Yahweh.

Another group of men was sent into the woods to cut strong poles, across the ends of which were pegged heavy bars long enough to knock down six men at one time. By drilling holes into the logs with spinning drills, they were able to fix handles to the rams so the men driving the chariots could slide them forward and lock them into place just before launching the final attack. The weight of the logs would thus be borne almost entirely by the wheels during the earlier part of the engagement, making the chariots more easily maneuverable and keeping the enemy from realizing the nature of the stratagem being used against them, until it was too late to prepare an effective defense.

The work went well, and by the fourth of the five days allotted him, Salmon felt free to turn his attention to the duties of physician, his first love. Since their victory over the

Amorites, he had made it a point to visit the surrounding villages regularly in order to treat the ills of the inhabitants, the elders having decided not to disturb any of the Amorites who made no trouble. Besides, Salmon had learned during their journeyings that if the people among whom they moved were healthy and free from plagues the camp of Israel was also healthier and less subject to the recurrent waves of illness that often attacked the nomad bands, sometimes killing more than the arrows of the enemy.

He came into Medeba late in the afternoon and was passing the shop of the charcoal seller, when the proprietor called to him, "Are you not the physician called Salmon?"

Salmon paused. "Yes. I am Salmon."

"Is it true that you command beneficent spirits and can heal any disease?" the man asked eagerly.

Salmon smiled. "I have some knowledge of medicine, having studied it in Egypt. But I know nothing of either evil or beneficent spirits. Why do you ask?"

"My little son, the apple of my eye, is sick. Unless you help him, he will surely die."

"I will do what I can," Salmon assured him.

"My name is Joel," the charcoal seller said as he lowered the curtain of split reeds hiding the inside of the shop from the street at night. Carrying the brazier of glowing coals that stood beside him while the shop was open, he led Salmon into the living quarters.

A child of about eight lay on a couch. His legs were drawn up, and his face was pale and beaded with sweat. The woman kneeling beside him held a small image of Baal in her hands to which she was intoning a prayer. When she looked up, Salmon saw with a start that she was the same one who had told him how Rahab had joined the caravan bound for Egypt. The woman seemed too distraught to recognize him, however, and Salmon did not remind her of their last meeting.

"I have brought a physician from the Israelite camp, Rebecca," Joel said eagerly. "He has great powers of healing at his command."

"Save my boy, please," the woman pleaded, throwing herself at Salmon's feet and placing his foot on her neck. "Save him and we will be your slaves."

The boy's belly was swollen, but the pulse at his wrist

103

beat only a little faster than it should have, and his skin was moist and normal in color. Nor did the physician's keen eyes miss the berry stains on the chubby dark-skinned fingers and about the child's mouth.

"When did this illness begin?" he inquired.

"He came in very hot and thirsty from playing on the mountainside this morning," Rebecca explained. "I gave him goat's milk to drink; he took a large bowl before he was satisfied."

Salmon had already made the diagnosis. The stains of berries on the boy's fingers and mouth meant that he had gorged himself with fruit, which was ripe now. Hot and thirsty, he had drunk large quantities of cold goat's milk, and the ordinary sequence of events had inevitably followed— colic and a swollen belly.

"I have prayed to Baal," Rebecca said, "but there is no time to make a sacrifice."

"Save your gold for a better purpose," Salmon advised. From his bag he took a jar of the balsam from the trees of Gilead. "Put a pot of water over the brazier," he directed. "And while it is heating, get some cloth to wrap around his belly and a little wine."

"I told Joel an evil spirit had entered the boy's belly," Rebecca chattered as she busied herself putting water on to boil in a copper pot over the brazier. "Is that not what happened, sir?"

Salmon gave the boy a dose of poppy leaves in wine. "A kind of evil spirit that often enters little boys," he agreed with a smile. "It lives usually in a berry patch."

The water was soon hot and he dropped into it as much of the balm of Gilead as could be lifted on the point of his knife. At once the room was filled with the pleasant, sharp aroma of balsam.

Baring the child's swollen belly, Salmon next wrung out pieces of cloth from the hot water and laid them on it. For two hours he worked with the steaming cloths, applying them as a poultice to the child's abdomen. During the second hour, improvement was rapid, and the distended belly grew soft. Soothed by the effect of the poppy leaves and relieved of the pain, the boy soon slept.

Joel walked with Salmon to the street when he was leaving. "Tell me your fee, O most illustrious of physicians," the charcoal seller begged, "and I will gladly pay it."

"You owe me only one thing," Salmon told him. "And that will cost you no gold."

"Name it and it shall be yours then," Joel said eagerly.

"Tell me what really happened to Rahab, the daughter of Chazan, on the day she came to Medeba bringing the bride price to her father."

The charcoal seller glanced quickly back into the shop. "I wish you had not asked me that, sir," he said in a low voice.

"Your wife lied, didn't she, when she told me Rahab had gone to Egypt?"

"No, no! The girl did go with the caravan of women slaves, as Rebecca told you."

"Of her own choice?"

"No," Joel admitted. "It was not of her own choosing."

"Tell me the whole truth of this affair," Salmon commanded sternly. "Tell it or I will send the evil spirit back into your son's body."

"Spare the child," the charcoal seller babbled, terror-stricken at the threat. "Spare him and I will tell you everything."

And so finally Salmon heard the sordid story as it really happened. "Do you know the name of this dealer in slaves?" he demanded when Joel paused for breath.

"I believe he is called Abda, sir. The people of Medeba have sold their daughters to him before."

"Where do his caravans go?"

"To Memphis, in Egypt. I heard him say that."

"Memphis!" Salmon groaned. Even if he dared go to Egypt and risk capture again as an escaped slave, only by a miracle could he hope to find Rahab in Memphis. The population of that one city was greater than that of both sides of the Jord, including the cities of Canaan to the west.

"Since Rahab was sold I have talked to fathers whose daughters were taken to Egypt by Abda," Joel volunteered. "They say he sells the women in the foreign quarter. Elijah's daughter Rachel was bought by a prince of Syria and is living in ease with her own slaves."

Realizing that he could learn no more from Joel, Salmon left Medeba. And as he rode through the starlit night he found his spirits rising. The foreign quarter of Memphis would hardly be much larger than Heshbon, he told himself. And if he could somehow reach Egypt he still might find Rahab and bring her back.

With that thought, however, his elation suddenly left him, for finding Rahab would only mean sending her back to Joshua. And yet, having been a slave himself, he could not leave Rahab to that fate if there was any hope of helping her. Freeing Rahab would almost certainly mean losing her immediately to another man, yet he must do whatever he could to help her.

Nine

IN THE LARGE CENTRAL HALL of Abda's establishment music and laughter were everywhere. A group of young women, clad only in the gauzy tunics that were the usual garb of singers and musicians in Egypt, played in one corner of the room. One dark-haired beauty, her garment of sheer white suspended from a single jeweled necklace so as to leave both lovely breasts bare, was playing upon a large harp with twenty-two strings and a broad hollow sounding board at its base. The instrument stood almost as high as she did, and she strummed it with both hands.

A second girl plucked a three-stringed lute with a long handle fretted near the outer end in order to vary the pitch of the strings. A third played an elaborately carved lyre of six strings, and a fourth blew upon slender double-reed pipes, while another beat out the rhythm upon large rectangular tambourines.

A slender girl with an elfin sort of loveliness was leaning against a pillar covered with red tiles, singing a love song in a plaintive high-pitched tone:

Put unguent and fine oil together to thy nostrils,
And garlands and lotus flowers on the body of thy beloved,
As she sitteth beside thee.

106

Set singing and music before thy face.
Cast all evil behind thee and bethink thee of joy,
Until that new day cometh when one reacheth port,
In the land that loveth silence.

The song ended, the musicians struck up a gay tune, and four girls began to dance. They wore black wigs of curled hair dropping to their shoulders, as did most of the women, and the nipples of their breasts were painted. About their hips were narrow girdles of brightly colored enameled pieces. From these, strips of finely tooled soft leather extended between their thighs and were attached to the girdles at the back. Other than this girdle for their loins and the jewels in their navels, they were naked. Their dance was a series of acrobatics in which they were marvelously adept, posturing and leaping about with startling grace in perfect rhythm with the music.

Rahab's eyes were wide, partly with wonder and partly with apprehension, as Abda escorted her along one side of the room toward a group of curtained small cubicles or alcoves forming the opposite wall. The curtains before some of them were already drawn, and once, when a girl's high-pitched drunken laughter sounded, Abda frowned in disapproval. The first lesson an inmate of this famous institution learned was how to lead a guest to drink much wine without becoming drunk herself.

Several of the cubicles were open so the couples who occupied them could witness the entertainment. The men, for the most part, wore the spotless short linen skirts, jeweled collars, and heavy wigs of the upper-class Egyptian. The lovely girls with whom they were eating and drinking were clad in the diaphanous robes that seemed to be the proper garment in establishments such as this.

A corps of waiters and wine girls with silver pitchers circulated among the guests, offering them viands of every description, spiced wine, and flowery garlands. One girl carried a silver tray on which were rows of cones made from perfumed wool fat. Each of the guests wore one of these cones on top of his wig. And as the air grew warmer, the fat slowly melted and dripped down along the head and face, filling the air with a heavy fragrance. Fresh flowers and fruit were

107

in vases and bowls everywhere, and slaves waited to supply the slightest request of the visitor.

Tamar, lovelier than Rahab had ever seen her in a brightly wreathed black wig and white robe, was sitting with a fat Egyptian in one of the alcoves. Her face was flushed with wine and her companion was already bleary-eyed and unsteady in his seat. A jeweled bracelet from his wrist was on Tamar's arm, and with one arm about his neck she toyed with his gold chain, no doubt intending to obtain that, too, before the night was over.

Nothing had been overlooked that catered to the guests' tastes in gaiety and opulence, Rahab saw as Abda led her through the room. Brightly painted wine jars stood on tables beside every column supporting the vaulted ceiling that was tiled in bright blue, red, and yellow. Cups, vases, and bowls of alabaster, gold, and the much more precious white metal, silver, lined the shelves beside them.

Male guests who were unwilling to pay for one of the cubicles occupied a row of cushioned couches lining one wall, with the feminine companions of their choice beside them, while the entertainment continued in the center of the room. For an establishment devoted to wine and voluptuous pleasure, everything was in surprisingly good taste, another tribute to Abda's shrewdness as a businessman in this field.

Abda went directly to one of the alcoves. He paused a moment before the drawn curtains to smile encouragingly at Rahab and reset one of the pleats in her gown so it would fit more subtly over the hips. Then, pulling aside a fold of the curtain, the slave merchant stood aside courteously for her to enter the small room, as if she were a noblewoman in her own right instead of simply a valuable piece of property being offered for sale.

Two men sat in the alcove on a cushioned divan, with a low table before them upon which were platters of fruit and silver goblets filled with wine. One was tall, with the erect carriage of a military officer and the lean, narrow-cheeked face of an Egyptian aristocrat. Rahab saw his eyes sweep over her body in a quick appraising glance. And at the fire that burned suddenly in their pale depths she felt as if her robe had been stripped from her, leaving her naked.

The Egyptian took a deep breath, and she could see the

smooth sinews ripple over his superbly muscled torso beneath the heavily oiled skin. "By the dwelling of Ptah!" he said in Egyptian. "This is indeed a gift from the gods, Abda." Rahab understood the language well enough to know the words, but the meaning of his speech would have been readily understandable to a woman in any language.

"Most noble Prince Hazor"—Abda bowed low to the other occupant of the alcove—"I promised to show you a dream of loveliness if you would but grace my humble establishment this night. Look now upon Rahab, a daughter of the Amorite people, east of the River Jord. Is she not fair beyond the dreams of man?"

"You speak truth, O mountain of flesh," the Egyptian said before the man to whom the question was addressed could answer. "Kanofer, son of Ptofer, has looked upon many women, but never one like this."

Rahab dropped her lids demurely as Tamar had warned her to do, but not so low that she could not study the other occupant of the alcove. He was not lean and sinewy like the Egyptian, although well formed for a man of perhaps thirty-five or forty. Nor was he dressed in the Egyptian fashion that most foreigners in Memphis affected in order to ingratiate themselves with Pharaoh and the officials of the court.

Prince Hazor's robe of alternating layers of blue and red was cut in the typical fashion of Canaan so that it appeared to have been wound loosely around his body in one long strip. In contrast to the Egyptians, who usually wore short white linen skirts and left their torsos bare, the Prince of Jericho was covered to his elbows. His only concessions to luxury were the embroidery of gold and silver in intricate patterns covering his robe, the plain gold chain about his neck, and a jeweled dagger at his belt. His short beard was curled, as were the dark waves of the hair falling to his shoulders. And the wrists were bare of bracelets above hands that were strong yet slender.

Prince Hazor's face, Rahab saw, was typically Canaanite, the cheekbones high, the nose bold and jutting, the mouth full and generous. His eyes, when she raised hers to meet them, were warm and brown. The light of tolerance and kindness in them startled Rahab at first, so much were they like another man's she knew, a man who could be gentle and kind when he wanted to be or as sharp-tongued as a bronze knife when he did not—Salmon, the physician of Israel.

Kanofer's tongue licked out to wet thin lips, like the darting head of a viper, Rahab thought with a sudden feeling of revulsion. There was something almost viperish, too, about his eyes as they devoured her, like a snake seeking to charm its prey. "Truly, Prince Hazor," he said, "if you do not buy this jewel I will have her though it means beggaring myself to pay the price this flesh merchant is sure to ask."

"Have you watched the clouds wreath the top of Mount Nebo with white in summer, O beautiful one?" the Prince of Jericho asked Rahab in her own tongue.

"Truly, O Prince. And I have listened to the music of the Jord tumbling over the rocks."

"I long to hear those sounds again, for this land is a weariness to me. If I buy you, will you sing to me of the flowers upon the mountainside in springtime and the trilling of the birds as they build their nests?"

"I am but an indifferent musician," Rahab admitted. "But I can model such things for you in clay. And I will paint them in many colors so you will think they are alive, just as in our own country."

Hazor turned to Abda. "She is all you said she was, my friend. All and more."

"As soon as I heard the noble Prince Hazor was in Memphis, I knew she was for you," Abda assured him. "All of Canaan sorrowed with you in your bereavement, but it is not good that a strong man should grieve and live alone forever. In the arms of one so fair as Rahab, you will find peace and joy again. And," he added shrewdly, "perhaps an heir for the throne of Jericho."

Hazor's eyes came back to Rahab. "What say you, daughter of Medeba?" he asked. "Will you come with me willingly if I pay gold for you?"

Rahab bowed her shining head. These were the words she had feared to hear, but from this man's lips they troubled her hardly at all. "I will come willingly, O Prince," she said. "For I know you are wise and kind, like Yah, whom I worship."

"You do not follow Baal?"

110

"My family are of the children of Abram. We worship only Yah."

"You may keep your god then," he promised. "I have known some worshipers of Yah in Jericho. They are gentle people, industrious and considerate. Draw upon me for the sum you mentioned," he instructed the eunuch. "It will be paid at once."

"Has the Prince of Jericho taken leave of his senses?" Kanofer asked incredulously. "This is like buying a horse without even examining the teeth. Show yourself, girl," he said to Rahab, "so this nobleman will know he is not being cheated—if you are indeed a virgin, as the flesh merchant claims."

Tamar had warned Rahab that a prospective buyer would almost surely require her to strip herself before him so he could be sure there were no blemishes on her body. Nor did she mind so much exposing herself to the kind eyes of Hazor. It was the thought of Kanofer's lustful gaze that filled her with shame and apprehension, making her recoil involuntarily.

Abda, too, seemed to think it quite reasonable for a buyer to examine the merchandise as closely as he wished. "I will help you, Rahab," he offered, "lest this beautiful gown be damaged."

"I——" Rahab stammered. "If Prince Hazor——"

"It will not be necessary for you to expose your body, Rahab," Prince Hazor said quietly. "You are obviously modest and a maiden."

"To buy even a maiden without examining her is a foolish thing," Kanofer protested. "Truly, you are trusting beyond your own good, O Prince."

"It is I who am buying her," Hazor reminded the Egyptian with a slight but quite perceptible edge to his tone. "And my gold is paying for her."

Kanofer shrugged. "You have no one but yourself to blame if you are cheated then."

Hazor rose. "My *merkobt* is waiting outside," he said, giving Rahab his hand. "Come, my dear. I will send the *kat'ana* back for you, Kanofer." It was a pointed reminder that he did not expect the Egyptian captain to accompany them.

The festivities in the outer room were going at full blast

111

when Hazor led Rahab from the building, wrapped in a long cloak that Abda had thoughtfully provided. A number of carriages waited in the outer courtyard; when they emerged, one of them left the line and drew up before the door. It was driven by a grinning black coachman with a wizened face, hunched back, and bright intelligent eyes.

"Drive us home, Senu," the Prince of Jericho instructed the coachman. "Then you can return to wait for Captain Kanofer."

The *merkobt,* as the carriage was called, was a very light vehicle, resembling a chariot, with room for three people to stand and a bar against which they could lean to steady themselves while it was in motion. The axle carried the body of the carriage, consisting of a floor surrounded in front and at the sides by a lightly hung wooden railing.

The pole by which the horses pulled the conveyance was let into the floor and secured there with additional leather straps holding the base to the railing. At the end of the pole was a crossbar with its ends bent into the form of a hook, serving as a fastening for the harness worn by the horses.

The harness was quite simple, consisting of a heavy strap fastened around the breasts of the animals and attached to the end of the carriage pole. To keep this strap from rubbing the necks of the animals, a broad piece of leather was secured beneath it, while a smaller strap passed beneath their bellies to hold it in place. The bridles with their metal bits were adorned with feathered plumes in a sort of headdress, and from the bits long reins passed back to the driver. The wheels of the *merkobt* were covered with thick tires of leather to lessen the noise as they rolled over the heavy stones with which the streets were paved.

Hazor helped Rahab courteously into the carriage and stood beside her, steadying her with his arm about her waist as the vehicle rolled through the streets at a fast clip. His strength was very comforting and reassuring, and for the first time since that terrible day when she had been carried away from Medeba, unconscious and trussed on the back of an ass like a sack of grain, Rahab began to feel as if she were really herself again and not some other person living a nightmare.

Remembering the frank lust in Kanofer's eyes and knowing instinctively what sort of life she would have had as his slave,

Rahab moved closer to her new owner. Prince Hazor smiled and, as if he sensed her thought, his arm tightened about her. Rahab was content to lean against him, reassured by his quiet strength and dignity.

The house where the Prince of Jericho lived during his mission in Memphis was not far away. Two flaming cressets burned before the door. In their light Rahab saw that the house itself was not large, but it was set in a jewel of a courtyard, where a fountain burbled softly in the warm summer night and flowers filled the area with a sweet fragrance.

A slave came to meet them, an older woman in Canaanite dress. Her wrinkled face broke into a smile when she saw Rahab.

"This is Myrnah, who nursed me as a child," Hazor explained. "She looks after my household and spoils me when I let her. And this is Rahab, Myrnah," he continued. "She will be my concubine; I would have you treat her as you would my wife."

The slave woman nodded approvingly. "Your loins have too long lacked the warmth a young woman can bring, O Prince of Jericho," she said. "My heart is gladdened that you have brought such a beautiful and modest maiden to this house."

"Rahab is an Amorite from Medeba, almost one of our own people. Bring us wine and food of my own country, Myrnah. I do not like these highly spiced Egyptian dishes."

The room to which Hazor ushered Rahab opened at one side upon the inner courtyard. It was fragrant with a delicate incense rising from a small burner on a table in a corner and the perfume of flowers blooming in the garden. A heavy curtain hung in place, ready to be drawn across the garden side of the apartment in cold weather or when privacy was desired. It was midsummer now, and the whole side of the room was open, illumined by a small oil lamp set high in a sconce on the wall.

The couch—evidently Hazor's sleeping place—was broad and covered with richly embroidered cushions. A bottle of wine stood on a low table with a silver goblet beside it. And to Rahab's surprise a pile of papyrus rolls was stacked in one corner of the luxurious apartment.

Myrnah took Rahab's outer cloak and brought another

113

silver goblet for wine, with a tray of delicacies prepared after the Canaanite fashion, preserved figs and olives pickled in vinegar, sweetmeats with the slightest flavor of Gilead's balsam, and little spiced cakes. She poured goblets of wine for them and then left discreetly.

"I noticed your surprise when you saw the papyrus rolls," Hazor said, handing Rahab a goblet of wine. "What I like most about Egypt are the libraries containing their history and the writings of the poets. Someday I will read you the ones I love most."

"I read Egyptian," Rahab told him. "My father is a scribe in Medeba."

"He must be a very fine man to have so lovely and talented a daughter. When we return home you can send for him. We can always use good scribes to see that we are not cheated by the travelers who pay tribute to cross the River Jord at the fords of Jericho."

"It—it would make me very happy," Rahab said shyly. "But I would not be a burden to you."

Prince Hazor smiled. "Why should I not wish to please you, my dear? Only to gaze upon you brings me more happiness than I have known for years."

"You must have loved your wife very much," she said softly.

He nodded slowly. "When she died of a plague, it was as if my very heart had been torn from my body. I swore never to look upon another woman and retired into a seclusion from which I thought never to emerge."

"You have no children?"

"No. I think being unable to bear me a son was what finally broke her spirit and led to her death."

"Let me make up to you for all your sorrow, master," Rahab said impulsively, because she pitied him the years of his loneliness and was grateful to him for rescuing her from the brothels of Egypt.

"It is already fading just from your being here," he assured her. "Let us drink to your beauty and gentleness; they have already shown me how much I have to live for."

Rahab drank, but the warm feeling in her heart was not entirely because of wine. No little of it came from a sense of gratitude to the man sitting beside her. Gratitude for what he had saved her from and for his consideration and tenderness.

"I know Kanofer and Abda thought me a fool for not making you show yourself tonight," Hazor said when he put down the cup. "But I could not bear watching Kanofer's eyes devour your loveliness, or the thought of his lusting after you."

"I know," Rahab said softly. "But it was not right for you to buy me until you were sure I was without blemish." Moved by the conviction that she must be honest and fair with him, she added, "Captain Kanofer is not here now, and if I am not all that Abda told you I was, you can still refuse to pay the draft when he draws upon you tomorrow."

Hazor smiled. "I knew you were lovely and intelligent the moment I saw you, my dear," he said. "Now I know more, that you are honest beyond what any man could expect. If you say you bear no blemish upon your body, I will accept your assurance."

Rahab did not pause to question the impulse that made her want to be fair to this gentle man who had bought her for his slave. Going to the curtains, she drew them across the side of the room opening upon the courtyard. Then with a quick, lithe movement she dropped the white linen robe she wore in a soft pile about her ankles.

Her fingers were trembling, but not from shame, as she loosened the jeweled pin fastening the strip of fine linen wound about her loins. Then, her heart beating quickly and her skin rosy in the soft light of the oil lamp, she dropped it to one side and stood gloriously beautiful and naked before him.

"Look well, O my master," she said tremulously as she turned so that he could survey every lovely line of her body. "Look well at what you have bought this day and be sure you have not been cheated."

"O my love!" He was on his feet and took her in his arms before she finished turning. "O my dearest love," he whispered against her lips. "What have I done to deserve such a gift from the gods as this?"

In Hazor's tender embrace Rahab learned that a woman may find pleasure and happiness—although not the soaring

115

ecstasy that comes only at the first yielding—with a man she admires and respects, even though she cannot give him her real love.

Ten

EVEN THOUGH actually a slave, Rahab would have found it difficult not to be happy in the home and in the embrace of the Prince of Jericho. The house was small but luxuriously furnished. It was ideally suited to the warm Egyptian climate, being constructed of sun-baked bricks with small, airy rooms and hangings of matting over the windows.

Located among the shady trees near the cool fountain that formed the central feature of the courtyard, the house had three doors along its longest measurement and one at the end. Above each was a latticed window covered with matting except at night, when it could be opened to catch the breeze.

Graceful, slender pillars projecting from the outer walls supported beams on which rested the flat roof. Inside, rugs covered the floors and the walls were hung in many places with carpets. The windows were small and barely high enough for a person to look out, with a wooden rod at the top of each for rolling up the mat which hung over the opening.

On the side facing the courtyard, where the walls of the rooms were largely absent, a colorful canopy borne by six blue wooden pillars projected from the walls. Thus a shady porch was provided in front of the bedrooms, as well as the large room that served for dining and entertainment. To one side, at the corner of the courtyard, was a smaller building, less ornate, where the slaves lived.

Hazor had leased this house from a rich man, hence its comfortable and luxurious furnishings. The chairs and couches were especially handsome, several being made of ebony inlaid with ivory, with the feet of the supporting legs carved like the paws of a lion. A pair of wooden stools covered with thick cushions had legs exquisitely carved in the form of a lotus flower. And against the wall was a long, low bench, also covered with cushions.

Broad couches in the main room needed only the addition of wooden headrests, used everywhere in Egypt as pillows, to serve as extra sleeping accommodations. Rahab shared Hazor's own chamber, in which was a large bed carved from sussuku wood and inlaid with gold leaf.

Since there was little rain in this climate, cooking was usually done over open fires or upon a conical clay stove in one corner of the courtyard. The Egyptians favored roast goose and other fowls, which were prepared by placing the bird over the coals upon a spit turned by Senu, the black coachman. Fish were roasted in the same way, and pots were held by tripods or racks over a charcoal-filled brazier.

For preparing bread the ritual was a little longer. A fine flour was first made by rubbing corn between two stones, after which the dough was kneaded thoroughly. Shepherds in the fields baked their cakes, after beating the dough in earthen bowls, by placing them in the hot ashes, removing them with little sticks which also served as forks. Here in Memphis, however, the dough was baked in the houses of the richer people by fashioning it into various shapes and placing it on the conical stoves.

The stove used most was a blunted cone of Nile mud open at the top. Smoke from the fire burning inside escaped through the opening, and the cakes were plastered on the outside for baking. A common part of all Egyptian kitchens, too, was the "pure," a small brewery where beer was prepared from ground barley, the "corn" of upper Egypt. Wine was made either from grapes or fermented date pulp.

Rahab and Hazor ate their meals at a low table served by Myrnah and Senu. At one side stood a jug and basin from which water was poured over their hands at the beginning and end of each meal. Fresh flowers were always in the house, for the gardens of the courtyard produced them the year round.

Although Rahab was technically a slave, neither Myrnah nor Senu would let her do any work. Her task, they informed her, was to make their master happy; nothing else was required of her. And Hazor was so kind, so tender in his affection and his embraces, that she found herself wanting nothing else save to earn his smile and his words of praise.

The day after she came to his house Hazor took Rahab on

117

a shopping expedition to buy clothing, for she had come to him in only the thin robe provided by Abda as a part of the purchase price. Wrapped in a long outer cloak of fine linen which Myrnah bought for her at a nearby shop, Rahab rode with Hazor through the streets of Memphis in the *merkobt*, stopping at various shops to make purchases.

The foreign quarter, she discovered, was close to the river and the great docks where boats loaded and unloaded. Some came from the upriver cities, particularly Thebes, which, as the seat of Pharaoh, required a constant traffic with the cities downstream.

Here, too, were docked the long craft with their double sails that engaged in commerce between the cities along the shores of the Great Sea and those of the Nile. The shops in the foreign quarter of Memphis were filled with products of Canaan, whose skilled artisans were famous the world over for their cleverness with the loom, the dyeing pot, and the cutting and sewing of cloth.

In the street of the potters they stopped while Rahab watched with fascinated gaze the work of the men who prepared the exquisite kilnware of Egypt. Squatting beside their wheels, the craftsmen fashioned their products with deft hands and placed them in kilns to be fired. Nowhere else in the world had the technique been developed so highly as in Egypt for creating *faïence*, a glazed, brightly colored pottery with flat decorations resembling enamel and favored by the upper-class Egyptians.

In another section worked the jewelers, who made delicate little figurines and amulets, which were an important part of every Egyptian household. Because of her own interest in this type of artistic work Rahab would have been happy to spend long hours learning the secrets of their finished products. But she did not wish to exhaust her master's patience, so they moved on to still another area. Here she watched glass blowers at work with long blowing tubes and soft masses of molten colored glass, from which they constructed exquisitely fashioned bottles, jugs, and vases.

Altogether this teeming city upon the Nile formed a very cosmopolitan world in itself, representing the meeting place of Egyptian culture with that of Canaan, only a few weeks' journey by ship in the swift Phoenician craft that regularly plied the river and the Great Sea.

The shops of Memphis also sold products from the Land of Punt, such as ivory for carving, ebony, and rich exotic woods. And even the less skilled products of the nomad tribes living in the great wastelands across the Red Sea to the east were on sale, as well as jewels from the turquoise mines of Paran, and copper from far-off Alashiya, the island west of Byblos in the Great Sea where the finest copper mines in the world were found.

Most of all, however, Rahab loved to walk through the busy streets where the weavers, the dyers, and the makers of garments displayed their wares in typical open-fronted shops. For wear at home, Hazor preferred that she follow the Egyptian style, which meant two types of garments. One was the narrow dress of thin white material worn by most Egyptian women. Draped so as to leave the right shoulder bare, it covered the left and was fastened with a jeweled pin. Cut to hug the body closely, it hung in pleated folds from the waist, with the hem at the ankles.

Over the dress, when going out, a white cloak fastened across the breast was worn. At home Rahab wore nothing beneath the almost transparent inner garment save a strip of fine linen wound about her loins. But when they had guests she put on a thicker underdress that hid the intimate details of her body.

With the natural beauty of her own hair, Rahab needed no wig. Sometimes to please her master she put on Syrian dress, consisting of a narrow, close-fitting plain robe in which blue threads alternated with dark red, the whole being adorned with rich embroidery. But like many Egyptian women in the intimacy of their own homes, when the weather was warm Rahab wore only a short skirt of white linen, leaving the upper part of her body and her legs bare.

Once a week was washday in all Egyptian households. In the establishment of Pharaoh the various duties were apportioned to the nobles, one being "royal chief washer," another "royal chief bleacher," and so on. Here in Hazor's house, however, the work was done by Myrnah and Senu.

Early in the morning on washday Myrnah would be busy at the small tanks with the laundering while Senu beat the wet

119

clothes with wooden staves. The washing finished, the clothes were then sprinkled by being held up high while water was thrown upon them with the fingertips. The open end of each folded piece of linen was next hung over a post, a stick was thrust through the other end, and the whole wrung with a good deal of force in order to remove the water.

When the linen was nearly dry, Myrnah began the delicate task of pleating it into the regular folds favored in Egypt. For this purpose she used a strip of wood, cut in cross grooves like a fluting, into which the garments were pressed before drying in the sun. It was an operation requiring considerable skill and in larger households was the task of one slave who did nothing else.

Hazor had stayed very much to himself before he purchased Rahab, but with a beautiful concubine in his home he began to entertain more. And since there were many other Canaanites and Syrians of high degree in the foreign quarter of Memphis, they had an active and busy social life. Most of all, however, Hazor liked to hunt, so they often spent the day among the papyrus marshes, where the marsh birds were found in vast numbers.

With their roots bathed in the lukewarm water and their feathery tufts waving upon slender stalks, the papyrus reeds and other water plants of the low ground near the river formed a floating forest, above which swarmed thousands of marsh birds. For hunting them, sportsmen used light boats formed of papyrus reeds. Hazor would stand at the front of the boat, with Rahab in the middle to gather lotus flowers and hold the birds he killed, while Senu poled the boat skillfully from the rear.

Noiselessly the light craft would glide along beside a papyrus thicket while Hazor stood upright in the bow with his throw-stick in his right hand. When a bird was sighted he would send the stick humming through the air with a powerful throw. Usually one bird would fall into the water with each cast, for he was very skillful. But if the bird was missed, the thin piece of hardwood, bent in a peculiar way, continued in a graceful curve and returned to fall at the feet of the marksman.

This type of marsh bird hunting was mainly sport, however. The great number of fowl needed for the markets were caught in a much more utilitarian fashion, by means of a large net spread on a small expanse of water. First the birds were enticed into the net by bait, then it was quickly drawn shut by means of a purse string.

Fishing was also popular, a thin spear with a long handle and two barbed points being used. More dangerous prey were the hippopotamus and the crocodile which were hunted by royalty but not much by people of lower rank.

Sometimes great crowds would attend bullfights, where powerful, highly bred animals battled each other until the long sharp horn of one put an end to the conflict. There were also public wrestling matches and "sailor stabbings," where boatmen stood up in slender skiffs and thrust at each other with long poles. Prize fighters, too, fought with short sticks, each wearing a piece of wood tied to the left arm with which to protect himself against the blows of his opponent.

Sometimes Hazor would entertain at home with dinner parties. Then a troupe of dancers and singers might be brought in to entertain the guests. Clad in long transparent robes and sometimes in nothing save a wreath of flowers about their hips, the beautiful girls danced with tambourine and castanets, clapping their hands together in rhythm with the music and performing intricate and remarkable gymnastic feats.

Or two young girls with flutes might play for another to sing a song, perhaps in praise of the happiness brought by the annual inundation of the Nile:

> "The earth god causes his beauty to grow in the
>   heart of every creature,
> This is the work of Ptah's hands, this is the balm
>   to his breast,
> When the tanks are full of fresh water, and the
>   earth overflows with his love."

Altogether it was a pleasant life into which Rahab found herself fitting as naturally as if she had been born to such luxury, whether she was entertaining noble guests or playing draughts at home with Hazor, using the elaborate boards for *senit* and *tshan* that were found in every Egyptian home.

Even the memory of Joshua dimmed a little when the weeks passed with no sign that he had made any attempt to find her and take her back to Israel.

Eleven

FOR SIX DAYS the army of Israel had marched slowly northward, attended by a train of pack asses and carts carrying supplies and equipment and the weapons taken from the arsenal of King Sihon at Heshbon. Each of the battering-rams with its crossbar head was slung between two chariots, as Salmon had planned, so the drivers could become accustomed to handling them. The chariots, too, were bound together with rods so they could not become separated and drop the logs at the most important moment. Repeatedly, when they stopped and set up camp for the night, Joshua ordered out the ram-bearing chariots for a review of their actions once the attack had begun.

The plan of battle was simple enough. The twenty chariots bearing the ten rams would dash across the field of battle before the might of King Og, but out of spear or arrow range. Then at a trumpet blast by Joshua, who would ride in the lead chariot, they would turn suddenly upon the massed ranks of the defenders, swinging the rams into place with the bars prepared for that purpose. With the horses driven at breakneck speed, the strange new engines of war would smash directly into the ranks of the enemy, breaching great gaping holes in the opposing lines. Into these openings would pour the fighting men, led by Joshua on the right and Caleb on the left.

On both sides of the River Jabbok, marking the southern boundary of the domain of Bashan, was the area called Gilead. It was a well-watered upland plain with many springs and lesser streams arising in the hills and tumbling westward down the steep declivity to reach the River Jord in its great north-south cleft, extending from Mount Hermon in the north to the Salt Sea, which lay just west of the kingdom of Moab.

On the third day of the march they had crossed the River Jabbok and come upon well-watered plains. Beyond these the country became rougher and hillier, with patches of the black basalt layer that meant former volcanic activity. It was in this region, they had been told by the Amorites, that earthquakes sometimes shook loose great masses of earth, even blocking the flow of the River Jord on occasion and leaving its bed dry for days, until the pent-up waters behind the earth dam finally cut their way through and re-established a channel.

Scouts had ranged far ahead of the main body to survey the situation and spy upon the enemy. On the fifth day of the march, word came back that the forces led by King Og of Bashan had chosen their own battleground below the town of Edrei. This small city lay almost at the edge of the great desert that extended eastward to the end of the fertile crescent formed by the basin of the rivers Tigris and Euphrates in the territory of the Babylonians. A halt was called on the fifth day and a base camp set up only a few miles away from the enemy lines.

Salmon had traveled near the head of the column with his medical supplies on an ass-drawn cart. Although he hated war, he could not help feeling proud as he looked back at the long line of troops marching in regular formation behind the leaders, with the pack trains in the center of the column for protection, and a wing of skirmishers flung out on either side to guard against a surprise attack.

Not so long ago this had been a mere rabble of ex-slaves escaping from Egypt, fortified and strengthened to endure the tortures of hunger and thirst, hot sun and cold nights, by the conviction that the God who had spoken to their leader Moses from the smoking mountain would lead them to victory. Already they had accomplished the first part of the plan whose completion—in the mind of Joshua at least—included the whole sweep of the rich land of Canaan to the west as far as the Great Sea, in addition to this well-watered region of upland pastures, orchards, and fields east of the Jord.

What Salmon saw now was no rabble of ex-slaves but a band of confident, skilled fighting men able to hold their places against any army they met. Load after load of arms

123

and supplies followed them where previously they had carried everything they owned on their backs or on a few pack asses. No longer was this simply the band of nomad fighters Sihon, the Amorite King, had considered them to be when he sent back the emissaries with bleeding stumps where their hands had been. This long column of hard-bitten fighting men was now an army, the army of the people of Israel, feared and respected everywhere in this land of Canaan they hoped to conquer for themselves.

Joshua, Salmon was the first to admit, had been responsible for much of this new sense of confidence and certainty of purpose in the men of Israel. Salmon, it was true, had planned the strategy. And dogged, loyal, brave, and unbrilliant Caleb had supervised most of the rigorous training. The priests, too, had encouraged the people with the assurance that theirs was a god of battle, thunder, and storm, ever at their sides to give them victory.

But when the first trumpets sounded the call to battle, the first clash of weapons swept the field, and the first cry of pain told of a fatal spear thrust, it was Joshua who led the fighting, a tall, handsome, heroic figure always in the thick of the combat, equaling in prowess and courage any ten of the enemy. And it was Joshua who saved the day when the tide of battle sometimes threatened to turn against the men of Israel. Standing there like a rock and fighting like the great leader that he was, he had rallied the warriors of Israel to beat off the counterattacks and surge on to the final victory.

So far they had met only small groups of skirmishers on this march, obviously sent to feel them out and fall back to report their strength and numbers. Obeying Joshua's instructions, the Israelites had surrounded all such bands before cutting them to pieces. Thus they had managed to prevent any word being sent to the enemy of the strange double chariots traveling with them.

Now, as they waited for the battle to be joined tomorrow, the soldiers of Israel were confident. Whole goats and calves from the supply train were roasting over the cooking fires, and there was much laughter and singing. For some reason, though, Joshua was silent and did not boast as usual around the evening campfires about the coming victory.

Knowing Joshua as he did, Salmon surmised that the defeat of the skirmishers under his command in their first contact with the forces of King Og a few days ago still rankled in the Israelite leader's mind. There had been much talk lately of appointing Joshua commander of all the fighting men of Israel after the victory tomorrow on the plains before Edrei. This post had never existed before, the leadership being decided by common consent among the captains of a thousand and captains of a hundred, but most of the military leaders agreed now that it was time to choose a supreme commander. A defeat tomorrow would be more than just a simple setback for Joshua, as the skirmish had been; it could mean the failure of a secretly nursed ambition that might one day make him—as Salmon believed would happen—the first King of the united tribes of Israel.

When the evening meal was finished and the cuts and bruises sustained by the men on the march had been bound with the healing balm of Gilead, Salmon made his daily report to Joshua where he sat before his goatskin tent.

"What of the men?" Joshua asked. "Do many have blisters from their sandals?"

"Only a few. They will forget them tomorrow when the *shophar* sounds."

The Israelite leader turned to stare at the fire. "It will not sound unless the ranks of Og are broken by the chariots and the rams."

"You have rehearsed the chariot drivers well," Salmon pointed out. "Nothing could possibly go wrong."

Joshua drew a deep breath. "I am a man of battle, Salmon. With spear and bow, yes, even with the battle-ax, no man can stand against me. But when the outcome of a battle depends upon a thing that runs on wheels and is drawn by horses, I am not sure any longer."

"How do we know the men of Bashan have not been trained to throw saplings through the wheels of chariots as you proposed once?" he demanded. "We have twenty chariots to carry the battering-rams, but twice that many men could break the spokes on the outer wheels of each pair and drop them to the ground."

"The enemy will not know what is happening until you have smashed through their ranks," Salmon assured him. "The Hornet of God will triumph tomorrow, and then it will

125

be time to call the people together and name a single leader for all of Israel. Who could that be save Joshua, the son of Nun? Think only of that, and stop worrying about tomorrow's victory."

Joshua's shoulders lifted a little. "I have thought much of this thing since you first spoke of it," he admitted. "And I can see now that we do need a single leader to take and hold this land promised to the descendants of Abram."

"Would you let yourself be crowned King then?"

"If Israel should choose me for that trust. But say nothing of it now, the time is not yet ripe."

"A king will need a queen."

"You are ever busy at matchmaking for me, my friend," Joshua said with a smile. "Who have you selected now?"

"In Medeba I discovered that Rahab did not go away to Egypt of her own free will."

Joshua's face grew dark with annoyance. "Nevertheless, she did go," he said heavily, "and made me the butt of rough jokes from my men."

"You did not seem to mind," Salmon said, surprised.

"Could I let them believe the son of Nun is like a simpering youth, pining for a woman no matter what she does to him?"

"But Rahab did nothing to you, Joshua. I found proof in Medeba that she was carried away to Egypt by a slave merchant and sold to him by people she trusted so they could take the bride price and divide it among themselves."

"She went to Egypt—and I *was* shamed," Joshua said darkly. "That is enough."

"Then you do not intend to wed her if somehow she manages to return?"

"Would a king of Israel take a queen from the brothels of Egypt?" Joshua snapped. "You are not such a fool as that, Salmon."

"If I loved a woman, what she had done or what she had been would be of no importance to me."

"You are a poet and about some matters also a fool," Joshua said savagely. "Speak to me no more of this girl, lest you goad me into striking one I count as my friend."

Caleb was crossing the camp and bumped into Salmon as

he walked along after his talk with Joshua, deep in thought. The slender physician would have fallen had not the sturdy captain seized him by the arm and steadied him.

"A soldier who forgets to look where he is going usually winds up with his head on the point of an enemy's spear," Caleb warned bluntly.

"I am a fool, not a soldier," Salmon said bitterly. "Joshua just told me so."

Caleb's quick glance moved to where Joshua sat before his tent, then back to the physician. "By what authority does the son of Nun pronounce judgment upon his fellows? He is not yet a king, or likely to be one for a long time."

"What do you mean?"

"Israel is still a group of tribes where each man has an equal voice in our affairs. The men of Reuben and Gad, with half the tribe of Manasseh, are already saying that we should cease fighting. They claim there is more than enough fertile land here east of the Jord for all of us."

"What they say is true. This is a good land."

"Yahweh has promised that Canaan will be delivered to us," Caleb reminded him. "But if we are divided we can be conquered easily. The others think only of settling in this land, building themselves homes and stopping our wanderings. They are concerned more with their hungry bellies than with the glory of a nation."

"We will have no army if the people choose to settle here," Salmon said. "How could you fight then?"

"If we win tomorrow's battle, it is already arranged for some to demand that Joshua be made leader of all the fighting men. The tribes of Reuben, Gad, and Manasseh can settle on the east bank of the Jord here if they will, but the young men will follow the son of Nun into battle for the sake of the spoils and women. Joshua has persuaded the elders to invoke *herem* against the people of Bashan," Caleb added. "That always stirs the passions of the young men."

"The curse?" Salmon exclaimed. "Why should he do that?" *Herem*, the destruction of every living thing in the ranks of a conquered enemy, whether man, woman, child, or animal, was usually invoked only against a particularly hated country.

127

Caleb shrugged. "It makes sense not to leave the enemy alive to plot against us later."

"But why kill women and children just because the men fight against us?"

"Joshua suggested it," Caleb said matter-of-factly "There was no objection."

"I still don't understand why."

"Have you forgotten that the men of Bashan were the first to defeat him in battle?"

"That was a skirmish, not a battle. He was only feeling them out."

"Joshua was defeated, according to his way of seeing it. And in a battle plan that he devised himself." Caleb put his hand on the young physician's shoulder. "You are not like the rest of us, Salmon. Perhaps it is you who are right and we who are wrong. I do not know. The priests agreed that it was the will of Yahweh when Joshua suggested invoking *herem* against the men of Bashan. Perhaps as that girl called Rahab said in the cave on Mount Nebo, Yah is a god of peace in this country. But with Israel he is a god of war."

"What sort of a god looks with favor upon killing innocent women and children?" Salmon demanded angrily. "I heard nothing like that in the teachings Moses received from Yahweh."

"Leave such questions to the priests," Caleb advised. "A soldier's job is to kill the enemy."

"But I am not a soldier."

"If we win tomorrow, it will be your strategy that gave us the advantage," Caleb pointed out. "So you will be responsible in a sense for what happens."

"I planned a campaign against soldiers, not women and children," Salmon said bitterly. "I wish now I had never thought of a way to win battles."

"Hush," Caleb warned. "It is blasphemy to speak against the will of Yahweh."

"I will repeat my words before the council of elders," Salmon insisted.

Caleb sighed "Nothing is harder than keeping a man with good intentions from making a fool of himself. Go to your tent, Salmon, and think no more of why men do as they do A physician's job is to relieve suffering and bind up wounds.

You do that well, so leave the rest to the soldiers and the priests."

The morning dawned clear and bright. Before many hours passed, the heat of the approaching midday would be intense and the hot, dry wind from the vast desert waste to the east would sweep the plains, scorching men's throats and making their eyes sting from dust and sweat. But in the hours just after dawn it was still cool from the night, and Joshua hurried the men with their morning preparations so the battle could be joined as early as possible.

In little clumps between the cooking fires they ate a brief meal of dried dates, cheese, and hunks of bread, prepared the night before and washed down with huge drafts of wine. Enough wine, as everyone knew, could make a brave man of a coward. And a sparse meal of strong food like cheese made from goat's milk strengthened the belly against the sickening cramps of fear that would assail him at the first sight of the naked spear points of the enemy.

The sun was just rising over the hills when the Israelite army moved out on the brief march to the plain where scouts had reported the forces of King Og of Bashan to be deployed and waiting. The war machines devised by Salmon moved at the head of the column now, for they would be the first to engage the enemy.

While the long column of fighting men was being deployed upon the plain before Edrei, Salmon busied himself arranging his medical supplies in a shady glen sheltering a spring of clear water. He had chosen the spot carefully for the comfort of the wounded, but also because it was elevated above the plain, much as had been the Cave of Yah on Mount Nebo. Thus he could do his work and still watch the progress of the battle below him.

Caleb swung by at the head of the picked troops whose task it would be to rush into the breach and widen it, once the mobile battering-rams had broken the ranks of the enemy. He grinned at Salmon and shook his short sword over his head in salute, the blade pointing ahead to where Joshua rode in the lead chariot, standing tall and straight above everyone else on the field.

Joshua had selected this position himself, although he

would be a target for the arrows of Bashan. The heavy tunic of chains would protect him, however, save for the unlikely occurrence of a direct hit at close range.

Salmon could not help admiring Joshua's courage, for all that the Israelite leader had called him a fool last night. And he could see that Joshua's placing himself in the very forefront made sense, even though dictated by his determination not to let anyone precede him in battle. In order for the whole stratagem to succeed, the foot soldiers must join battle directly behind the battering-rams, before the men of Og could heal the first break in their lines. And with their leader plainly visible in the forefront, the Israelite warriors would have an additional incentive not to fail him.

Just as Salmon had planned, two Israelite soldiers marched behind each of the chariots, holding to a strap of leather attached to the frame of the vehicle itself. These men formed a hard core of the toughest fighting men in Israel, many of them having been a part of the small band who had won through the gates of Heshbon under Joshua's leadership by dressing themselves in the captured garb and weapons of the Amorite soldiers.

When the chariots with the battering-rams hurtled down upon the enemy, the men holding to the leather straps would be literally flung through the breach behind the vehicles, with the task of holding open the break. Victory would be certain if they succeeded. But if they failed, Joshua at their head would be cut down with the rest.

Salmon found his resentment against Joshua fading in a surge of admiration for this display of courage. That it was a display, he recognized at once. But that, too, was characteristic of the man called by the Israelites the Hornet of God, a naturally flamboyant figure with a shrewd sense of drama that made his courage and fighting ability even more spectacular.

Joshua was risking his life today, it was true, but he was playing for high stakes. Should he come through the battle alive, he would be the natural choice as leader of all the tribes, acclaimed by the fighting men, who could control the future of the people of Israel if they wished.

Salmon busied himself with his own work as he watched the preparations on the plains below from the vantage point on the hillside. At one side he laid out his instruments, the bandages of good cloth from the shops of Heshbon, and an ample supply of medicines. In the cool shade beneath the trees he marked out the place where the sorely wounded could be left to die in the greatest comfort, shielded from the sun. In preparations such as this, plus his ability to work rapidly and skillfully, lay Salmon's particular genius in ministering to the wounds and needs of the fighting men who fell upon the battlefield.

Across the plain, before the white walls of the small city of Edrei, the opposing army was drawn up like a rock wall, blocking further progress northward. Against them, like a wave preparing to dash itself upon the rocks, moved the men of Israel in battle array, with the chariots at their head. In numbers, Salmon estimated, the odds were weighed slightly in favor of the forces of Og. In fact, from his elevated position the strung-out column of Israel moving across the plain seemed almost puny against the solid human wall arrayed before it.

The battle plan of the enemy seemed to be exactly what the wounded Sherdan had described to Salmon. The men of Bashan wore conical hats of metal, and the front rank was made up of a solid wall of what appeared to be their tallest and strongest warriors. Each was armed with a large shield and carried as his principal weapon a heavy battle-ax. In the rays of the morning sun the forces of Og seemed literally to form a wall of metal, the hard metal of the Hittites, capable of turning the point of a spear and splintering an arrowhead.

Behind the front rank of the shield-bearers stood a second rank of spearmen, each with the point of his weapon thrust forward between two men in front of him, the butt held firmly against the ground. In this way the forward wall became literally a hedgehog of spear points upon which the attackers would be forced to spit themselves before they even reached the solid phalanx of the shields.

Behind the first two ranks of warriors was a third composed of bowmen, lightly armed so as not to interfere with their rapid shooting. Every few places along the rear line, however, stood other men carrying shields, whose job it was to protect the whole forward wall from an arching rain of weapons by raising the heavy metal bucklers above their heads.

Joshua had deployed his forces into a line at some distance from the enemy so that they would be in the position from which he planned to launch the attack before any actual fighting began. The whole success of the battle today depended on the element of surprise inherent in the battering-rams, and the Israelite leader did not intend to reveal his new weapon to the enemy until the last moment.

As for the forces of Bashan, they seemed content to make the Israelites attack them so they could utilize to the full the advantages of their wall of shields. While he waited for the clash of battle to begin, Salmon prayed silently to Yahweh that all would go well.

In spite of the taunts hurled across the field by the enemy, Joshua did not allow himself to be hurried into the attack. The safer tactic, initially, might have been to concentrate on one of the flanks, seeking to turn it and thus get behind the enemy line. Were this to succeed, the risk might be less, it was true, for thus behind the massed troops, the Israelites would have them at a disadvantage.

If a flanking attack was not immediately successful, however, the men of Bashan could simply retreat and fold their flank back around themselves, as had been the custom of the Babylonians years before. Then the Israelites would have revealed to the enemy the particular stratagem by which they hoped to break his ranks, and the value of surprise would be lost. For the weakest point in the strategy of the battering-rams lay in the fact that if the enemy were forewarned he could neutralize the effect, simply by placing bowmen behind the front ranks and letting them shoot through at close range, bringing down the horses and rendering the chariots useless before they could make contact with the enemy.

With magnificent courage and daring, Joshua had chosen to stake everything on the initial effect of the rams. Now, as the chariots reached the center of the enemy line, Salmon felt his heart begin to pound with excitement and suspense.

Even at a distance he could see Joshua's tall figure when he lifted the ram's-horn trumpet to his lips. And the blast that floated across the field was clear and sharp in the morning air. At the signal the chariots wheeled into line. And as the whips slashed down upon the backs of the horses, the drivers slid the rams forward smoothly and locked them into place, ready for the smashing drive into the enemy wall.

Twelve

THE BLAST of Joshua's signal trumpet on the field before Edrei and the sudden swinging into line of the chariots with their unwieldy burdens acted like the release of a bowstring upon the Israelite army, committing them irrevocably to an action that must now go on through its prescribed course to whatever fate awaited it. A shout of surprise and sudden apprehension went up from the massed warriors of King Og when they saw what the chariots carried.

At least one enemy officer seemed to grasp the meaning of the mobile battering-rams, for from his vantage point Salmon saw a sudden surge near the center of the line as a group of skilled bowmen were rushed forward to kneel and direct their arrows point-blank between the shield-bearers at the breasts of the horses thundering down upon them. But Joshua was executing the battle plan with his usual daring and speed, so there was not time for any effective change in the defense before the rams struck the solid phalanx of iron shields making up the first rank of the enemy.

The screams of dying horses as their breasts were transfixed by the hedgehog of spear points projecting before the shield-bearers floated across the battlefield. But Salmon had taken this into consideration, counting on the headlong charge of the chariots to gain enough momentum, even with the horses dying, to take them through the ranks of the enemy. One instant the forward wall of Bashan's warriors stood like a rock; the next, the air was filled with the crash of wood against metal, the screams of the horses, the shouts of the enemy, and the war cry of the Israelites as they rushed into the great breach created in King Og's lines.

The enemy officers laid about them with their golden-handled whips of authority, trying desperately to rally the badly disorganized phalanxes to take the initiative. They might have succeeded had not the men who raced behind the chariots attacked just then, stabbing and hacking while they kept up a shouting that made their size seem ten times the real number. In the forefront of the battle, as usual, was Joshua, a heroic figure plowing through the enemy as he swung a giant battle-ax with both hands, taking staggering blows on his tunic of metal armor, but moving on still.

While the small advance party exploited to the full the momentary panic created in the center of the enemy lines by the battering-rams, Caleb drew his short sword and led the main body straight into the breach, splitting the forces of Og in two. The warriors of Bashan were caught in a quandary, as Salmon had intended, for the third wave of Israelites still faced them. These had not yet been committed to battle, but the threat of their presence kept the enemy from turning to fight the men led by Joshua and Caleb, who had now passed completely through the lines and were fanning out to attack from the rear according to Salmon's plan.

The short period of indecision by the front rank of his troops proved to be King Og's ruin. Leaderless and paralyzed by the fury of the attack, some of his men turned to meet the thrust from the rear. Others did not, and in a matter of moments the battle line became a milling shambles, with their heavy shields now hampering the men of Bashan more than they helped.

The battle was not yet won, but the initial advantage possessed by the enemy was gone. With Joshua and Caleb leading them, the Israelites fought like the demons their enemies had labeled them more than once. Most of the horses had been killed by the spears, and the chariots now lay useless on the field, but there was no need for them any more. This was a battle to the death, and when after an hour of bloody fighting the enemy cried for quarter, none was given. The kingdom of Bashan was under *herem,* the terrible curse of Yahweh which doomed every living thing to destruction.

Watching from the hillside, Salmon saw a giant of a man on a horse engage Joshua in combat while the conflict was at its height. That this was the famed King Og, whose bedstead of iron was said to be twice as long as a man was tall, Salmon had no doubt, for no one else on the field equaled him in size.

The horse gave the enemy King a momentary advantage, but Joshua quickly evened it. Plucking a spear from the hand of a dying Israelite warrior, he drew back and threw it, plunging the point halfway through the body of the charging steed.

King Og was a worthy adversary, however. Leaping clear of the horse as it fell, he charged upon Joshua with his iron shield before him, his battle-ax swinging. Joshua was forced for the moment to give ground and, recognizing this as a duel to the death between the two leaders, the soldiers drew back and formed a ring around the battling men. This was what Joshua wanted, they knew, a personal combat with the enemy's leader that could end only with one of them lying dead on the battlefield.

Joshua leaped to one side, forcing King Og to turn, and thus destroyed the momentary advantage. While Bashan's King was swinging the heavy shield, Joshua moved in again to attack with his spear. Og had barely time to turn the shield enough to deflect the sharp blade point of Joshua's spear from his body.

The thrust placed the Israelite leader within range of the battle-ax carried by the King of Bashan, and Joshua took a mighty buffet on his armored tunic. The blow would almost certainly have killed him had he not been wearing the armor. As it was, he staggered but managed to stay on his feet and hack at King Og with his short sword, bringing blood as a long wound was opening in the huge man's cheek.

Even from a distance Salmon could see that Joshua had almost found his match at last in the great size and strength of King Og. But as the fight continued, the Israelite captain's superior agility began to tell against the weight of the shield and ax borne by his opponent. Gradually Og began to slow down, making him more vulnerable to Joshua's attack. And exulting in his growing advantage, Joshua somehow seemed to find new reserves of strength.

Finally a blow by Joshua on the conical helmet of his opponent stunned him momentarily. And as King Og reeled without defenses, the Israelite captain plunged his spear into the doomed man's neck, cutting nearly through it at one

135

thrust and almost severing the head from the body. As the massive form of the King of Bashan crumpled to the ground, a great shout of triumph went up from the Israelites, and they turned once more to the attack with renewed vigor.

Demoralized by the loss of the leader they seemed to have thought invincible, the warriors of Bashan gave ground and retreated toward the town of Edrei. This was the signal for the third wave of Israelites, who had been held in reserve, to race across the plain and outflank them, cutting to pieces the remnants of what had been a formidable army.

Salmon could watch no more, for the wounded were beginning to drift back to the glen where he had set up his dressing station. He worked without stopping through the day and into the night, administering large doses of poppy leaves and wine to those whose wounds were hopeless, so that death would be as free from pain as possible, binding up wounds, stopping bleeding, and performing the hundred and one duties that a physician must discharge in battle.

After the first hour of the battle, reports came back that all organized resistance had been stamped out, and the troops were busy now with the wholesale butchery called for by *herem*. All night long the flames from the burning village of Edrei lit up the plain. And although he was much too far away, Salmon still fancied he could hear the screams of the dying women and children as the Israelites relentlessly killed everyone who escaped from the flames.

It took a month in all to complete the destruction of Ashtaroth, King Og's seat of government, and subdue the city of Ramoth-gilead. In each instance the Israelites followed to the letter the application of the curse. Only those who showed descent from Abram and worshiped the god called Yah in this part of the world were allowed to live.

Finally, arrangements having been made for the northern land around Ramoth-gilead to be occupied by the half tribe of Manasseh, and that below the River Jabbok by the tribe of Gad, the main body of the army retired victoriously to Heshbon, where the rest of the Israelites were camped. Laden with spoils, they were received as heroes, and the days that followed were given over to feasting and celebration.

Joshua was named chief of all the fighting men by ac-

136

clamation soon after their return, but the elders still jealously guarded the right to rule in all civil matters and decisions of policy. At their insistence it was decided to do no more fighting for the moment, but to rest and consolidate their gains. Nor did Joshua object, for with the east side of the Jord now in their hands, he was looking westward, where the rich and populous cities of Canaan stood on their hilltop strongholds. And in this campaign he would need all the strength and wealth that Israel could muster.

It was also decreed that the three tribes who had chosen to remain east of the Jord were to furnish their quota of fighting men when the others moved on to attack the fertile land of Canaan. Even Joshua agreed that this phase of their conquest of what they termed the "Promised Land" had best be deferred many months, until the army could recover from its wounds and new fighters be trained among the younger men who had as yet seen no military action.

Now that the active fighting was over, Salmon felt himself becoming restless. The leeches who practiced their trade among the people could take care of ordinary illnesses, so his services were no longer needed badly by the camp. When he had told Chazan about what had happened to Rahab, the old scribe had wanted to journey at once to Egypt to try to find her. But Chazan was old and in poor health, so Salmon had persuaded him to remain, with the promise that he would go to Memphis as soon as the campaign against Bashan was completed. He raised the question of the journey to Caleb one night as they sat beside the campfire before the latter's tent.

"Why go to Egypt?" Caleb demanded. "You would only be putting the chains of slavery around your neck again."

"I plan to travel as Samma, a physician of Egypt, returning from a visit to Canaan," Salmon explained. "Many such travel the caravan roads. I would be just another one."

"With a full purse, fine clothing, and a new name, no one would suspect you were once a slave," Caleb agreed. "Besides, you escaped from Tanis, which is a long way from Memphis. But you studied healing in the temple at Thebes; why would you want to see Memphis now?"

"Rahab was taken there by the slave trader."

"If anyone should seek her out it is Joshua," Caleb said. "They were betrothed."

"Joshua does not want her to return," Salmon explained. "When I mentioned her he became very angry and said a leader of Israel could not take a wife from the brothels of Egypt."

"The son of Nun takes his new position very seriously," Caleb agreed. "Perhaps he is right. We are no longer a band of wanderers, but already a nation to be reckoned with. Why not leave the girl in Egypt, since Joshua does not want her?"

"I love her myself," Salmon said quietly.

"Suppose you do find her in a brothel. Would you wed a harlot?"

"Whatever Rahab may have been forced to do was not of her own choosing," Salmon told him. "It would not matter to me."

Caleb shook his head. "What you propose is foolish, but you are my friend. How can I help you?"

"If my real reason for going to Egypt were known I think Joshua would oppose it," Salmon told him. "So it must apparently be for another reason."

"What?"

"Suppose we knew Pharaoh would oppose us with his own troops if we attack Canaan. Would that make any difference in Joshua's plans for the future?"

Caleb snorted. "Not even the son of Nun would be such a fool as to fight the armies of Pharaoh. Remember the vengeance of Harmhab?"

"Then it is important for Israel to know what Pharaoh will be likely to do, isn't it?"

"By the altars of Baal!" Caleb cried. "I will never cease to wonder at that mind of yours, Salmon. But how would you discover Pharaoh's purpose?"

"A physician goes places where other men cannot, and hears things others might not consider important."

"That may be. But how will you find the girl? Memphis is the largest city in Egypt."

"I know she was taken away from Medeba by a slave merchant named Abda," Salmon told him. "And I am told he sells women in the foreign quarter of Memphis. If you will propose to the council of elders that I be sent to Egypt to try to discover the intentions of Pharaoh concerning the defense of Canaan, I will take care of the rest."

And so it came about that Samma, a physician of Egypt, joined the next caravan passing southward along the King's Highway, bound for Ezion-geber, from which a water route led to the cities of the Nile. Nor did anyone think his Semitic features odd for an Egyptian; since the sojourn of the Hyksos people in Egypt centuries before, many of the Nile dwellers showed traces of their occupancy in the prominent noses of the Semitic people.

The journey was without event as far as Ezion-geber. Here, rather than essay a long trip across the desert wilderness where he had so nearly lost his life several years before, Samma took passage on a galley bound for the Nile.

Down the Gulf of Aqabah the fleet craft moved, by sail when there was wind, by long banks of slave-powered oars when there was not. Turning northwestward up the narrow sea called Red and through the "bitter lakes," the galley reached the body of water known as Lake Timsah. From here the long, many-oared galley with its large square sails floated through a canal that had connected the Red Sea with one of the many mouths of the Nile for hundreds of years.

Only a few weeks after leaving Heshbon, Salmon reached the great river a short distance downstream from Memphis. And one day in late summer, now metamorphosed so completely into the rich and learned physician Samma that no one suspected him of being anything else, he debarked upon the docks of Memphis and set out on an undertaking which, on the face of it, seemed impossible: the task of finding one lovely girl named Rahab in the teeming brothels of Egypt's largest city.

Thirteen

ONLY ONE THING marred Rahab's enjoyment of her life in Prince Hazor's household, and that was the presence of Kanofer, the Egyptian captain. She had not missed his open admiration for her when Abda had exhibited her to him and Hazor on the night the Prince of Jericho had bought her for his slave-concubine, or his offer to buy her himself if Hazor had not taken her first. And as the weeks passed, she had more and more evidence of Kanofer's ardent desire for her.

The Egyptian captain did not live in Prince Hazor's small house but dwelt nearby. And since he was in attendance at most of the social functions by virtue of his rank and influence as a captain of mercenaries, Rahab could not help coming in contact with him often. Whenever they met, she often felt his eyes following her as she moved about. Kanofer lost no opportunity to get her alone, when he would whisper compliments and occasionally lewd suggestions to her. Sometimes he came to the house when Hazor was away, obviously to see her and equally obviously convinced that she could not long resist him.

Rahab hesitated to speak to her master about this, partly because she did not wish to disturb him, but also because Kanofer seemed to have a great deal of influence in the Egyptian court. And Hazor could not well afford to antagonize the handsome captain, she knew, since he still hoped to obtain Egyptian troops for the defense of Jericho, the reason why he had come to Memphis originally. Rahab avoided Kanofer as much as she could, but she never got over her fear and dislike of him, or her instinctive premonition that he posed a threat to the quiet happiness she had found in Prince Hazor's household.

As the weeks passed and the troops did not come, Hazor began to be more and more concerned. "If the money does not come soon from Thebes to employ mercenaries, I shall have to go on back to Jericho without them," he told Rahab as they lay on soft cushions under the canopy outside their bedroom one summer evening, listening to the quiet voices of the night.

"Are the Habiru making trouble?" she asked quickly.

"They are still on the east side of the Jord, according to the last report I had from Urusalim, brought by the captain of a Phoenician galley." Urusalim was the most important city in central Canaan and the center of Egyptian control in that area. The King of Urusalim had been assigned the duty by Pharaoh of watching over invaders who might seek to take the fertile land of Canaan for themselves and, as a result, kept in touch with the many other Canaanite kings.

"What is the trouble then?" Rahab asked.

"I have never spoken of this to you before," Hazor said. "But you are a part of me now, so you should know all my secrets. My father is old and no longer rules with the strong hand that kept Jericho peaceful and prosperous for so many years. A few years ago he married a new wife, a woman of the Hittite people called Cesera. Her brother, Kalak, lives in my father's palace and is the high priest of Baal in Jericho. I believe they are plotting to gain control of the kingdom when my father dies."

"Shouldn't you return at once then?"

"I cannot delay much longer," he agreed. "But as long as there is any chance of obtaining the mercenaries Pharaoh promised for the defense of Jericho, I cannot afford to leave."

"Why are the Egyptians so important? You must have soldiers of your own."

"Jericho is not a large city. At most, we could hardly put more than a thousand men upon the field of battle. But the presence of Egyptian troops inside the walls of Jericho, under an Egyptian captain, would remind any possible invader that we are still a part of the empire of Egypt. I would see that this was made known to the Habiru, and they would no doubt hesitate to attack. People in our part of the world still remember how Harmhab put down the revolt against Ikhnaton."

"But Jericho has strong walls."

"Not so strong as they seem. The city has been destroyed several times by invaders, and each time the walls have been

141

built back, but on flimsy foundations. A few years ago an earthquake made a great crack in them, but we plastered it over quickly with mud so the weakness would not be apparent. Another earthquake might break through the walls and leave us defenseless."

"Then you think the Habiru will really attack Jericho?"

"They must if they intend to enter Canaan. The city stands across the road to Urusalim. Some of the Amorites who escaped from Heshbon say the Habiru openly boast that their god has given Canaan to them."

Remembering that Joshua and Caleb had said much the same thing in the Cave of Yah, Rahab was silent. Nor could she help being troubled by what she had heard An Israelite attack on Jericho could only mean that Joshua, whom she loved, and Prince Hazor, who had been so kind to her and for whom she felt such a tender concern, would almost certainly face each other one day upon the battlefield. Then she would be forced to choose between them, and although she could only choose Joshua, it would still pain her greatly to see any harm come to Prince Hazor.

"Couldn't you let the Habiru pass by Jericho?" she asked.

"That would earn me the hatred of the other kings of Canaan."

"Then they should come to your aid if Jericho is attacked.'

"I think the other kings are waiting to see whether Pharaoh will help defend Canaan. It seems that he has already decided to let the lands east of the Jord go to the Habiru"

"But the cities of Canaan must have many times more fighting men than they do. If all of you stood together, the Habiru could not attack."

"The kings of Canaan have never joined together, and I doubt if they will now. Each one looks to Egypt to drive out the Habiru, as they did the Hyksos and the Hittites a long time ago. Kanofer wants me to go back to Canaan now and try to persuade the other kings to hire mercenaries, with him in charge. But unless I can bring troops from Egypt, I am afraid we will have to fend for ourselves."

"If the Habiru mean to conquer Canaan, why did they attack my country first?" Rahab asked.

"The kingdoms east of the Jord have given only slight allegiance to Egypt for many years," Hazor explained. "But those of Canaan are much closer. We trade directly with Egypt by water, and the taxgatherers of Pharaoh are in every town. The Habiru could be fairly certain that a weak Pharaoh would not be too much concerned by the loss of the region beyond the Jord, and they gained weapons and chariots by conquering King Sihon, so it was worth the risk. But Canaan is prosperous and rich. It would be a tremendous blow to Egypt to lose it, and a rich prize indeed for the Habiru if they succeeded in taking it."

These were almost the same words Salmon had used, Rahab remembered now. She could see how important it would be for both the Habiru chiefs and the kings of Canaan to know what the intentions of the Egyptian government were. Which, of course, made Hazor's mission in Egypt all the more important.

"If gold for paying the mercenaries does not come from Thebes in another month," Hazor continued, "we will take ship for Joppa with Kanofer. Perhaps King Adoni-zedek in Urusalim will stand with us against the Habiru." His face darkened. "That is, if Kalak and Cesera have not stolen the kingdom for themselves while I have been away."

"Should you wait then?" Rahab asked.

"I must take the risk," he said. "If I fail here, there may not even be a kingdom for the sons I hope you will bear me, Rahab."

Knowing how disturbed he was, she comforted him in the only way she could. But long after Hazor was asleep in her arms, she lay awake thinking of the strange pattern of events whereby her betrothed husband and the master she admired and respected so much seemed destined to be pitted against each other, with the life of one of them at stake. And her dilemma was made infinitely more difficult a week later, when she knew for certain what she had half suspected for several weeks—that she would bear one of them a child.

Fourteen

PRINCE HAZOR was overjoyed by the news that Rahab was to bear a child and naturally concluded that he was its father. And, in truth, Rahab herself could not be sure now whether she would rather it be Hazor's child or Joshua's. To Joshua she had given the surging passion that sweeps away all restraint, all reservation. And she had thought—as every woman secretly thinks in the ecstasy of surrender—that she could feel the new life surging into being within her body while she lay in Joshua's arms.

But then Prince Hazor had saved her from the slave market and she had learned from him that there are two kinds of love. For her master she felt a tender, deep, and mature affection that made her happy in rewarding him for his love with the gift of her body. And now—if he were the father of the child she was to bear—she knew she might be bringing him the most precious thing she could possibly give, a son and possibly an heir to the throne of Jericho. Before the reality of Hazor's love and tenderness, the ecstasy she had shared with Joshua seemed far away now, like something experienced in childhood and remembered but faintly.

Only one thing about bearing Hazor's child troubled Rahab. Her master had left her free to worship her own god, but since Baal was the god of Jericho, his child would have to be dedicated to him rather than to Yah. Still, with all that a child would mean to Hazor, she knew she could not object to such a little thing as his being reared in the worship of another deity.

The foreign quarter of Memphis was so much a separate section of the city, with its teeming streets and many nationalities, that the Egyptian authorities had allowed temples for the worship of foreign gods to be erected there. Most prominent among these were the great temples of Baal and Ashtarth, where Hazor worshiped.

Baal, in his many incarnations, was the god of most of the

144

people from Canaan, Syria, and the kingdoms to the north who made up the foreign quarter. And wherever Baal was worshiped, his consort, under the various names of Ishtar, Astarte, Asherath and Ashtarth, was also adored by her followers, particularly women, who looked to the "Earth Mother" to make them fertile.

Among the structures dedicated to the worship of lesser gods, Rahab had found one belonging to Yahweh, or El as he was more commonly called here. It was only a small building served by one old man, but here she had prayed to the god known to her as Yah, not to determine the paternity of her baby—for that of course had been settled at its conception—but that it would be strong and handsome, yet good and kind, qualities which, had she stopped to consider it, characterized Prince Hazor more than they did Joshua.

As soon as Rahab told Hazor she was to bear a child, he insisted that they go to the temple of Ashtarth and make a sacrifice to the goddess of fertility in thanksgiving. She had not accompanied him before when he went to the temple but, sensing that he wished her to be there because of the child within her womb, she went with him this time.

Rahab was somewhat familiar with the worship of Ashtarth, who was a favored goddess in every country because she brought fertility to both animals and humans. It was the day of the full moon, a time of special celebration, when their *merkobt,* driven by Senu, deposited them before the great temple located in a large garden overlooking the broad reaches of the Nile.

The whole foreign quarter was in festive array, for this was one of the major feasts of the Earth Goddess. Those who sacrificed this day, it was believed, would be far more generously rewarded than on less important occasions, when the goddess might not look with so much favor upon the supplications of her adherents. Bright-colored pennants and streamers rippled in the breeze on poles projecting from the roofs of the buildings and shops. Groups of gaily shouting children danced in the streets, clad only in wreaths and garlands of bright-colored flowers that grew in such riotous abandon here in the fertile alluvial plain of the Nile Valley.

The temple itself was a building of considerable size, for Ashtarth was a popular and wealthy goddess. It was built

145

of brick and stone, the design that of a world in miniature, the ceiling being identified with the sky and the floor with the earth. Two large columns at the entrance simulated the pillars upon which the heavens rested, and the stone blocks surmounting them were carved in the form of an opening lily, in itself a symbol of fertility. Behind the temple shone the blue waters of a small artificial lake, simulating the cosmic ocean.

Because the weather was clear and warm today and the crowd large, a small incense altar of stone bearing four horns had been set up in an open courtyard before the broad pillared entrance to the temple.

As Hazor and Rahab made their way to the special area near the altar reserved for those who had paid liberally to sacrifice today, hoping for the especial favor of the goddess, little girls besieged them on every hand, thrusting up small clay figurines of the goddess.

"Buy a goddess for your wife," they implored. "Ashtarth will be gracious and make her fertile."

Rahab's vivid beauty made her a target for all eyes whenever she went abroad. She was richly dressed in the Egyptian fashion, and Hazor's bearing stamped him as royal in position, so she held up her head proudly as they found their seats near the front, knowing that she need feel inferior to none.

Soon after they found their seats a strange and colorful procession emerged from the temple itself. Leading it was a tall man in rich robes, such as a bridegroom might wear. Over his head he wore a mask of the pale yellow metal called *electrum*, shaped in the form of a bull's head. He bore in his hands a golden tray upon which was another exquisitely modeled figurine of Ashtarth. And as he carried it at arm's length around the open space, Rahab could see two live snakes of brilliant green color coiled about the feet of the goddess.

"He is the *Mtrh*," Hazor explained in a whisper. "The bridegroom of Ashtarth who represents Baal."

Behind the *Mtrh* came a half dozen lesser priests, wearing only loincloths and carrying bronze knives that gleamed in the sun. They leaped about with utter abandon and in their frenzy gasped and mutilated themselves with the knives.

146

Blood dripped from hundreds of shallow cuts before they had completed the circle of the open space before the altar, but they seemed impervious to the pain and kept up a high-pitched shrilling cry, imploring the goddess to show favor to the sacrifice.

Now the sound of female voices singing was heard from the temple as a sacristan emerged, bearing a beautiful carved bowl of *electrum* filled with wine. Behind him filed a double line of the sacred women of Ashtarth. They wore chaplets of flowers on their heads and transparent robes of the incredibly fine white linen preferred by the Egyptians.

The sacristan approached the altar with his bowl of wine and set it down, while the women began a slow sensuous dance to the music of a group of priestly musicians who emerged from the temple behind them. As they circled the open space before the altar the women approached very near the massed onlookers in the special area reserved for those who had contributed liberally to today's sacrifice. Rahab was startled to see them turn inviting eyes upon the men and a few of the latter nod back to a particular one of the dancers, as if making an assignation.

When she turned inquiring eyes to Hazor, she found him smiling. "Those who buy a special sacrifice today may visit the sacred women of the goddess afterward," he explained. "It is considered a part of the worship of Ashtarth." He gave her hand that lay in his a quick squeeze. "I do not plan to exercise my own rights, although I paid the priests well," he whispered. "No man could want a woman more beautiful than you are."

As the women finished their dance and sank to the ground in graceful postures, a group of naked children wearing garlands ran from the temple portal, carrying loaves of bread and jars of wine. These they placed upon the altar and also upon several small clay stands which stood here and there in the open space of the court.

At each corner of these small altars were cherubim, those in front with female heads, bodies modeled in the form of lions, and wings. At the back corners of each of the stands the cherubim were male. Hazor explained to Rahab that they represented other gods who had been invited to attend the ceremony honoring the Earth Mother.

147

Now a giant gong clashed somewhere within the temple, and the high priest—a tall, commanding figure in a richly brocaded robe and tall conical headdress adorned with figures of the goddess and her consort embroidered in gold and silver —began a slow march to the altar. As he walked he intoned in a rich, vibrant voice:

> *"I will summon the gods, gracious and beautiful,*
> *Children of princes eat of the bread with me,*
> *And drink of the wine, my weary ones."*

"He is calling the gods to the feast," Hazor explained in a whisper. "Ashtarth and Baal are already here but unseen. Your god Yah may even be present."

"Yah does not dwell in places such as this," Rahab said with a smile. "His home is a cave upon a hillside, or a small temple by the riverbank."

Suddenly there was a crash of cymbals, and a group of priests ran into the open court. Dressed as laborers, they carried small pots containing grapevines, which they began to trim and prop up with sticks as if erecting a miniature arbor. Behind them trudged a disconsolate-looking priest in a black robe, his face and head covered with soot and ashes. He carried a broken reed in his hands, but the crowd gave him no sympathy. Instead, they laughed happily at his dejection.

"That is Moth, the god of death," Hazor whispered. "The crowd is happy at his disappointment because he will not be able to kill the vines this year."

Their pruning finished, the priests began to sing as they drove Moth before them from the court. The crowd joined in, clapping their hands and stamping their feet in rhythm with the song:

> *"Moth shall sit,*
> *In his hand the scepter of bereavement;*
> *In his hand the scepter of silence;*
> *The pruners shall prune the vines;*
> *They shall cast the stones from the field."*

As the laborers and the god of death retired, a herdsman came out leading a she-goat and carrying a kid in his arms.

Behind him was a priest, followed by slaves bearing a stove of fired clay and a large copper pot. The priest blew up the fire from the pan of glowing coals in the stove while the herdsman quickly milked the goat. Then while the milk was set to boil in the copper pot, the herdsman carried the kid to the altar, where the high priest dexterously killed it by cutting its throat with a jeweled knife.

Quickly the kid was dressed by the priest attendants. And then, to Rahab's amazement, they put it in the pot where the milk was now boiling.

"The goddess loves the smell of the meat from a kid boiling in its mother's milk," Hazor told her. "She will come to the feast now with Baal, and the bridegroom of the goddess will bless all women."

The sacred women rose now and began to dance before the priest in the bull's-head mask. And as the women passed before him, their bodies writhing in the voluptuous movements of the temple dance, the divine bridegroom sang:

> *"The women, the wives of Baal, shall cry,*
> *O Moth, we shall cut down thy scepter,*
> *We shall tear away the staff of thy hand,*
> *By kindling the seed of men to life in our bodies,*
> *By bringing forth new life from our wombs."*

The priest wearing the golden bull's head touched each of the women with his staff as these words were being chanted, while they continued the slow dance around the altar where the meat of the kid was boiling in its mother's milk. And as they danced they sang:

> *"We are women, each the wife of Baal, and his slaves,*
> *He shall cleanse our lips with his, he shall lift us up.*
> *Our lips will be sweet, like the pomegranate,*
> *With us is kissing and conception.*
> *By embracing, she who is passionate shall bring forth."*

As they finished their dance, the women filed back into the temple, casting inviting glances toward the men who had bought sacrifices. The crowd began to disperse too, signifying that the festivities were over.

Senu was waiting at the edge of the courtyard with the *merkobt*, but so great was the press of the crowd that they could not leave at once. Standing in the carriage, Rahab looked idly across the small sea of faces reflecting every nationality of the world gathered here in this great metropolis of its greatest nation. Suddenly she went rigid and gripped the rim of the chariot frame for support. Across the crowd she had glimpsed momentarily a man's head in profile, but even with only a glimpse she knew it was Salmon.

Fifteen

"IS ANYTHING WRONG, Rahab?" Hazor's voice brought her back to the present. "You look as if you had seen a demon."

She leaned against him for support and drew a deep breath. "It is nothing," she said quickly. "I am a little tired, that is all." She must not betray Salmon's presence in Memphis, she realized, remembering now that he had been an escaped slave and would still have a price on his head.

The realization that Joshua had sent Salmon to look for her—she did not consider that there could be another reason for his being in Memphis—sent Rahab's heart to pounding with a surge of emotion that she had almost forgotten during the past few months in the security and comfort of Hazor's love. Joshua's sending for her could only mean he wanted her so much that his love had reached across the world to her. And everything—her debt to Hazor, even the fact that the child within her body might be his instead of Joshua's—faded before a sudden yearning for the rapture she had shared with him.

But then came the chilling reminder that she could never hope to find Salmon in this city of two million people. And if she did not find him, she could not hope to return to Joshua.

"This morning at the temple of Ashtarth, I came to a decision," Hazor told Rahab as they refreshed themselves with wine and fruit after returning from the religious ceremony. "You cannot be my Queen—our laws forbid that—but if the

150

child you are to bear me is a boy, he will one day be the King of Jericho."

For a moment Rahab's heart was so filled with gratitude that she could not find words to thank him. Even though she could never be Queen, the place of Hazor's wife-concubine and mother of the Crown Prince would be an honored one, honored above all women in the city. If she did find Salmon, she realized now, a difficult choice would face her, the choice between the palace of the King of Jericho and the goatskin tent of a captain of a thousand in the army of Israel. And most of all, of course, she must think of her unborn child.

More than once in the weeks since she had left Abda's establishment Rahab had thought of going back to thank the eunuch and Tamar for the good fortune they had arranged for her. But although she knew Hazor would not refuse her permission, she sensed that he would rather she was not seen visiting a well-known brothel. She was surprised and pleased one afternoon when a visitor was announced who turned out to be Tamar.

Rahab kissed the other girl happily and led her into the cool garden beneath the shade of the trees. Tamar looked around her with an appraising glance, taking in the unobtrusive luxury of the house and the courtyard, the obvious respect with which Myrnah treated Rahab when she brought water for their hands and a cool dish of fruit mixed with honey.

"I owe all of this to you and Abda," Rahab said when they were alone. "How can I ever thank you?"

"If Prince Hazor had not considered you a jewel well worth any price, he would not have bought you that night," Tamar assured her. "And rest assured that Abda made a tidy profit on the transaction."

"How is he?" Rahab asked eagerly.

"The fat one has gone to Syria by ship to buy fresh young maidens. Like most husbands everywhere, the men of Memphis are tired of their wives and pay fine prices for virgins."

Tamar's prosperity was evident in the rich stuff of her robe, its fashionable revealing cut, the bracelets about her wrists and ankles, and the jeweled necklace about her neck. "Fortune has obviously been kind to you," Rahab observed. "I am happy for you, Tamar."

151

"I am prosperous enough. Most young women will not tolerate the embraces of stupid old men, but I learned long ago to shut my eyes and pretend they are young and handsome. Besides," Tamar went on, "Abda discovered that during his absences the chief eunuch had been making an extra profit for himself on the food and wine. I persuaded the mountain of flesh that I could do a better job and cheat him only a little, so he placed me in charge."

"No wonder you are prosperous then."

"Are you happy, Rahab? Or should I ask, with all this?"

"I have every reason to be happy," Rahab admitted. "Prince Hazor is the kindest man who ever lived; he treats me more like a wife than a slave."

"But you still long for the Habiru," Tamar observed shrewdly.

Rahab looked away quickly, to make sure that Myrnah was not nearby to overhear. Hazor and Kanofer had gone up-river by boat to Thebes to make a last inquiry about the gold for the mercenaries before giving up hope that Pharaoh would help defend Jericho and Canaan. "Everyone remembers the man to whom she gives her first love, I suppose," Rahab admitted. "But until a few days ago it all seemed like a dream."

"Let the Habiru captain stay a dream then," Tamar said bluntly. "It is better to be an old man's favorite."

"Prince Hazor is not old," Rahab protested. "He is not old at all."

Tamar smiled. "I only saw him once, but I was sure he would be an adequate lover. The young ones are so busy with their own pleasure, they forget everything else."

Rahab blushed. "I am happy in his love. He does not know there was ever anyone else. Besides," she added, "I am with child."

Tamar's eyes widened. "Even the young ones do not always get a woman with child in the first few weeks. Prince Hazor must indeed be a man."

"I am not even sure he is the father," Rahab admitted.

"So? When did you first suspect you were pregnant?"

Rahab told her, and Tamar frowned. "It could be either," she agreed. "But it makes no difference, so long as your master does not know."

"If it is a boy he has promised to make it his heir."

"Then you would be the mother of a king!" Tamar cried. "This is truly a thing to boast about."

"I—I can't believe it yet," Rahab admitted. "Why should Yah especially choose me for such an honor?"

"Because you are yourself," Tamar said crisply. "But after this news, I wonder if I should tell you why I came."

Rahab looked up quickly. "What do you mean, Tamar?"

"A man came looking for you the other night. He asked for Abda, and they brought him to me."

"What was he like?" Rahab asked eagerly.

Tamar gave her a keen glance. "Were you expecting someone?"

"I saw a man I used to know in the crowd the other day at the temple of Ashtarth," Rahab explained. "I am sure it was Salmon, Joshua's closest friend."

"This one was slender and wiry. He was handsome, but more like a poet or a musician than a soldier. He pretended to be a physician of Egypt called Samma, but I could tell that he was an Israelite."

"It was Salmon!" Rahab cried. Then her animation faded. "Did he seem to enjoy the—the entertainment?"

Tamar laughed. "He did not stay, if that is what troubles you." Then her face sobered. "Why are you concerned about whether or not he found pleasure with another woman? Does this physician mean anything to you, Rahab?"

"Salmon is a good friend," Rahab explained. "That is all."

"If he were looking for a wife, I would take him before either your Israelite captain or your Canaanite prince," Tamar said bluntly. "Besides, he obviously does not lack for money."

"Did Salmon say Joshua sent him to find me?" Rahab asked.

"That one is not the kind to tell his business to everyone," Tamar assured her. "He said only that he sought a girl called Rahab who was sold into slavery at Medeba."

"What did you tell him?"

"Nothing, except that Abda had sold you to an older man and that you were alive and well. After all, you have everything here a woman could wish, Rahab."

"But Salmon is my friend. Joshua must have sent him to look for me."

"I would judge that he sought you for himself," Tamar observed. "He was very much concerned when I told him you had been sold as a concubine."

"When is he coming back to see you?" Rahab asked.

"We made no engagement, and he is not the kind who frequents brothels."

"Don't you know where he is staying?" Rahab cried.

"I could not ask, else he would suspect I knew more about you than I told him."

"But I must see him, Tamar! I must."

"Listen to me, foolish one," Tamar said bluntly. "You are the concubine of a prince who adores you. No woman could wish for more. Let this Habiru physician go back with the news that he could not find you. It is better to be the favorite of a prince and the mother of a king than to yearn for a nomad captain who might be killed in battle tomorrow."

Sixteen

IT WAS the day after her conversation with Tamar before Rahab thought of a way by which she might find Salmon, even among the teeming millions of Egypt's largest city. And the answer, when she found it, was amazingly simple. Since Salmon knew of her devotion to the god at whose sanctuary on Mount Nebo she had first met both him and Joshua, she hoped he would think to look for the temple of Yah in Memphis in the hope of finding a clue to her whereabouts there. She lost no time, therefore, in dressing herself in her finest raiment and setting out for the small temple devoted to the worship of the god known here as both Yahweh and El.

The city was teeming with people as usual, but Rahab did not even stop in the street of the jewelers to watch the skilled craftsmen fashion exquisite gems of lapis lazuli, chalcedony, and mussirru stone. Nor did she ask the price of a wash-basin of bronze engraved with scenes of the marsh-bird hunts

154

which was held up for her inspection by a street vendor when the *merkobt* was stopped for a moment by the press of the foot and wheel traffic near the riverbank.

At the small temple of Yah, Rahab instructed Senu to drive on a little way and wait with the carriage as usual while she went inside alone. The temple was cool and peaceful, its dimness lit only by a shaft of sunlight slanting through a window high up in the wall. From the dim recesses behind the altar an old priest with a long beard came to meet her.

"The peace of El and Yahweh be upon thee, daughter," he said. "Would you make a sacrifice?"

"I seek one recently come from the lands east of the River Jord who may have been here looking for me," she told him.

The old priest squinted at her in the dim light. "A man has been here each day asking for a woman called Rahab. He gave no name—but he did say he was a physician."

"When did he last come?" Rahab asked breathlessly.

"He has not missed by so much as one hour for the past three days," the priest told her. "I remember that I had not yet turned the clock at the sixth hour when he first came."

It was well into the fourth hour, now, Rahab remembered. She had noticed the time on a large shadow clock before the shop of a jeweler as they had driven to the temple. Consisting of a crosspiece elevated slightly above a narrow bar of wood so as to throw a shadow across it, the clock was placed with the crosspiece toward the rising sun each night to record the morning hours as its shadow moved along the wooden bar. At the sixth hour, which was noon, the clock was turned so that the declining rays of the sun could register the hours of the afternoon.

"I will wait here for him," she decided, and took a coin from her purse. "Please offer up a sacrifice to the god in my behalf."

The priest accepted the gift and disappeared, leaving Rahab alone in the cool sanctuary. While the old priest busied himself with the sacrifice in the dim recess where the altar stood, Rahab reviewed in her mind the events of the past few months. And the more she thought, the more it seemed— as she had felt deep inside her more than once since that day when Salmon and the litter-bearers had brought Joshua up the slope of Mount Nebo—that what was happening must be part of some grand pattern determined by the single all-powerful god she believed Yah to be.

Absorbed in her thoughts, Rahab did not hear the door at the back of the temple open or Salmon's light footsteps as he came down the long room to where she sat with the rays of the sun from the small high window turning her bright hair into gold.

"Rahab!" The word was the first intimation she had of his presence. "Rahab! It is you at last!"

At the sight of Salmon's familiar lean face and deep-set dark eyes she was suddenly overcome with happiness at finding him and threw herself into his arms. He held her gently and let her weep, sensing as he always seemed able to do that she needed this relief.

Finally she raised her head and he looked down at her, his eyes shining. "You have not changed, Rahab," he said wonderingly. "Except to become more beautiful. It is like a miracle, finding you here."

"Tamar told me you were in Memphis," Rahab said. "I was afraid I would not find you, until I remembered you might think to search for a temple of Yah."

"I knew you would come here to worship if you were in Memphis," he told her. "So I decided to return every day until I found you."

Rahab dried her eyes on Salmon's robe. "I should have known Joshua would send for me," she said happily. "And that you would be the one to come, Salmon."

In her excitement she did not notice that he looked away quickly, lest she see the sudden look of pain in his eyes. "Joshua is the leader of Israel now and has very important duties," he said. "And I needed to buy drugs and instruments."

"Is he all right—from his wound, I mean?"

"The wound healed quickly. Since Joshua fought King Og of Bashan and overcame him, he is the leader of us all. The people listen to him instead of to the elders and the priests."

"I wish I could have seen the battle. Joshua must have been magnificent."

"He was." Salmon smiled. "I discovered a suit of armor in Heshbon for him to wear in battle so he would be preserved for you."

156

"No one thinks of me as you do, Salmon." Rahab was holding his strong, slender hands in her own. Now she led him to one of the benches and drew him down beside her. "Does all go well with you?"

"I dress the wounds of Israel as usual. And treat their children when we are not fighting."

"How did you know to look for me in Memphis?"

He explained how he had learned that Abda had carried her off to be sold in the foreign quarter of Memphis, and how, with that much to go on, he had been able to trace her as far as Abda's place of business.

"Then Joel and Rebecca told you what happened in Medeba that day."

"They claimed that you went with Abda willingly to be a harlot."

Rahab looked at him, aghast. "A harlot!"

"I never believed it," Salmon assured her quickly. "And I finally did learn the truth from Joel."

"Then my father must think——"

"Chazan knew they lied too. He would have come after you himself, but I persuaded him that I could make the journey better than he."

"It was bad enough to stone me just to steal the *mohar,*" Rahab cried indignantly, "but to tell it abroad that I came to Egypt of my own accord to be a harlot!" Her eyes took fire. "I will make Joshua destroy them; he will put the whole town of Medeba to the torch."

"Tamar told me you had been bought by a rich man," Salmon said. His first quick glance had noted her jewelry, the rich stuff of her robe, and the cloak she wore over it, as well as the obviously expensive perfume and cosmetics that served to heighten her already striking beauty.

"My master is good and kind," Rahab told him. "He is Prince Hazor of Jericho."

"Jericho! In Canaan?"

"Yes." She smiled. "I knew you would be surprised."

Salmon recovered himself quickly. He must not reveal even to Rahab the other purpose of his coming to Egypt. For if Samma, the physician, were identified with Salmon, the strategist of the Israelite armies and an enemy of Egypt, things might go bad for him indeed. And the fact that Rahab

157

was now a concubine of the heir to the throne of the very frontier city the Israelites must attack first, when finally they began the march into Canaan, made the situation even more tense.

Salmon's every sense of justice rebelled against using the girl he loved to obtain information that might help them when the attack upon Jericho began. Yet, on the other hand, he was obligated to discover anything that could help in the invasion of Canaan and thus lessen the bloodshed among his own people.

"Is anything wrong, Salmon?" Rahab asked.

"We are encamped near Jericho," he explained, "at the city of Heshbon. Your belonging to the Prince of Jericho is a coincidence."

"Are the Habi—your people going to remain at Heshbon?"

"For a while, at least. Several of the tribes have already settled down in the lands east of the River Jord. Chazan is the chief scribe now," he continued. "He was very happy when I told him I was coming to seek you and bring you back to Israel."

A troubled look came over Rahab's face. Salmon saw it and asked quickly, "Don't you want to go back, Rahab?"

"Yes, but——" She stopped, not knowing how to tell him.

"Have you come to love your master so much that you don't wish to leave him?" he asked gently.

Rahab looked up, and he saw that her eyes were filled with tears. "I love Prince Hazor," she admitted, "but not the way I love Joshua. Prince Hazor saved me from being what the people of Medeba said I was—a harlot in a brothel of Memphis. I owe him a great deal, Salmon."

"Surely he knew you were not sold as a slave willingly."

"Yes. He did know that."

"Then you owe him no allegiance. He bought you, anyway, just as he would have bought an animal."

"It would still make him very unhappy if I ran away. And besides, they would send guards after me."

Salmon smiled. "Who would look for an escaped female slave in a youth apprenticed to a physician traveling to Babylon by way of the Red Sea and the King's Highway? We'd have to cut your hair, but in a Canaanite robe you could pass for a boy."

"But I haven't told you everything," Rahab said. "I am with child."

"With child!" Now she could not help seeing the hell in his eyes—or realizing its cause.

"I—I'm sorry, Salmon," she said gently. "Really sorry."

For a long moment he did not speak. When he did his voice was harsh, almost as it had been that day on Mount Nebo when he had first seen her. "Is Prince Hazor the father?"

"He thinks so."

"And you?"

"I don't know," she admitted.

"It could be Joshua's child then?"

She nodded. There was no point in trying to keep anything from him; he seemed to know already that she and Joshua had spent the night in each other's arms in the Cave of Yah on Mount Nebo. Nevertheless, the realization that Joshua had told even Salmon about that precious night hurt her deeply. She tried to tell herself that men felt differently about such things than women, but a voice somewhere in her mind kept warning her that, had it been Salmon to whom she had given herself instead of Joshua, he would not have told anyone else.

Salmon got up from the bench and moved with that quick lithe stride of his across to the opposite wall and back again. His face was set in thought and his eyes bleak with a misery he made no attempt to hide now. Finally he sat down beside her once again.

"If this child is Joshua's," he said, "you owe it to him to come back with me to Israel." He did not add that he was not at all sure Joshua would accept her even with his child in her body. That was an eventuality neither of them could foresee, but even if Joshua refused to accept Rahab as his wife, Salmon was not concerned about her future. However much it had pained him to learn that another man's seed had germinated into life within the body of the woman he loved, the fact that he loved her had not changed in the least. And loving her, he would willingly make her his wife, even with Joshua's child yet unborn in her womb.

"But I don't know, Salmon," Rahab protested. "I don't know which one of them is the father."

159

"You could always say it was Joshua," he pointed out. "No one will know but you and me."

"I will know," Rahab said quickly. "As soon as I see the child."

"Many a man has been happy thinking himself father to another's child."

"I would not deceive Joshua," Rahab protested. "It would not be right."

"Suppose Prince Hazor is the father?"

"That is what troubles me," Rahab admitted. "He plans to make the child his heir if it is a boy."

"Then your son might one day be a king." Salmon frowned. "I can see that this does change things."

"If the child is Prince Hazor's, I must remain with him," Rahab said, crystallizing a decision she knew now had been made when she had first known that she would bear a child. "He has been good to me, Salmon. I could not take his son away from him."

Salmon took her hands in his strong, gentle fingers. "I have heard men say women know no loyalty save to themselves, Rahab." He smiled wryly. "I may have even said such a thing myself before I knew you. But I know now they were the words of a fool. No one could show a greater loyalty than you have just done."

"Joshua loves me, so I know he will understand," Rahab said confidently. "Promise me that you will explain how it is to him."

"I will do my best," he assured her, knowing in advance that it would be a hopeless task.

"When will you return to Heshbon?"

"In a week or so. I have some other things to do here."

"Prince Hazor will be back in a few days. Stay until he returns. We can meet here in the temple of Yahweh every day."

"Would he go away and leave you alone at a time like this?" Salmon asked in surprise.

Rahab laughed. "I am not exactly alone, Salmon. I am actually a slave, but two others wait upon me day and night. Senu, the coachman, would give his life for me. And so would Myrnah, who keeps house for us."

"Where is Prince Hazor?"

"In Thebes. Pharaoh promised to send money for mercenaries to help defend Jericho." She stopped, remembering now that Salmon was one of the very people against whom her master sought help.

"Did you say Pharaoh is sending help to Jericho?" he asked quickly.

At the urgent note in his voice Rahab's face sobered. "Is that the real reason you came here, Salmon?" she asked. "To find out if Pharaoh will fight to defend Jericho and the other cities of Canaan?"

"I came to find you," he assured her, truthfully enough. "But if we knew Pharaoh's intentions, it would help us a great deal."

"The Israelites mean to attack Jericho, don't they?"

"I cannot tell you that, Rahab."

"Because I am the concubine of Jericho's prince?"

"Partly that," he admitted, "and partly because we have no definite plans as yet. But if you remain with Prince Hazor, your loyalty must be to him. I would not ask you to betray him, so forget my question about Jericho. Anything I need to know about—political matters—I will learn elsewhere."

She smiled and squeezed his fingers. "We are cut from the same cloth, I think, Salmon. Your loyalty is to your people, and mine must be to whoever is father of my child. Will you stay until Prince Hazor comes back?"

He nodded. "We need medical supplies, drugs, knives of bronze, and cloth for binding wounds. I can be buying them while I wait."

"It will be only a few days," she promised. "You can meet me here; it would not be safe elsewhere."

"I will come each day at the fifth hour," he promised. "We can be together until noon."

She stood on tiptoe and kissed him gently on the cheek; her lips were soft and warm, like a child's. "Dear, good Salmon," she said. "Why is it not you I love and your child I bear? You deserve as much, and more."

She was gone then, up the narrow aisle between the benches and out into the sunlight. Salmon stood watching her lovely, graceful figure, not yet distorted noticeably by pregnancy, until she disappeared through the door. When he was alone, he raised his eyes to the window through which

161

sunlight still streamed and prayed—not that Rahab would one day come to him as a reward for his love, for that seemed hopeless now—but that she would bear her child safely and find happiness, whatever choice she made.

Seventeen

RAHAB continued to meet Salmon daily in the small temple of Yahweh, but she was careful to have Senu wait outside so word would not get back to Hazor that she was meeting a man. In the peaceful coolness of the temple they talked at length of many things.

She was thrilled by Salmon's description of the stratagem by which Heshbon had been taken and the crucial battle before Edrei, when King Og of Bashan had been defeated. Knowing what she wanted most to hear, he gave Joshua full credit for the important part his bravery, his daring, and, above all, his flair for dramatic leadership had played in the ultimate victory.

Rahab listened with sparkling eyes, but when he finished she said gently, "You have not told your own part in all this, Salmon."

"I am only a physician. My job is to bind up the wounds of the warriors."

"The battle plan was yours as usual, wasn't it?"

"What do you mean?"

"But for the way the soldiers of Heshbon were lured into opening the gate, your forces might not have won against the Amorites," she pointed out. "And you yourself said breaking the wall of shields at Edrei with the battering-rams enabled Joshua to win that battle. Were they your idea or his?"

"I may have thought them out," he admitted, "but the bravery of our soldiers under the leadership of Joshua and Caleb brought about the real victory."

Rahab smiled. "Do you know that the first time I saw you I was afraid of you?"

"Why?"

162

"You were so stern. And you spoke so sharply to me."

He smiled. "That was when I thought you were an enemy."

"But when you held up Joshua's head to give him a drink of wine," she continued, "your movements were gentle, like a woman's, and I knew your harshness was only a pose. And when you sang to me the song of Ikhnaton, I was sure it was the most beautiful thing I had ever heard."

"It still is," he said quietly. "I sing it to myself sometimes, when I have seen too much of war and killing."

"But you still plan the strategy that lets your army win," she reminded him.

"Only because I can save our people from more bloodshed."

"Do you approve of the Habi—the Israelites attacking Canaan?"

Salmon shook his head. "Half of our people are settled now in what were the domains of King Sihon and King Og. The fertile lands west of the River Jord are sparsely populated outside the cities; there is more than enough room for the children of Israel to settle in peace."

"Would the kings of Canaan allow it?"

"I think they would if they really knew that we are shepherds and tillers of the soil, not bloodthirsty brigands. Besides, small bands have been escaping from Egypt, as we did, for many years. One group, called the Jebusites, holds several important cities in Canaan."

"You would have to pass Jericho first to get into the land," Rahab reminded him. "Prince Hazor says it will be the first city of Canaan to be attacked."

"Jericho does lie astride the main road leading into Canaan between the Salt Sea and a lake far to the north called Chinnereth."

"I have heard of the Sea of Chinnereth," she said. "My father spoke of it."

Salmon's eyes glowed. "One of the Amorite soldiers who was wounded told me about it. He says it teems with fish and the waters are like a green jewel in a golden setting. The shores of its northern tip are a garden where all kinds of fruits and other plants grow in abundance."

Rahab smiled. "You sound as if you had seen it yourself."

"I have, in my mind. One day, when we have finished with

163

war and bloodshed, I hope to build a house there. From my garden I will watch the fishing boats with their sails of many colors upon the water and listen to the shouts of children at play."

"I will ask Yah to make your dream come true," Rahab said softly.

Salmon smiled wryly. "Caleb says I dream too much. Perhaps he is right."

"But this could still be," she protested.

"In such a place a man could not be happy alone, Rahab. And I would share it with only one woman."

She dropped her eyes to hide the tears. She knew he had dreamed of her as sharing the house above the beautiful lake with him, and the knowledge brought only pain now. "I am sorry, Salmon," she whispered. "You know I love you, but——"

Gently he laid his fingers across her lips. "Say no more," he said. "Your heart belongs to one man and your body is owned by another. As for Salmon, the physician, be sure he will always come when you need him."

"I can give you nothing in return."

"I ask nothing," he said quietly, "save to know I have helped make you happy."

When she returned to the house that day, Rahab found that a papyrus roll had come for Prince Hazor in her absence, brought by the captain of one of the Phoenician galleys that traveled on a regular schedule between the cities along the eastern end of the Great Sea and those of the Nile. The roll was sealed with wax upon which was imprinted a device she did not recognize. Myrnah, however, knew it at once.

"It is the seal of Milkili, the vizier of Jericho," she said excitedly. "The King must be worse, and that means Cesera will be plotting with her brother Kalak to steal Prince Hazor's place."

"What can we do?" Rahab asked.

"Nothing until our master returns," Myrnah said darkly. "I told him he should kill her when she first came into his father's house, but Prince Hazor is too kind for his own good." Then she grinned. "When we get back to Jericho I will take care of it for him. A sorcerer here in Memphis can mix a potion that brings death through sleep so gently no one

164

can tell it is not a natural thing. He sells much of it to young women with rich fools for husbands."

"You wouldn't kill them, Myrnah!" Rahab protested, horrified.

"Why not?" the old slave demanded. "Cesera and her brother would like nothing better than to destroy our master." She touched Rahab's body where the swelling of her pregnancy was just now beginning to be noticeable. "Within your womb you carry the heir to the throne of Jericho and the happiness of Prince Hazor. Be sure I will let no slut who calls herself Queen deprive the child of his birthright."

Rahab shivered and turned away to put the papyrus roll into the drawer of a cabinet beside the bed she shared with Hazor. Suddenly she felt a vague sense of dread, a feeling of impending disaster, which she could not throw off. For a moment she felt a strong temptation to seek out Salmon and beg him to take her away at once, back to the familiar surroundings of Heshbon and Medeba, the towering heights of Mount Nebo and the Cave of Yah, where she had always been able to find peace and reassurance.

She yielded only momentarily to the panic that assailed her, however. As she had told Salmon, she owed too much to Prince Hazor to deprive him of the child, if it were his. If it were not, then somehow she would find a way to reach Joshua after the baby was born and bring him the news that she had given him a son. That the child would be a boy, she had never allowed herself to doubt for a moment.

Prince Hazor and Kanofer arrived from Thebes the following day. A glance at her master's face told Rahab their mission had been a failure. She waited until Kanofer had gone to his own quarters nearby before entering the chamber where Hazor was refreshing himself with wine after the journey.

"Rahab!" He took her in his arms and kissed her tenderly. "I have missed you very much. Is it well with you—and the child?"

"We are well," she told him. "Did Myrnah tell you of the papyrus roll that came yesterday?"

"She said you had put it away for me."

Rahab went to the cabinet and took out the roll, still with its seal unbroken. "The seal is Milkili's," Hazor said with

165

quick concern. "It must be an urgent message, for him to write me himself."

Quickly he broke the seal and glanced at the message. His face darkened as he read it and his lips set in a tight line. Rahab never remembered seeing him look so angry before.

"Is it bad news?" she asked.

"Very bad, on top of that I bring from Thebes. All these months at Memphis have been wasted, and now the kingdom itself is in peril." He handed the papyrus roll to her. "I'd forgotten you could read, Rahab. See for yourself what the situation is."

Rahab read quickly. The message was short and to the point.

> Milkili, the vizier of Jericho, to my lord, Prince Hazor. Thus sayeth Milkili, thy servant, seven times and seven times I fall down in the dust at thy feet. Let the Prince, my lord, know that his father, the King, grows weaker and would fain see his son's face again before he dies. But there are those, of whom the Prince, my lord, knows, who destroy the King's letters to him. May the Prince, my lord, return quickly to Jericho; else he shall not see his father's face, save in the tomb. And let the Prince, my lord, take care to guard himself well, lest they who wish evil against him bring about his death, too, by stealth. Seven times seven times I fall at thy feet, O Prince, and beg thy early return, else Jericho be left without a king of thy line. Verily this is for thy information alone, from Milkili, thy servant.

Rahab put down the roll. "Your father must be much worse."

"My father is dying," Hazor said, "or Milkili would not have written. We must leave by the first galley sailing for the Great Sea. Even then we may be too late."

"But the gold for the mercenaries——"

"There is no gold. Pharaoh's vizier has been playing cat and mouse with us, or he has taken it for himself. Kanofer will return with me to take charge of Jericho's defenses." He drew Rahab to him again.

"Can you travel to Canaan without danger to the child?"

"Of course. Myrnah will be with us."

"I will employ a physician to accompany us if you wish."

For an instant Rahab thought of suggesting Salmon but put the idea from her. As much as his presence would comfort her, she could not subject him to the torture of being with her, loving her as he did and knowing she was possessed by another man. Besides, there was Salmon's own safety to think about, for should Prince Hazor discover that he was one of the hated Habiru, his death would be certain.

"I need no physician," she assured him. "When shall we leave?"

"As soon as I can find a ship. But do not trouble yourself with the preparations. Myrnah and Senu will take care of that."

"Will you take any soldiers with you?"

He shook his head. "Only Kanofer. He is an experienced captain and can help train our men to defend Jericho. I may still be able to hire mercenaries from Adoni-zedek in Urusalim, and some of the other kings of Canaan may join us in an alliance against the Habiru."

Hazor found that a Phoenician galley was sailing for the ports of the Great Sea in two days, and the house became a beehive of activity. Rahab managed to get away the next morning to bid Salmon good-by. They met in the temple of Yah as usual.

"I cannot stay long," she told him hurriedly. "We leave for Canaan and Jericho tomorrow."

"Prince Hazor must be in a hurry to get the mercenaries to Jericho," Salmon observed.

"He is not taking any," Rahab said without thinking that she might be betraying an important secret of Hazor's to a potential enemy. "Pharaoh did not furnish the gold."

"Are you going with him?" Salmon asked quickly, lest she realize how much she had revealed to him.

"I have to go, Salmon," she said. "Surely you see that."

"What if the child should be Joshua's?"

"I will find some way to let him know," she promised, "and to bring the child to your camp."

Salmon did not remind her that should Joshua go ahead with his plans to attack Jericho he might see her even sooner.

167

He had learned what he sought in Memphis: first, that Rahab was safe, although the slave of another man; and second, that Pharaoh would not defend Canaan from attack by the Israelites. There was no point in letting her know that she had unwittingly revealed to the enemies of her master a fact that might in the end mean his own destruction and that of his city.

Salmon waited until Rahab was safely away from the temple, then hurried to make his own arrangements for departure. Thus it came about that as the great Phoenician merchant ship plowed down the Nile, with its huge square sail bellying from the mast amidships to catch the morning breeze, it overtook and passed a smaller sleek galley bound for the canal in the delta leading to the Red Sea, the Gulf of Aqabah, and the King's Highway stretching northward from Ezion-geber along the fertile crescent of the caravan routes to Babylon. On the latter, the physician called for the moment Samma, his mission in Egypt completed, had embarked once more upon his travels.

Book Three

THE LAND OF CANAAN

Behold the land of Canaan, which I give unto the children of Israel for a possession.

DEUTERONOMY 32:49

One

THE ENERVATING HEAT of summer was already giving way to the cooling breezes of autumn when the caravan of Hazor, Prince and uncrowned King of Jericho, approached its owner's native city late one afternoon. The caravan was not large, for trade was not its purpose, but it was well guarded. Behind Prince Hazor and Captain Kanofer marched twenty-five Egyptian mercenaries. Leathery-skinned Sherdans, they were the finest warriors among the desert tribes who regularly sold their most stalwart sons into the military service of the Egyptian Pharaohs.

The presence of the mercenaries in the caravan was due to the persuasive arguments of Hazor with King Adoni-zedek of Urusalim, representative in Canaan of the Pharaoh, to whom the land gave at least nominal allegiance. Pharaoh himself seemed unable to recognize the threat to Canaan posed by the possible fall of Jericho to the invading Israelites, but it had been perfectly apparent to his Canaanite representative.

Adoni-zedek—with the traditional hesitancy of the Canaanite kings to join in any sort of alliance that might involve them in the quarrels of the neighboring city-states—had been reluctant to weaken his own defense, but the arguments of Hazor and Kanofer had finally prevailed. The addition of even so small a number as twenty-five trained fighting men to the garrison of Jericho would increase its strength considerably. Word of his father's death several weeks before had reached Hazor at Joppa, when they had debarked from the Phoenician ship which had brought them from Egypt. The fact that Hazor would enter the city at the head of a column of Egyptian troops would be of considerable weight in establishing himself upon the throne.

When Jericho first came into view ahead of them, Hazor reined in his horse for the fighting men to swing by, their weapons rattling against the metal-studded shields slung on their backs, then guided his mount beside the mule-borne litter in which Rahab rode.

"The way will be easier now that we are coming down from the hills," he told her. "We should reach Jericho in another hour."

Rahab smiled. "How does it feel to be King?"

"I have not yet been crowned. Trouble may still wait ahead of us."

"With Egyptian troops as your bodyguard? And a captain of Pharaoh's army in command?"

More than once on the journey eastward from Urusalim, Kanofer had stopped beside Rahab's litter to speak to her. His manner was very pleasant, but she felt no more favorably inclined toward the Egyptian captain than she had in Memphis. Because of his importance to Hazor and the throne of Jericho, however, she had decided to treat him as civilly as she could. And she had even begun to hope that, since her body was already swollen from pregnancy, some of his lustful interest in her might have subsided.

"Kalak will hardly dare to make trouble, with Kanofer and his men to back me," Hazor agreed. "I only wish I had been more successful in drawing the other kings of Canaan into an alliance."

Rahab looked ahead to where the deep cleft marking the valley of the Jord divided the rolling plain in the midst of which Jericho stood, with the mountains of Gilead rising from its eastern bank. Those mountains, she knew, were in a territory now occupied by the Israelites. And her pulse quickened at the thought that Joshua himself might be standing upon one of the distant hills, looking down into this land of Canaan

170

which she herself had heard him say was given to his people by their god.

"You can almost see your home." Prince Hazor's voice brought her thoughts back to the present. "Does it make you happy to be so near it again?"

"Medeba is in the hands of the Israelites," Rahab reminded him gravely.

"I tried to learn something about the purpose of the Habiru from Adoni-zedek in Urusalim," he told her. "But he could tell me nothing I did not already know."

"They may have given up the idea of attacking Canaan."

Hazor shook his head. "The Habiru are led by a great general called Joshua. All Canaan knows how they captured Heshbon and defeated King Og of Bashan. The caravan drivers say they boast openly that Canaan will be theirs one day."

"You can still let them pass Jericho without giving battle," Rahab suggested.

"Before Adoni-zedek would let me have the mercenaries I had to give my word to hold Jericho against the Habiru if they move against Canaan."

"But Jericho cannot fight the Israelites alone. They have thousands of soldiers."

"With hardly four thousand people in all of Jericho, we *are* badly outnumbered," Hazor agreed. "But we have our walls, even though they are dangerously weak where the earthquakes breached them. If we can only hold out for a few weeks, the other kings will have time to send troops to aid us."

Jericho—still several miles distant—with the verdant fields surrounding it, made a picture of both strength and beauty in the afternoon sunlight. Widely known throughout the lovely region of Canaan and the fertile valley of the River Jord as the "City of Palms," the city's towering battlements rose from the elevation of a large knoll, white and shining above the cool, green canopy of palm fronds that formed a roof against the hot summer sun of the Jord Valley.

A continuous wall more than two paces in thickness, built of stone at the bottom and brick in the upper portions, surrounded the city. Inside this bastion, separated by a space through which a chariot could have been driven, was another wall, narrower and less formidable in appearance, but no

171

mean protection in itself. The area between the two was filled in places with rubble. In many places houses of dried mud bricks were perched upon the very walls, spanning the space between them, with narrow windows overlooking the outside.

There was only one opening—located in the eastern wall near the large spring that burst forth from the rocky foundations. Above it the walls rose abruptly, towering over all but the tallest of the palm trees.

So close was Jericho to the range of hills from which the caravan was descending that their shadow was already beginning to fall upon the walls as the sun set in the west. The ridge itself was rough and desolate. Its river beds were dry at this time of the year, although in spring the freshets that swelled the Jord to the east would turn these rivulets into small torrents.

The face of the cliff bordering the caravan road was cracked in places by the successive heat of summer and cold of winter, and the rocks had been eaten away by the centuries until they were pocked by numerous shallow caves. In places such as these, robber bands often lay in wait for the caravans, ready to fall upon those too weak to defend themselves. But none dared to attack the armed Sherdans of Hazor's party. These tough warriors from the desert were feared wherever Egypt had dominion, for one of them was easily worth three of the poorly armed and trained Canaanites.

The caravan had reached the plain now and was approaching the city itself. At close range Rahab could see why Hazor had said the walls of Jericho would be poor protection against a strong invader. Great cracks extended almost through them in places, with piles of loose brick and dried mortar proving their recent origin. Streaks of fresh mortar across the face of the walls showed where other breaches had been repaired by plastering the deepest ones over.

Like all cities in this region, the area surrounding Jericho was divided into a geometric pattern of fields and groves watered by the overflow from the spring. As the caravan approached the gate it became part of the crowd of people pouring back into the protection of the walls with the coming of the night, after a day in the fields. They made room for the soldiers, for the golden crest of Kanofer's helmet openly advertised the might of the Pharaohs. The Canaanites had long ago learned not to offend the haughty mercenaries of Egypt.

Prince Hazor eagerly scanned the crowd for familiar faces. Suddenly he pulled his horse out of the line and reached down to seize the shoulder of a rugged-looking old man with a rude bronze hoe over his shoulder.

"Elath!" he cried. "Have you forgotten your Prince?"

The old man looked up, and tears suddenly filled his eyes. "Prince Hazor!" he cried, and dropped to his knees in the dust, pressing his lips against Hazor's foot in the stirrup. "Our prayers to Baal have been answered; you have come back to Jericho."

Others recognized the Prince now and took up the cry. All about them people pressed closer to touch him and kiss his boot in the stirrup.

"Make way for the King of Jericho," someone shouted. And as others echoed the cry, what had been only a small caravan was turned into a triumphal procession that surged up the ramp to the gate.

Armed guards stood on either side of the great stone hinges in which the gates themselves turned, but they could not have stopped the triumphant entry of Prince Hazor if they had tried. Through the gate and into the narrow crooked streets of the city the people surged with the caravan in their midst. Looking at the eager faces of the crowd as they jostled her litter, Rahab could see only a great joy that their Prince had come home. In fact, it seemed as if they looked to him to free them from some evil that had been pressing upon them.

The houses of Jericho in this part of the city were thin-walled, Rahab saw. Some appeared to be only one brick in thickness, and many of them leaned against the walls of the city itself. As the procession moved through the streets, people popped out of the doorways to stare incredulously at Prince Hazor and the Egyptian mercenaries for a moment. Then, shouting his name happily, they joined the jostling, pushing crowd, lifting their own voices with the others in praise of their new sovereign. There could be no doubt that the people of Jericho loved Hazor, as they had loved his father before him.

173

Halfway through the city, the procession ran into a large crowd of people and was forced to a halt. Myrnah was walking beside Rahab's litter, shouting with the others. When Rahab sat up to see what had stopped them, Myrnah said quickly, "Do not be disturbed, beautiful one. The priests of Baal are blessing the new house of a rich merchant. It will be over in a little while and we can go on."

Curious to see everything of interest in the city that was now her home, Rahab had the mule driver take her litter closer. The crowd good-naturedly made room for the beautiful young woman who was so obviously a prized possession of their Prince. At the edge of the open space before the new home where the ceremonies were being conducted, the litter came to a halt in a position where Rahab could see everything that was taking place.

A fat man wearing the robes of the high priest of Baal embroidered richly with designs of the god in silver and gold was ceremoniously tossing small images of Baal and his consort into a square hole dug just at the portal of the new house. The house itself was a much more imposing structure than the others Rahab had seen in Jericho, evidently being the dwelling place of a man of substance. And since the people of Canaan, like those of Medeba, looked to Baal for supervision of every activity of life, the blessing of a new house was an important thing to them.

Having tossed the images into the square hole dug at the entrance to the new house, the pudgy priest now took up a curiously shaped jar standing just beside it. The jar was bulbous in its middle, with a broad flaring mouth, and could hold as much water as a strong man could carry. That it was not intended for water, however, was immediately apparent when the high priest handed it to a lesser priest and turned to a woman who had been standing by with a young baby in her arms, weeping quietly.

"What is he going to do, Myrnah?" Rahab asked in a whisper.

Before Myrnah could answer, the high priest took the baby from the sobbing mother, and, bending it until its tiny head touched the drawn-up knees, slid it dexterously into the jar.

Turning, the lesser priest set the jar into the hole and, with the cries of the child oddly muffled now, began to shovel dirt

174

into the wide mouth. The mother gave a strangled cry when the child's wailing was suddenly shut off by the dirt being shoveled into the jar. She fell on the ground in a faint, but the fat priest only frowned and urged the man filling the hole to greater effort.

"Myrnah," Rahab gasped, "they are burying the baby alive."

"Certainly." The old slave did not take her eyes from the scene. "Now Baal will bless the merchant's house and his business. He will become very rich."

"But to kill his own child!"

Myrnah shrugged. "His wife will have another. The favor of Baal can be worth much to a man. Many people sacrifice their first-born in this way to bring good fortune to a new house."

The hole was filled now and the fat priest raised his hands above it. "O most omnipotent Baal," he intoned, "accept this offering by the merchant Zador to thy glory and bless his house with good fortune."

"Myrnah," Rahab whispered as the crowd opened up and her litter began to move, "who is the priest, the fat one?"

The old slave spat into the dust. "That is Kalak, brother of the she-devil called Cesera, and your master's most bitter enemy."

Two

THE CAMP of Israel was a scene of peace when Salmon returned from Egypt, having traveled with a caravan bound for Damascus and Babylon, which he had joined at the seaport city of Ezion-geber. Sheep and goats grazed on the hillsides around Heshbon, and the people were working in the fields and vineyards. The shepherds dwelt in tents outside the walls in order to be near the flocks, but many of the Israelites had chosen to live inside the city itself.

As Salmon walked through the streets of Heshbon from the gate, the tramp of feet and the rattle of arms came to his ears from the open parade ground before the palace of King Sihon. When he reached that imposing structure, he saw that it had been taken over entirely by the army of Israel, with Joshua himself occupying the former royal apartment.

The Israelite leader was dictating to Chazan when Salmon entered. The old scribe was sitting cross-legged on the stone floor, writing swiftly on a papyrus roll with pen and ink, but he started up from his seat at the sight of Salmon, spilling the pens on the floor in his excitement.

"Salmon." Joshua embraced the slighter form of the physician. "You are back sooner than any of us expected—or were you stopped before you reached Egypt?"

"I went to Memphis."

"Did you see Rahab?" Chazan broke in eagerly. "Is she alive?"

Joshua's face darkened with annoyance. "Did you lie to me, Salmon? Was this trip only to look for a harlot?"

Chazan gave a strangled cry of protest, but Joshua continued with rising anger, "I will not have people deceiving me, not even you."

"I went to Egypt on business for Israel," Salmon said curtly. "And I found out what I sought to learn."

"Did you see Rahab?" Chazan dared brave Joshua's displeasure to ask again.

"Yes, I saw her," Salmon told him. "She is well and happy."

"Did she return with you?"

"Rahab is the concubine of Prince Hazor of Jericho and will bear a child," he explained. "In fact, she may even be in Jericho already. They left Memphis when I did and traveled directly to the Phoenician coast of the Great Sea."

Chazan prostrated himself on the floor and would have put Salmon's foot upon his neck in a gesture of eternal debt, but the physician quickly reached down and lifted the old man to his feet. "She sent you her love, Chazan," he said. Then he turned to face Joshua once more. "And to the son of Nun also."

"Leave us, Chazan," Joshua ordered brusquely. His lips were tense with annoyance and his cheeks flushed with anger. "Send word for Caleb as you go out. He will want to hear what Salmon has to say about his journey—if he visited anything but brothels."

The old man hurried out, stumbling in his excitement. "Must you treat him like a slave, Joshua?" Salmon demanded angrily. "After all, he is the father of your betrothed."

"Chazan is a scribe and paid to do my will," Joshua snapped. "Speak to me no more of that harlot."

"Rahab is no more a harlot than you are," Salmon said hotly. "The people of Medeba sold her into slavery that day when she brought the bride price from the cave. A slave merchant named Abda bought her and sold her directly to Prince Hazor of Jericho. No one else has owned her."

Joshua pounded the table with a heavy fist, sending clay tablets and papyrus rolls tumbling in every direction. "I warn you, Salmon," he shouted. "Say no more of her."

"Not even when she bears your child?"

"My child? A harlot's brat is fathered by the last man to lie with her. And that honor, it seems, was not mine." Joshua planted both hands on the table, his face thrust forward and his cheeks purple with anger. "For the last time, I warn you, Salmon. Say no more to me of that whore, else you will find yourself a slave again."

Salmon faced him across the table, his own face white with anger. "Make me a slave," he challenged, "if a few military successes have made you so drunk with power. Make me a slave—and see what happens when next you go into battle."

"Are you saying that you win battles and not I?" Joshua demanded scornfully.

"Ask your captains what would have happened before Edrei if I had not planned the stratagem for breaking the ranks of the men of Bashan."

"They will say that, but for the son of Nun, King Og would still have won the battle."

Neither of them realized that Caleb had come into the room until his broad, sturdy body was interposed between them. "Blood brothers do not shout at each other in anger," the grizzled old warrior said soothingly. "Remember, we three swore a pact in the desert. We should be celebrating Salmon's safe return from Egypt instead of quarreling."

"I found this—this leech dying of thirst and saved his life," Joshua snapped. "Now he thanks me by daring to dispute my decisions."

At the sight of Caleb's rugged face, the memory of that

177

day came flooding back upon Salmon, the awful torment of thirst as he had crawled across the hot sands of the wilderness south of the Salt Sea, with no oasis in sight, driven only by the need to do something even in the face of certain death. At first he had thought he was already dead—or at least delirious from thirst and fever—when the coolness of the waterskin had touched his lips to allay his thirst. Afterward Joshua had lifted him on massive shoulders and carried him to the camping place that he and Caleb had set up beside a spring, from which they had been spying out the southern part of the land of Canaan.

"You are right, Caleb," he said quietly. "I owe Joshua my life; I must never forget that."

"And he owes the same to you," Caleb said gruffly. "Let the son of Nun never forget that but for the skill of Salmon, the physician, he would be dead now from the poisons of an Amorite arrow point."

Joshua snorted indignantly, but before he could add fresh fires to the argument, Caleb continued, "Chazan said you wanted to see me, Joshua. Was it because Salmon had returned?"

"He says he brings news of the intentions of Pharaoh," Joshua sneered. "But I suspect he spent his time in the brothels of Memphis."

Salmon curbed his anger with difficulty. "Joshua is offended because I sought out Ra——"

"I warned you, Salmon," Joshua snapped. "Speak not to me of that who——"

"Then do not lie about the woman you once loved," Salmon said curtly. "Her guilt is less than yours. It was you who cozened her into lying with you by a promise of marriage and deserted her the moment she was in trouble."

Caleb pulled up a bench to the table. "Sit down, Salmon. What did you learn about Pharaoh and the cities of Canaan?"

Salmon took a seat on the bench and drank the cup of wine Caleb poured out for him. Joshua paced the floor on the other side of the table, his face still suffused with annoyance.

"I went to Memphis, as I said I would," Salmon began. "It was open knowledge in the foreign quarter there that many of the kings of Canaan and Syria have sent emissaries to Egypt asking Pharaoh to defend them against us."

"Hah!" Joshua said triumphantly. "Even Egypt now cringes before the might of Israel."

"Pharaoh seems concerned only with pleasure," Salmon corrected. "He hardly ever stirs from his palace at Thebes."

"Did you go there?" Caleb asked.

"I learned what I needed to know in Memphis without going any farther," Salmon explained. "Egypt is full of emissaries from the subject kings, but they can get nothing from Pharaoh. His vizier promises all sorts of things but does nothing."

"How do you know he will not send help to Canaan then?" Joshua demanded tartly. "You should have gone to Thebes instead of chasing harlots in Memphis."

"I told you I learned what I needed to know in Memphis." Salmon turned to Caleb. "Rahab is now the concubine of Prince Hazor of Jericho. He was in Memphis seeking Egyptian mercenaries."

"I have heard travelers speak of Hazor," Caleb said. "He is reported to be much loved by his people, and the walls of Jericho are thick and strong."

"They will fall before the favored of Yahweh," Joshua boasted. "Just as did Heshbon and Ashtaroth and Ramoth-gilead."

"The walls of those cities still stand," Caleb reminded him dryly. "They were captured by tricks—tricks devised by Salmon here."

Joshua snorted angrily, but before he could speak Caleb said, "Go on, please, Salmon. Finish your story."

"Prince Hazor went to Thebes twice," Salmon continued. "He did not ask for Egyptian troops, only for gold with which to hire mercenaries."

"And Pharaoh refused him?"

"They gave him vague promises, and the vizier refused him gold."

"Then Jericho got no help from Egypt?" Joshua asked.

"Only one captain of the Royal Guard, a man named Kanofer. He is said to be very clever——"

"One man cannot stand against us. I will cut him down myself, as I did King Og of Bashan."

"Are you absolutely certain that Prince Hazor got no mercenaries from Egypt, Salmon?" Caleb asked eagerly.

179

"I talked to the captain of the vessel upon which they were sailing for the coast of the Great Sea. No Egyptian troops accompanied Hazor and Captain Kanofer."

"By the beard of Pharaoh!" Caleb exclaimed. "You bring good news indeed. All Israel is in your debt." He looked at Joshua meaningly. "Say you not so, Joshua?"

The big man hesitated a moment. "You have served us well, Salmon," he admitted reluctantly. "Tell Chazan to give you a purse of gold as a reward."

"I do not serve Israel for gold." Salmon got to his feet. "Chazan will give you a record of what I spent on the journey. I will take that and nothing more."

Caleb's hand was on the physician's arm, guiding him from the room before the quarrel could break out anew. "I was just about to eat the evening meal," he said. "Come join me and we will talk more about the wonders of Egypt."

They were halfway to the door when Joshua called in a gruff voice, "See that the physician has good quarters, Caleb. And provide him with whatever he needs."

Caleb's quarters were in a far less luxurious apartment than those of Joshua. A low table had been spread with the evening meal, and the old general waved Salmon to a bench before it. He poured a mug of wine and shoved it across the table to the physician, then filled a second for himself and sat down.

"I heard the son of Nun threaten to make you a slave." Caleb hacked off a liberal helping of roast meat with his knife. "He knows the captains would not stand for that. We would have been defeated before Edrei but for your trick of breaking the ranks of King Og with the battering-rams."

Salmon grinned wryly. "I told Joshua as much. That was when he really became angry."

"Some men wear power like a fine garment, increasing their stature. The son of Nun must hold it always before him like a shield."

"But why? He is the champion of Israel. The elders usually do what he wants."

"The elders *always* do what Joshua wants now," Caleb corrected. "Since the tribes of Reuben, Gad, and half of Manasseh have settled here east of the River Jord, hardly anyone in the council opposes him."

180

"Why not crown him King of Israel then?"

"A king would have to be supported by the captains," Caleb explained. "We accept Joshua's leadership; he is a great champion and men are inspired by his example to new heights of bravery. But we will give no man absolute power over us, such as a king would have."

"Is that why he has become so stiff-necked?"

"That may be part of it. But I think deep down inside him the son of Nun realizes that most of his strength is in his sinews and in his limbs, not in his mind. That is why he resents you, because all of us accept the fact that you possess the power to think beyond any of us. Joshua can admit no man to be greater than he is in anything."

"Perhaps it would be better if I left Israel," Salmon suggested.

"Where would you go?"

"There is a lake far up the River Jord, and a town called Chinnereth overlooking it. The caravan drivers say it is a beautiful and fertile region whose people are farmers and love peace. If I came into that country and pretended to be a physician of Egypt, as I did on the journey to Memphis, they would not know I was an Israelite."

Caleb looked at him keenly. "What of the girl called Rahab? You saw her in Egypt, didn't you?"

"Yes. She was taken by a slave merchant to Memphis and sold as a concubine to Prince Hazor of Jericho."

"Then Joshua's betrothed is now the concubine of our first enemy in Canaan!" Caleb exclaimed. "This is a strange thing indeed."

"Rahab is with child, and Joshua may be the father. They were betrothed, so it would be his heir under the laws of Israel."

"How will she know who is the father if she is Prince Hazor's concubine?"

"A mark runs in Joshua's family," Salmon explained. "The small pits upon his shoulders."

"I remember hearing the son of Nun say his father and his father's father before him bore these marks," said Caleb. "If the child's body bears them when it is born, Joshua will have no choice except to admit he is the father."

"Any judge would accept the marks as evidence," Salmon agreed.

"This is like something sung by a teller of tales," Caleb marveled. Then his face sobered. "But you love the girl too. Where is your place in this affair?"

"I have none," Salmon admitted. "Rahab still loves Joshua, but she also feels that she owes Prince Hazor a debt for saving her from the brothels of Memphis. She will stay with him at least until the child is born."

"Suppose Joshua is the father."

"She intends to bring the child to him here in Israel if the marks are on its back. I couldn't bring myself to tell her he has sworn to have nothing to do with her."

Caleb pursed his lips thoughtfully. "She will not be the first woman to make a fool of herself over Joshua. But I don't see what you can do, Salmon, even though you love her yourself."

"That is why it might be best for me to leave Israel."

"You are not one to run away."

"A physician can always profit by observing disease in other lands," Salmon reminded him. "I would like to know more about the black metal of the Hittite smiths, and in Egypt I heard wondrous tales concerning the copper mines of Alashiya. They even say that Phoenician ships have sailed through a great gateway to the west giving access to a sea larger than any now known to man. One ship, I was told, sailed westward through this gateway around the land of Egypt and the country of the Nubians, returning by way of the Land of Punt on the east."

Caleb shook his head. "You have been listening to tellers of tales and sorcerers, Salmon. Such things cannot be—except by magic."

"They could happen if the world is greater than we think it is."

"Leave such things to the wise men," Caleb advised earnestly. "The destiny of Israel is greater than Joshua—or you, or me. Your place is here with us, where your counsel in war is worth a thousand men."

"When will you move against Canaan?"

"Not until spring—and the rains."

"Will Joshua wait that long?"

"He has no choice. The men from the tribes east of the Jord will not be free from their fields and herds until winter. And then they must be trained in scaling walls and battering down gates."

"Is he going to attack the walls of Jericho?" Salmon asked in surprise.

"How else can we surmount them? The Canaanites will hardly let themselves be duped a second time by the stratagem you devised to capture Heshbon. Besides, the priests tell us Yahweh will level the walls before us when we march against Jericho."

"Does Joshua believe that?"

Caleb smiled. "Since the people chose him leader, the son of Nun holds himself above his old comrades in arms. I think he really believes that, if he commanded it, the sun would stand still in its course." The old soldier's face was suddenly grave. "You can see now why I want you to stay in Israel, Salmon. Once before Joshua thought he could subdue the giants of Bashan by hurling spears over their heads. That time he came near to paying for his confidence with his life. I am counting on you to give us a better plan for taking Jericho than storming the walls."

"You set me a hard task, my friend."

"Only because I know of no other man in Israel—not even Joshua—who can measure up to it."

"When will the attack on Jericho be made?" Salmon asked.

"In the spring. We cannot move a large body of people far without water, and most rivers in that region are dry now. But if we wait until spring, the dry stream beds on the mountainsides will be full. Then we can make our camp wherever we wish and launch our attack. Jericho should yield to our siege in a few weeks, and the whole of Canaan will lie before us." He filled the cups and lifted his own. "Let us drink to victory for Israel."

"It is better to invoke the favor of Yahweh," Salmon said soberly. "Without that, we will surely fail."

"To the favor of Yahweh upon our arms, then," Caleb agreed. "And to victory over Jericho."

Three

AFTER Hazor's triumphant entry into Jericho with a body of Egyptian troops at his command, Kalak and Cesera could hardly have dared to deny him the throne of Jericho, which was rightfully his. In fact, they had no recourse save to welcome him with pretended exuberance. Kalak lost no time in doing just this when he recognized Hazor in the triumphal procession that had been interrupted by the ceremony. Pushing through the crowd to where Hazor sat his horse with Kanofer, waiting for the people to make way once again for the procession, the high priest of Baal bowed before his lawful sovereign.

"Welcome to Jericho, Prince Hazor," he said effusively. "Had we known of your coming, we would have prepared a celebration in your honor."

"I have been too long away from the house of my father," Hazor answered the fat priest politely, "so I pushed on without notifying anyone."

"It is obvious that your mission to Pharaoh was successful," Kalak observed, his shrewd eyes taking in the gold-crested helmet that Kanofer wore as he sat his horse with easy grace beside Prince Hazor, the golden whip of authority carried by all Egyptian officers, and the line of armed Sherdans behind him.

Hazor turned to Kanofer, who was observing this parrying with a sardonic light in his eyes. "Captain Kanofer of the Imperial Egyptian Guard," he said. "Kalak, high priest of Baal in Jericho."

"I bring greetings from Pharaoh to the people of Jericho and to their god," Kanofer said easily. "May you be successful in all your undertakings."

"Be sure the great god Baal, my master, will favor a warrior of such importance," Kalak said with equal insincerity. "I shall walk beside your stirrup to your father's house, Prince Hazor. My sister is grieving for your late father and does not go abroad."

184

The priest's eyes flicked to the litter in which Rahab rode. "The Prince of Jericho has obviously brought a beautiful female slave from Egypt to console him in his grief," he said slyly. "Truly a man's heart cannot long remain cold if his loins are warmed by a beautiful woman."

"This is Rahab, my beloved concubine and wife," Hazor said. "She bears in her womb an heir to the throne of Jericho."

Kalak's gaze had been harmless enough until now, merely a shrewd appraisal of Rahab and the implications of her presence. But at the mention of her child, she saw a startled light appear in the small eyes of the priest. Whether or not Kalak had made any plans covering the return of Hazor—and only the future would give the answer—the presence of an unborn heir to the throne of Jericho was something he could not have figured upon. Nevertheless, he recovered his composure quickly. "One so beautiful as thou, Rahab, must soon have everyone at her feet," he said effusively.

As the procession moved toward the royal palace at the head of the broad central avenue, from which lesser streets led off in either direction, Rahab saw that this part of Jericho compared favorably with Heshbon itself in the magnificence of the houses belonging to the nobility and the shops of the richer merchants. Located on the main east-west trade route in this area—as Heshbon was on the main north-south route east of the Jord—Jericho naturally engaged in a great deal of profitable commerce, in addition to exacting tribute from travelers along the caravan trail.

Away from the central avenue, however, the splendor was less marked. Closely packed rows of low, one-story houses lined the narrow, crooked streets. These dwellings were of brick with a few stones, from the rocky hillsides adjacent to the city, buried in the mud walls. In some, the outer door was open and Rahab caught a glimpse of the small court with a few rooms beyond it where the family lived.

Women were busy in the courtyards or at the edge of the street before the houses, washing in pots of kiln-baked ware and occasionally in vessels of copper, grinding corn for the evening meal or plastering thick dough on the outside walls of the small clay stoves that served for baking. Chickens, goats, and children ran about everywhere, and a literal bedlam of sound followed the procession toward the royal dwelling against the farther wall of the city.

Near the center of Jericho they passed an open space with a thin roof of rough cloth supported by upright beams and ropes forming a protection from the sun. Piles of vegetables, fruits, goat's cheese, and crocks of soured curds, bolts of cloth in regular rows, and metalsmiths' wares hanging from the poles marked this as the central market for the city.

All towns in this area had such markets forming the center of their daytime activities, with buyers and sellers shouting in each other's faces and gesticulating frantically. In addition, the jeering voices of the men who were always standing around waiting to be hired contributed to a constant din that was as much a part of the market as the rough cloth canopy shading it.

The palace of Jericho's King was easily the most imposing structure in the city, rising almost to the height of the walls. It was built on a foundation of stone, the upper walls of brick but plastered over with white clay that shone in the late afternoon sunlight almost like the snow on the tops of the higher mountains in winter.

Located at the extreme end of the broad avenue, with an open flagstone-paved court before it, the palace abutted directly against the city wall, with its flat roof almost on a level with the ramparts. Two flights of steps opened on the courtyard. One led to the palace roof—in this climate serving also as a place of refuge in the evening from the day's heat—the other to the top of the wall, where the guards maintained a constant vigil.

The lower three courses of the palace walls were constructed of the hewn stone of this region called *ashlar*. Upon them lay a single course of cedar beams, and above these were brick walls with corners of stone like the foundation. A slave waited beside the open door of red cedar planks studded with rounded boltheads of polished bronze.

Acting as host, Kalak led the way through the open doors of the palace into a small foyer whose floor was paved with a beautifully colored pattern of seashells embedded in mortar and smoothed by the passage of many feet. In the center of the foyer was a shallow basin of black basalt filled with water.

186

A slave waited beside the basin to wash the feet of visitors and another knelt to place soft, fibrous slippers on the feet of each of the guests. The washing finished, Rahab was startled to see the first slave empty the bowl simply by over-turning it and letting the water flow through a drain hidden in the floor.

From the foyer they entered a paved inner courtyard whose walls were painted in bright colors. Here, as every-where in the city of Jericho, palm trees gave shade from the midday sun. At one side of the court a door led to what Myrnah explained were the servants' quarters and the rooms for cooking and washing. Another door, elaborately deco-rated with an intricate patterning of bright gold, led into the apartments of the royal family. Still another opened into the large throne room that served as the official audience cham-ber of the King. The broad, flat roof with its elaborate garden was reserved—as with all houses in this region—for sleeping and enjoying the cool breezes of evening.

Rahab's chamber was a small room adjoining the some-what larger one that Prince Hazor would occupy. While Myrnah ordered water brought to fill a large shallow basin of black basalt so Rahab could wash the dust of the road from her body before the evening meal, Rahab gave vent to her curiosity by exploring Hazor's bedchamber.

The room was somewhat larger than the one she had shared with her master in the house at Memphis, and much more elaborately furnished. The bed itself was of *sussuru* wood, inlaid with an intricate paneling of ivory and carved with hundreds of tiny and incredibly beautiful scenes.

The center of the broad polished headboard depicted a king on his throne, which was supported by two winged lions with human heads. Another scene showed a smaller throne and near it a woman with a tall crown of feathered plumes, while a minstrel squatted before her, strumming a harp. To Rahab, these exquisitely carved scenes were a source of great delight. She was still moving about the bed, exclaiming over them, when Myrnah returned with another slave and jars of warm water for the bath.

While Myrnah filled the shallow basin, Rahab hurried to strip off her clothing, for her skin was hot and caked with dust from the journey. The water was delightfully warm, and

187

she was content to listen to the old slave's chattering while her body was washed gently with a soft cloth.

"The slaves say Cesera was taken with a fit of shaking when she heard our master had returned," Myrnah confided. "She and Kalak had been telling the nobles our master would not return. They say that in another month the priest would have been crowned King of Jericho."

Milkili's letter had said almost as much, Rahab remembered now. In all probability, only Prince Hazor's premature return at the head of a column of Egyptian troops had ensured his ascending the throne of Jericho—if indeed it were certain even now.

"Was the vizier here to meet our master?" Rahab asked.

Myrnah's face hardened. "Milkili died a few days after the old King. Kalak and Cesera must have learned of the message he sent to our master in Memphis."

"You don't think they killed him, do you?"

Myrnah shrugged. "It would not be the first time they have murdered. Cesera is the strong one there, the one we must watch."

"But they wouldn't dare do anything against Prince Hazor now. Not when the people are so happy at his return from Egypt."

"But for the Egyptian troops, our master would have gotten no farther than the city gate," Myrnah said darkly. "The slaves say an order was issued the day the old King died to arrest him as soon as he entered Jericho."

Rahab shivered, and Myrnah hurried to rub her body dry with a soft towel. "What will happen now?" Rahab asked.

"As soon as Prince Hazor is crowned King, he must order Cesera and Kalak executed at once."

"Our master is not a murderer."

"Then someone must do it for him."

"Not you, Myrnah," Rahab said quickly.

"I visited the sorcerer I spoke to you about before we left Memphis," Myrnah assured her. "There are plenty of slaves in the palace who will be glad to slip the drug into their wine."

"Myrnah!" Rahab said sharply. "I forbid you to do such a thing."

The old slave cackled and picked up an exquisitely carved

188

alabaster cruet of perfumed oil. Pouring a liberal measure into the palm of her hand, she began to rub it into Rahab's skin. "Don't trouble yourself about such things, beautiful one. Your job is to please our master and give him a fine son."

"She could not please me more than she does now," came Hazor's voice from the door leading to his bedroom. Neither of them had heard him enter the adjoining room. Rahab turned her head quickly to smile at him.

"How do you like your quarters?" Hazor asked.

"They are lovely," she assured him. "I have never seen anything like the ivory plaques in the *sussuru* wood of your bed."

"They are interesting," he agreed. "Much of the history of Jericho is engraved upon them."

"Come over to the couch," Myrnah told Rahab. "I will rub oil into the skin of your belly so your beauty will not be marred by the swelling of pregnancy."

Rahab stretched out on the soft couch while Myrnah expertly massaged her skin with oil. This was the part of the day she liked best. Hazor often came to visit while Myrnah dressed her for the evening meal, and knowing how much he loved to watch her naked body as the perfumed oil was rubbed into her skin, the cosmetics applied to her lips and cheeks, and the nipples of her breasts painted a glowing red with carmine, she was happy to have him there.

"Kalak insists upon giving a state dinner for me tonight," Hazor said. "There will be much rich food and many toasts to be drunk. I thought you might rather stay in your quarters, Rahab, or up on the roof where it is cool."

"Do you ever think of yourself, master?" she asked with a smile.

"Sometimes." His face sobered. "Perhaps when I persuaded King Adoni-zedek to hire out the mercenaries to me I was thinking of myself more than I was of defending Jericho against the Habiru."

"It is a good thing you thought of yourself at least once then," Myrnah said with the familiarity bred of long years of servitude, "else all of us would be in prison now."

"With my father and Milkili dead, this is not the same city we knew years ago," Hazor agreed.

"It could be again," the old slave said promptly. "You need

189

only to crush a few lice who have crawled in, to make it as good as ever."

Hazor smiled. "If all of Jericho were as loyal to me as you and Rahab, Myrnah, I would have no cares."

"The crushing of lice can easily be arranged," Myrnah suggested eagerly. "There are many here in the palace who would take care of it for you."

Hazor shook his head. "I will not fight evil with evil, Myrnah. Tomorrow I am to be crowned King of Jericho. We will see then just how strong are the forces arrayed against me." From beneath his arm he took a small papyrus roll. "I have here some poems of Egypt, Rahab. When you are dressed you can read them to me while I dress for the feast."

On Rahab's cheeks Myrnah rubbed white antimony paste and with a tiny brush of soft hairs gently stroked kohl on her eyelashes to darken them. Then she brought a gossamer light robe of wool, so finely woven that it was almost as transparent as a veil, and dropped it over Rahab's shoulders, girdling the fragile fabric about her waist with a cord of silver thread. While Myrnah laced Rahab's fragile silver sandals, Rahab attached a pair of golden earrings set with turquoise and pearls in her pierced ears and bound the long hair about her forehead with a silver chaplet.

"I am ready," she said then, turning to her master.

"In all of Jericho—nay, even in all the world—there is no one lovelier than you, my dear," Hazor said, taking her into his arms. "Were I not a king I would still be the richest man in all the world."

"And I am the most honored of women," Rahab assured him in a sudden rush of warm gratitude. "Honored to be the slave of such a master."

Myrnah and another slave had brought Hazor's robe for the banquet. While they helped him dress, Rahab read from the papyrus roll of poems, choosing a group titled *The Beautiful Joyous Songs of Thy Sister Whom Thy Heart Loves, Who Walks in the Fields.*

"The love of my beloved leaps on the bank of the stream.
A crocodile lies in the shadows;
Yet I go down into the water and breast the wave,
My courage is high on the stream,

190

And the water is as land to my feet.
It is her love that makes me strong,
She is a book of spells to me.
When I behold my beloved coming, my heart is glad,
My arms are spread apart to embrace her;
My heart rejoices forever . . . since my beloved came.
When I embrace her, I am as one who is in Incense Land,
As one who carries perfumes.
When I kiss her, her lips are open,
And I am made merry without beer.
Would that I were the Negress slave who is in attendance
    on her;
So should I behold the hue of all her limbs."

"I think I would rather be the poet who wrote those lines than King of Jericho." Hazor was carefully attaching to the girdle of his robe a jeweled leather sheath containing a slender dagger with a handle of ivory. "Then I could speak them to you with my own lips, Rahab, my dearest."

Rahab ate the evening meal on the roof of the palace, where the night breeze from the River Jord brought a refreshing coolness after the heat of the day. She was served by Myrnah and another slave, but when the meal was finished she dismissed them and went to lean on the low parapet surrounding the roof.

In the city below her, torches were moving everywhere, for Jericho was in a ferment tonight over the return of Prince Hazor and the announcement that he would be crowned King tomorrow. It was common knowledge that the presence of Captain Kanofer and the mercenaries had caused Kalak and his sister, Queen Cesera, to hasten Hazor's coronation. And hating the two of them as they did, the people rejoiced at the pair's discomfiture as well as because now a kind and understanding ruler would be over them.

Rahab was not concerned with the merriment going on in the city below her tonight, however. Instead her eyes were drawn to the east, where the dark shadows of the mountains beyond the Jord loomed in the soft moonlight. Remembering another night like this, when she and Joshua had been alone in the Cave of Yah upon the slope of Mount Nebo, she felt a

191

sudden warmth begin to fill her body and the quick throbbing of the pulse in her throat.

Prince Hazor was a tender lover and Rahab had known much happiness in his arms, but she knew that nothing in the experience of a woman ever equals the surrender, the welcome pain, of the first embrace, the first yielding of her body to the will of a strong and masterful lover. And for a long moment she allowed herself to wonder if somewhere out there where the dark shadows of the mountains of Gilead blanketed the land Joshua might be thinking of her and longing for her, as she had longed for him so many times these past months since their idyll had been so rudely shattered.

Feeling a little guilty because she had thought of Joshua while occupying a favored position in the palace of Prince Hazor, Rahab turned back to where Myrnah had arranged a low couch for her, with some fruit on a table beside it and a small flask of wine in case she became thirsty. Her master, she knew, would be sitting late at the banquet table, and she had decided to remain up here, where it was cool and pleasant, until he finished. Myrnah had been instructed to come for her when Hazor returned to his room, and she hoped, if he were not too exhausted from the dinner, that they could talk together of their situation in Jericho and what the future held for them.

No one could have been more fortunate than she, Rahab thought dreamily as she burrowed comfortably in the soft cushions of the couch. She possessed the love of two strong men, and the seed of one of them was already kindled within her body into a child—a fine son, she was sure—that she would one day proudly show to his father. Upon that pleasant thought she drifted off to sleep.

Four

AT FIRST Rahab was not sure just what had awakened her. The moon had sunk low enough in the sky for the palm trees growing in large tubs on the roof to throw much of it in shadow. Then the sound of voices came from the other

192

side of the roof and she was able to see that two people were leaning on the parapet, a man and a woman. Hoping that her presence would not be discovered, she did not move from the couch on which she lay.

When the man spoke, she recognized his voice immediately; Captain Kanofer's amused and often insolent tone was quite familiar. The woman with the low, throaty laugh, however, was as yet only a shadowy figure in the darkness.

Knowing Kanofer as she did, Rahab could easily understand what had brought him to the roof garden. Bored by the tediousness of a state dinner, the Egyptian captain had no doubt lured a pretty slave girl up here for reasons of his own, thinking the roof would be deserted because of the social function. Or perhaps he had snared a quarry even more to his taste, the wife of one of the nobles attending the dinner, young and foolish enough to have her head turned easily by the attentions of the handsome Egyptian captain.

The two were laughing and talking as they moved along the parapet overlooking the city walls. Just then they came out of the shadows into a band of moonlight and Rahab saw the woman clearly.

"I was surprised to find the widow of the King of Jericho so young and beautiful," Kanofer said in his most ingratiating voice, and Rahab almost betrayed her presence on the rooftop by a gasp of surprise.

Kanofer's companion was Cesera, Prince Hazor's stepmother, and—according to Myrnah—his worst enemy.

She would not have called the former Queen of Jericho beautiful, Rahab decided. Handsome seemed a better word. Cesera was tall for a woman, almost as tall as Kanofer. And she quite obviously possessed a magnificent body, even hidden as it was by Canaanite dress. Her features were bold and her nose prominent—seen in profile in the moonlight.

"You are a flatterer, like all Egyptians, Captain," Cesera said lightly. "But we women love it. The men of Canaan are not so clever with words as you of Egypt."

"Perhaps because my inspiration is greater," Kanofer replied gallantly.

"You must find Jericho a mean city after Memphis and Thebes. We have little to offer a man who has already seen so much of the world."

"When you have seen so much," Kanofer said, his voice still low and intimate, "you are quick to recognize a jewel beyond price." He moved closer to the woman, and their shadows seemed to merge for a moment, before Cesera moved casually away, allowing a narrow shaft of moonlight to show between them.

"It is possible that you might find real jewels here in Jericho, Captain," Cesera said. "We are not poor, even if our city is small compared to others you have seen. The merchants do a good business with the caravans, and we exact a tribute from all who pass on the road."

"Prince Hazor pays me and my mercenaries well," Kanofer parried, pretending to misunderstand her meaning. "I am lucky to have such a generous employer."

"Indeed you are," Cesera agreed, just as lightly. "But if Hazor's need of you should happen to end, I shall be glad to recommend you to others who will perhaps be even more generous."

"You are most kind, noble lady," Kanofer assured her. "Prince Hazor was telling me only tonight how grateful he is to you and the most noble Kalak for preserving the kingdom after the death of his father, until he could return and take up his rightful place."

"Why should we not hold the throne for the rightful King of Jericho?" Cesera's laugh was still light. "Especially when we knew he had earned the favor of our master in Egypt." Her voice dropped again to a more insistent note. "I am sure Pharaoh gave his approval in advance to Hazor's taking the throne upon his father's death. Else he would not have sent you and the mercenaries."

Kanofer laughed. "You are wise as well as beautiful, noble lady, and well versed, I see, in the affairs of kings and their ambassadors. Naturally Pharaoh would wish the son of the King of Jericho to be its ruler—especially when the people love Prince Hazor so much."

"And naturally he would send troops with Hazor as a sign of his approval," Cesera agreed.

"Why else would we be here?"

"To guard the city against the Habiru, perhaps," Cesera said bluntly. "It is no secret that their leader, Joshua, covets power and intends to conquer all of Canaan."

194

"You may be sure that Pharaoh is concerned with the welfare of *all* his people," Kanofer assured her blandly. "With the love the people of Jericho have for their new King, plus our presence here as a sign of Pharaoh's approval, they will naturally defend the city strongly if it is attacked."

Cesera had found a match for her own wiliness in the Egyptian captain, Rahab decided. As yet Kanofer had shown no sign of disloyalty to Hazor, but she could not believe he was as sincere as he pretended to be.

"You are a very attractive man, Captain Kanofer," Cesera said. "And a clever one. You should go a long way."

"I do not deserve the compliment," Kanofer demurred with mock humility.

"But you do," Cesera assured him. "If only because you manage to speak so much, yet say so little."

Kanofer laughed and lifted the Queen's hand to his lips. "Even if you were not so beautiful, noble lady," he said smoothly, "I could not but admire one who can speak so little—yet say so much."

Cesera laughed again. "I knew we would have no trouble understanding each other, Captain. You will find Jericho a very attractive place to a man of ambition such as yourself."

"With such a sponsor, how could I fail?"

"We should go back now," Cesera said, "but it may be just as well if you return to the banquet before me. After all, I am only recently widowed and you are a very handsome man."

When the echo of Kanofer's footfalls had died away on the stairway to the ground level, Cesera turned back to the parapet overlooking the city. Rahab heard her laugh softly to herself and divined that Jericho's Queen was very pleased by her conversation with the Egyptian captain.

A sudden gust of cool wind flowed across the rooftop from the distant mountains. Clad only in the thin robe, Rahab was not prepared for the sudden chill and sneezed. The sound was startlingly loud in the quiet of the rooftop, and before she could move, the tall woman was standing over her.

"Who are you?" Cesera demanded angrily. There was nothing beautiful about the contorted features now.

Before Rahab could answer, another sneeze came. "My name is Rahab," she gasped when she could speak again.

The Queen leaned forward and stared at her. "How dare you come up here? You, a slave?"

"Prince Hazor told me to wait for him on the rooftop."

Cesera's eyes narrowed. "Then you must be the harlot he bought in Memphis?"

"I am no harlot," Rahab cried indignantly. "No man owned me before Prince Hazor."

"You are a slave—and an insolent one. I could have you whipped for this. Stand up so I can look at you."

Rahab got to her feet a little awkwardly because of her swollen belly.

"What does Hazor see in you?" Cesera demanded contemptuously. "You are not even graceful."

"I am with child," Rahab said spiritedly.

Cesera lifted a jeweled hand as if to strike her, and Rahab braced herself for the blow. It did not come, however, and finally the Queen let her hand fall. "Kalak said it was true, but I could not believe it," she muttered, as if to herself. "I thought Hazor was im——" She turned upon Rahab again. "When will this child of yours be born?"

"In about three months."

"Surely Prince Hazor is not fool enough to believe a harlot's brat is his own?"

Rahab did not answer, for at the moment there was nothing she could say. She herself was not sure Prince Hazor was the child's father.

Cesera prowled about the shivering girl like a lion savoring its kill before delivering the final blow. "You do have some measure of beauty," she admitted finally, "although hardly enough for the concubine of a king. From whence do you come?"

"My father is a scribe and an innkeeper of Medeba, across the Jord at the foot of Mount Nebo." With the people of Jericho already convinced that the Israelites would strike them, it seemed sensible not to mention the closer tie of a common ancestor that bound her to Israel.

"So? Did the Israelites sell you into slavery when they conquered King Sihon?"

"I was betrothed to—a very great man," Rahab explained. "Some people in Medeba were envious. They stole the bride price from me and sold me to Abda, the slave merchant."

196

"I know of this man Abda," Cesera said. "He is a shrewd trader. Did you say Prince Hazor was your first owner?"

"Yes. Abda sought him out because Jericho is near my own country."

"Well, at least the child will be of Canaanite blood!" Cesera's voice hardened. "How long have you been here on the rooftop?"

"Since the evening meal," Rahab confessed.

"Then you heard me talking with the Egyptian captain?"

"I—I was asleep. You woke me up."

"What did you hear?"

Rahab's mind moved quickly. Unless she was careful, she might be in grave trouble indeed, for the Queen had as much as guaranteed that Kanofer would be well paid if he deserted Hazor and came over to the faction controlled by her and her brother Kalak. To admit such knowledge now, Rahab realized, would be the same as signing her own death warrant.

"Go on." Cesera's voice was like a whiplash now. "Tell me what you heard."

"I was trying to remember. It meant nothing to me."

Cesera looked at her keenly. "You were clever enough to gain a hold on Hazor, so you cannot be the fool you seem. What was I talking about to the Egyptian captain?"

"I remember your saying that Pharaoh approved of Prince Hazor becoming King of Jericho."

"Naturally I said that. Pharaoh did give his approval, did he not?"

"I did not go to Thebes with my master," Rahab said truthfully. "He and Captain Kanofer went alone."

"Was that before or after Hazor received the letter from Milkili?"

The question told Rahab a great deal, verifying, in fact, Myrnah's statement that Cesera and Kalak had undoubtedly murdered the old vizier as soon as the King was dead.

"It was before," she admitted.

"Hah!" Cesera cried triumphantly. "Then Hazor did not know he would soon be King."

"My master said his father could not live much longer. I suppose he told the same thing to Pharaoh."

Cesera's elation evaporated as suddenly as it had risen. But she lost none of her concentration or her venom. "You

197

may be right," she admitted. "Someday I will find out for sure from the Egyptian captain. Meanwhile"—she leveled a finger at Rahab warningly—"say nothing to anyone about tonight if you know what is good for you."

"How could I say anything, O Queen?" Rahab asked innocently. "I have told you what I heard, and it was nothing."

Cesera studied her closely for a long moment. "You may not be as stupid as you pretend to be, young woman," she said finally, "but don't make the mistake of trying to trick me. One false step and you will rue the day Hazor first saw you in that Memphis brothel Abda runs."

When Cesera left her, Rahab lost no time in fleeing to the safety of her own quarters. Prince Hazor was very late in returning from the dinner and did not waken her, so she did not see him until the morning meal, which they always ate together.

Myrnah served them fruit and fresh goat's milk with a dish of curds and a thin slab of bread from the clay stoves of the bakery that formed a part of the palace. Remembering Cesera's warning the night before, Rahab wondered if she should speak to Hazor about what she had overheard on the rooftop. But since it concerned him even more than it did her, she decided to tell him everything, regardless of the Queen's warning.

He listened, his face grave, while she repeated the conversation as nearly as she could word for word.

"Captain Kanofer has been to see me already," he said when she finished. "He told me practically the same thing."

Rahab looked up in surprise from the pomegranate she was peeling. "Why should he do that?"

"Perhaps because he is loyal to me. After all, it is to the best interests of his Egyptian master for Jericho to stay in the hands of those legally entitled to rule it."

Rahab shook her head. "Captain Kanofer is loyal only to himself, master. If he told you about last night, it was because the Queen warned him and he knew I would tell you what happened."

"You may be right," Hazor admitted. "But Kanofer is a fine soldier and leader of men. We never needed those qualities in Jericho more than we do right now."

"You are the King, master. Look how the people love you."

198

Hazor took her hand in his and kissed the fingers tenderly. "That is for your loyalty and your confidence in me, dearest one. I may make Jericho a good king—at least I shall try—but I am not a soldier or a leader of soldiers. They respect their own kind more than any other."

"She tried to bribe Captain Kanofer to turn against you," Rahab warned.

"I expected Cesera to try that. But there may be another reason for her interest in him. It is no secret in Jericho that she cuckolded my father with half a dozen men, so she would hardly overlook a fine prospect like Kanofer."

"Why does she hate you so bitterly?"

"Because I would not jump when she swung the whip!" His face grew sober. "Cesera tried to make me her lover years ago, soon after she was married to my father. She has hated me ever since I spurned her."

"Why didn't you denounce her then?"

"Perhaps I did make a serious mistake," Hazor admitted. "She was always good to my father, though; I will give her credit for that. She treated him like a baby, and he could see no wrong in her. I hesitated to make him unhappy."

Rahab leaned over and kissed him warmly. "There was never anyone as good as you are, master," she said impulsively. "In all my life I have known only two other men whose kindness and understanding were anywhere near as great as yours. One was my father."

"And the other?"

"The other? He was a physician—an Egyptian named Samma."

Five

HAZOR entered upon the duties of kingship with a zest and a genius for ruling that demonstrated at once his right to follow in his father's steps. For several years while the old King had been declining, Cesera and Kalak had been looting the royal treasury and the coffers of Baal for their own good. To this Hazor put an end immediately following

199

his coronation. As a result, he was able to lower taxes, an act that endeared him even further to the people.

From the very beginning the new King's rule was a period of prosperity for Jericho. The people were happy and well fed; the poor were given food from the state funds; and a heavy program of public works was undertaken to strengthen the walls that were their sole protection against the feared and hated Habiru across the Jord. This forthright attack upon the weaknesses of the city itself stood out more than anything else in Hazor's program of reform. And since it was paid for by taxing the richer nobles and merchants, this, too, brought him great favor with the common people.

Anyone who wished work could find it in Jericho during the early months of Hazor's reign, repairing the walls where the frequent earthquakes of the spring and summer seasons had cracked them over the years. Teams of men labored every day blocking cracks with stone and brick and plastering the repaired places with mortar that dried rapidly in the sunlight to a smooth hard layer.

Under Kanofer's direction, men of fighting age were also trained in warlike arts, using the small group of mercenaries from Urusalim as a nucleus. Before many months had passed Jericho was able to muster nearly a thousand men possessing at least some skill with bow, arrow, and spear, a force of no mean stature when it was remembered that they would fight from behind a strong double wall which any invader must attack across open ground and scale before reaching the city itself.

Rahab went out but little during those early and busy weeks of Hazor's reign. As the time of her confinement approached, he insisted that she remain most of the time in their quarters in the palace, or in the cool shade of the inner courtyard, with Myrnah and Senu waiting upon her slightest wish.

She rarely saw Cesera, and although Myrnah reported that Kanofer continued to be very attentive to the tall handsome ex-Queen, the pair gave no grounds for suspicion that they might be up to any mischief. Rahab never saw Kalak, for she did not worship Baal and therefore did not visit the temple adjoining the palace.

That intrigue was continually going on was not to be

doubted, however, even for a moment. Hazor's reforms had endeared him to the ordinary people of Jericho, but they antagonized the nobles and the rich merchants, from whose well-filled purses came most of the gold for rebuilding the walls and training their defenders. Nor did Hazor diminish his attempts to bring the neighboring city-states of Canaan into an alliance against the constantly growing threat of the Habiru across the Jord.

One of the first of the rulers he approached was the King of Ai, a neighboring city located on two of the possible routes toward Urusalim, the most powerful citadel in this part of Canaan. Ai's position was an important one indeed, for it served as an advance post of the people dwelling on the central plateau in this section of Canaan. From its commanding highland location Ai overlooked the lower foothills where Jericho stood and the deep north-south rift in which the cold, sparkling waters of the River Jord tumbled to the Salt Sea.

Both cities would have profited by a treaty of mutual defense, but all of Hazor's persuasions were not sufficient to convince the King of Ai that his people should commit themselves to the defense of any other

Hazor next sought an alliance with a group of people to the north called the Gibeonites because their largest city bore the name of Gibeon. Actually the key to a confederation that included Beeroth, Chephirah, and Kirjath-jearim, with a total fighting population of close to two thousand men, Gibeon and its sister city-states would have been an important ally indeed.

Another reason why Hazor hoped for success with the Gibeonite confederation was because they were not ruled by kings. In fact, their manner of government was very similar to that of the Israelite tribes, being administered by elders chosen from among the people themselves. And since Hazor had himself lessened the burden upon the common people of Jericho and was in reality their champion against the nobility and the rich merchants, it seemed for a while that he might succeed in this alliance where he had failed with the others.

In the end, however, the reluctance of the Gibeonites to be drawn into a war not directed against themselves prevailed, and the proffered alliance failed. As for Adoni-zedek in Urusalim—the logical center from which a body of warriors could have been sped by chariot to the defense of any beleaguered city—he seemed content to rely upon his own city's strategic position on two hilltops and its strong walls to repel any invader.

Thus Jericho faced the strongly developing strength of the Israelites to the east without allies. And as more and more evidences of the Habiru might were reported by travelers crossing the Jord at the fords below Jericho, a state of tension bordering almost on panic began to grip the city in spite of the active preparations for its defense by Kanofer and the men under his command.

In this tense situation, on a cool frosty morning in midwinter, an heir was born to the throne of Jericho.

As with all first-born, Rahab's travail was great. But Myrnah was skilled in midwifery and did everything she could to allay the agony of bringing forth the child. Throughout a night and part of a day Rahab suffered the pains of labor. When it was evident that the child was about to be born, Myrnah brought out a birth seat made after the Egyptian fashion. This was simply a three-legged stool of heavy wood whose central portion had been cut away. On it the old slave perched the weeping young mother, supported by a female slave. Thus, sitting erect according to the Canaanite custom, Rahab gave birth to the baby. Kneeling before the stool, Myrnah received it directly into her hands as she had many other children in Jericho.

It was early evening when Rahab awoke. She turned her head slowly, still half unconscious from the drug Myrnah had given her in wine as soon as the child was born. But when she saw the exquisitely carved crib of sandalwood standing in the corner of the room, she was suddenly wide awake.

Hazor came in from the other room and went over to the couch to put his arms around her.

"Where is the baby?" Rahab asked.

"Sleeping there. In the crib."

Rahab relaxed gratefully in his arms with a sigh of relief. From Hazor's grave manner she had feared for a moment that something was wrong with the child. "I—I don't seem to remember much about what happened," she admitted.

"Myrnah gave you a sleeping draught as soon as the child came."

"Is anything wrong in Jericho, master?"

"No. Why?"

"You seem so—so disturbed."

Hazor groaned but got up before she could speak. "I will send Myrnah," he said quickly, and Rahab was sure now that there were tears in his eyes as he left the room.

Myrnah came almost at once and began to putter about, making Rahab comfortable, bathing her face and insisting upon putting a fresh robe on her. Even the old slave was not like herself, though, and Rahab began to feel a rising certainty that all was not right. In the middle of the toilette she suddenly gripped Myrnah's arm.

"Did our master tell me the truth when he said the baby was sleeping in the crib?" she asked.

"It is sleeping," Myrnah said quickly.

"There is nothing wrong then?"

"What could be wrong?" the old slave asked gruffly, but she did not meet Rahab's eyes. "You are young and you have had a baby. Women have been doing that ever since the world began."

"I want to see my baby," Rahab cried. She started to get up, but Myrnah pushed her back.

"All right," the old servant said. "I will get the young Prince."

"The young Prince! It is a boy then? From the way our master acted, I thought it might be a girl."

"It is a boy." Myrnah bent over the crib and lifted a small bundle of blankets. Bringing it over to the couch, she knelt on the floor beside Rahab's couch and parted the blankets so that Rahab could see the baby's face.

"Give him to me!" Rahab cried, her eyes shining with happiness. "He's beautiful." It was a big, handsome boy, digging at his eyes with sturdy fists and opening his mouth to protest this indignity.

"All babies are beautiful." Myrnah placed the child in its cocoon of soft cloth on the couch beside Rahab. "Be careful with it, now."

"Look at his hair," Rahab cried excitedly. "See how black it is? And his eyes! He knows me already!" She lifted the child in her arms. "And feel how sturdy his body is, Myrnah! Surely you have never seen a finer baby than this."

"He is strong and sturdy," Myrnah agreed. In her excitement Rahab did not notice that the old slave was near to tears.

"And beautiful!" Rahab insisted. "No baby was ever more beautiful than mine."

Myrnah turned away quickly but could not hide the trembling of her shoulders or the racking sobs that shook her body.

A chill of terror gripped Rahab. "What is it, Myrnah?" she asked in a whisper. "What is it you don't want to tell me?"

But Myrnah only continued to sob. Sure now that there must be something wrong with the baby, Rahab, with trembling fingers, unfolded the layers of swaddling clothes in which the child was wrapped. Its body was as strong and as sturdy as she had felt it to be through the cloth. And the legs were perfect, too, just as she had been sure they would be. Only when she looked at the baby's feet did she realize—with a sudden sense of horror—why Prince Hazor had acted so strangely and why Myrnah had been overcome with grief.

The right foot was straight and well formed. The left was twisted and deformed, with the toes pointing sharply downward.

Now Rahab herself experienced the agony that had tortured Hazor and Myrnah. But with her it was many times worse, for she was the child's mother. She had seen many of these deformed children—and adults too—in the Canaanite villages. And while she had always felt pity for them, it had never occurred to her that a child of hers might be born with such a deformity.

Being crippled was perhaps an even greater tragedy than being stillborn. Had it died, her heart would have been torn, of course, but in time her grief would have faded and become only a scar deep in her heart. In Canaan, however, a cripple lived as an outcast, despised by his village, a shameful thing to be hidden away by the family or condemned to life as a beggar, spurned and kicked contemptuously by the strong and straight children, groveling in the dust for food and shelter in company with lepers and sufferers from other loathsome diseases.

Able to weep at last, Rahab clutched the baby to her breast, as if somehow she could protect it from the insults, the pain it would know as an outcast throughout its life. And the baby, sensing her fear, began to wail loudly.

Myrnah had regained control of herself now. She came to take the baby back to its crib, but Rahab stopped her.

"Wait," she said. "I must see its back, Myrnah."

"The back is strong. Only the foot is crooked."

"I must see it—for a reason." In her concern about the child's deformity Rahab had almost forgotten the marks that would tell her who was the baby's father.

Myrnah unwound the wrappings. At the sight of that strong little back with its broad shoulders, Rahab caught her breath in an audible gasp.

The child was Joshua's! She would have known it from the sturdy body, the broad shoulders, the mane of black hair, and the wide-set serious eyes. The inherited marks only confirmed the father's identity beyond question.

Less than a year ago Rahab would have been certain that the happiest day of her life would be the one when she looked upon her and Joshua's child. Now everything was changed. She was the favored wife-concubine of the King of Jericho, but she had borne another man's child. And worst of all, the baby was destined, because of the crippled foot, to be an outcast. Neither of its fathers would want it now.

Fighting back her tears, Rahab watched the old slave put the baby back into the crib. And then suddenly an idea came to her.

"Myrnah!" she called. "Do you suppose a skilled leech might be able to straighten a twisted foot?"

The slave's eyes brightened. "In Egypt it is said that physicians sometimes bind crooked bones and make them straight while they are still soft." Then her face fell. "But Egypt is a long way off. Our master could not go there now, with the Habiru about to attack Jericho."

"I know a skilled physician nearby," Rahab said excitedly. "On the other side of the Jord."

"One of the Habiru?"

"Yes."

"He would never be allowed to enter Jericho."

"Not as an Habiru, but there are other ways. If anyone can help my baby's foot, he can do it."

"Kalak and Cesera would stir up the people against our master if he let one of the Habiru into Jericho," Myrnah warned.

"I saw him in Memphis just before we left. He was traveling as an Egyptian physician named Samma, and no one took him for an Israelite."

"Physicians from Egypt and Babylon do travel through the cities of Canaan plying their trade sometimes," Myrnah agreed. "I remember seeing them here in Jericho. But how can you get word to him?"

"Senu can take a letter," Rahab said eagerly, "when he goes to the river for fish. It is only a little farther to the Habiru camp."

"Tell the physician to approach Jericho from the west, as if he came from the other cities of Canaan," Myrnah advised. "Nobody will suspect that you sent for him then."

Six

AS THE WINTER HEIGHTENED and Joshua continued his preparations for the spring invasion of Canaan by way of Jericho, Salmon found himself getting more and more restless. For the first time in anyone's memory the Israelites were well fed, well housed, and healthy, so he had little work to do. And having exhausted the resources of Heshbon as far as learning any new thing was concerned, he was thoroughly bored.

Caleb set himself to devise some way to occupy his friend's mind, for with the approach of the greatest battle the Israelites had yet fought, the old general wanted to be certain that Salmon would not decide to move on to some far-distant land, as he had spoken of doing, before his services as a planner of military strategy would be needed. Caleb and Salmon were watching the captains drill the warriors in the uses of scaling ladders to surmount the defenses of walled cities under the protection of a hail of arrows, when the former broached the subject.

"Our losses will be heavy when we storm the walls of Jericho," he observed casually.

Salmon nodded. "I have tried to think of a way to lessen the toll, but my mind doesn't seem to work any more."

"Still thinking about the girl?"

"She is not for me, Caleb. I have tried to put her out of my thoughts."

"You spoke once of traveling again," Caleb reminded him.

Salmon shook his head. "Just traveling aimlessly around would not help."

"Suppose you had a mission?"

"But I don't have one."

"Before we invade Canaan in the spring we will need to know something about the lay of the land and the defenses of the cities," Caleb told him. "I know of no one who could obtain that information better than you."

"I would only be helping to kill more people. There is too much of that already."

"You told me once that you devised strategy for us in order to keep so many of our own soldiers from being killed."

"The Canaanite cities have strong walls and are well defended," Salmon pointed out. "No strategy will help climb walls or protect soldiers being shot with arrows and stabbed with spears."

"There may be weaknesses in their defenses," Caleb reminded him. Then he added shrewdly, "You might even discover that some places are stronger than others and should be passed to attack weaker ones."

"I would have to enter the Canaanite cities," Salmon said thoughtfully. "It would be difficult."

Caleb's eyes gleamed. "But not too much for a physician of Egypt named Samma."

Salmon grinned and clapped Caleb on the back affectionately. "You grizzled old fox!" Then his face sobered. "What would be the reward of this physician for risking his neck?"

"Much gold, and the gratitude of his people."

"He has both."

"Plus the knowledge that he had saved many lives by discovering hidden weaknesses," Caleb added shrewdly.

"Is there a chance that Joshua might pass around Jericho if I showed him a better way to enter Canaan?"

"Of course. Even the son of Nun has no wish to sacrifice men needlessly."

"I will go then," Salmon said. "Perhaps I might travel as far north as the sea called Chinnereth."

"Go wherever you like in the land of Canaan," Caleb told him. "And if you find a better way than through Jericho, I will be the first to back you."

So it came about that a few days later the physician Samma set out once again upon his travels. And when a hunchback came to the camp of Israel, bearing a letter for Salmon, he was told that the physician had gone on a journey from which he would not return for several months. So, having destroyed the letter as Rahab had instructed him, Senu returned to Jericho.

Samma, the physician, traveled upon an ass while another, loaded with his medicines and the instruments of his trade, was led by a servant. A half day's journey to the north along the King's Highway from the military camp established by Joshua at Abel-shittim, between Heshbon and the river, the traveler took a side road heading northwestward. He came in the late afternoon to Adamah, the first crossing of the Jord north of the fords that were east of Jericho, and halted for the night.

Located on a small knoll in the Jord Valley, Adamah overlooked a road leading westward into central Canaan. The river cut through a canyon here, and a lofty mound of earth formed its west bank, with the swift waters of the Jord tending to undermine the craggy surface of the mound. There was no rocky face to hold the cliff thus formed, and Salmon was not surprised to learn that earth falls frequently took place, particularly during the tremors that were often felt in the spring and summer. He was even told that a great earth fall many years before had actually blocked the Jord's flow entirely for more than a day. But since there were no tremors while he was in town, he had no opportunity to witness the phenomenon at first hand.

Leaving Adamah the next day, Salmon crossed the river and followed a road leading northwestward along the bank of a smaller stream that tumbled into the Jord from the high-lands of the central plateau. The way here was hard, for the road was narrow and rose steadily. He did not try to make rapid progress, and stopped that night in the Canaanite town of Tirzah, beneath the towering shadow of Mount Ebal.

Salmon did not visit the city of Shechem, a short distance to the south, since he was bound at the moment for the Sea of Chinnereth, which he had been told lay about two days' journey to the north. Shechem, he learned, was a large city with a great temple and altar of Baal in its midst, and he hoped to visit it on the return journey.

The cities of northern Canaan, the traveler discovered, were in many ways quite as advanced as those of Egypt—and far more so than, for example, the towns of Bashan across the Jord. Their artisans wove cloth of an exceeding fineness. Their smiths were experts at working copper and bronze, al-though he saw little of the Hittite metal called iron. And their potteries produced all sorts of earthen and glazed ware, exquisitely painted and decorated and much in demand, he was told, in the Phoenician cities along the coast and in Egypt.

At Tirzah, Salmon paused for a day to treat the sick and help preserve his masquerade as a physician of Egypt. He learned little of interest to Joshua and the Israelites, save that these cities were not so well fortified as Jericho and those to the south, and that the inhabitants were fearful of the Israel-ites, whom they expected to attack the whole land of Canaan after the coming of the spring rains.

From Tirzah, Salmon followed a well-traveled road north-eastward and soon came down from the hill country into the lowlands paralleling the Jord on its west bank. Late on the second day he came to a cleft in the hills through which the river seemed to tumble, like water pouring over the lip of a cup. Toiling up the slight elevation down which the water flowed, he stopped upon its crest. And knew that he had reached the distant place of beauty for which every man secretly yearns in his heart—but which so few ever find.

Lying in a cup surrounded by hills—some of them quite precipitous—and looking like a beautiful blue-green jewel in a setting of gold was the small inland sea of which he had been told and which he had journeyed these weary days to

209

see. Only a narrow shore surrounded the lake here at the southern end of the cup—perhaps a day's journey in length, he estimated—for the hills dropped almost into the water.

On the east side of the Sea of Chinnereth a range of steep hills rose directly from the water itself. At several places, steps had been cut into the slope descending to the lake, where fishing boats rode at anchor. Far to the north he could see that the land around the lake was more rolling and less precipitous, and he imagined it was here that the verdant gardens, the rich groves, and the fertile fields of which he had heard so much were located.

The road northward wound along the western shore of the lake, almost at the water's edge, where the waves had piled up white sand beaches on which fishing boats with multicolored sails were drawn up. As he rode along he passed many wooden racks from which came the pungent odor of drying fish.

Farther along the shore of the beautiful lake Salmon noticed a strange sight. At times progress was completely blocked by a procession of the crippled and deformed. Some dragged themselves painfully with gnarled and horny hands. Others stumped along on rude crutches and walking sticks. A few, apparently possessing more substance than the rest, were carried in rude litters by slaves or members of their families.

Such a thing as this naturally aroused the curiosity of a physician. When Salmon inquired among the sufferers, he learned that they were bound for the village of Hammath, about a third of the way to the north end of the lake. Here, they assured him, mineral springs of extraordinary healing power burst from the very rocks of the mountainside, and people from all sections of northern Canaan journeyed there to drink the waters and bathe in them, with much benefit to inflamed joints and deformed limbs.

When he shortly came to Hammath, Salmon halted for the night, welcoming the opportunity to observe this strange natural cure for one of the most obdurate of diseases. He found many people drinking the bitter water and bathing in the pools where hot streams gushed forth from the rocks. Thousands were helped here every year, he was told, and sometimes miraculous cures seemed to take place.

The next day Salmon continued his journey northward along the shore of the lake. This was the most populous area he had seen in Canaan outside the larger cities, especially when he approached the northwestern rim, where the land spread away almost level just above the surface of the water. Here was a veritable garden in itself where winter seemed never to lay its hoary touch. Flowers bloomed everywhere, and the green of olive groves almost hid the ground itself from view.

The village of Chinnereth was perched halfway up the western slope, overlooking both the lake and the spot where a stream poured into it after leaping from rock to rock down from the northwestern hills. Standing on the hillside, with the lovely green jewel of the lake in its cup before him, Salmon felt as if he had finally come home from his travels.

For a moment he considered going no farther. Here he could build a home of his own, a cool house with thick walls of sun-dried brick in a region where the flowers forever bloomed and the birds sang always in the trees. Below him lay the lake, with the multicolored sails of the fishermen's boats arranging and rearranging themselves in a never-ending, always different pattern of quiet beauty.

As lovely as the prospect was, however, Salmon knew he could find no happiness anywhere without Rahab. That she would love this hillside overlooking the lake, he did not doubt for a moment, for he knew she felt as he did about natural beauty, with the instinctive feeling for it of the poet and the artist. Had things been different, he was sure they could have found a happiness here granted only to few people. Without her, however, it could never be anything else but a dream.

Not wishing to torture himself any longer with thoughts of what might have been, Salmon urged his mule up the path that ascended the precipitous hillside while his servant hauled on the lead rope of the pack animal. At the summit he paused for one more look before the winding road through the highlands shut the beauty away from his range of vision.

Far to the north in the clear afternoon air he could barely distinguish the white-topped crest of a tall mountain from which the people on the lake had told him the River Jord took its source. In the rocky passes of the hillside the cooing of thousands of doves filled the air with soft music, joining with the rushing murmurs of the water in a hymn of praise to the Creator of a scene with so much beauty. And a little to the north, currents of molten silver seemed to pour from the hillside and down across the shore to enter the lake at the spot called by the people around it the "Place of the Seven Fountains."

Reluctantly Salmon finally turned his face westward along the caravan road known in this region as the "Way of the Sea," because it led southwestward from Damascus around the Sea of Chinnereth and on to the shore of the Great Sea, thence southward through the Phoenician cities to Egypt. One of the two most heavily traveled caravan routes in the world—the other being the King's Highway east of the Jord—it was a logical route for an itinerant physician to follow southward.

Traveling leisurely, Salmon came within a few days to Megiddo, a strongly fortified city on the southwest side of a plain where the Way of the Sea cut through a sharply defined pass in a long mountainous ridge. As guardian of this important pass, Megiddo was a fortress city like Jericho, and Salmon wished to seek information here that might give him some idea of how that city might be reduced without the inevitable losses that must result from a direct assault.

The walls of Megiddo, he saw as he approached it, were strongly made of stone and brick. They were wide enough, too, for soldiers to move easily from one section to another and thus keep their defenses flexible. Since the city was on a regular caravan line and Salmon had taken the precaution to join a long line of pack asses moving southward on the road, he was admitted to Megiddo upon payment of a token tribute.

As was his custom when entering any new city, he went immediately to an inn. Here he set up his place of business in the courtyard with a small table to hold his instruments and his medicines. These preparations completed, he sent his servant through the streets, crying the news that Samma, the renowned physician of Egypt, was ready to treat all ills to the best of his ability, using the latest methods of treatment. And as always—since Egyptian physicians were known

212

to be superior to local ones—he shortly began to enjoy a brisk trade.

From the sick who visited him Salmon learned two important things. One was that even the inhabitants of this distant city knew of the people called the Habiru and of Pharaoh's failure to provide for Canaan's defense. The other was that, barring some subterfuge, a direct attack upon the walls of such a city as Megiddo could be a very bloody affair even if it succeeded—which did not seem likely.

The latter information came from a talkative officer in the Royal Guard, grateful for the cure of a painful carbuncle on his neck—upon which Salmon used the drastic but remarkably effective remedy of burning it out at the center with a glowing bronze spear point. The officer not only described in detail how Megiddo would be defended, but took Salmon on a tour of the city's pride, an underground water supply protecting the inhabitants from thirst even in a time of siege.

As in most Canaanite cities, the water supply was derived from a spring outside the walls and had originally been carried in by the women using jars borne upon their heads. But since the spring was too far away for effective defense, the rulers of Megiddo had long ago devised a way of bringing water into the city. For this they had sunk a shaft just inside the wall, opposite the spring, extending down to the rock base upon which the city's foundation stood. Next they had cut a sloping tunnel through the rock itself with steps along one side. Finally another, almost horizontal shaft ran directly outward to the spring, but sloped so that water would run down to the foot of the steps where the women could reach it.

The officer even took Salmon through the tunnel, indicating with great pride the details of its construction. Salmon, in turn, made careful notes of how long the tunnel was, the distance from the walls, and other details. These he set down on papyrus as soon as he was alone. From these facts he was sure that, should Israel ever attack Megiddo, he could direct the sinking of another shaft by which the soldiers could reach the water tunnel and thus gain an entrance by stealth into the city.

His mission in Megiddo accomplished, Salmon next headed southeastward along the central caravan trail that followed

213

the eastern rim of the highlands. Knowing that Joshua had no immediate designs upon the cities of the coast or the northern strongholds of the Hittites—whose use of the new metal might make them formidable opponents in battle—Salmon turned away from that branch of the great caravan trail that paralleled the shore of the Great Sea. Instead, he followed the more centrally located road to the west of Mount Ebal until he came to Shechem, a poorly fortified town, which he judged would offer little resistance to the Israelites. Thence he moved southward to the cities of the Gibeonites—or Hivites—Gibeon, Beeroth, Chephirah, and Kirjath-jearim. Here he stayed several weeks, for if Jericho fell, the city of Ai, as well as the Gibeonite towns, would be the next barriers to the passage of the Israelites deeper into Canaan.

Gibeon, the central city of the group, stood only a few hours' walk northeast of the great city of the Jebusites called Urusalim, which occupied an imposing position on a knoll in a small plain. Strongly fortified, it was a thriving population center. Beeroth, about an hour's walk to the northeast of Gibeon, was a powerful fortress town, its great walls wider than a man could leap even with a running start.

Chephirah stood to the west of Gibeon, on a spur jutting out between two steep watercourses commanding the approaches from the west. Kirjath-jearim was roughly an hour's walk to the south, commanding one of the main routes from the coast to Urusalim.

Altogether, Salmon saw, the four Hivite cities formed a powerful bastion. And he soon learned that they stood solidly together, with similar governments by groups of men chosen by the people themselves and binding treaties holding each city responsible for the defense of the others should any of them be attacked.

This last fact made them particularly formidable in Salmon's opinion, for there were no kings to be jealous of each other and thus weaken the strength of the group. Here, too, he learned that Hazor, King of Jericho, had made unsuccessful overtures to the Hivite cities, seeking to join in their federation and thus invoke their protection against the Israelites when the expected attack finally came.

From Gibeon, Salmon moved on to Urusalim, the greatest and strongest city of central Canaan. Tradition had it that the city was already nearly two thousand years old and, looking at its massive walls on a commanding hilltop, Salmon could easily believe that this was true.

The walls themselves seemed impregnable. Salmon paced them surreptitiously one day, finding them nine paces in thickness and well built of rock, mortar, and brick. Any attack upon Urusalim, he decided, would have to be launched uphill and over these massive walls, a bloody task indeed. Meanwhile its defenders would form poor targets for bowmen forced to shoot almost directly upward in order to protect the men who stormed the walls. When he left Urusalim it was with a profound respect for its defenses, as well as for those of Gibeon and the other Hivite cities guarding the roads into northern Canaan.

Caleb had suggested that Salmon not enter Jericho, and he had agreed willingly. Certain that Rahab was inside the city, he was equally sure that nothing was to be gained, except torture to himself, by seeing her again. And so he turned off into the hills and, moving eastward with the walls of the city in plain view, came again to the road between Jericho and the fords of the Jord, less than an hour's walk from the gate itself. From the hills he saw what seemed to be a great deal of activity inside the city, but he could not make out any details of what was going on.

On a day when the warmth of spring was already in the air and flowers were beginning to open their blossoms to the sun, the physician called Samma during his travels rode into the great camp of Abel-shittim. With everyone busy preparing for the imminent march on Jericho and the land of Canaan promised to the children of Israel by their god, no one thought to tell him of a hunchback who had sought vainly for him a few days after his departure and had then gone away without revealing to anyone whence he came or for what reason he sought the physician.

Seven

RAHAB had been bitterly disappointed when Senu
returned with the news that Salmon had left the Israelite
camp on a journey that might take several months. But she
was comforted by the thought that the slave had been told
the physician would return. Confident as she was of Salmon's
skill, she told herself there would still be time for him to
straighten the baby's foot when he returned.

The child, called Jaschar after an ancestor of Hazor, was
strong and healthy; Rahab loved him perhaps more than if
he had been whole. Wrapped up in the boy, she paid little
attention to what was happening in Jericho. But from certain
mutterings and dark hints from Myrnah, she gathered that
all was not entirely well.

Partly as an antidote to his bitter disappointment at
Jaschar's deformity, Hazor had thrown himself into a new
project for the defense of Jericho, rebuilding the great gate
into a strong bastion guarding the breach in the walls that
was the city's weakest point. Most of each day he spent with
the workmen, directing the erection of two strong towers beside the only entrance into Jericho and constructing a new
and heavier gate of hewn timbers, swung on great pivots that
turned in hollowed-out blocks of black basalt.

Only at night, when they were in Hazor's quarters together
or on the cool roof, did he confide in Rahab as he had previously done. She sensed that deep inside him he blamed
her at least a little for the child's deformity, but being kind
and good, he would never mention that feeling to her. And
knowing how he felt in his bitter disappointment, she exerted
herself to be as tender and considerate as she could.

"Does the building of the gate go well, master?" Rahab
asked one warm night as they were eating their evening meal
on the roof, where the breeze dispelled some of the heat of
the day.

"Not fast enough to suit me," he admitted. "Joshua has
moved his camp to Abel-shittim, and his captains buy food

216

from farmers who cross over at the fords. They bring back great tales of the Habiru strength and their preparedness for war."

"Don't the people have confidence in the walls of Jericho?"

Hazor shrugged. "Most of them are too much afraid of the Habiru to have confidence in anything."

"Are you still convinced of Captain Kanofer's loyalty?" she asked.

"He labors as hard training the men as I do strengthening the walls. I have yet to see any evidence that he is anything but loyal."

"Myrnah says he has purchased a large house on the wall. Where does he get the gold?"

"Kanofer gambles a great deal and wins much of the time. The house serves as quarters for the mercenaries and also as an inn."

"She says it is a brothel."

Hazor smiled. "Are not all inns thought to be brothels? And with considerable reason?"

"My father's inn was not," Rahab said spiritedly.

"I promised to send for your father, didn't I?" Hazor said. "But if he were to come to Jericho now, the people might regard him as a spy."

"I think we should wait until later." Rahab frowned. "If there were only some way to get the people interested in the defense of the city."

"Kalak may have the answer," Hazor told her. "When the new gate is finished a few days from now, he wants to hold a great ceremony and invoke the favor of Baal upon it and the other defenses. He thinks that if the people believe the god favors them they will not fear the Habiru so much."

"Did the high priest suggest it himself?" Rahab asked quickly.

"Yes. Why?"

She shivered. "I'm afraid of him—and of Queen Cesera and Captain Kanofer."

"Kalak has been very helpful," Hazor said. "He even gave temple funds to help with the work on the walls. And Cesera stays to herself, as a widow in mourning should."

"Don't trust them too far," Rahab begged. "Remember, they planned to kill you when you came back from Egypt."

217

Hazor took her chin between his fingers and lifted it until he could look into her eyes. "If I could be as sure of everyone's loyalty as I am of yours, Rahab, I would not worry about the fate of Jericho." He kissed her gently. "But Kanofer and the mercenaries are behind me, so I hardly think Kalak and Cesera will cause any trouble. Come, my dear. I must be up early to supervise the work on the gate. And Kalak has requested an audience at the fifth hour to make plans for the ceremony."

The announcement of a great celebration and feast in honor of Baal and his divine spouse did indeed seem to dispel some of the apathy and fear that had gripped the people of Jericho. They busied themselves decking the city in festive array, hanging strips of bright-colored cloth across the streets and preparing great cooking pits in the open space inside the new gate, where whole oxen would be roasted the night before to provide meat for the feast. Long lines of asses plodded up the ramp to the gate each day, bearing all kinds of rare foods and many skins of wine in preparation for the feast.

On the day before the celebration, Myrnah wakened Rahab early and put the baby to her breast. "Our master has promised the people that he will be shown to them for the first time tomorrow. They are talking of nothing else in the city.'

Rahab started up from the couch, breaking off the nursing, and the baby immediately set up a lusty howl of protest. "I will not have it," she cried. "Jaschar must stay here."

"Don't be foolish." Myrnah pushed her back on the couch and dexterously slipped the nipple into the child's mouth again, stopping his wailing at once. "It is time the people saw what a fine young Prince they have."

"But the foot," Rahab protested. She could not have told why she felt such a sudden chill of terror at the idea of letting Jaschar be seen publicly. But whenever she had felt this way before, some danger had always threatened.

"The crowd will not see it," Myrnah assured her. "I will hold Jaschar and keep him wrapped in a blanket. The people will see how strong and fine-looking the baby is and what a kingly voice he has."

"I won't do it," Rahab cried desperately. "I won't show my baby to the crowd."

The old slave stopped her puttering and came over to the couch. "Don't forget you are a slave, Rahab," she said severely. "If it had not been for our master, you would be in a Memphis brothel instead of the favorite concubine of a king."

"I know, but——"

"Our master wants to show the young Prince to the people and let them know he believes Jericho will go on and on, with the child as their King someday."

"This may be only a plot by Kalak and Cesera," Rahab protested. "A plot to harm us all."

"Those two know what is good for them," Myrnah assured her. "And right now nothing is more important than saving Jericho from the Habiru. After that is done, our master will have time to take care of them. The people will love the little Prince as we do, and he will be King of Jericho one day, even if your physician friend does not straighten his foot."

"But cripples are despised in Canaan."

"Not when they bring good fortune. Some make their living letting sick people or those with bad luck touch their deformity. Senu often does that; his hump acts like a charm to bring good luck."

Rahab shivered. "I could never let my baby be used for that."

"He will never have to," Myrnah told her cheerfully, "if you don't do anything foolish. Let Jaschar be shown to the people at the ceremony tomorrow. Then when the Habiru fail to conquer Jericho, the people will say the little Prince brought the favor of the god. After that they will forgive him anything."

What the old slave said could well be true, Rahab knew. If the people of Jericho thought Jaschar had brought them good fortune in the coming struggle with the Israelites, they would almost certainly accept him as Crown Prince—and later as King. Of course, if that happened, all chance of returning to Joshua would be removed—unless she left Jericho without Jaschar, which was unthinkable. And yet even her love for Joshua would not let her keep Jaschar from becoming a king.

"What are you going to do?" Myrnah's blunt voice broke into Rahab's thoughts. "Make a fool of yourself because you despise the Egyptian captain and the other two? Or help your

219

master gain a firm hold upon the people through the child?"

"If you put it that way, I have no choice," Rahab admitted.

"Get up from that couch then, lazy one," Myrnah said crisply, "and go to the bath. Your hair must be washed and we will have to take up your best robe a little. Your breasts are still full, but the rest of you is as slender as it ever was. Many a man will sigh tomorrow when he sees you, and all the wives will hate you for being more beautiful than they are—and the concubine of a king."

Eight

THE day after Salmon's return from his journey a council of the elders and the leading captains of Israel was called to hear what he had to report. Joshua, as usual, presided and harangued them at great length before Salmon was given an opportunity to speak. He reminded them that Yahweh had promised the land of Canaan across the Jordan to the descendants of Abram and that it was now Israel's task to seize and hold it for themselves. He pointed out how they had been able to defeat the forces of King Sihon and King Og in battle and attributed the victory to the combination of their arms and strength and the favor of Yahweh.

When he finished, Caleb rose and faced the crowd. "It may be as Joshua has said, that Yahweh favors us in this undertaking," he admitted. "The priests tell us so, but even the favor of a god will not help him who fights foolishly against too great odds. A little over the span of a moon's course ago I asked Salmon to cross over into Canaan and study the strength of their cities and their defenses, because, being a physician, he can go where none of the rest of us could go."

"And being a physician, not a warrior, he is also liable not to interpret what he sees correctly," Joshua pointed out a little sharply.

"That may be," Caleb admitted. Then he added dryly,

"But I would give my right arm for Salmon's quick mind any day."

A murmur of agreement went up from the captains. "Let Salmon speak," one of them said, "and tell us what he heard and saw in Canaan."

"So be it," Caleb agreed. "I wanted you all to know that Salmon went at my request, because I wished to make sure before we move into battle that we are doing what is best for Israel."

Salmon got to his feet and looked around him at the old men of the elders' council and the younger faces of the captains, their skins leathery and seamed by the wind and sun, their bodies scarred by the effects of many battles. For the most part, they were friendly countenances, eager to hear him. But a few showed hostility, which startled him, for he was sure he did not have an enemy in Israel. Joshua, too, sat with his feet planted sturdily on the ground, scowling, as if he had already decided not to agree with whatever Salmon had to say.

"I left this place with the rising of the sun a moon's course ago," Salmon began. "With me I took two asses and a servant, traveling as I have done before in the disguise of Samma, a physician from Egypt, serving all who have need of my skill."

"And who can pay your price?" one of the captains asked.

"I withhold my skill from no man because his purse is empty," Salmon said; then he added with a twinkle, "But it is well known that the rich have more need of a physician than the poor."

There was a round of laughter at the sally, and he waited for it to cease before continuing. "On the first day I journeyed only as far as Adamah, where the next road above the fords of Jericho crosses the River Jord."

"Why did you stop there?" Joshua asked. "It is only half a day's journey away and a village of no importance."

"I had heard that the earth sometimes falls here and dams the river," Salmon explained.

"Does it?" Caleb asked.

"The old men say they have seen such a thing when the land was cleft by an earthquake," Salmon replied. "They even showed me where the banks of the river had cracked and fallen away."

"Of what importance is this?" Joshua demanded. "I myself heard rumors of this thing, but it could not help us."

"A great earth cliff forms the west bank of the Jord at Adamah," Salmon explained. "If we decided to cross into Canaan there, I believe a few men could dig into the bank where the stream cuts under it and cause the earth to fall into the river. Then we could cross over almost dry-shod and drive the chariots and carts across without wetting their loads."

A murmur of agreement went up from the captains at this information. The fords before Jericho were deep and the current would be strong from the spring freshets at the time they planned to cross into Canaan.

"Why should we choose to cross at Adamah?" Joshua demanded tartly. "It would only mean marching back down the riverbank to Jericho on the other side, with no road to follow."

"Why must we take Jericho?" Salmon countered.

Joshua flushed angrily. "Jericho is the gateway to Canaan. With the city in our hands, the rest of the land promised us by Yahweh lies before us."

"What of the thousands who will be slain upon the walls?" Caleb asked. "Canaan will do us no good without men to hold it and till the fields and plant the grain."

"Even though you take Jericho easily," Salmon added, "Ai and the Hivite towns of Gibeon, Beeroth, Chephirah, and Kirjath-jearim lie beyond it. I have been within their walls and seen their defenses. It will be no easy thing to overcome them."

"The Lord fights on our side!" Joshua pounded the table with his fist. "He has given the lands east of the Jord to us and he will deliver the cities of Canaan in the same way."

"Salmon has seen the land and knows whereof he speaks," Caleb said sharply. "Let us listen to what he has to say and then decide what must be done."

Joshua subsided with poor grace. "Tell us of your travels, Salmon," he said. "But leave military decisions to soldiers."

Salmon flushed at the rebuke but controlled his anger. The most important thing now was the welfare of Israel and the hundreds, even thousands, of men whose lives might be saved if he gave good advice here. Against that, even his

atural wish to spare the city in which Rahab now lived must
bear no great weight. But he must be careful, he reminded
himself, careful lest he allow his own desires to change either
the facts he was laying before the group or his interpretation
of them.

"From Adamah, where I crossed the Jord," he continued,
"the road led northwestward to a tall mountain called Mount
Ebal overlooking both Tirzah and Shechem."

One of the elders, a very old man with a long beard and
palsied hands, spoke. "I remember my father's father telling
now our forefather Jacob came first into the land with his
flocks and herds near a place called Shechem and settled
here."

"My father's father told a story handed down to him," another old man broke in excitedly. "He said that Yahweh put
into the hands of Jacob all the strange gods of that land with
all their wealth and buried them under a great oak near Shechem."

"Since Yahweh delivered the gods of Canaan into the hands
of our forefathers, he will once again destroy them before
us," Joshua boomed triumphantly.

There was a murmur of assent among the captains and
the elders, until Caleb interposed dryly. "It may also prove
that the land promised to our people by Yahweh lies in the
region of this place Shechem, not in the south where the
heavily fortified cities of the Jebusites and the Hivite peoples are located."

"Shechem and Tirzah do not have such strong walls as the
cities to the south, or even Jericho," Salmon added.

"Are they rich?" a younger captain inquired.

Salmon shook his head. "These are a peaceful people, tending their flocks and planting their fields and battling but
little amongst themselves."

Joshua shrugged. "It hardly seems worth the effort to conquer them, then. When the main cities of Canaan with their
wealth are in our hands, the others will fall to us like plums
from a tree."

"There *are* great riches in the cities of the Jebusites and
the Hivites," Salmon admitted. "They told me in Canaan,
too, that the Phoenician cities on the coast of the Great Sea
are richer still."

223

"We have no quarrel with the Phoenicians," said Joshua. "They communicate directly with Egypt by ship. Pharaoh might take action to save them when he would not defend the other cities of Canaan."

"In Urusalim I learned that the King of Jericho has hired mercenaries from Adoni-zedek, the King of that city, to help in the defense of Jericho," Salmon informed them.

"By the beard of Pharaoh!" Caleb exclaimed. "This is news, indeed."

"How many did he hire?" Joshua demanded.

"Some said twenty-five; some fifty."

"But no more?"

"No. Hazor arrived from Egypt with only one Egyptian captain, the man called Kanofer I told you about before. And he had no more than fifty men when he departed from Urusalim."

"You were right, Salmon," Caleb cried. "Hazor got no aid from Pharaoh. He must have hired the mercenaries himself."

"And Jericho will get no aid when we attack," Joshua agreed jubilantly. "What else did you learn, Salmon?"

"I visited the Sea of Chinnereth and the country round it. It is a fair land, flowing with milk and honey. The fruits are sweeter than any in the world, and the fish tastier."

"You shall have it for your domain after we have conquered the country to the south," Joshua promised. "Caleb and I will sit in the sun there and dangle your children upon our knees."

A roar of laughter went up from the captains at this. "Are there no fortified cities in that region?" Caleb asked when the gathering quieted again.

"Megiddo is the greatest." Salmon went on to outline his plan for attacking that center by tunneling underground, but as he talked he realized that his audience was only half listening. Many were already estimating the loot that would be theirs from the rich cities of the Jebusites and the Hivites west of Jericho. With such tempting prizes little more than a day's hard marching beyond the River Jord, they were not interested in such a faraway place as Megiddo.

Joshua, however, was listening intently. Suddenly he interrupted Salmon. "This tunneling method of yours, could it be used to undermine the walls of Jericho?"

224

"I believe so," Salmon admitted. "But it would take much longer. The shaft to the spring already passes beneath the walls of Megiddo."

"If we build a shelter and move it up to the walls," Joshua said excitedly, "could the men tunnel under them with that protection?"

"Not if the defenders poured hot coals down and set the wooden shelter afire." Salmon paused, for an idea had come to him, an idea so simple that he wondered why he had never thought of it before. It was true that this stratagem might mean suffering for Rahab and her baby. But if it delivered the city up without bloodshed, it would be a boon to everyone.

"This idea of a shelter could be carried further," Salmon continued. "We could build it of hewn logs laid close together and covered with dirt as a protection against fire. By placing the shelter on great carts, the whole thing can be pushed up to the spring. Once it is in place, the water supply of Jericho will be cut off and the city will be forced to surrender soon because of thirst."

"By the Baal of Heshbon!" Joshua exclaimed in wonder. "That is an ingenious scheme indeed. And from the shelter we can tunnel under the walls as I proposed. Then I will lead a party of warriors through the tunnel and into the city to open the gate from within. We will take Jericho as we did Heshbon."

Salmon glanced at Caleb and saw that the old captain was grinning broadly. Suddenly Caleb leaped to his feet. "To the fall of Jericho!" he cried. "And to the triumph of Joshua, son of Nun!"

With one voice the men echoed in a mighty shout, "To the fall of Jericho, and the triumph of Joshua."

The matter was decided then and a jubilant Joshua clapped Salmon on the back. "An extra share of the plunder from Canaan will be yours, Salmon," he said magnanimously. "You have done Israel a great service." He strode away, followed by many of the captains, who gathered around him as he walked, eager to hear his every word.

Only Caleb and a few of the others remained behind with Salmon. A quizzical smile on his face, the old warrior watched Joshua's tall form until it disappeared from sight around a row of goatskin tents. Then he turned and put his arm across Salmon's shoulders. "Come to my tent," he said. "We will drink a glass of wine together in honor of your success."

"I had no success," Salmon protested as he followed the sturdy form of his friend to the tent. "I did not even persuade them to march north and cross the river at Adamah."

Caleb poured the wine and handed Salmon a cup. "I long ago gave up trying to convince people of something they don't want to believe, Salmon."

"But northern Canaan as far as the Sea of Chinnereth would fall to us with hardly a battle," Salmon protested. "And we could even take Megiddo by digging into the water tunnel."

"You said yourself the northern cities are not rich," Caleb reminded him.

"But the saving in lives! Don't they consider that?"

"We would still have to attack the cities of the Hivites and the Jebusites, even if we held all of northern Canaan. And since we have to take them anyway, why not do it first?"

"Have you forgotten the bloodshed?"

"No. But sometimes a great leader must expend lives in order to hold the allegiance of his people and tie them solidly together."

"Now you are talking like Joshua," Salmon said bitterly.

"Perhaps that is the reason Joshua is the leader of Israel and I am only second in command," Caleb admitted. "You see, Salmon, to hold his people a military leader must win victories. If he wins booty with it, so much the better. Suppose a thousand men are killed when we storm the walls of Jericho? A thousand women will weep for their sons and husbands, but the rest will see only the plunder. It is hard to be very sad when you are rich, my friend—especially when you have been hungry and a slave all your life."

"What of the priests and their talk of Yahweh giving the land of Canaan to our people?"

Caleb shrugged. "They will love God all the more if He gives them wealth too. Priests are as greedy as anyone else." He poured another cup of wine. "Joshua sees this whole land as belonging to our people and us as a great nation and he may be right. Certainly we will never know for sure until we try to conquer it."

"He could conquer more of Canaan in less time by attacking in the north," Salmon protested. "I have seen the walls of Urusalim and of Gibeon and Beeroth. We will not take those cities in a day."

"Nor a week, I grant you," Caleb agreed. "But with the gold of Jericho, we can hire mercenaries from among the Sa-Gaz and the other peoples besides us that the Canaanites call Habiru. When they see what riches are falling into our hands in Canaan, the young men of Reuben, Gad, and Manasseh will flock to Joshua's standard, too, so we will not lack for warriors."

Salmon shook his head sadly. "Then I am a fool to hope for a time when men will place peace and understanding and love for one another above war and plunder and killing."

"The time may come soon—if we take Canaan for ourselves," Caleb pointed out. "Our people are herdsmen and farmers by choice. When nothing is to be gained by fighting longer, they will settle down to enjoy the fruits of the land that Yahweh gives them. Just now a great soldier is needed to lead us, though, and Yahweh has raised up Joshua to fulfill his promise to our father Abram that this land would belong to his descendants." He looked at the physician keenly. "You are a young man, Salmon, but already you have earned the respect of Israel because of your power to heal and the keenness of your mind——"

"What good does it do me?" Salmon interrupted. "I only use it to further war and bloodshed."

"Your time will come," Caleb assured him. "Either through you or your sons, who will inherit your cleverness and your spirit. When Joshua and Caleb are too old to fight and have no place in the councils, men like you can still show Israel the rewards of peace. Meanwhile, we will attack Jericho in a few weeks and Israel will have no stronger weapon than the power to heal the sick and wounded that Yahweh has put into your hands. Believe me, my son"—the older man put his hands on Salmon's shoulders—"your task may still be greater in the sight of Yahweh than either Joshua's or mine."

Salmon squeezed the grizzled soldier's arm gratefully. "It is you who should lead Israel, my old friend," he said.

Caleb shook his head. "Once I was envious of Joshua, but I can see now that once again Yahweh has raised up the man to fit the task. When we were escaping from Egypt, it was Moses who led us and persuaded Yahweh to send food from the sky and water from the rocks. Now that we must take what is ours by force of arms, he has set up a great hero in Joshua to stir our hearts to deeds of valor. Someday another will come—perhaps you, Salmon, or one of your line—to bring a message of healing and peace and love. God grant he will fire the people to follow him then as Joshua has fired Israel here on the banks of the Jord."

Nine

THE CEREMONY dedicating the new gate of Jericho to Baal was to be held in the late afternoon, but preparations for it had gone on during most of the night before. Whole oxen roasted in pits while attendants basted the flesh with savory herbs and hot spices. Wineskins were placed at convenient spots, for Hazor had wisely decreed that on this day of days, when the Crown Prince would be revealed to his people, no one should either hunger or thirst.

In every house people were up early to bathe themselves and rub perfumed oil into their skins. Hair and beards were clipped and combed and the finest raiment was put on. All the day before, women had been gathering flowers along the river bed where the hot midday sun pouring into the deep cleft through which the Jordan ran brought them into full blossom weeks before they bloomed in the highlands. Now the children were busy plaiting flowers into chaplets and garlands to wear during the merriment that would follow the ceremony.

Myrnah's arguments and Hazor's obvious desire to have the baby shown to the people at the ceremony had finally prevailed over Rahab's premonitions of trouble. She still felt no enthusiasm for the coming celebration, however, although the streets were filled with gaily dancing people and the noise of flutes and drums mingled with shouting and laughter.

Hazor was all smiles when he came in from the gate for

the noonday meal. He seemed happier than Rahab remembered seeing him since the baby was born. "This will be a day long remembered in Jericho," he said. "The people have not been in such a happy mood since the Habiru first appeared across the Jord a year ago."

"You think the city will hold out then?"

"At least until the other kings realize they must come to our aid and stop them before they go any farther. The new gate is strong; it could hold against ten thousand men. And the towers will protect the spring."

Myrnah, too, was happy and clucked over Jaschar like a mother hen as she bathed him and wrapped him in a rich new blanket. "When the people see what fine shoulders the Prince of Jericho has and what a head of hair, they will know that Baal favors him," she said. "And who knows? Our master might even be able to make you his Queen, Rahab, once Cesera and Kalak are out of the way."

"Out of the way?" Rahab looked up quickly from the rouge pots on her dressing table, where she had been brushing color into her cheeks.

"Senu listens to talk everywhere. It is no secret that those two have been plotting against the King and would kill him if they had a chance. But this time they are in for a surprise."

"Our master will not harm them unless they first make a move against him."

Myrnah smiled mysteriously. "The sons of Milkili have not forgotten who killed their father. When the time is right— perhaps tomorrow, when the ceremony is over—they will act."

"The King would not permit it."

Myrnah shrugged. "If people die of a strange malady, who can say what killed them?"

"What about Captain Kanofer?" Rahab asked. "Is he plotting with Kalak and Cesera?"

"That one is too clever for his own good," Myrnah said darkly. "He will hold back and choose the winning side."

Rahab shivered. For a moment she felt an almost overpowering urge to escape somehow from the city and make her way to the Israelite camp at Abel-shittim across the Jord. But she put that thought away at once. In the first place, it would be almost impossible to leave Jericho without being stopped, for Hazor had doubled the guards. Besides, everyone leaving the city was questioned closely lest they give the Habiru important information about its defenses.

In the late afternoon the din of flutes, drums, and the shouting of many voices announced that the people had come to escort their King to the place of celebration. Hazor went first, and a shout of approval greeted him. He was arrayed in his costliest robe and wore the golden crown of authority upon his head, surmounted by the golden serpent that was the symbol of Baal and his divine spouse, the Earth Mother, Ashtarth—or Ashtoreth, as she was sometimes called in this region.

Captain Kanofer, resplendent in a gold-crested helmet and a tunic of snowy-white cloth, and wearing a sword of the new Hittite metal, fell in behind the King with his personal guard. The mercenaries wore the snowy-white short skirts of Egypt beneath embroidered tunics, and their weapons and armor were polished until they shone in the afternoon sun.

At a command from Kanofer, the guard formed an open-sided square surrounding the King and marched out of the courtyard at the head of the royal procession. Next, a litter borne by four giant Nubians stopped before the palace door for Rahab.

She wore a costly robe cut in the Canaanite fashion and richly embroidered in gold and silver. Behind her, Myrnah proudly carried Jaschar upon a brocaded pillow, his body wrapped in a rich cloth that also hid his face so the crowd could not see it until the climax of the ceremony.

Rahab stepped into the litter and took the baby on her lap, while Myrnah walked beside it. The Nubians lifted the carrying handles and the elaborately decorated chair fell into place behind the mercenaries guarding the King. After it marched a long line of the nobles of Jericho, followed by the soldiers recruited from the city itself.

So great was the press of the crowd that the procession was forced to move at a crawling rate down the broad central avenue. And as the crowd shouted good-natured compliments upon her beauty and requests for the child to be held up so they could see it, Rahab felt some of her worries beginning to evaporate. It did indeed seem that no harm could possibly come to a king who was so well liked by so happy a people, or to his concubine and the little Crown Prince she had borne him.

Two costly canopies had been erected in the open space before the gate to shade the viewers from the sun. Beneath the one reserved for the royal family, Hazor took his seat upon a chair covered with a richly embroidered cloth. Rahab's litter stopped before the canopy, and the Nubians lowered the carrying handles. Giving Jaschar to Myrnah, Rahab moved to a seat just behind Hazor, while the old slave placed the baby on a cushioned stool beside her.

While the nobles who had followed the procession were deploying themselves along a row of chairs and sumptuously cushioned benches prepared for them, Rahab looked around her. As captain of the military guard, Kanofer stood beside the King, with his mercenaries flanking him on either side. Rahab had not seen the Egyptian for several weeks, except momentarily when she had happened to pass him in the palace. When her eyes met his now he smiled boldly at her and bowed his golden-crested head in a mocking salute.

Something in Kanofer's manner seemed different—even from his usual impudence and unconcealed lust where she was concerned. It almost seemed as if he knew something, perhaps concerning her, that gave him considerable satisfaction. And yet, Rahab assured herself, nothing could possibly go wrong here before thousands of people who worshiped their new King second only to Baal.

"People of Jericho!" the chamberlain in charge of the ceremonies announced in a loud voice. "Your King will speak to you."

The shouting of the crowd and the sound of flutes, drums, and singing subsided as Hazor rose to his feet. Across the open court from the temporary throne, an altar of Baal had been erected, with a golden image of the god in the familiar form of a bull's head resting on a cabinet behind it. To one side of the image stood Kalak, arrayed in the rich robes of his office. Flanking him on either side were the sacred prostitutes of the temple in gauzy robes with bright-colored flowers in their hair. Just behind them waited other priests, one of whom led a mother goat and her kid, waiting for the ritual sacrifice and the boiling of the kid in its mother's milk

231

that would lure the god from his heavenly abode to bless those on earth.

As Hazor waited for the tumult to subside, Rahab's gaze moved on to the massive gate of hewn logs that had been devised to resist the battering-rams of the Israelites should they try to bring up the engines of battle introduced into warfare centuries before by the fierce warriors from the north. The gate did indeed look powerful enough to withstand even the massive battering-rams, she thought. And beside it the two wooden towers built during the past several weeks towered well above the top of the walls.

Hazor had explained to Rahab that the towers were intended to fulfill a twofold purpose in case of a siege. From the slotted ramparts at their tops, bowmen could lay down a barrage of arrows to keep an invader away from the city's water supply. The other purpose was to place the defenders above the movable siege towers used sometimes by attackers to bring fighting men right up to the tops of the very walls themselves. Word had already come—from farmers visiting the camp of Israel to sell food—that the Habiru were building towers of this type.

"People of Jericho," Hazor began, "I greet you upon this festive occasion when none shall hunger or thirst and not be filled."

A roar of acclamation went up from the crowd at his words. Many had already visited the huge wineskins that had been hanging since early morning at practically every street corner near the gates.

"As you know, a cruel invader waits across the Jord to attack us," Hazor continued. "But the strength of Jericho's walls is exceeded only by the courage of its people." Again he was forced to stop while another roar of approval came from the people.

"With the god of our fathers fighting beside us, we cannot be conquered. I have decreed this day as a time of joy and of intercession with our lord Baal for his favor. Be sure that if our hearts are filled with love and praise for him, our god will not withhold his blessing from us, and Jericho will stand against all her enemies."

"Baal!" A great roar from the crowd. "Bless us, O Baal."

Hazor turned to Kalak. "We invoke the favor of the god

you serve, O Priest. Intercede with him to bless this gate and these towers and the walls that we have built. Beg him to preserve our city from the enemy and to show his favor to us."

A gong sounded at the back of the canopy beneath which stood the golden image of Baal. As Kalak knelt before the image, a low chant was begun by the women, rising in volume. Suddenly it was drowned out by a shout of wonder from the crowd when two doves appeared as if from nowhere to settle down upon the golden horns of the image. Rahab was sure they had been hidden in the flowing sleeves of Kalak's robe, but to the awe-struck crowd it seemed a divine act.

Kalak now rose and, with the help of lesser priests, began to prepare the sacrifice of the kid by boiling it in its mother's milk, the sacrifice whose sweet savor rising to the heavens would lure Baal and his divine consort to earth and win the godly favor for the city. They moved quickly with well-rehearsed precision, while the women chanted softly in the background.

Finally, when the kid's flesh was boiling rapidly in the copper pot, Kalak stepped before the altar and prostrated himself in the dust seven times—invoking the mystic number —before rising and lifting his arms into the air in a gesture of supplication.

"Descend to us, O Baal," he implored. "Fill the sacred image with thy presence." Every eye was fixed expectantly on the golden bull's head under the canopy before Kalak, and hardly a sound came from the great crowd.

"Descend upon us, O Baal," Kalak shouted again. "We have sacrificed to thee, now fill the sacred image with thy presence."

When nothing happened following the second appeal, a murmur went through the crowd, a murmur in which a rising note of fear was easily recognizable. Hazor started to rise, but before he could speak, a man's voice sounded from the crowd.

"Exhibit the young Prince to the god," he shouted. "Surely, Baal will favor us then."

Hazor, too, seized upon this method of placating the crowd and pleasing the god. Signaling Myrnah to lift the child upon its cushion, he stepped down from the throne and walked across to the canopy beneath which Kalak stood. As a slave, Rahab had no right to follow except at her master's order, but she did not stop to think of that. Rising quickly, she walked beside Myrnah, steadying the cushion upon which the baby lay. Hazor gave her a quick approving smile, but she could see that he was concerned by this unexpected complication in the ceremony.

Kalak had stepped from beneath the canopy to meet them. The four, with the child, now stood almost in the center of the circular open space just under the gate. At a word from Hazor, Myrnah knelt before the high priest and extended the cushion upon her outstretched arms. Gently Kalak parted the wrappings to expose the baby's head, then turned and faced the golden image, lifting his arms to the sky once more.

"O god of Jericho and of Canaan," he intoned. "Look with favor, we beg, upon the child Jaschar, son of him who rules this people in thy name."

The crowd waited expectantly, but still nothing happened. And now the swelling murmur was pregnant with a rising hysteria. Rahab sensed that the sign they were awaiting must be something more dramatic than the simple announcement by Kalak that the god approved, but had no idea yet what it would be.

Suddenly Kalak turned back to Myrnah and the child. Before either Rahab or Hazor could divine his intention and move to stop him, he had lifted Jaschar from Myrnah's startled grasp, holding him aloft naked, except for a diaper of fine linen. And at the sight of the twisted foot, a great baying note of terror went up from the crowd.

"Baal has spoken his anger against Jericho and its King," Kalak shouted. "See how the god crippled the child as a sign of his wrath."

"Have mercy, O Baal," someone shouted, and the crowd took up the cry in a frenzied wail of terror. On all sides people were falling to the ground, beating the dust with their hands or jerking in convulsions of fear, crying out to Baal for his mercy.

Rahab had started forward to wrest the child from Kalak's grasp, but two lesser priests seized her arms, holding her back. Hazor, too, seemed struck dumb, and Myrnah had fallen to the ground, prostrating herself before Kalak and the image on the cabinet.

In the midst of the pandemonium the same loud voice that had demanded that Jaschar be shown to the people now sounded again. "A sacrifice! Let us make a sacrifice to the god!"

"Let the god speak," Kalak shouted above the turmoil, as if, Rahab thought in a sudden moment of revelation, he were speaking a part in a well-rehearsed drama. "Baal will tell his people what sacrifice will appease his wrath."

All eyes were drawn once again to the golden bull's head. At any other time it would have been obvious to Rahab that the cabinet upon which the image rested was quite large enough for a man to hide beneath and thus manipulate the so-called god as he wished. But she was too concerned now to think of anything except the threat to her baby.

"Speak, O Baal!" Kalak implored. "Speak to thy people."

As if in answer to his plea, two twin jets of smoke shot from the open nostrils of the golden bull.

"The sign!" Kalak shouted. "Baal has given us a sign!"

Again as if Kalak's announcement were a cue, the man with the loud voice shouted at the back of the crowd: "Bury the child beneath the gate of Jericho, and the god's wrath will be appeased."

"No! No!" Rahab cried in futile protest, but the high priest had already turned to the image of the god.

"Speak, O Baal," he begged. "Tell us thy will."

Once again twin jets of smoke spurted from the nostrils of the golden bull. And at the sight of it, the crowd roared as one man, baying with the blood lust which—Rahab realized now in an instant of clear thought even amid the pandemonium—Kalak had carefully built up to this climax.

"The god has spoken!" Kalak announced. "Place the child in a jar and bury it beneath the gate so Baal will forever keep the enemies of Jericho from entering."

"Stop them!" Rahab pleaded with Hazor, tugging at his sleeve. "Kalak arranged this so he could kill Jaschar and leave you without an heir."

Indecision and doubt were mirrored in the face of the King of Jericho as he fought between his love for the pitifully deformed child and submission to the god he had been taught to fear since childhood.

"You heard it all!" Rahab cried. "Don't you see how he is using all this to turn the people against you?"

Hazor's face cleared then. When he spoke, his voice was loud and clear, stopping the clamor of the crowd at once.

"The child will not be harmed," he ordered, and turned to Kanofer. "Arrest the false priest Kalak, and——"

Standing close beside Hazor, Rahab heard the whir of the arrow, like the angry buzzing of a hornet in her ear. But to the crowd it must indeed have seemed to come from no-where—or from the hand of an invisible god.

The thud as the missile struck Hazor's body was a sound Rahab would never forget. Just as she would never forget the startled look on her master's face as he sank to the ground, blood already beginning to gush from his mouth, the point and shaft of an arrow driven completely through his heart.

Ten

LATER, when she found time to think about the tragedy, Rahab could easily see how the whole affair had been planned by Kalak to achieve Hazor's death and yet have the crowd believe it came from divine displeasure. The arrow itself had been the simplest part. A skilled bowman at the top of the tall gate tower had only to rise momen-tarily, aim, and release the bowstring, falling back out of sight once he had loosed the murder weapon. In the con-fusion, however, she thought of none of these things, her first concern being for Jaschar. And since the priests who held her had been startled, too, at the seeming intervention by Baal to cause Hazor's death, she was able to wrest the baby from Kalak's grasp.

An angry roar had gone up from the crowd at Hazor's re-fusal to do what they considered to be the will of Baal in allowing the child to be buried beneath the gate, as was the common custom in Jericho. Whether the people would have

236

forced their King to capitulate, tearing Jaschar to pieces themselves in a fury of fear lest the anger of Baal be visited upon the city would never be known now. No one except Rahab seemed to realize that this whole affair had been cleverly planned from the start to place Hazor in a position where he must refuse to obey the apparent will of Baal and thus stir the wrath of the people. That Kalak had expected Hazor to recognize his stratagem and refuse to obey seemed evident, too, by his having placed the bowman in the tower, ready to shoot down the King at the proper moment.

Kalak broke the awed silence of the crowd as Hazor's body slowly collapsed to the ground. "The arrow of Baal has struck the King down for his blasphemy," he cried. "The god has spoken."

There was no response from the crowd, stunned by the suddenness of the King's death. But the wily priest was taking no chance that they might put a different interpretation on what had happened. "Baal has spoken," he repeated. "Let the child be sacrificed."

At that announcement, the crowd found its voice again in a low animal note of fear. In an instinctive but futile effort to escape, Rahab turned and started with Jaschar toward the empty throne where Hazor had been sitting, as if it might still possess some power to give refuge to her. But she was immediately ringed in by the hard-faced mercenaries and could go no farther.

Suddenly a new note of drama was added to the scene. Kanofer had been standing beside the empty throne, and as Rahab turned, desperately seeking some way to save her baby, he spoke an order. Four of the mercenaries formed a cordon around her with drawn spears, and Kanofer's trumpeter sounded a blast that stopped the few members of the crowd who had surged forward to keep Rahab from escaping with the baby.

"The child Jaschar is the heir to the throne of Jericho," Kanofer announced. "I hereby place it under the protection of Pharaoh."

Kalak looked as if the arrow had struck him instead of Hazor. He opened his mouth to speak, but no words came. Before he could grope for something to say, Kanofer continued. "It is the will of Pharaoh that Kalak shall rule as

237

King," he announced, "until a successor to the throne of Jericho can be decided."

Belatedly Kalak seemed to realize that the crowd was waiting for him to play the next scene in this macabre drama. Moistening his lips with his tongue, he managed to speak, but as if each word caused him pain. "The noble Kanofer speaks well. I accept the task of preserving Jericho until the decision of Pharaoh is made known to us."

The crowd seemed to realize for the first time now that their beloved ruler was dead and the hated Kalak King in his place. An angry murmur arose, but Kanofer obviously had no intention of letting a public demonstration against Kalak begin. At his order, the soldiers who lined the front ranks of the crowd turned, their spears ready. And in the face of this show of force, the people subsided meekly.

For the first time the Egyptian captain spoke directly to Rahab. "I will take you and the child where you will be safe under guard," he said in low tones without turning his head. "Do not resist."

"Can't—can't they show even a little respect for their King?"

"The dead are dead," Kanofer said curtly. "I am concerned with the living. Obey my orders and you and your brat may come through this alive." He gave a sharp command, and the hollow square of soldiers—with Rahab, Myrnah, and Jaschar in the center—moved away from the open place where tragedy had so recently struck. For a moment it seemed that the now half-rebellious crowd would not let them through, but the forefront fell back before the naked spear points of the mercenaries, making an aisle for them to pass through.

Rahab had naturally assumed that they would return to the palace, but a little way beyond the gate, the column turned and halted before a two-story house standing against the wall, with a small courtyard before it. Unceremoniously they were herded into the house and up to a chamber on the second floor. The door was slammed shut with equal brusqueness, closing them up inside. In the silence that followed, Rahab heard the measured tread of the soldier on guard and knew that, even though Kanofer had publicly announced Jaschar as heir to the throne of Jericho, they were actually his prisoners.

The room that formed their prison was sparsely furnished, containing a broad couch, a bench, and a chest of rough workmanship, evidently for storing clothes. One side of the house seemed continuous with the wall of Jericho, for from the window Rahab could see the hills of Canaan, now mantled with dusk at the approach of the night. The other window looked down upon a courtyard from which came the rattle of arms, the loud voices of the mercenaries, and the occasional shrill laugh of a woman.

"Whose house do you suppose this is, Myrnah?" Rahab asked.

"Captain Kanofer's," the old slave said dully. "He calls it an inn, but it is really a brothel."

From belowstairs came the sound of men's voices, followed by a woman's squeal.

"I have heard scandalous things about this place," Myrnah said, brightening a little at the chance to gossip. "The Egyptian captain quarters the mercenaries here so the women can steal their pay when they are not robbing travelers. Then he makes the harlots give him part of their earnings."

"Why would Kanofer bring us here?"

"Where else could he take you? Kalak is King now." Myrnah drew a long sigh. "If only I had put the Egyptian poison in Kalak's and Cesera's wine. Then the priest would never have been able to invoke the wrath of Baal."

"He did not invoke it, Myrnah."

"But the arrow——"

"I was standing beside Prince Hazor and heard the whir of the arrow. It was shot from one of the towers beside the gate."

Myrnah started to weep again, and Rahab put her arm around the old slave's shoulders to comfort her. "I loved our master too, Myrnah," she said. "But he is dead and all our weeping will not bring him back. We must think of a way to protect Jaschar and ourselves."

"What can we do? Captain Kanofer has us at his mercy."

"Whatever we must do we will do," Rahab said resolutely. "I have friends in the Habiru camp, if we can manage to reach them. Our job now is to find a way."

Jericho was in a ferment that night, but toward morning the tumult subsided somewhat. Shortly after dawn Senu appeared, having hidden in the crowd after the murder of Hazor until he could follow them to the inn. From the hunchback they learned that Kalak had been crowned King of Jericho shortly before midnight and that he and Cesera were in control of the palace. Kanofer was the real ruler, however, by virtue of his control of the soldiers. He had chosen to let Kalak sit upon the throne, but only because at the moment that suited his purpose.

Rahab, the servants, and the baby were treated well enough. A guard continuously paced outside the door of the room in which they were prisoners, blocking the only route of escape, but Myrnah was allowed to descend to the courtyard, where fires had been kindled for cooking. She was given food for them all and even allowed to bring water for bathing from a cistern that was filled daily by slaves from the spring outside the gate.

Rahab had been expecting momentarily to hear from Kanofer, but it was early evening before he appeared. He was obviously tired, and his tunic appeared not to have been changed since the day before, but there was a satisfied look on his face. He ordered the servants from the room and, removing his helmet with its golden crest bearing the emblem of Pharaoh, sank down upon the couch.

"Bring me wine," he ordered, and Rahab thought it best to obey, filling his cup from the wineskin Myrnah had brought up with the food.

"Why did you bring us here?" she asked.

Kanofer took a long draught of the wine and wiped his lips with the back of his hand. "To save your lives, why else?"

"Why would you save us after killing the King?"

"Hazor was struck down by Baal in just retri——"

"He was killed by an arrow from a bowman hiding in the tower beside the gate," Rahab said sharply.

"So?" Kanofer grinned. "You have not lost your spirit, beautiful one. I had hardly hoped for as much."

"I can recognize murder when I see it."

Kanofer shrugged. "Hazor was a dangerous man. He thought more of the people than he did of filling his own purse and letting the nobles enrich themselves. It was inevitable that someone would kill him from the moment he was crowned King."

"Why did it have to be you? He trusted you, and you were sent by Pharaoh to protect him."

For the first time Kanofer showed anger. "I did not place the bowman. He came from Kalak's own guard."

"But you knew he was there."

"Let us rather say it fitted my own purpose for him to be there."

"Then you could have prevented the King's death."

"I suppose I could have," he admitted, "but someone would have assassinated him tomorrow. There are plenty of people in Jericho who hated Hazor."

"And more who loved him."

"Granted. But those who hated him are rich and the people who loved him are poor. Naturally the rich would win out eventually. They always do."

"So you chose the winning side?"

"I always choose the winning side," Kanofer assured her urbanely.

"Why didn't you kill me and the baby then?"

"Because it suited my purpose to keep both of you alive."

"For how long?"

He studied her appraisingly, and now she saw a familiar light begin to burn in his eyes.

"That will depend on you," he said frankly.

If Rahab had ever doubted his meaning, she could no longer. From the very moment Kanofer's mercenaries had surrounded her after Hazor's death, there had been no question of his purpose as far as she was concerned.

"I am glad we understand each other," Kanofer continued. "It will save a lot of explanation."

"Suppose I refuse to—to bow to your will?"

He smiled. "I think you *would* refuse, Rahab—if you were the only one concerned." His eyes flicked to the baby sleeping in its wrappings in the corner of the room. "But you are a mother! I hardly think you will condemn your child to death."

Rahab caught her breath. She had half—perhaps more than half—expected this. But the bald statement could still shock her.

Kanofer's manner had been light so far; now his voice hardened. "I have desired you since the first time I saw you,

241

Rahab, at that brothel in Memphis. Hazor was able to out-bid me for you then, and it suited my purpose to let him have you—for a while. But what I want I usually get - eventually. Please me, and you live—with the child. Displease me, and the child dies. It is as simple as that."

"Why not kill me too?"

"You are beautiful enough to bring a good price in the slave market. Besides, I can always use beautiful girls here."

"In a brothel!"

Kanofer shrugged. "The first time I saw you we were in a brothel. Your fortunes almost made you a queen, Rahab, but you were still a harlot."

"I was never a harlot," Rahab cried. "You know that."

Kanofer shrugged. "A concubine, then," he conceded. "I suppose there is a difference. From now on, though, you will sell your body to me—and whoever else it pleases me to let use you—in exchange for the life of your child." He got to his feet. "I am weary today, and a beautiful woman should be enjoyed only when a man is rested. See that your servant bathes you and rubs perfumed oil into your skin tomorrow. And put on one of the Egyptian robes, the kind you wore for Hazor. In the evening we will dine together and . . ." He did not finish the sentence, but she had no doubt of his meaning as he lifted the golden-crested helmet from the couch and went to the door. With his hand upraised to push it open, he turned back to her. "And don't think you are not being honored," he reminded her. "I could have any woman in Jericho. You should be flattered that I chose you."

Strangely enough, Rahab found that she could look upon him—and herself—with complete detachment, as if she were seeing this drama from a distance. "Desire for me is not the real reason you spared us," she told him. "You would never let such a thing interfere with your main purpose."

Kanofer's full lips curved in a smile of admiration. "You are something very rare, Rahab. A beautiful woman who is not also a fool."

"Then there is another purpose?"

"Of course. You heard me tell Kalak he could be King un·til the successor to the throne of Jericho can be determined.'

"By Pharaoh?"

He laughed. "By me, in the name of Pharaoh."

"Do you dare to gamble that Pharaoh would uphold you?" Rahab challenged.

"Our master in Egypt will not intervene in Jericho, whatever happens here. The Habiru will attack soon, in a few weeks at most. If the city stands, I will depose Kalak when the danger is past and rule here as regent for Hazor's heir—in the name of Pharaoh and with Hazor's concubine as my own."

"Suppose the city falls?"

"I shall stop the fighting when there is no longer hope. The Habiru are no fools; they will hardly molest the representative of Egypt, especially when he hands the city over to them."

"So you win either way?"

"Of course. I planned it that way a long time ago. Just as I planned to have you. I shall be busy with the political affairs for several weeks," he added. "In addition to pleasing me, your duties will also include managing this establishment."

"Must I be a brothel-keeper too?"

Kanofer shrugged. "I saw you first in one, remember? And since you are a harlot now, it is no more than fitting. Until tomorrow . . ."

With a mocking bow he was gone.

Myrnah came back into the room, her eyes still wide with fear. She gave Rahab a quick look and went over to the improvised crib. Realizing that Jaschar, too, was safe, she turned back with a puzzled look in her eyes. Rahab answered her question before it was voiced.

"We are all safe, Myrnah, for the time being at least."

"The Egyptian captain decided to be generous?"

"The Egyptian captain is protecting us—for a price."

"What price?" The old slave's eyes were round.

"What other price can a harlot pay when she has no gold?" All emotion had gone out of Rahab's voice. "As long as I please him and the men whose favor he seeks—and run this brothel at a profit—we all live. When I fail—we die."

The old slave looked at her for a long moment. "One day your god will avenge you, Rahab, and reward you for your sacrifice. I know he will."

Rahab laughed, and the sound was like the cracking of blown glass.

"It is more a time for weeping than laughing," the old slave said severely. "Weeping—and praying."

"I will weep no more, Myrnah," Rahab said in a hard, bitter voice. "The people of Medeba named me a harlot first, when I did not deserve it. Now I do. Henceforth I shall be known as—the harlot of Jericho."

Book Four

THE HARLOT OF JERICHO

And they went, and came into an harlot's house, named Rahab, and lodged there.

JOSHUA 2:1

One

NEITHER the *moreh*, the autumn rains that made it possible to plow and sow the winter grain crops, nor the *gesem*, as the winter rains were called, had been great during the period that the children of Israel dwelt in the land of the Amorites, hard by the fords of the Jord between Abel-shittim and Jericho. As a result, the land was parched and dry except for a narrow band on each side of the river. But the *malquosh*, or spring rains, were abundant, filling the springs and rivulets in the mountain country west of the Jord and bringing ample water to supply an army and a people on the march.

Joshua was impatient to move the army he had assembled westward across the Jord against their first target, the walled city of Jericho. Travelers had reported, however, that the defenses of Jericho were being strengthened and also that some sort of political upheaval had taken place inside the walls, so he was anxious to obtain information as to the exact conditions inside the city before they attacked. Salmon was not surprised, therefore, when he received a summons one rainy morning to appear in the magnificent tent, captured from King Og, that Joshua used as his headquarters in the military camp at Abel-shittim. Caleb and several of the leading captains were also present.

"Israel has need of you again, Salmon," Joshua said without preamble when the physician had seated himself on a cushion in the circle of men and accepted a cup of wine.

"My supplies are ready," Salmon assured him. "We have ample medicine and cloth for dressing wounds."

"Your skill will be needed when we go against Jericho," Joshua conceded. "I have another task for you now—or rather for the physician called Samma."

Salmon smiled. "He is probably the only Egyptian who would serve Israel now."

"Before we launch the attack against Jericho," Joshua continued, "we must learn everything we can about the city's defenses."

"Don't you have patrols watching the city?"

"The information we seek can be found only within Jericho itself. As the physician Samma, you were able to penetrate the strongholds of Canaan without difficulty, so Jericho should be easy for you."

"The people of Jericho are on guard," Salmon pointed out. "They will be suspicious of any stranger."

"That was exactly my argument against asking you to go," Caleb interposed. "I don't think we should ask it of you or anyone else, Salmon."

"Nor I." Another of the captains, named Khalith, spoke up. "It is one thing to send a man into battle where he has an even chance against his enemies. But if Salmon is taken inside Jericho, he will lose his head."

"The life of every one of us must be sacrificed if it is for the good of Israel," Joshua said sharply. "No one person is better than another."

"Then why not go yourself?" Caleb asked.

Before the argument could go any further, Salmon intervened. "Joshua is right," he said. "Any Israelite would be sure of death if he entered Jericho. But as Samma, the physician, I can pretend to come from Urusalim on my way to Damascus. When I display my medicines and skills in the courtyard of an inn, no one will suspect me of being other than what I pretend to be."

"It is settled then," Joshua said with satisfaction. "Now we must decide who will go with you."

"Why should anyone else risk his life?" Salmon objected.

An odd silence descended upon the half circle of men.

When no one spoke, Salmon looked inquiringly around at them. "Is something wrong?" he asked.

Joshua spoke, his tone hearty. "We were discussing the risk before you came, Salmon," he said. "And we had decided a soldier should go with you, one of the captains."

"If there is trouble, it would be fine to have a strong sword arm beside me," Salmon agreed. "But with the odds against us if we are discovered in Jericho, fighting skill will make little difference."

"The son of Nun is not concerned about fighting skill," Caleb said dryly. "He wants one of the captains there to inspect the military preparations."

"You are not a soldier, Salmon," Joshua hurried to say. "It would not be fair to ask you to estimate the military strength of Jericho."

"Why not say what you mean?" Salmon said quietly. "You want me to go into Jericho, but you do not trust me to bring back an honest report."

"It is just that we believe a warrior could tell more about the defenses of the city."

"Tell him your real reason, Joshua," Caleb said gruffly. "Because Salmon suggested crossing the Jord at Adamah and attacking the northern cities, you no longer trust his judgment."

Salmon nodded slowly. "Joshua may be right at that. There are—reasons—why I might not advise you well in the case of Jericho. I will take whoever you decide should go with me. He can be disguised as my servant."

"I will go," Caleb said quickly. "If they catch us in Jericho," he added with a grin, "we will at least have the satisfaction of taking a few of their men with us."

The very next day the physician Samma embarked once more on his travels. With him went his slave, Ammiel, a powerful, grizzled man with a craggy face. They journeyed north to Adamah and thence westward across the Jord and into the Canaanite uplands. When finally they approached Jericho, several days later, it was from the direction of Urusalim. And since the physician boasted of healing the sick in that city, as well as in Megiddo, Gibeon, and Beeroth, no one suspected that he was actually one of the hated Habiru from across the Jord to the east.

Two

IN JERICHO, Rahab had long since learned the third lesson of love; namely, that to protect her child, a woman can prostitute her body and feel no shame, no real degradation, only a cold hate for the man who forces her to do so—and a burning determination to kill him at the first opportunity.

The political situation had settled down into a contest that resembled nothing so much as a tense game of *tshau,* or robbers, between skilled players, with the life of each hanging on the outcome. Kalak and Cesera ruled upon the sufferance of Kanofer but plotted constantly against him. And the Egyptian captain busied himself increasing his hold on the military forces. Meanwhile the rains poured down and the hour of doom for Jericho grew daily nearer.

Rahab was busy with preparations for the evening meal in the establishment she supervised for Kanofer—the Egyptian being in Gibeon on a mission to make one last appeal to the Hivites for a defensive union against the Habiru—when Myrnah came running excitedly to her.

"Rahab!" she cried. "I have good news."

Rahab smiled, and some of the harsh lines that had been etched into her face these past weeks were momentarily softened. "It will be a welcome change from what we usually have, Myrnah. What is this news of yours?"

"A physician has just set up shop in the courtyard. He claims to come from Egypt."

Rahab caught her breath. It could not be Salmon, she told herself. Even he would not dare come into Jericho at such a time as this, when every newcomer was suspected of being a spy.

"Let me show Jaschar to him," Myrnah begged. "He may be able to straighten his foot."

"Take the physician to my room," Rahab directed Even

if the newcomer was not Salmon, it would do no harm to let him see the baby's foot. "I will come as soon as I finish what I am doing."

Rahab hurried through her work and upstairs to her room. She heard voices inside and hesitated, her hand on the door, reluctant to enter and hear the verdict of the physician, lest it be unfavorable. Then, straightening her shoulders, she pushed the door open and stepped into the room.

Salmon was examining Jaschar, who lay on his face on the couch, kicking and cooing. Even before she met the physician's eyes, Rahab knew he had already recognized who the baby's father was. A quick warmth burned in Salmon's eyes when they met hers, but he made no other sign of recognition, for Myrnah was in the room.

"I brought the physician and his slave up here as you told me," Myrnah said. "He says he never saw a finer boy."

With an effort Rahab forced a note of calmness into her voice. "You did well, Myrnah. Our guest and his servant must be tired and thirsty; go down and bring them food and wine."

As soon as the servant departed, Rahab ran across the room and threw herself into Salmon's arms. He held her while she sobbed on his breast, and when finally she recovered from her momentary breakdown he dried her eyes with his sleeve. Realizing for the first time then that someone else was in the room, she drew away from him.

"It is only Caleb posing as my servant," Salmon said with a smile. "You remember him from the Cave of Yah, don't you?"

Rahab began to laugh, a little hysterically. "Are all the captains of Israel your servants now, Salmon?" she asked.

"They should be," Caleb said with a grin; then he added, "You have changed since last I saw you, girl."

Rahab's face hardened. "For the worse. You find me a harlot, running a brothel."

Caleb shrugged. "Yesterday I was a general; today I am a slave to help my people. I'll wager you are not a brothel-keeper by choice."

"No," Rahab admitted. "And now that you are here, I pray it will not be much longer. What do you think of Jaschar, Salmon?"

"He is a fine, strong boy, like his father."

249

"You saw the marks on his shoulders then?"

"We did not need to see them," Caleb said. "I would know Joshua's child anywhere."

"I sent for you when he was born, Salmon," she said. "But they told Senu you were away. I—I was hoping you could straighten his foot."

Salmon bent over the baby once more, moving the deformed foot with strong, skilled fingers. When he raised his head Rahab saw the answer to her question on his face. "Nothing can be done then?" she asked.

"If it were only twisted, I might straighten the bones and hold them until they grew in the right position," he said. "But see how the foot points downward because the cord here behind the heel is too short. I can try to stretch it, but there is little hope."

Coming on top of all the things that had happened lately, this was a heavy blow to Rahab. "I suppose this is a—a punishment from Yah because I lay with Joshua when we were not wed," she said slowly.

"The god you worship is a god of kindness," Salmon assured her. "Many children are born deformed. Yah would not do such a thing to you merely because you loved Joshua."

Rahab shook her head slowly. "It seems that I left Yah behind in the Cave on Mount Nebo. Sometimes I think I will never find him again."

Salmon took her gently by the shoulders and made her face him. "You told me once that the temple of Yah is in the hearts of those who love and serve him, Rahab. Never let yourself doubt that for a moment."

"But my baby is a cripple, an outcast," she wailed.

"He is Joshua's son. In Israel he will be respected, if only because of that."

With an effort she gained control of herself. "Do you expect to take Jericho soon?"

"Joshua sent us to study the defenses of Jericho, but Caleb thinks one of the mercenaries at the gate may have recognized him. The man looked closely at us when we came through."

"Then we have no time to lose," Rahab said quickly. "What is it you want to find out?"

Salmon shook his head. "You told me in Memphis how kind

250

Prince Hazor was to you. I would not ask you to betray him by giving us information about Jericho."

"The King is dead, struck down by a traitor's arrow." Quickly she gave them an account of what had happened in the past several weeks, the tragic ending of the ceremony dedicating the gate, Kanofer's taking control, and the uneasy truce that now existed between him and Kalak and Cesera.

"What of the walls?" Caleb asked. "Have they been strengthened?"

"Only at the gate. The towers are mainly to protect the spring. The cracks in the walls have only been plastered over with mud."

"They are still strong," Caleb pointed out. "If the city is well defended by the people——"

"There is no courage left in the hearts of anyone in Jericho. They know Yahweh has given this land to you. Such a fear has fallen upon them that they will melt away before you once the walls are breached."

"That may be," Caleb admitted. "But how shall we breach them?"

"That I do not know," Rahab told him. "But all of Jericho has been filled for months with talk of what you did to King Sihon and King Og."

The door opened and Myrnah came in, her face white. "Soldiers are in the courtyard," she gasped. "They say two of the Habiru are in the house."

Three

AT MYRNAH'S WORDS, Caleb's hand dropped to his side where his sword always hung. But as the slave of a physician he wore only a small dagger, a useless weapon against armed soldiers.

"Did you betray us, woman?" he demanded, seizing Myrnah by the wrist.

The slave's eyes almost popped out. "Then you are Hab——"

251

"Quickly, did you tell them we were here?"

"No," Myrnah gasped. "I did not know they were seeking you."

"These are the friends I told you about, Myrnah," Rahab explained hurriedly. "Where can we hide them while the soldiers are searching the house?"

"I was drying rushes on the roof this morning," Myrnah said. "It is dark already, and they could hide up there beneath the grasses."

"The roof can be reached from just outside this door," said Rahab. "We must move quickly."

"Don't involve yourself in this, Rahab," Salmon begged. "Show us where to go and we will do the rest."

"I owe Kalak a debt," she assured him grimly. "For King Hazor's sake. Hurry up the steps to the roof."

Darkness had already fallen and the night breeze was beginning to ripple the piles of rushes on the roof when they reached it by way of a ladder from the second story. Caleb and Salmon burrowed beneath the piled-up rushes, pulling the dried grass over them until they were completely hidden. But as Rahab turned back to descend the ladder to her room, the sound of men's voices on the floor below stopped her.

She was trapped on the roof.

Rahab's mind raced as she considered the best thing to do in the desperate situation in which she now found herself. At all costs she must keep Salmon and Caleb from being captured, for the information they would take back to Joshua concerning the fear that gripped the people might help capture Jericho. And if the city were taken, she would be free at last from Kanofer and the hateful servitude into which he had forced her.

Suddenly she thought of a way of hiding the presence of the two men beneath the rushes. The soldiers knew her for a harlot—as did all Jericho—so the logical thing to do was to play the part. Quickly she pulled her robe from her shoulders and dropped it to her waist, exposing the upper part of her body as she moved to the opening where the ladder gave access to the roof.

By now the soldiers had reached the second floor in their search and were at the foot of the ladder. "I am up here," Rahab called. "Are you looking for me?"

252

One of them held a torch above his head and peered upward. "You are early," she called down. "I was cooling myself on the roof before the evening begins." Belatedly she pretended to realize that she was naked to the waist and slowly pulled up the top of her robe.

A man wearing the helmet of an officer elbowed his way through the others to the foot of the ladder. "We do not seek pleasure tonight," he told her. "At least not yet. One of the guards at the gate thinks he recognized a pair of men who came through a few hours ago as Habiru. He says they came here to the inn."

"Two men did come here," Rahab said. "But they left just after dark in time to get out of the city before the gate was closed."

The officer frowned. "We know nothing of their going out. They were seen to come here."

"You can search the roof if you like," Rahab offered.

The captain climbed the ladder and came out on the roof. As he looked around, Rahab moved closer until her body was touching his, hoping to keep his attention from centering on the piles of rushes drying on the roof. "You can see there is nobody here but me," she assured him, then added in a lower tone, "Unless I have a visitor later."

The officer put a hard arm around her waist. He drew her against him and bent to kiss her roughly. Rahab rigidly controlled the shiver of revulsion that went through her and with a lithe movement freed herself from his embrace.

"I don't know where the men went," she said. "But you will have to pursue them quickly if you hope to overtake them in the darkness."

"We will go after them," the captain promised. "They must have gone toward the ford of the Jord and the Israelite camp. But when I return——"

"Rahab waits for no man," she assured him with a shrug. "Except Kanofer?"

"The Egyptian has gone to Gibeon and will not return for several days. Shall I sit alone and pine for him?"

The captain was already descending the ladder. To keep from rearousing his suspicions, Rahab followed him down and out into the courtyard. She stood watching until the soldiers disappeared in the direction of the gate. Going back into the house then, she went to the storeroom and searched until she found a length of strong cord. It was scarlet in color, having been wrapped around a dyer's pack, but there was nothing else strong enough to hold a man.

Hiding the cord under her robe, Rahab went quickly up to her room, where Myrnah was guarding Jaschar, and examined the window opening on the west side, away from the city. The distance to the ground was still greater than the length of the rope, she estimated, but she was sure Salmon and Caleb could drop the rest of the way without being hurt. The way of escape was clear at the moment, for the soldiers had gone eastward toward the fords of the Jord.

Salmon and Caleb were still hidden under the rushes when Rahab reached the roof again. They shoved the grass aside and crawled out, picking bits of straw and leaves from their clothing.

"The soldiers have gone toward the fords looking for you," she told them breathlessly. "If you hide in the mountains to the west tonight, you can make your way to the river later."

"We cannot get through the gate," Caleb objected. "They will have doubled the guards by now."

"I have a rope in my room," Rahab explained as she led the way down the ladder. "You can climb through the window and down the wall."

"By the Tablets of the Law!" Caleb said admiringly. "You have a clever head on those beautiful shoulders of yours, girl."

Working swiftly, the men tied one end of the rope to the bench and let the other out the window. Salmon, being the slenderer one, leaned out, Caleb holding his feet, and strained his eyes down into the darkness. When he wriggled back into the room, his face was flushed, but there was a look of satisfaction on it.

"We will have only a short drop from the end of the rope," he reported. Then his face sobered. "But how will we get the baby down the rope?"

"You two must go without us," Rahab said. "We would only hold you back."

"The guards will return and——"

"They will think you escaped them in the darkness. Hurry

now, but promise me one thing. When Jericho falls, swear that we will be saved."

"I swear it," Caleb said promptly. "By the name of Yahweh."

"And I," Salmon agreed. He picked up the slender rope by which they planned to escape. "Bind this scarlet cord in the window. Then no one can fail to recognize your house."

"You need have no fear," Caleb assured her. "You nor anyone in your house."

At Salmon's insistence, Caleb went first. He let himself down feet first, while Rahab, Salmon, and Myrnah steadied the bench to which the rope was tied. For what seemed an eternity the rope was tense with the Israelite captain's weight, then suddenly it slackened and they heard a soft thud from outside.

Tensely they waited for a sign that Caleb had safely negotiated the descent. Then a low whistle sounded from the darkness outside and Salmon gave Rahab's arm a quick squeeze in farewell. Wiry and agile, he had no trouble lowering himself from the window. Myrnah and Rahab held the bench until the sudden slackening of the rope told them he had fallen clear, then Rahab climbed up on it and put her head and shoulders through the window.

She could see little outside, but when Salmon's low whistle sounded beneath her, Rahab was able to distinguish two dim figures moving across the rocky ground outside the wall toward the towering black shadows of the mountains to the west. Only when they were out of sight did she step down from the bench and draw the scarlet cord back through the window. Quickly she untied it from the bench and hid it beneath the baby's wrappings where he lay asleep in an improvised crib in the corner.

Dawn was just beginning to break when Rahab awoke with the same strange feeling of impending disaster that had warned her before of danger. She did not realize at first what had awakened her. But when the couch on which she lay seemed to be tilted slowly by a giant hand, she was no longer in doubt, for she had experienced this sensation many times before.

It was an earth tremor, a shaking of the land like an

255

animal aroused from sleep, which often presaged an earthquake at this time of the year.

With no thought for her own safety, Rahab leaped from the couch and ran to the corner where Jaschar lay. She took the baby in her arms, protecting it with her body. As she knelt there, another tremor shook the room and a large crack opened in the side that was part of the wall of Jericho. Plaster and broken mud bricks rained down upon the floor, and the groaning of the timbers supporting the roof was like the moaning of giants in pain.

When a few moments passed with no more of the tremors, Rahab called to Myrnah to follow and ran down to the lower floor and out into the courtyard, where they would be better protected from falling debris. Here they crouched, staring wide-eyed at a giant crack that had split the inner wall from top to bottom only a few paces from the house. Had it occurred in the outer wall, which actually supported the building, the whole thing would have collapsed, burying them in the debris.

People were pouring from their houses now, white-faced with terror. The crash of falling masonry was heard from other parts of the city, and amid the din hundreds of voices could be heard crying out, "Jericho is doomed! Baal has cursed the city."

No one tried to leave the city, for they knew that the Habiru waited not far away, ready to destroy them once they left the protection of the walls. And as the hours passed, reports of the damage were more reassuring. Although the inner wall was breached in a dozen places or more, the outer one had held with only a few cracks. Jericho's main defense was still intact.

To Rahab, the earthquake seemed indeed to be a sign from Yah, sent to reassure her. She even dared to hope now for an early release from the hateful situation in which Kanofer had placed her.

Four

CALEB AND SALMON felt the trembling of the earth where they were hiding in the hill country to the west of Jericho. The tremor had not been as severe in the uplands as on the lower ground where the city stood, but as they looked down on Jericho in the early dawn, they could detect some of the damage that had been done to the inner wall.

"Perhaps Yahweh is preparing for the fall of Jericho, as Joshua expects," Salmon suggested.

Caleb grinned. "I care not who breaches the walls, so long as they are breached. But we must get this information to Joshua as quickly as possible. These earth tremors sometimes last a week or more in the springtime. Whatever happens, we must be ready."

"They will be guarding the fords below Jericho," Salmon pointed out. "But we can go back by way of Adamah."

Stopping only to gather fruit and berries on the mountainside to allay their hunger and to drink from the springs that burst from the rocks all through the highlands here—now that the *malquosh* had soaked the earth once more—Salmon and Caleb made their way northward toward the next crossing of the Jord above the fords of Jericho, opposite the town of Adamah. The way was rough, for there were no roads here. And in truth, they did not dare follow a traveled path for fear the soldiers of Jericho would be lying in wait along the roadside to capture them.

Every few hours they felt a new tremor of the earth, but since none was as strong as that which had occurred during the first night, they pushed on each day until darkness fell and then slept in a cave. Early the third morning they reached the road leading from Tirzah in the uplands eastward to the Jord and shortly came down into the deep valley where the river flowed.

On Salmon's previous visit to Adamah, when he had been spying out the cities of Canaan, he had noted the great earth cliffs on the west bank of the Jord. He had been certain then that a few men could block the river here by digging away the undercut bank and allowing great masses of dirt to fall into the stream. Now, they saw, this had already happened to a small degree. A section of the overlying bank had fallen into the Jord during the recent earth tremors, slowing the flow of its waters.

More significant, however, was a giant crack that had cut almost halfway through the cliff, leaving a mass of earth large enough to block the Jord completely, hanging, so to speak, in the air.

Salmon discovered the crevice while inspecting the crossing. He stopped at the edge of the earth cliff, for it seemed that hardly more than a nudge would send the whole mass tumbling.

"Come here, Caleb," he called, and when the gnarled captain stood beside him he pointed down into the great crevice. "A hundred men digging here could dislodge this mass of earth into the river and block it."

Caleb knelt at the edge and dropped a stone into the crevice. A moment later they heard it strike water well below them.

"Ten men could do it," he agreed, "but we will take no chances. A hundred should be more than enough. Then the carts with our supplies and even the battering-rams and siege towers can pass over the Jord without any trouble." He got to his feet. "Joshua must know about this at once."

On the east bank of the Jord they met an Israelite patrol stationed there to give warning of any attempt by the Canaanites to deliver a flanking attack. Supplied with fresh sandals and food by their fellows, the travelers trudged on southward and reached the Israelite encampment at Abel-shittim in the late afternoon.

To their surprise, they found the place almost deserted and were informed that the main body of the troops and the people were encamped on the banks of the Jord at the fords, waiting for the river to lower before crossing into the region controlled by the King of Jericho on the west bank. No one seeing the battering-rams and the rude siege towers on their great wooden wheels waiting on the bank of the river could doubt that the armies of Israel were embarked at last on the long-expected attack against Jericho.

Joshua's tent was pitched on the very bank of the stream, near the sumptuous canopy housing the Ark of Yahweh, which was said to contain the tablets of a covenant made by their god with the Israelites.

Joshua had been studying a rough map drawn on a sheet of papyrus. He looked up quickly when Salmon and Caleb were ushered in, and the physician was almost shocked at the burning light in the Israelite leader's eyes.

The Joshua with whom he had conferred in this very tent a few days ago had been strong and secure in the belief that he was obeying the will of Yahweh. But the man who faced them now was fired by something more, the consuming flame of a fanatic zeal that neither knows nor admits opposition.

"Salmon! Caleb!" he cried. "I was afraid you had been taken in Jericho. We were moving against it to take the city and release you."

"We were almost captured," said Caleb grimly. "But you would have found only our heads."

"Three days ago when the earth began to tremble," Joshua told them, "I recognized it as the voice of Yahweh urging us on against Jericho. We began to move that very day in preparation for crossing the river."

Salmon had the strange feeling that he was already watching a great event from a distance, as he had watched the destruction of King Og and his men from the hillside above Edrei. Nor could he throw off the conviction that everything taking place here had somehow been ordained already and nothing any of them could do would really hinder or help it, leaving all of them to play out their appointed roles with no volition of their own.

"When will you cross?" he asked Joshua.

"When Yahweh cuts off the waters of the Jord."

Caleb shot him a startled glance. "And when will that be?"

"He spoke to us once in the earthquake, telling us the time had come to move on Jericho. When it is time to cross the river, he will speak again."

"We found a great crack in the earth cliffs at Adamah," said Caleb. "It was made by the tremors we have been feeling these past few days. Salmon thinks a hundred men could push it loose and block the river."

"Yahweh has already spoken then," Joshua said, as if he

259

had expected to hear this information all along. "Take the hundred men tomorrow, Salmon, and loosen the earth cliff. Did you learn anything else in Jericho?"

"One of the mercenaries guarding the gate recognized Caleb," Salmon explained. "We were forced to escape at night before the earth tremors occurred and learned but little of their defenses. But we could see from the hills the next morning that the inner wall was breached in several places by the earth tremors."

"And the outer?"

"It is still strong," said Caleb. "Only battering-rams can break it down."

"We will make camp on the plain before Jericho and wait for the voice of Yahweh," said Joshua. "If he does not breach the walls for us, then we will attack them with rams!"

Caleb shook his grizzled head. "Yahweh has given us victory so far, Joshua, but only when we fought for it. I say move up the rams and the siege towers at once. The people of Jericho are afraid. When they see our strength arrayed before the city, they might even open the gate to us."

Joshua shook his head. "They will not surrender without a battle. I have caused *herem* to be invoked against Jericho."

"The curse!" Salmon exclaimed in horror. "Why would you doom everyone in Jericho to death for defending themselves?"

Joshua's face hardened. "You know the Lord God of Israel has given the land of Canaan to us, Salmon."

"Would you kill every living thing because of that? Our god also teaches kindness and love one for another."

"I intend to destroy everything until they yield up the whole land to us."

"We promised immunity to one family," Caleb told him. "The house of a harlot. She let us down from the wall with a scarlet cord when the guards sought us."

"I will give orders that the harlot and her household be spared," Joshua agreed.

"Her name is Rahab," Caleb said quietly. "She will mark her window with the scarlet cord."

"And she will have with her a babe," Salmon added, "bearing the same marks as those on the back of the son of Nun."

For a moment it seemed that Joshua would strike them both; he even raised his fist. Then he dropped it. "I have

260

given my word and the woman will be saved," he said harshly, but suddenly his anger broke the bonds within which he had been rigidly holding it. "I will be father to no harlot's brat, Salmon," he snapped. "It could be yours as well as mine. You were in Egypt with her."

"The child is yours," Salmon said evenly. "Caleb knew that without seeing the marks upon its back. Rahab will not ask you to acknowledge it if you are so stiff-necked as to deny your own seed. She asks only that she and hers be spared when Jericho is destroyed."

"That shall be—but no more." Joshua turned abruptly back to his map.

Outside, Caleb found his voice in an explosive burst of indignation. "By the altars of Baal!" he snapped. "What has come over Joshua? He must be possessed by a demon."

"He is possessed," Salmon agreed, "but not by a demon. You might say he has been possessed by a god——"

"I wager he did not resist," Caleb said shortly. "He was already beginning to *think* himself one."

"Joshua cannot let anyone be superior to him in anything," Salmon agreed as they walked across the camp toward Caleb's tent. "Remember when he lost the skirmish to the forces of King Og?"

Caleb nodded. "It was then that he invoked *herem* against Bashan. Jericho is a similar case."

"How? Joshua has never even been in the city."

"He hates Rahab for shaming him," Caleb explained. "The King of Jericho honored her by making her his concubine, so now the whole city has become a target for Joshua's anger."

"Hazor is dead."

"But his city still stands."

Salmon shook his head slowly. "I don't want to believe that of Joshua, Caleb. He must be convinced that Israel cannot live in Canaan side by side with the Canaanites."

"We live here with the Amorites," Caleb pointed out.

"Look what is happening to our people since they began to intermarry with the Amorites and the Moabites. You can find a golden image of Baal in half the tents, and the men openly visit the temple of Ashtarth to lie with the sacred women.

"Joshua may be right, Caleb," Salmon continued. "And

261

you and I could be wrong. Yahweh may indeed have given him the power to conquer Canaan and destroy its people so that we of Israel will turn away from the false gods we have been pursuing."

"Then you will have to believe Yahweh will block the waters of the Jord for us to cross. And that he will shake down the walls of Jericho and let us in." The old warrior shook his head. "That is asking too much, Salmon. Battles are won by fighting, not by praying."

"Remember the crevice in the earth cliff at Adamah? It needs but little help from us to block the Jord."

"I will not sit by and wait for rivers to cease flowing or walls to be shaken down before me." Caleb clenched his massive fists. "If these two hands grip a sword in a good cause, Yahweh will give victory to my arms. But I must make the first thrust." He smiled. "If you don't understand my words, I am saying, 'Take the hundred men to Adamah tomorrow morning and make sure the earth cliff does fall into the Jord.'"

Salmon, too, smiled. "I had no intention of waiting," he admitted. "Yahweh has put a gift of healing into my hands. But I must still dig out poisoned arrowheads and dress wounds with soothing balm."

"One thing I do know," said Caleb. "I have not eaten a full meal for three days, and my belly cries out for meat and wine. Let us go and find some."

They had just finished their meal when the trumpets blared out a summons for the people to assemble. As Caleb and Salmon joined the crowd on the riverbank, they saw Joshua standing on one of the portable siege towers high above the crowd. With the sun shining on his dark head, he seemed godlike as he waited—lost in some distant contemplation—for the people to come together.

The trumpet blared out again, and as the echoes from the opposite bank of the Jord died away Joshua spoke. Even his voice had changed, Salmon realized with a start. Its tones had become deeper and more sonorous, like the voice of a king.

"Sanctify yourselves," Joshua told the waiting throng, "for tomorrow the Lord will do wonders among you." Turning to the priests, he ordered, "Take up the Ark of the Covenant, and pass before the people."

262

A hush claimed the whole of the camp of Israel while the priests brought the Ark of the Covenant from its tent, covered with a rich cloth against the profane gaze of those not holy enough to approach it. Moving slowly with an impressive tread, the priests bore the Ark up and down along the bank of the swiftly rushing stream, passing twice before the silent people and the tall figure standing on the siege tower with arms folded. Only when the sacred symbol once more reposed within its tent did Joshua speak again.

"Come hither and hear the words of the Lord your God," he commanded. "Hereby you shall know that the living God is among you and he will without fail drive out from before you the Canaanites, the Hittites, the Hivites, the Perizzites, the Girgashites, the Amorites, and the Jebusites. Behold, the Ark of the Covenant of the Lord of all the earth is to pass before you into the Jord.

"Now, therefore, take twelve men from the tribes of Israel, from each tribe a man. And when the soles of the feet of the priests who bear the Ark of the Lord, the Lord of all the earth, shall rest in the waters of the Jord, they shall be stopped from flowing, and the waters coming down from above shall stand in one heap."

That night Salmon was awakened in his tent by another strong earth tremor. There was no fear in the camp of Israel, however, for Joshua had told them the trembling was caused by the footsteps of Yahweh walking upon the earth to aid them. And such was the trust of Israel in their leader and in the favor of Yahweh that no one dared to doubt his words.

Nor was Salmon surprised when, halfway to Adamah with a hundred men shortly after dawn, he met a patrol from that city bringing the exciting news that the tremor during the night had loosened the great cliff of earth on the west bank of the river where the waters had undercut it. In the early hours of the morning the earth had tumbled into the river with a great crash, blocking the flow of the stream completely. The waters were piled up far above the crossing, according to the report of the patrol, while the stream below the newly formed obstruction had trickled to a mere brook, carrying only the flow from a few springs that entered the Jord between Adamah and the fords east of Jericho before which Israel was encamped.

Five

ALL DAY LONG, the Israelites crossed the Jord almost on dry land, women leading children and domestic animals, asses, goats, dogs, and sheep. Horses pulled the chariots, heavily loaded with supplies of war, as well as the great clumsy battering-rams, and mobile siege towers on huge wooden wheels. They were helped by the strongest men, who labored in the mud of the ford, pushing the great wheels and levering them up with heavy poles when they gouged holes into the river bottom.

At the head of the multitude moved a band of the best fighting men, guarding against attack. Behind them, the mass of the people with their possessions were strung out in a broad pattern like a V. The flocks came first after the fighting men, followed by the herds, and behind them were more warriors protecting the flanks from attack. By the time the first column had reached the place called Gilgal chosen for the new camp, a little more than halfway between the river and Jericho, the end had not yet finished crossing the Jord.

Gilgal was located in a flat area particularly suited for such an encampment, with an ample water supply from a stream forming its southern boundary in a small canyon. Long after night had fallen the Israelites labored, setting up tents, dispersing the flocks on the grassy hillsides with shepherd boys to look after them and armed patrols to guard against a surprise attack by the enemy. When morning dawned, a formidable sight indeed met the eyes of the soldiers patrolling the walls of Jericho. Spread out in full sight was the might of Israel, with the great war machines waiting for the beginning of the final attack.

Joshua had not yet ordered moved up a portable shelter Salmon had devised to cover the spring that supplied Jericho with water and deny it to the inhabitants. The shelter was ready when it was needed. Meanwhile, since this was the season of the Passover, when the children of Israel were accustomed to celebrate their escape from Egypt, it was decided to defer any more intensive movement against the city until the celebration was finished.

On the morning after their arrival at Gilgal, Joshua called the people together and announced that on each of the succeeding six days the entire forces of Israel would march around Jericho, with the Ark of the Covenant borne before them and the ram's-horn trumpets of the priests blasting out defiance to the city's defenders.

At the announcement, a murmur of surprise ran through the crowd. None of the captains spoke, however, until Caleb asked, "What is the meaning of this play-acting, Joshua?"

"Do you dare call the commands of Yahweh play-acting?"

"I will obey the commands of Yahweh," said the old soldier, "when I know they come from him."

"I speak words which the Lord our God puts into my mouth," Joshua told him.

"What shall we do on the seventh day when the play-acting is finished?" Caleb inquired. "Will the soldiers cease to prance and boast and be ready to fight like men?"

"On the seventh day we will march around the walls seven times."

"And when we are all too exhausted to fight? What then?"

"Our god will deliver Jericho to us," Joshua said evenly.

For a long moment there was a deep silence while the people stared up at Joshua in a state of awed wonder, as if he had indeed become, as he claimed, the mouthpiece of Yahweh. Only when Caleb snorted and stamped away was the spell broken.

Joshua dismissed them then, and they scattered to their tents to discuss this strange method of warfare about which none of them had ever heard before and which, in truth, had never been used in the history of mankind. A second important topic of conversation, particularly among the captains, was the rapidly approaching breach between Caleb and Joshua.

Salmon found his old friend sulking in his tent and gnawing his beard. "Now I *know* Joshua is possessed," Caleb burst out angrily as soon as Salmon came in. "Were those the words of a soldier—or a self-chosen prophet?"

"I could not help believing it will all happen as he said."

"You are not alone," Caleb admitted reluctantly. "I too had to fight hard not to believe it."

"Why do you try then?"

"Why do I try?" the old captain spluttered. "Because after Joshua I am the first captain of the hosts of Israel. Suppose the army of Jericho decides to attack us on the seventh day when we have marched ourselves into exhaustion? What better time could they choose?"

"Remember how the waters of the Jordan were stopped?"

"You saw the reason for that at Adamah. It was caused by the earthquake."

"Joshua was waiting for the river to go down before we brought news concerning the condition of the earth cliffs at Adamah," Salmon pointed out.

"He might have waited a month then. Or a year."

"But the cliff *did* fall into the river," Salmon reminded him. "And just when we needed it to be blocked."

Caleb threw up his hands in disgust. "Have I no friend in Israel any more? You, of all people, Salmon, should not be taken in by this business of Joshua posing as a god."

"You and I have been friends for a long time, Caleb——"

"And shall continue to be, I hope."

"If we are not, it will not be of my choosing," the physician assured him. "Are you sure you don't fight Joshua because of envy? After all, but for him you would be chief of our armies."

Caleb poured a cup of wine with a shaking hand. He drank it slowly and wiped his lips with his sleeve before he spoke. "I had not thought my friend would accuse me of envy," he said, a little sadly.

"I too envy him," Salmon admitted.

"You envy Joshua?" Caleb asked in surprise. "In your own field of work you are greater than he is in the art of war."

"I envy him the love of Rahab, for one thing," Salmon admitted. "Once, too, the captains looked to me in matters of strategy. Now Joshua makes such decisions for himself and I am not consulted."

"Nor am I—or any of the captains," Caleb growled. "Take this foolishness of walking around Jeri——"

"It may not be foolishness, Caleb."

"Why not?"

"We have decided to celebrate the Passover before attacking Jericho. If we only sat here, the people in the city might decide we fear to attack and be heartened. But if we parade our might, they will know we outnumber them at least several times and can attack whenever we choose. Besides, this is still the season of earthquakes. Who knows whether or not by the time we launch our attack another earthquake may damage the walls more than they have already been damaged."

"You will be telling me next that Yahweh will deliver Jericho to Joshua by shaking down the walls—while we only stand by and watch," Caleb said disgustedly.

"It could happen," Salmon reminded him. Before Caleb could snort his disbelief, Salmon went on, "We know Yahweh raises up a leader for Israel when she is in need. He gave us Moses to lead us out of Egypt. And now he has raised up Joshua to lead us in conquering Canaan. Neither you nor I can go against the will of Yahweh, Caleb. And we should not want to if it is for the welfare of Israel."

"Not even when it means I must yield to the son of Nun?"

"I have yielded, although it meant giving up the woman I love—because I believe Joshua's way is Yahweh's will."

"You are stronger—and more forgiving—than I am then," Caleb growled. "But I will try—if Joshua does not push me too far."

And so the armies of Israel paraded around the walls of Jericho the next day in all their warlike might, with the trumpets sounding before them. Joshua marched immediately behind the Ark, which was borne by the priests, with Caleb just behind him at the head of the army, as befitted the second-in-command. Marching in the rear, as usual, Salmon looked up at the walls, and his heart took a sudden leap when he saw a scarlet cord hanging in the window of one of the houses.

On the first day the soldiers of Jericho, safe within the protection of the thick walls, peered and shouted insults at the marching Israelites. But as the days passed, the mockery died away. Soon they only stood and watched while the long line of fighting men daily wound its way around the city, their arms clanking in a martial din. Soon the fear of Jericho's people was a heavy dank miasma, palpable even at this distance from the walls.

All during the week they had felt earth tremors. On the sixth day Salmon climbed one of the hills west of Jericho in order to look down into the city, and saw that considerable damage had been done to the inner wall. It still held, however, and the outer one appeared to be intact, a formidable barrier to an attack by frontal assault.

More than once during that week, when he returned from treating one of the minor complaints that always seemed to arise with nightfall, Salmon saw Joshua standing at the edge of the camp, a majestic and somehow lonely figure, staring across at the forbidding walls of Jericho. Whether or not there was any doubt in Joshua's mind that Yahweh would indeed deliver up Jericho as he had promised the people, Salmon could not know, of course. A year ago he would have felt free to stop and talk to his former comrade, but an invisible wall seemed to have been reared between them now, a wall he did not know how to surmount.

When Joshua addressed the troops on the morning of the seventh day, however, Salmon could detect neither doubt nor lack of decision in his voice. "Today Jericho will be delivered up to us," he promised them. "When we have marched around the walls the seventh time, the priests will blow a loud blast on the trumpets and we will launch the attack against the city."

As his words died away a sudden tremor shook the earth, throwing many of them to the ground and overturning one of the siege towers with a mighty crash. Plainly audible in the hushed silence that followed were the terrified shouts of the people inside Jericho and the sound of falling masonry.

"Hear me, O Israel!" Joshua shouted, his face suddenly aglow. "Yahweh marches with us today! Forward!"

Again the long line filed around Jericho, with the priests marching as before in the lead, each blowing on a long, curved ram's horn. The wailing of the people within the city was like a deep animal howl of despair as the army of Israel continued the slow, deliberate march. When the seventh turn had been completed Joshua, resplendent in full military regalia and wearing his armored tunic, lifted his hand.

"At my command, you will shout," he ordered. "For the

268

Lord has given you the city. All that is within Jericho shall be devoted to the Lord for destruction. Only Rahab, the harlot, and all who are with her in her house shall live, because she hid the messengers that we sent.

"But you," he warned, "keep yourselves from the things devoted to destruction, lest you take away any of the devoted things and make the camp of Israel a thing for destruction and bring trouble upon it. All silver and gold and vessels of brass and iron are sacred. They shall go into the treasury of the Lord."

Joshua's upraised fist swung downward in the agreed-upon signal. As one man, the multitude set up a great shout, not only the soldiers, but the people in the camp who were watching.

At the shout and the sudden blast of trumpets, the massed troops began to close in upon the city, pushing before them the battering-rams and the siege towers, from which bowmen were already laying down a covering hail of arrows to protect the men who would place the long scaling ladders against the walls.

The attack upon Jericho had finally begun!

Six

THINKING OF IT LATER, Salmon could not remember whether or not the earth had been trembling before Joshua finished speaking. But he knew he would never forget the sudden shock that threw him and many of the attackers to the ground before they were halfway across the open space separating them from the walls of Jericho. Joshua—miraculously, it seemed—stayed erect, although the earth was quivering now like a living, demented thing and a great crevice had opened out before them, stretching straight toward the doomed city of Jericho.

"It is the voice of Yahweh!" Joshua shouted again, and his voice carried to all the troops, even above the crashing roar of the earthquake and the terrified cries of the people, attackers and attacked alike.

Salmon staggered to his feet, but another shock sent him to his knees once more. He rose again and stumbled on, his eyes fixed on the window looking down from the wall of Jericho in which the scarlet cord was displayed.

The crash of masonry and the screams of the dying made a pandemonium of sound now. Salmon saw a great crevice open up and swallow a group of Israelite soldiers like ants, but had no time to wonder at the strange phenomenon of the god of Israel killing his own troops. He could not take his fascinated gaze from the walls of the city, which were slowly tilting outward, as if pushed from within by a giant hand.

Almost intact, a huge section of the outer wall collapsed and overturned, revealing the great breaches torn through the inner bastion by the previous shocks. Houses were tumbling everywhere, but through the dust of falling masonry he could see that several sections of wall were still standing. In the midst of one was a window, and across it, plainly visible, was bound a scarlet cord.

At Joshua's shout of exaltation the Israelite warriors who had been thrown down struggled to their feet. Seizing their spears, they moved toward the walls, which were still crumbling apart and falling to the ground. Dust filled the air, but Salmon held his breath and plunged on with only one thought in mind, to reach the house where Rahab would be waiting. In the excitement and the blood lust that always went with *herem*, he knew that something could easily go wrong and she and those with her might still be injured in spite of Joshua's order.

Stumbling over great boulders—so recently shaken loose from the masonry of the wall that they were still moving—coughing and choking from the dust and barely able to see, Salmon pushed on.

Now he was past the first wall and into the rubble-filled area between it and the inner one. Pausing for a moment, he peered through the haze, looking for Rahab's house, which, since it was built across the walls, could be entered only from the inner one.

Already the butchery of the inhabitants had begun, and the screams of the dying penetrated even through the roar of falling rocks and the groaning of those sections of the walls that had not already fallen. Above the screams sounded the

270

exultant cries of the Israelite warriors as they went about the bloody task of carrying out the *herem*.

An Israelite soldier loomed suddenly out of the dusty haze beside Salmon, instinctively stabbing at him with his spear until he recognized the physician and deflected the point at the last moment. Belatedly Salmon remembered that he was armed with nothing save the bronze knife he carried at his belt for cutting away clothing and slitting cloth for bandages.

The air cleared for an instant and he was able to distinguish the wall of a house that looked like Rahab's, still standing to the right of him. Turning, he plunged toward it and lurched into a courtyard that seemed familiar. He moved on, caroming against a wall as he stumbled over a pile of rubble, and half falling through a door leading into the lower floor of the house.

"Rahab!" he shouted. "Rahab! Where are you?"

Guided by a woman's scream, Salmon turned toward another room and found himself facing a soldier of Israel with spear upraised, ready to strike a woman cowering in the corner. Even as he struck the spear aside, Salmon recognized her as the old slave who had brought him to Rahab in this very house only a short while before.

"This is the house with the scarlet cord," he shouted into the astonished face of the soldier. "Harm these people and Joshua will have your heart."

The man still stared stupidly at him, but Salmon paid no more attention to him. Kneeling, he lifted Myrnah's head and saw that she was not hurt, only pale with fear and shock. "Where is your mistress?" he demanded.

"In—in there," she gasped, pointing toward another room. "With the baby."

"Guard this house well," Salmon ordered the soldier. "It is under the protection of Joshua."

The man nodded and lifted his spear once more. Whimpering with fear and relief, the slave woman scuttled through the open door leading to the adjoining room. There Salmon found Rahab with the baby clutched to her breast. Her body was bent over so that if the walls fell they would strike her first, so she did not see him.

He touched her shoulder gently, and she looked up with

271

eyes that were wide with horror. Then a sudden light of gladness burned in them.

"Salmon!" she cried. "Yahweh has delivered up Jericho to Joshua."

Salmon felt as if a band of the Hittite metal had been forged about his heart, but this was no time to consider his own feelings. "We must get out of the house," he told Rahab, lifting her to her feet. "This section of the wall may fall at any time."

With Rahab carrying Jaschar and followed by Myrnah and Senu, who had appeared out of the dust and rubble from somewhere in the building, Salmon led them from the house. Hardly were they clear of it when the roof collapsed with a groan of rending timbers and the outer wall tilted slowly away to crash upon the rubble pile forming all that was now left of the once formidable defenses of Jericho.

"Yah protected us, Salmon!" Rahab cried, her eyes shining. "He kept the walls standing until you could find and save us."

An Israelite captain came into the courtyard, followed by a dozen warriors, their spears and knives dripping blood. With a surge of relief Salmon recognized his friend Khalith.

"This is Rahab and her family," Salmon called to him. "Give me soldiers to protect them."

"The harlot?" Khalith peered at them through the murky dust-filled air that shrouded the city in a pall of destruction.

"Did Joshua call me a harlot when he gave the order, Salmon?" Rahab asked quickly. At the hurt in her voice he knew he dare not tell her the truth. And yet if he could, he would have spared her some of the heartbreak she must experience when she met Joshua again.

"The house where you were staying was known to be a brothel," Salmon explained. "He spoke without thinking."

Khalith detailed six Israelite warriors as a guard for them. "You will be safe with these men," Salmon told Rahab. "I must see to the wounded."

"Where is Joshua?"

"He led the soldiers across the walls," said Khalith. "You will find him wherever the fighting is thickest for the rest of the day."

As Rahab and her guard moved off into the dust cloud, Khalith wiped sweat from his face. "You will have little work today, Salmon," he said. "Jericho's defenders were jellied with fear. Only a few mercenaries and one Egyptian captain dared to fight against us. Joshua cut him down in one thrust."

And indeed, as Salmon went about the city looking for those who might need his services, he saw that Khalith had been almost correct. Stunned by the earthquake that had leveled the walls and let the armies of Israel pour into the city unimpeded, the people of Jericho had resigned themselves to death from the very beginning of the attack.

Sickened by the butchery, Salmon made his way through the gate shortly after sunset and down the ramp to the spring outside what was left of the walls of Jericho. His elaborate plan for securing the spring would not be needed now—further proof, it seemed, that Yahweh did indeed speak through the voice of Joshua.

Salmon doused his head with water and drank deeply, but even quenching his thirst could not cure the sickness in his heart. Butchery like this, even in the name of Yahweh, he could never understand. Nor could he believe that it was really the purpose of the god they worshiped, however war-like they believed him to be.

Parts of the city were aflame already. As the raging fires swept through the flimsy roofs of the houses—most of them covered with dried rushes that caught like tinder—the people who had hidden in the hovels and huts built into the very walls of the city were driven out, along with the rats and vermin who skulked there. Rats and vermin the soldiers spared; they had no quarrel with them. But men and women, old and young, and children of every age they cut down with their spears and battle-axes.

A ring of soldiers surrounded the entire city now, driving back with naked spears anyone who managed to burst through, forcing them to choose between death upon the weapon or in the raging holocaust that had once been the proud city of Jericho.

A line of men led from the gate to the camp, carrying the wealth of Jericho, ornaments and utensils of gold and silver, images of Baal and other gods, tools of iron, cooking pots of copper, metal-reinforced helmets and shields—all the loot that fell to the conquerors of a fallen city. Some of the booty, Salmon knew, would find its way into the tents of the people, in spite of Joshua's strict order that everything of value was to be dedicated to Yahweh by being placed in the temple treasury. That was expected, however, and not even the priests worried about it, so long as the major share found its way into their hands.

At the Israelite camp at Gilgal the priests were busy in the open space before the tent housing the Ark of the Covenant, counting and recording the booty in the light of flaming torches. There, as he had expected, Salmon found Rahab's father, Chazan, busy at his task as chief of the scribes, recording on a long papyrus roll each item and its estimated value.

"Yah will bless you for giving Rahab back to me, Salmon," the old man cried, embracing him.

"She earned her freedom," Salmon assured him. "But I am glad I reached the house first."

"Rahab told me that but for you they would have been killed." Chazan's face sobered. "Have you seen Joshua? She has been asking for him."

"He is still in the city, seeing that it is burned, down to the last stone."

Chazan looked across the plain toward the red glare that now masked what had been a proud city. "What can I tell Rahab about the change in Joshua? I would like to soften the blow for her."

"Don't say anything yet," Salmon advised. "When Joshua sees the baby, he will know it is his beyond any question. He may feel differently then."

The old scribe shook his head slowly. "It takes an understanding and tolerant person to play god, Salmon. I am afraid Joshua is neither."

"Where is Rahab?"

"In my tent, over there at the edge of the camp."

Salmon frowned. "I thought your tent was in the center of the camp, near Joshua's."

"The women are already saying Rahab bewitched you and Caleb so she would be spared from Jericho. It seemed better for her to be at one side of the camp, at least until the *herem* is over."

As Salmon moved through the camp he saw that the women were already beginning to gather in little groups. And as they talked their eyes went to Chazan's tent, where Rahab and those who had escaped from Jericho with her were quartered. A few even stopped him to demand why a harlot should have been spared from the curse put upon Jericho and to predict that bad luck for the whole camp would come because of her.

Seven

RAHAB was kneeling beside Jaschar's crib, improvised from a pile of goatskins, when Salmon opened the flap of the tent. She looked up quickly, her face radiant. Obviously she had expected Joshua, and her disappointment showed momentarily in her face.

"The son of Nun is still at the battlefields," he told her. "Are you comfortable?"

"My quarters are not so luxurious as the palace of the King of Jericho," she admitted with a smile. "But oh, Salmon, I am so happy to be with my own people again."

She would not have said as much if she had heard the talk of the women, Salmon thought. But if Joshua took her under his protection, as he must because of his son, it would quickly die down. After today—or until he suffered a defeat, which hardly seemed likely now—Joshua could do no wrong in Israel.

"Is the fighting still going on?" Rahab asked. "I didn't think Jericho could resist very long after the walls fell down."

"What you hear is the carrying out of the curse," he told her soberly.

"The curse?" She frowned. "What do you mean?"

"Joshua invoked *herem* against the city—the curse of Israel."

Rahab caught her breath, and the color went out of her cheeks. "You mean they will all be killed?"

"When the curse is invoked, every living thing is destroyed and the city itself is burned to the ground."

"But there were innocent people in Jericho. They loved their King and harmed no one."

"You and your family were the only ones exempt from the

275

curse," he explained. "And that was only because you saved Caleb and me."

She looked down at the ground, her face grave. "I lived many months in Jericho, Salmon, and many of its people were my friends. Please don't blame me because I grieve for them." Then she raised troubled eyes to his. "Why did the priests invoke the curse?"

"Joshua is the leader of Israel now. There are no more councils; he decides what is to be done."

"Is he responsible for all those people being killed?" she asked quickly.

"He gave the order, but you must try to understand that even Joshua is not responsible. What he orders is the will of Yahweh."

"The will of Yahweh—or the will of Joshua?" Her face was grave now. "Will he listen to me when I bring his child to him?"

"Please try to understand what I am saying, Rahab." Salmon took her hands in his. "Our god promised the land of Canaan to the descendants of Abram many generations ago. He gave us the strength to escape from slavery in Egypt, and now he has raised up a great leader to guide us in taking that land for ourselves. It is not Joshua's will that the people of Canaan and their cities must be destroyed. It is the will of Yahweh."

Rahab shook her head slowly. "You told me once that my god and yours are the same, Salmon. But Yah, the god of our father Abram, would not kill innocent women and children like those in Jericho. In your heart you know that is true."

Outside the tent a sudden chorus of shouts sounded, and Rahab ran to open the flap and look outside.

"It is Joshua!" she cried, her fears of a moment before forgotten. "I must go to him."

She turned back quickly and picked up the baby, wrapped in a cocoon of blankets against the cool of the night which came quickly here in the valley of the Jord once the sun had set. Salmon tried to stop her, but she pushed him impatiently aside in her eagerness to see the man she loved. His heart already sick with dread of what he was afraid would happen, Salmon hurried after her.

276

A great press of people was gathered around Joshua, and Salmon lost sight of Rahab momentarily in the glare of the torches that lit the scene. As he pushed his way through the crowd, searching for her, he heard Joshua's sonorous tones rolling over the people from where he stood upon a cart, quieting the clamor by the very power of his voice.

"Hear the words of your god, people of Israel," he shouted. "Jericho is ours. The hand of Yahweh crumbled the walls before us."

A great shout of victory went up. Joshua waited, smiling, for it to subside.

"In the name of Yahweh," he continued, "I have laid a curse upon this city and even upon the ground where it stands. Cursed before the Lord be the man that rises up and rebuilds this city of Jericho. At the cost of his first-born shall he lay its foundation. At the cost of his youngest son shall he set up its gates."

Another roar of approval went up from the crowd, forcing him to pause momentarily. "Of all those who dwelt in Jericho," Joshua continued, "only those in the household of the harlot——"

"Joshua!" Salmon heard Rahab's strangled cry and saw her now, a few paces from him. He tried to reach her before she could get to Joshua, but they both came into the clear space around the cart upon which the Israelite leader stood at the same time. Before Salmon could stop her, Rahab had lifted the blanket-wrapped bundle containing her son, her head uplifted proudly and her eyes shining.

"Joshua!" she cried again. "Don't you know me?"

A hush fell over the crowd as they sensed the drama inherent in this meeting and waited for the next act in the swiftly developing play.

Joshua's face seemed to have turned to stone. "I know you, woman," he said finally, and there was no warmth in his voice. "You are Rahab, the harlot of Jericho, whom I spared from the curse upon the city."

The rich color in Rahab's cheeks drained away suddenly, as if he had slapped her in the face. "I am no harlot," she said slowly. "Who should know that better than you?"

"You have been saved, you and your family," Joshua said harshly. "What more do you want?"

277

Rahab lifted her head proudly. When she spoke, her voice was strong and unafraid. "Look upon the face of your child," she said. "Look upon it and tell me whether you still call its mother a harlot."

"Enough, woman," Joshua shouted, his face suffused with anger. "I am father to no harlot's brat." Leaping down suddenly from the cart, he strode through the crowd to his tent and disappeared inside it.

For a moment there was an awed silence. It was broken when a woman in the crowd stepped forward and spat deliberately on Rahab, the spittle striking her forehead and dripping down across her face.

"Joshua has denounced the harlot!" a voice shouted from the crowd. "Let her be killed like the others in Jericho!"

Realizing the grave danger that threatened Rahab and Jaschar, Salmon moved to her side and faced the crowd. He saw only blood lust in every eye, for the excitement of the *herem* and the butchery that had followed was still burning inside them.

"If you harm this woman you must kill me first," he announced.

For the first time since Joshua had denounced her as a harlot Rahab seemed to realize what was happening. "Let them do what they will with me, Salmon," she begged. "Only save Jaschar."

"You, Carmi," the physician called to a man in the crowd. "Did I not set a broken bone so you could walk again?"

"We wish you no harm, Salmon," the man mumbled. "But you know we allow no harlots in Israel."

"Separate them," another voice cried. "The woman has bewitched the physician."

The circle about them was closing in as eager hands reached out to tear Rahab and Salmon apart, but suddenly there was an interruption.

"What mockery is this?" a familiar voice growled. "Rahab is under the protection of Israel." It was Caleb, shouldering his way through the crowd and beating men and women aside roughly with the flat of his sword. "This woman saved our lives when we entered Jericho to spy out its defenses," he told the people sternly. "Is this the way Israel rewards her? Move back and let us through."

Perhaps because Caleb never let them think for a moment that he expected resistance, or more likely because no one wished to be the first to feel the old warrior's steel, the crowd made way for them. Sobbing hysterically, Rahab collapsed as soon as they reached her tent.

Setting Myrnah to care for the baby, Salmon poured a sleeping potion from a pouch of medicines that he always carried hanging from his belt and stirred it up in wine. Rahab drank the bitter mixture without protest and lay down on the cushions in the tent. But when he started to leave she clung to him until he promised to sleep nearby where he would be within immediate call.

Caleb was sitting on a rock outside the tent, a grave look on his face. "You came just in time, old friend," Salmon said gratefully. "If you hadn't happened to be passing, Rahab would be dead."

"I didn't happen to be passing," Caleb said quietly.

"What do you mean?"

"I was at Joshua's tent, waiting for him. Just as he came in, a soldier brought word that the people were about to kill you and Rahab."

"Then Joshua sent you to help us?"

"Joshua made no move to help. I came of my own accord."

Shocked by the implication, Salmon did not speak for a long moment. "Surely you don't think he would have let the crowd destroy us," he said finally.

"I try to tell myself Joshua knew no one in Israel would possibly harm you, Salmon."

"He did not know that about Rahab and the baby—his own child."

"Joshua has acknowledged neither of them, remember? For his purposes it would even be better if they did not exist."

"I can't believe that of him," Salmon insisted.

"Not of the Joshua who was our comrade," Caleb agreed. "But that one exists no longer. When you believe anything you do is God's will, it is easy to get rid of those standing in your way, without troubling your conscience."

"What shall I tell Rahab?"

"Tell her the truth," Caleb said bluntly. "How could she love him, after the way he denounced her tonight?"

279

"Let me think about it awhile," Salmon begged. "I may find a better way."

"Now is your chance to put Joshua out of her heart," Caleb insisted. "You love her, Salmon, and she would be far happier with you. Don't let any idea of loyalty to Joshua make you do anything foolish. Believe me, he would not think of you."

In the morning Salmon made the rounds of the camp before he visited Rahab, rebandaging whatever wounds needed further treatment and administering to all who had need of his medical skill. When he came back to Chazan's tent, where he had left Rahab, he found Myrnah squatting beside a cooking fire, baking cakes of flour on a flat rock.

"The beautiful one is awake," the old slave said. "She has been nursing little Jaschar."

Salmon found Rahab inside the tent, brushing her hair. When she turned to face him, he saw a hardness in her eyes and a tenseness about her normally generous mouth that he had never seen before—nor liked to see now.

"Did you rest well?" he asked.

"Could I help myself? After the potion you gave me?"

"You needed rest more than anything else." He went over to the crib where little Jaschar was asleep in his nest of blankets and stood looking down at him. "He is a fine boy."

"Fine enough to be the Prince of Jericho," Rahab said in the same hard, brittle voice, "but not to be acknowledged by his own father."

"I told you Joshua had changed. Perhaps when there is an end to war——"

"There will never be an end to war where Joshua is concerned. You should know that by now."

"But he has a great responsibility——"

"You have a great responsibility," said Rahab hotly. "You hold people's lives in your hands, and Caleb controls the fate of thousands of soldiers when he leads them into battle. Has that changed either of you?"

"No."

"Then there is no excuse for the change in Joshua. Fortunately," she added, "I know his weakness."

280

Salmon noted now that she had dressed herself as if for a feast. "What are you going to do?" he asked.

"I care nothing for myself, Salmon," she said curtly. "Joshua can spurn me if he likes. But Jaschar is of his seed and entitled to an inheritance and a position in Israel."

"Last night he refused even to look at the boy."

"Last night I was a fool," she said bluntly. "But I am no longer. I will make him acknowledge the child."

"How?"

"Joshua branded me a harlot publicly, so I will use harlot's wiles." She got to her feet abruptly and turned before him, swaying her hips and smiling the same hard, brittle smile. "Am I not beautiful still?"

"More than before," he told her truthfully. Motherhood had only served to accentuate the lovely lines of her body.

"Is there a woman in the camp of Israel more attractive to a man than I am?"

"None," he admitted.

"Then Joshua should be easy for one who knows the harlot's wiles. Tell me, will the caravans continue to travel this route now that Jericho is destroyed?"

"On the other side of the Jordan they came among us freely and traded their goods without hindrance. Why do you ask?"

"I will need new robes cut from the cloth of Byblos. And gold to buy jewelry and cosmetics and perfumes."

"I would let you have whatever you need," he told her. "But not for this evil purpose you have in mind."

"Is it evil to force a father to acknowledge his son?" she demanded. "Is it evil to want your child to have his rightful place among the people?"

"No," he admitted. "But to arouse a man's lust deliberately for any purpose is dangerous."

"Who should know that better than I?" Rahab asked. "But this time I will make him pay the bride price and speak the vows first."

Salmon shook his head slowly. "I can understand your being hurt after last night, Rahab. And wanting revenge, for a little while at least. But it is not like you to talk this way."

"How do you know what I am like?" she cried angrily. "Many men have held me in their embrace this past year."

281

"But only to save your child. Myrnah told me the whole story."

"That still makes me what Joshua's branded me—a harlot."

Salmon shook his head. "To me you had not changed, Rahab—until I came this morning."

"Then you are a fool!" she cried. "And too softhearted for your own good. No wonder Joshua has taken credit for your accomplishments these past years."

"What I did was for Israel, not for Joshua."

"And how has Israel rewarded you? Are you rich as Joshua is? Do the people bow down before you as they do him?"

"A physician serves others, whether he is paid or not. He expects no honor for what he does."

"You are a worse fool than I thought then," she said bitterly. "You let others enrich themselves and take nothing for yourself."

"What do you mean?"

"The soldiers who brought me to the camp told me all gold and silver was dedicated to the treasury of Yahweh."

"It is. Your father set down the record when it was counted."

"Yet they joked openly that hardly any man who went into Jericho had come out without a golden image of Baal or a cup of silver hidden in his robe."

"Some small things are always stolen," Salmon admitted. "That is well known."

"Some small things?" she cried. "Are two hundred shekels of silver and fifty shekels of gold small enough?"

"What do you mean by that?"

"Early this morning Jaschar cried and woke me," she told him. "I heard people talking and went outside. The voices came from a tent next to mine; a man and a woman were burying something in the ground inside it. I heard them speak of two hundred shekels of silver and a bar of gold weighing fifty shekels."

Salmon knew who dwelt in the tent next to Rahab's. It was Achan, son of the same Carmi to whom he had spoken in the crowd last night, reminding him how he had set a broken leg. Achan had a bad reputation, but his father was a leader in the tribe of Judah, the most powerful and influential of all the tribes of Israel, so he had not been called to account as yet.

"Have you mentioned this to anyone else?" he asked quickly.

"No."

Salmon gave a sigh of relief. "Then they would have no way of knowing you overheard them."

"I tripped on a piece of wood in the darkness." Rahab's face was sober now. "The man opened his tent just as I came back inside here. I—I think he realized I had been outside."

"Perhaps he didn't see you." Salmon forced a confidence into his voice that he did not feel. "And anyway, he wouldn't know how much you overheard."

"Shouldn't we report to the priests that they buried the gold and silver?"

Salmon shook his head. "Achan may have moved it since you overheard them. Caleb saved us last night, but even he could not stay the wrath of the people if you accused a man from an important family of being a thief without proof."

"Then what can we do?"

"Wait and see—for the moment. If Achan makes a move against you, we will know he saw you last night."

Rahab's eyes went to the improvised crib where the baby lay sleeping. "No one would dare harm Joshua's child," she said thoughtfully. "Where is he now, Salmon?"

"With the captains, I imagine. They usually receive his orders in the morning in front of his tent."

"Then I must be on my way."

"Where?"

"To the spring, of course. How better can a harlot be seen than when bringing water from the spring while the leader confers with his captains?"

Eight

INTENT on her campaign to arouse Joshua's desire for her once more so he would marry her and acknowledge her child as his own, Rahab lost no opportunity to flaunt her beauty before the Israelite leader. When he sat with his captains, she made a point of walking by, hips swinging and bracelets jangling. At first Salmon could not understand where she got her money, until he discovered that the women were willing to pay her well to teach them how to paint their cheeks and lips and darken their eyelids and eyelashes with kohl. And when a caravan paused at Gilgal on its way along the east-west route from Damascus to the cities of Canaan, Rahab was able to purchase a store of jewelry and cosmetics with money her father gave her. These she subsequently sold to the other women at a considerable profit.

The older women grumbled at Rahab's behavior, but the younger ones admired her openly. They flocked to listen to her stories about the wonders of the courts of Egypt and the cities of Canaan which she had visited. Only one family spoke openly against her, that of Carmi, whose son Achan, according to the story Rahab told Salmon, had stolen a fortune in gold and silver from the spoils dedicated to the treasury. Noting the way they whispered to others in the tribe of Judah against her, Salmon set himself to watch them—and Rahab—constantly.

As for Joshua, he seemed not to notice Rahab's behavior, for he was busy planning another military campaign. This time he did not consult the captains until a week after the fall of Jericho. And then they were only called together to hear his plan of action. Salmon was not invited to the meeting—a deliberate slap by Joshua, he was sure, for only he in all of Israel had actually been inside the city of Ai, which it was proposed be attacked next. He did go, however, but only because Caleb insisted.

Salmon saw Joshua frown when he came to the meeting

place before the commander's tent with Caleb, but the Israelite general did not order him away.

"Three days ago," Joshua announced, "I sent two of the captains, Migda and Annath, to spy out the city of Ai. Yesterday they returned, and I would have you all hear what they have to say."

Migda rose to his feet. He was a stocky man who had never shown any particular proficiency in battle but was always quick and loud in agreeing with anything Joshua said. The other spy, Annath, was of the same ilk. No one questioned the choice of the spies, however, save for Caleb's eloquent snort when their names were announced.

"We went up to Ai and studied its defenses from a ridge that lies to the west of the city," Migda began.

"Well to the west, as I remember," Caleb said in a loud whisper.

Migda flushed and a low undercurrent of laughter ran through the group. Joshua rapped sharply for order.

"As I said," Migda continued, "we studied the defenses of Ai and found the walls tall and strong but the numbers of people small."

"What do you advise then?" Joshua inquired.

"Let two or three thousand men go up and attack Ai," Migda suggested. "The people of the city are but few."

"What Migda says agrees with my own decision," Joshua announced. "We are well encamped here at Gilgal, and it is foolish for the whole army to climb the hills to attack one city. Even as Yahweh delivered Jericho into our hands, he will give us Ai."

"The earth tremors have ceased," Caleb pointed out. "How will we break the walls?"

"With so few people inside to defend the city, we can scale the walls with ladders," Joshua told him.

"And stain them with our blood?" Caleb observed caustically. "Have you discussed the defenses of Ai with anyone who has been *inside* the city, Joshua?"

"There was no need. My decision has been made."

Caleb rose slowly to his feet. The tension between the two men was palpable, filling the air. "Israel has not yet crowned the son of Nun King," the old warrior said heavily, "although each day he acts more and more like one. As for me, if I am to risk my life in an attack upon Ai, I want to know everything I can about the nature of its defenses."

"I told you——" Joshua began furiously, but Caleb cut him off.

"Let us return to the old way, when the captains decide by vote what we shall do," he suggested.

About half the men present joined in a shout of assent, for many of the captains resented the way in which Joshua had relegated them all to the background in matters of policy. A startled look came over Joshua's face, and although his fist was upraised to strike the table and silence all argument peremptorily, he let his hand drop back. "Very well, Caleb," he said with a shrug. "What do you propose?"

"Salmon visited Ai when he spied upon the cities of Canaan for us. I would hear what he has to say."

"Let Salmon speak then," Joshua said stiffly.

Now that Caleb had injected him into the controversy Salmon had no choice save to tell what he knew. As he rose to his feet and looked at the faces staring up at him he thought how much the war councils had changed in the short space of less than a year. They had been real councils once, with every man's opinion respected and the decisions made by vote. Now the fighting men of Israel were divided into two factions. The group dominated by Joshua composed more than half, he judged. They stared at him resentfully, with disapproval of what he had to say already written on their faces. The others, with Caleb as their leader, waited for him to speak.

"I believe, as Joshua has said, that we should move next against the city of Ai," Salmon began. "Of the three routes westward into Canaan, that to the south leads to the city of Urusalim, which has the strongest walls and the largest army in all of Canaan. It is also defended by Egyptian mercenaries."

"I say leave the Egyptians to themselves," Khalith said promptly, and a chorus of assent arose, even from those who supported Joshua.

"The other two routes," Salmon continued, "lead to Ai and converge before it. We could move our army by either road and still reach the city."

"What of its defenses?" Khalith asked.

"Ai has only one wall, but it is stronger than the wall of Jericho was. I saw many men capable of bearing arms in the city, and well-trained soldiers guarded the wall and the gates."

"Would you go against it with only part of our forces," Caleb asked, "as Migda has advised?"

"I would hurl our whole strength against Ai," Salmon said without hesitation. "Then if the defenders are few—as Migda claims—our task will be light and our losses few. But if it is well defended, we can still overpower them."

"We are indebted to Salmon," said Joshua, cutting off further questions. "But it is well known in Israel that he is not a soldier and does not think like one. In fact—" and here his voice hardened—"Salmon's defiance of the voice of the Most High God sometimes comes close to blasphemy. Migda is a soldier, accustomed to sizing up a military situation, and I accept his opinion. I myself will lead the men who go up against Ai," he added with a confident smile. "You can be sure that Yahweh will give us victory."

"Put it to a vote!" Caleb demanded doggedly. "Those who favor a small body of troops against those who favor a large-scale attack."

"Of course," Joshua agreed, sure of his own following. "Let us vote on it according to our custom."

The vote went as Salmon had known it would from the first, with Joshua's following outnumbering the others. The decision made, the meeting broke up and the captains went to get their troops ready for the expedition against Ai. On Joshua's orders Caleb and the main body of warriors were to remain at Gilgal, but Salmon was instructed to accompany the party as chief physician for the armies of Israel.

"Why is Joshua so insistent upon attacking Ai with a smaller force?" Salmon asked Caleb as they were leaving the council.

"To prove that he no longer needs me and those who follow me," the old warrior said promptly.

"But he must know he cannot get along with only half the army."

Caleb shrugged. "When you believe that God fights at your right hand, it is easy to convince yourself you cannot lose."

287

"Do you think he will be defeated at Ai?"

Caleb shook his head slowly. "When we took Jericho, the earthquake breached the walls for us and we marched over the rubble into the city. If Yahweh does indeed fight on the side of Joshua, as he claims, the same thing may happen at Ai. Then a small force would be enough. If he does not——" He shrugged and left the sentence unfinished.

Salmon had not seen Rahab very often during the past week. She had been busy with her campaign to make Joshua notice her and, disapproving of what she was doing, he had stayed away. As he sat before his tent late in the afternoon before the departure for Ai, preparing medical supplies, she came through the camp and, kneeling beside him, began to tear cloth into strips for bandages.

"I came to tell you I am sorry for the way I talked to you, Salmon," she said half defiantly.

He smiled and put his lean brown hand on her slender white one. "There is nothing to forgive," he told her. "It was another who spoke harshly to me, not the Rahab I know."

She shook her head. "That was the real one, else why should I want to hurt someone I love dearly?"

"Sometimes when we are angry and hurt by others we lash out and strike anyone who is near. But those who love us understand and forgive."

She looked up at him then, and he saw that her eyes were filled with tears. "Except for my baby, Salmon, I would put Joshua out of my mind. I loved Prince Hazor because he was good and kind to me, and I love you for the same reason. Once I loved Joshua in a different way; perhaps I do still. But now I only want to make him give my boy his rightful place in Israel."

"There is a place waiting for Jaschar now."

She gave him a startled glance. "What are you saying?"

"That I would be proud to accept him as my son," he said simply.

"Even when you know Joshua is his father?"

"It would make no difference if I did not know who the father was."

"Would you feel the same way if I were really the common harlot the people here think I am?" she insisted.

"What you have or have not been makes no difference to

288

me," he assured her. "It is what you are now that I love, Rahab."

"Even though I taunted you with lies?"

"I told you that was another person."

"Where did you ever know the real Rahab?"

"At the Cave of Yah, when we talked of the Song of Ikhnaton. And when you taught me what our god is really like."

"If we could only find a place like that again," she said softly, "how wonderful it would be."

"I have found it," he assured her.

She turned quickly, her eyes aglow. "Where, Salmon? Where?"

"To the north of here, on the shores of a lake called Chinnereth. A place so beautiful you would want to paint it the moment you saw it." He put his hand on hers again. "Will you go there with me when the fighting is over? As my wife? We could take Chazan with us, and Jaschar can learn to sail little boats on the waters of the lake."

She turned her hand beneath his and gave his fingers a quick, grateful squeeze. "Thank you, Salmon," she said, and her eyes were wet. "Thank you for that."

"I am in earnest," he assured her. "Very much in earnest. All this bloodshed sickens me; I can't believe Yah intended it this way."

"You can't leave your people until the fighting is done," she protested. "They need your skill with the wounded—and the sick."

"But when the fighting is over——"

"Will it ever be?"

"If Yahweh has given Canaan to us as Joshua believes, we will soon capture it. And if he has not, then we will soon be defeated and will not be able to fight again for a long time. We could go to Chinnereth then, Rahab. It might even be only a few months from now."

She shook her head gently. "I have an obligation too, Salmon. You know how children torture those who are not like themselves. I don't want that for Jaschar," she said, a deep earnestness in her voice. "They wouldn't dare revile Joshua's son, so if I can make him want me enough to marry

289

me and acknowledge his son before all the people, I must do it—for Jaschar's sake."

"But would you—or Jaschar—be happy that way? You know how Joshua has changed."

"Sometimes—when I think of the good people in Jericho who were burned and killed—I almost hate Joshua," she admitted. "But the baby is mine, Salmon. My body bore him, and I will not see him shamed for something that is not his fault."

"Then the answer is no?"

She leaned over and kissed him quickly on the cheek. "I shall always love you and respect you for what you said today," she told him. "And I will ask Yah to keep you safe when the armies go into battle."

Nine

AS IT HAPPENED, Salmon had need of Rahab's prayers before the campaign against Ai was over. In fact, but for the courage and fighting skill of Joshua, he and all the party who went up against Ai the next day would have been beyond the help of anyone before the brief battle was finished.

The sun had not yet sent its first exploring rays of light across the mountaintops and through the steep-sided valleys when the group of about two thousand men chosen by Joshua for the attack moved out of the camp at Gilgal. So confident was he that Migda's estimate of the strength of Ai was correct that they carried no battering-rams or siege towers, only scaling ladders with which to clamber over the wall in a swift attack.

Ai's position as the easternmost advance post of the populous cities on the upland plateau of Canaan was a strong one. Firmly ensconced upon the crest of a low hill, the city looked eastward across a tangled wilderness of steep-sided valleys toward the Jord. Deep watercourses surrounded it and made the approach doubly difficult.

The only visible weakness of Ai, as the Israelites paused to reconnoiter before launching the attack, seemed to be its water supply. This was a tiny spring gushing from the rock on the northwest side of the hill upon which the city stood, reached by a winding path from above. But since they planned a frontal assault rather than a prolonged siege, the water supply would play little, if any, part in the battle.

From where they had halted to rest before attacking, Salmon could look down across the defenses of Ai. And indeed it did seem that Migda had been right in his estimate of the city's defenses, for they saw few soldiers upon the wall. Nor were there many people moving about on the streets.

A little over two hundred paces square—according to Salmon's estimate—the wall of the city was not so thick as Jericho's and not nearly so high. From this distance it appeared that a man standing on another's shoulders could see over the wall in places, but it was obviously strong and well built.

Joshua seemed to be pleased by what he saw, for he called out to Salmon with good-natured raillery, "Ai is poorly defended, as Migda reported."

"It was full of people and soldiers when I was there a few months ago," Salmon said dubiously. "Perhaps they heard of our coming and hid themselves to draw us on."

"They will have their wish soon then," Joshua said confidently. "When we flush them from their hiding places they will be sorry they did not fight us upon the wall." He raised his arm and swept it down. "Sound the trumpets for the attack."

As the long, curved ram's horns sent a blast of sound sweeping toward the city of Ai, the men of Israel swung to the attack, shouting the high-pitched yells that had struck fear into the hearts of King Sihon and his men before Heshbon and into the defenders of Jericho.

The land to the east of the city, across which they were moving, fell away from the wall in a series of descending terraces. These would have made excellent outer bastions for its defense, but they were completely undefended. Not even an arrow came from the wall as the Israelites swept up across the terraces. Scaling ladders were set up without opposition, and the men began to ascend them, shouting their exaltation

291

at the prospect of such a strong city as this being yielded to them almost without a battle.

Watching from the post he had set up near the spring for treating the wounded, Salmon saw the ease with which the attack had gone so far and wondered what could be happening inside the city. It almost seemed that fear of the Israelites had actually rendered the men of Ai helpless, or that Yahweh, as Joshua believed, was indeed delivering it into their hands.

He had no time for further conjectures, however, for the situation changed with almost magical swiftness. Where no defenders had been upon the wall a moment before, ranks of bowmen now appeared suddenly, aiming their weapons down at the Israelites on the scaling ladders and shooting as fast as they could fit arrows to the bowstrings. The first hail of arrows struck down those highest up on the ladders. And as they fell, those behind them were swept from the rungs and sent crashing to the ground.

The screams of the wounded and the dying drowned out the shouts of the attackers, but above them could be heard Joshua's voice, urging the men of Israel forward. The sudden surprise of the enemy's ruse had taken all the initial force from the Israelite attack. Men ran for shelter while the deadly hail of arrows rained down upon them, and the mass of attackers milled around aimlessly before the wall, helpless targets for the bowmen of Ai.

Now a trumpet sounded from inside the city. The gate swept open, and a body of spearmen poured through it to harass the flank of the now thoroughly demoralized Israelites. But for the courage and fighting heart of Joshua, the day would have been lost then and there. He moved at once to meet this new attack, shouting for his own troops to rally around him.

The shock of contact with the spearmen of Ai had set the Israelites back momentarily, but as more and more of them rallied around Joshua, the rout gradually slowed to an almost orderly retreat. Fighting like a man possessed, Joshua stabbed and hacked at the attackers while he gave ground slowly, shouting commands to the other captains to marshal their men and get the retreat under control.

Back down across the terraces they moved, fighting every

step of the way. Caught by the swiftness of the rout while he was working to staunch the bleeding wound of an Israelite soldier, Salmon was almost captured. Only when Khalith happened to see his plight and sent a party of men to guard his retreat with the wounded was he able to extract himself from what had almost been his last military experience.

Back down the rocky canyons and small valleys leading to the plain the harassed and broken forces of Israel stumbled in defeat. They dragged or carried their wounded as best they could while fighting off the men of Ai, who never let them rest until they were completely beyond the valley where the city lay. Only then did the pursuers finally turn back to their city and leave the pursued to limp home.

In the shelter of a tree at the Israelite camp of Gilgal, Salmon set up his boxes and his bags of balms and medicines and instruments. Rahab came to help him dress the wounds of the battered and broken Israelite troops. They worked together throughout the afternoon, staunching the flow of blood from wounds, applying splints to broken and wounded limbs, administering the sleep-producing poppy leaves to those for whom there was no hope.

When finally no one else waited, Salmon looked up and saw Caleb standing by with a wineskin in his hand.

"Drink," the old warrior ordered, handing them the skin. "And tell me what happened, Salmon. Joshua is raving so much I can't learn anything from him."

"Joshua fought magnificently," Salmon said as he waited for Rahab to drink from the wineskin.

"Joshua always fights magnificently," said Caleb dryly. "Khalith tells me that but for him the whole force would have been destroyed. What I want to know is why he had to fight a retreat."

"They must have had scouts watching for us. When we reached the city hardly anyone was visible, just as Migda said. But when the soldiers started up the scaling ladders, a host of bowmen suddenly appeared on the wall and shot them down."

"I thought it must have been like that," Caleb said soberly. "Joshua is blaming the defeat upon the wrath of Yahweh against us, but the truth is that the men of Ai outwitted us. They must have discovered Migda and Annath when they went up to scout the city, and arranged for only a few soldiers to be seen."

"It could have happened that way," Salmon agreed.

"What will you do now?" Rahab asked. "Leave Ai standing and attack another city?"

Caleb smiled grimly. "You don't know Joshua, girl. He will take Ai now and put it to the *herem*, or destroy Israel in the attempt."

"I had time to look the situation over before the attack," said Salmon. "A high ridge lies very close to Ai on the west, between it and the city of Bethel. And a road leading westward winds around the end of the ridge very close to the city, but hidden from it."

Caleb's eyes lit up. "The men of Ai will be confident after defeating us. If a small force like the one they just defeated repeats the attack in a few days, they might come out against it as they did today." He clapped Salmon on the shoulder. "It is a good plan. At the right time we will reveal it to Joshua."

Darkness had already fallen by the time Salmon and Rahab finished dressing the wounded. Noticing that a crowd had gathered before the tent covering the Ark of the Covenant, and hearing Joshua's voice, they joined them.

The Israelite leader stood before the tent, with the elders and the priests in the background. They had rent their garments and were dressed in sacks, and their faces were black with ashes and soot.

"Alas, O Lord God!" Joshua cried, lifting his arms in supplication. "Why hast thou brought this people across the Jord at all, to give us into the hands of the enemy to destroy us? Would that we had been content to dwell beyond the river."

Around them people were falling on their faces in the dust, tearing their clothing, and beating the earth as Joshua had been doing, in an agony of self-abasement.

"What can I say, when Israel has turned their backs before their enemies?" Joshua cried. "The Canaanites and all inhabitants of the land will hear of it. They will surround us and cut us off from the earth."

Again a great wailing went up. Emulating Joshua and the

elders, many of the Israelites prostrated themselves in the dirt before the tent that housed the Ark of the Covenant, crying out to their god to have mercy upon them.

As he watched this display of self-abasement, Caleb's lips twisted in a wry smile. "Only Joshua would dare blame his defeat upon the Lord. But he will have to find a more willing scapegoat, I think—one nearer home."

Joshua had been standing, arms upthrust toward the sky, his eyes uplifted as if he were listening to a voice none of them could hear. "He is listening to the commandment of the Lord," someone whispered, and like something passed from hand to hand, the words went through the crowd.

"Thus saith the Lord." Joshua spoke in solemn tones. " 'Israel has sinned; they have transgressed my covenant which I have commanded them. They have taken some of the dedicated things. They have stolen and hid and put them among their own things.' "

Salmon felt Rahab seize his arm and glanced quickly at her. To his surprise, he saw that her eyes were hot with indignation and her cheeks flushed. And yet he remembered nothing in Joshua's words that could have made her angry.

"Therefore, the people of Israel cannot stand before their enemies," Joshua shouted accusingly. "They turn their backs before their enemies because they have become a thing for destruction." He paused, and then his deep tones rolled out across the prostrate people, like the voice of doom itself. "Thus saith the Lord, 'I will be with you no more unless you destroy the dedicated things from among you. You cannot stand before your enemies until you take them away.' "

"Come, Salmon," Rahab whispered, pulling at his sleeve. "I have something to tell you."

As they were turning away, Joshua lowered his head. His eyes were blazing now as he looked upon the people. "Tomorrow you shall be brought near by tribes," he thundered. "The tribe which the Lord takes shall come near by families; and the family which the Lord takes shall come near by households. The household which the Lord takes shall come near man by man. Then he who is taken with the dedicated things shall be burned with fire, he and all that he has, because he has transgressed the Covenant of the Lord and because he has done a shameful thing in Israel."

"Yahweh must have indeed spoken to Joshua tonight," Salmon said, his voice filled with awe. "Else how would he have known of the silver and gold buried by Achan?"

Rahab did not answer until they were in her tent, where their words would not be overheard. "You heard Caleb say Joshua needs a scapegoat to blame for the defeat," she said. "Well, he found one. Tomorrow, when the lots are cast, the death of many people will be upon my conscience."

"Why?"

"Before you attacked Ai I was passing Joshua's tent, wearing my jewelry and painted like a harlot, hoping to make him notice me. This time Joshua came out and accused me of selling myself to the men to buy jewelry and fine clothes. In a fit of anger I told him about the gold and silver that Achan buried, so he would know his own people are no better than I am. Now he is using what I told him to shift the blame for his defeat." Suddenly she buried her face in her hands. "Why must I bring trouble to everyone, Salmon? Kanofer desired me and let Kalak kill Hazor so he could have me. And now, because I was angry at Joshua, many people will die."

"Achan took gold and silver that was dedicated to the Lord," he reminded her. "According to our laws, that is punishable by death."

"Everyone takes it," she cried. "You admitted that yourself. Joshua knew Achan was guilty, but he would have said nothing if he had not been defeated. If he had really been sincere, he would not have gone against Ai until the ones who had sinned were punished."

Caleb, Salmon knew, now believed Joshua to be only an opportunist, drunk with power and sure that whatever he decided to do was the will of Yahweh. But Salmon had not gone that far. He wanted desperately to believe that Joshua was merely using this method of bringing Israel to its senses and turning them away from greed and the worship of gold and silver. And yet Rahab's logic was hard to dispute.

"You see," she cried, "even you cannot defend him now. And if Joshua would punish others because of his own failure in battle, he would——"

"We don't know that," Salmon interrupted. "We don't

know that Joshua is shifting the blame. Yahweh may really be punishing Israel because so many have taken the devoted things."

"If he does this," she cried indignantly, "he would destroy anything that stood in his way." Suddenly her eyes widened and the color ebbed from her cheeks. "He may even destroy me—and his son—because I have tried to shame him before the people."

Salmon looked quickly away lest his eyes betray him. He remembered now what Caleb had said when he and Rahab had been on the point of being attacked by the crowd the night after Jericho was taken, and the memory troubled him sorely.

"You know something you are not telling me, Salmon," Rahab said suddenly. "You never were any good at hiding things. What is it?"

He reached up and took her hands from his shoulders, holding them in his own. They were trembling and damp with the cold sweat of fear now, not for herself, he knew, but for Jaschar.

"Do you remember the night you came to the camp from Jericho?" he asked.

"I remember," she said grimly. "Joshua called me a harlot and Jaschar a harlot's brat."

"Caleb was at Joshua's tent that night and heard the message brought to him that the people were about to kill you and the baby. He made no move to help, so Caleb came on his own account and saved us."

For a moment Rahab did not speak. When she did, her face was devoid of color. "Then these past few days," she said slowly, "when I was so bent on flaunting myself before Joshua and shaming him, I may have been sending Jaschar to his death."

"Caleb and I will protect you," Salmon assured her. "We still have a great influence in Israel."

"No one can stand against Joshua now." She seized his arms with fingers that dug into his flesh. "Take me away from here, Salmon, before it is too late," she begged. "Some terrible thing is going to happen. I've felt it before and I have always been right."

Concerned as Salmon was for Rahab, he could not help

297

feeling a warm sense of happiness because she had at last put herself wholly in his care. She might not love him freely yet—not in the way any man who loved a woman would want her to love him—but he could hope now that the rest would come when there was an end to the fighting.

"All of Canaan is armed against Israel," he told her. "We would be killed anywhere we went. But the Sea of Chinnereth will still be there when the fighting is finished."

She drew away from him then, and her words were a cry of despair. "The fighting will never be finished! You should know that by now. It will never be finished until Canaan is destroyed—or Joshua is dead."

Ten

THE CEREMONY of casting lots to determine a guilty person was a solemn occasion, and the multitude of Israel gathered on the open plain before the camp the following morning at the appointed time. Joshua himself, magnificently arrayed, stood before the priests with a box containing the Urim and Thummim, the sacred objects which were shaken to determine the selection by lot. There was no clamor today. The only sounds were the rattle of the Urim and Thummim in the box and Joshua's solemn voice announcing the verdict of the lots.

First came the leaders of the twelve tribes. One by one the innocence of each was established. At each fall of the lot in their favor, a sigh of relief went up from the involved family. It was a moment of great tension, rising to an almost unbearable height when only two tribes remained, those of Judah and Gad.

Joshua himself heightened the drama, it seemed to Salmon as he watched with Rahab and Caleb. As the choice narrowed, the Israelite leader's movements became more deliberate, his study of the position of the Urim and Thummim when they were cast more prolonged. Finally he raised his hand dramatically and let it fall in a gesture of decision between the two remaining tribes.

Judah had been taken!

A murmur of resentment against the guilty tribe—coupled with relief on the part of the others—went through the crowd. Those who had escaped relaxed and began to talk, but Joshua stopped them with an upraised hand.

"Silence!" he thundered. "Let the tribe of Judah come before me by families."

Judah was the largest of all the tribes of Israel, with many families, so this time the casting took longer. Again it was near the end of the choosing before the lot fell upon the family of the Zerahites.

Rahab had been standing beside Caleb and Salmon, observing the ceremony. Not being one of a family in Israel, she was not concerned, but she found herself watching with all the eagerness and suspense of those who were involved, so dramatic was the scene. While the households of the family of Zerah were arranging themselves for the next casting, she whispered to Salmon, "Why do the guilty always come last?"

"They let the others go first, hoping that some of them will be chosen by the lots because they are guilty of another crime."

"It is true," she marveled. "The household of Zabdi are the last family of the Zerahites waiting to be judged. Achan is among them."

Again the relentless casting of the Urim and Thummim continued. No one but Joshua would ever know, of course, whether the lots fell of their own accord into the pattern he was announcing, for only he saw them and reported the verdict. Finally the number of Zabdi, the father of Carmi—who in turn was the father of Achan, the guilty one—was chosen.

Caleb turned to Rahab and said with a grin, "Your tent is beside those of the household of Zabdi, Rahab. You must be glad you are not an Israelite by birth."

"Achan is the guilty one," Salmon said quietly so that only Caleb could hear. "Rahab heard him burying the loot inside his tent the night following the fall of Jericho."

"By the beard of Pharaoh!" the old soldier exclaimed. "The lot is falling true then."

"Rahab told Joshua yesterday, before he announced the casting of the lots."

Caleb's lips pursed in a soundless whistle. "The son of Nun

knows a windfall when he sees it. Casting the lots has taken the mind of the people off his defeat at Ai and will give him a scapegoat too."

The family of Zabdi were gathering before Joshua now. They moved slowly, for it was certain that one of them was the guilty party, according to the inexorable verdict of the lots from which there was no appeal by Israelite law. When all the men stood before him, Joshua took up the polished wooden box containing the Urim and Thummim. But before he could cast the lots, there was a diversion. Carmi stepped out from among the group and pointed an accusing finger at Rahab.

"There stands the cause of Israel's downfall!" he shouted. "The tent of the harlot is next to those of my family. The lot would point to her if she were on trial here. Instead, it pointed to us."

Knowing how the people had been stirred up against Rahab by Achan and his family, Salmon realized that he must act quickly, and stepped forward to face Carmi. "The guilty man must be in the household of Carmi," he accused. "Else why would he try to shift the blame to an innocent woman?"

"Rahab was in Jericho," Carmi shouted angrily. "The curse was put upon the whole city, but she was allowed to escape because of you and Caleb. Now the wrath of Yahweh has come upon us all because the harlot was not destroyed with the city."

A murmur of assent rose from the crowd, particularly the tribe of Judah. Here was a chance to pin the blame for the disaster at Ai upon someone not an Israelite, and they were ready to seize it.

"Let the harlot be destroyed as her city was," someone shouted from the crowd. "Then the curse will be fulfilled."

Rahab caught her breath as the full import of what they were saying suddenly became clear to her. The terrible curse of the *herem* meant destruction, not only for the person accused but all his family and even his possessions. Not only would she be burned with the symbolic fire of God's wrath, but also her baby and Myrnah and Senu, who had escaped with her from Jericho.

The crowd was shouting angrily now. Joshua had trouble making himself heard when he ordered them to be silent.

"Would you deny the voice of the Lord, spoken through the Urim and Thummim?" he demanded angrily. "The casting of the lots will continue."

"What about Rahab?" Carmi insisted. "Judah will not stand by and see the guilt cast upon us when the harlot is to blame."

It was a shrewd move, appealing to the whole tribe of Judah, the largest and most important group in Israel. After the defeat at Ai, Joshua needed the full support of the people for the second attack, which he must make if he was not to lose face in Israel and—most important of all—in his own estimation. And Judah would be an important part of that support.

Joshua hesitated only a moment, however. When he spoke again, his voice was that of authority, brooking no question.

"If the choice falls upon anyone in the household of Carmi," he said, "he may demand to have the lot cast between him and the harlot, Rahab."

"What if the guilt be hers?" Carmi insisted.

"She shall be burned with the fires of *herem*, she and all her household with her."

It was a fair decision according to the custom of the Israelites. The lot—traditionally the decision of Yahweh—would select only the guilty one and free the innocent. Salmon had no grounds for protest, nor did Rahab. And yet, he wondered, would the lot now fall according to chance? Or according to the will of Joshua?

Rahab understood his unspoken thought. "Do you think Joshua would let it choose me and destroy his own child?" she asked quickly.

"Of course not," Salmon said reassuringly. "Achan is the guilty one." But in his heart he was far from sure.

Rahab's return had been an embarrassment to Joshua, and her insistence that little Jaschar was his own son had been an even greater one. He had denied the child and Rahab before the people, but when the baby grew older and was out of swaddling clothes, it would soon be apparent to everyone that he was Joshua's son. Every line of Jaschar's strongly built little body—except the twisted foot—proclaimed his inheritance of his father's traits.

Nor could Salmon help remembering that the Israelite

leader would have let Rahab and the child be destroyed on the night following the fall of Jericho, when she had first come into the camp of Israel. Now Joshua had been presented with a seemingly God-given opportunity to throw the blame for their defeat upon Rahab and turn her over to the wrath of the people, thus ridding himself of both her and the child.

Could Rahab afford to put herself at the mercy of Joshua and the decision of the lots? Salmon wondered. And if not, what could he do to avoid the final decision that must condemn either her or a member of an important family of Judah to death?

"The lot has fallen to Achan," Joshua's announcement brought Salmon's busy thoughts back to the present—and with it an answer to the dilemma.

"The harlot is guilty!" Achan cried. "Our tents are side by side. The Urim and Thummim cannot distinguish them."

"Bring the harlot forward," Joshua ordered. "Let the lot be cast between her and Achan."

"Why should the lot be cast again?" Achan protested. "It is obvious that, since she is not of Israel, the Urim and Thummim chose the tent next to hers."

Achan's family, hoping to save him, set up a shout of agreement; and the tribe of Judah, wishing to escape the onus of having one of the number branded a thief, joined in. Since Judah was the largest tribe, many of the people followed her lead, and a great shouting arose. More than half the crowd, it seemed, was eager for Rahab's death as the clamor grew into an uproar, like hounds baying for the kill.

Joshua looked out over the crowd but made no move to quiet them. Watching him, Salmon could almost read the thought in the Israelite leader's mind. Sure now what that thought was, he decided not to wait any longer before putting into effect the stratagem that had unfolded in his mind during the tension-filled moments while Joshua had been making the final cast which had named Achan the guilty one. It was a desperate measure, but only desperate measures could save Rahab now.

"Rahab," he said, turning to her, "will you do just as I say?"

She too had seen the look on Joshua's face and had realized

302

its probable meaning. "Don't involve yourself, Salmon," she begged. "Only try to save Jaschar if you can."

"I can save you both," he promised, "if you do exactly as I tell you."

Joshua lifted his hand for silence preparatory to his decision, and the crowd gradually quieted. Before he could speak, however, Salmon moved quickly into the open space where the casting of lots was being carried out.

"I speak for Rahab," he announced. "She is willing for the question of guilt to be decided between her and Achan."

Salmon saw Joshua relax as he picked up the box containing the Urim and Thummim. "Let Rahab and Achan stand before me then," he said, and there was no mistaking the relief in his voice.

A smile curved Achan's lips, indicating that he too had heard the note of relief—and interpreted it as a sign that Joshua would not make the throw fall against a member of the powerful house of Judah.

"Rahab demands her right under the customs of Israel," Salmon announced.

"What right?" Joshua asked, startled.

"The right of choice," Salmon said quietly. "She chooses the ordeal by fire."

Eleven

THE ordeal by fire was but rarely invoked, although perfectly legal under the laws of Israel. It involved each of the contesting parties touching the tongue to a piece of hot metal. Whoever was burned was immediately damned as guilty without recourse.

Salmon was watching Achan closely and felt a sudden rush of exultation when he saw the color suddenly drain from the guilty man's face. Achan tried to swallow but seemed to have difficulty, for he gulped as if his throat were dry. His actions were in themselves sufficient evidence of his guilt, but Joshua seemed not to notice. He was looking at Salmon with a strange expression on his face, part relief and part frustration.

"It is a trick," Achan exclaimed hoarsely. "Salmon spends much time with the harlot. He seeks to evade the verdict of Yahweh."

"The ordeal by fire is recognized by our law as the decision of Yahweh," Salmon said quietly. "Ask Joshua if this is not true."

For a moment Joshua did not answer. Then he sighed as if carrying out a duty reluctantly. "The decision by fire is the voice of Yahweh under the customs of Israel," he admitted. "Let the spear be heated at once."

The preparations for the ordeal were simple enough. Coals were brought from one of the cooking fires, and a small flame, only enough to heat the point of a spear, was kindled. When it was burning freely, Joshua took a bronze spear and put the point into the fire to heat.

While the metal was heating, Salmon took Rahab by the hand and led her aside where they would not be overheard. She was pale, but when she lifted her eyes to him he saw that she was unafraid.

"Trust me," he told her. "Trust me and it will come out all right. Achan's guilt will be proved."

"Who can I trust if not you, Salmon?" she said simply. "Tell me what I must do, and I will do it."

"Touch the glowing spear point with your tongue when it is held before you," he directed. "Touch it quickly and draw away immediately. You will hear a hissing sound, but you will not be burned. Achan will have the right to be first, but he will hold back. I want you to go first."

"How can you be so sure?"

"You are innocent, we know that. And Achan knows he is guilty. The longer he waits, the more certain he will be to betray his guilt."

Caleb came over to them then, his face grave. "The spear is almost ready," he said. "Since Rahab chose the test, Achan insists that she go first."

Salmon spoke loudly enough for all to hear. "Did not the Lord say to Moses, *You shall purge the guilt of innocent blood from Israel, so that it may be well with thee*? Be sure that Yahweh will choose the guilty today and preserve the innocent."

The bronze point of the spear was glowing faintly in the flames when Rahab came forward for the test. Salmon walked on one side and Caleb on the other. The old soldier's face was set in a stern line, but Rahab showed no fear, and a murmur of wonder went up from the crowd at her composure. Glancing at Achan again, Salmon noted with a surge of satisfaction that he was still pale. When the guilty man saw Salmon's eyes upon him, he looked away and licked at his lips nervously with the tip of his tongue.

"May Yahweh choose whether Achan or the harlot, Rahab, is guilty for the wrath of God that has been visited upon us," Joshua said, and lifted the spear point from the flames. Holding it close to his face, he spat on the glowing metal.

The crackling sound of the spittle as it turned to steam was loud enough for all the people to hear. The nearest of them could even see the tiny drops dance on the hot metal before they suddenly burst and disappeared.

"You are to go first," Joshua said to Rahab. "Take the spear handle in your hand and touch the glowing point with your tongue. Draw it quickly away, and if you are innocent, you will be unharmed. But if you are guilty, the metal will burn you."

Unhesitatingly Rahab took the spear handle from him. With no sign of hesitation she lifted it to her face. When her tongue licked out and touched the hot surface, the frying of the moisture upon it made a sharp sizzling sound. Yet when she handed the spear back to Joshua and put out her tongue for him to examine, everyone could see that there was no sign of a burn.

"It is your turn, Achan," Joshua said quietly, holding out the spear. The guilty man stumbled a little as he came forward, and his throat worked as if he were trying to swallow.

With trembling fingers Achan took the spear and lifted it slowly. The contrast between Rahab's quiet assurance of innocence and the guilty man's obvious nervousness was so evident that a swelling undercurrent of sound came from the crowd. As Achan brought the spear slowly closer to his face he licked furtively at his dry lips with his tongue.

Twice the guilty man stuck his tongue out without touch-

305

ing the spear point, drawing it back as soon as he felt the warmth of the hot metal. Only on the third try did his tongue finally touch it.

With a scream of pain Achan dropped the spear and clapped his hand to his mouth, gibbering with fear and the agony of sensitive, burned flesh. Turning suddenly, he started to run, but Joshua seized him by the arm and jerked him back roughly.

"Put out your tongue," he ordered sternly. "Let all of Israel see the verdict of Yahweh."

Achan put out his tongue, and a cry went up from the people. Everyone could see the black band across it where the hot spear point had burned into the flesh.

"Take me away, Salmon," Rahab said urgently. "I—I don't want to see any more of this."

Held firmly in Joshua's compelling grip, Achan was already babbling his confession of guilt. And as Rahab and Salmon hurried toward her tent, a group of men passed them on the way to dig up the stolen things.

Salmon himself had no stomach for what would follow; he had seen criminals executed in Israel before. Achan and his immediate family, with all their possessions, would be stoned to death and then utterly destroyed by fire until nothing remained save the pile of stones customarily erected to mark the scene of the punishment handed down to those who broke the laws of Yahweh.

By midafternoon of that day Rahab was herself again. Salmon and Caleb ate the evening meal with her, but Caleb went to his tent as the moon was rising, leaving the two alone together. For a while neither of them spoke. Salmon was content to be near Rahab, and she seemed lost in thought. Finally she turned and put her hand on his; her fingers were warm and very much alive.

"Do you remember another night when we watched the moon rise, Salmon?"

"On the side of Mount Nebo, before the Cave of Yah?"

"Yes. We were happy then."

"I am happy now," he told her gently. "Just to be here with you."

"But you deserve more," she cried. "You deserve my love,

and it is yours, but a man should possess the woman he loves."

"I tell myself that will come in time if you love me and trust me now."

She laughed then, although a little shakily. "You should know I trust you. Didn't I obey you without question this morning?"

"And you came safely through the trial," he reminded her. "Let me look after you for all time and you will be happy. I promise it."

She shook her head slowly. "If I were selfish—and if I didn't love you—I would let you do that. But I must not put upon you the responsibility of another man's child—a cripple. You deserve more than that, Salmon."

"Not even if I am willing to take it?"

"I cannot seek happiness for myself by denying Jaschar his birthright. As Joshua's son, even the twisted foot would make little difference. But otherwise——"

She did not have to complete the picture for him. As leader of the victorious armies of Israel, Joshua's position was already a high one. He might even be a king one day, for he seemed to have a knack of turning defeat into victory, as had happened today when the punishment of Achan had taken away whatever odium had fallen upon him because of the defeat before Ai. Joshua's son would always be respected in Israel, even though a cripple.

As a physician, however, Salmon would never be rich. His family would dwell in a house like others in whatever village they chose as their home. His stepson would be on the same level with the other children of the village, with only Rahab's love and his own to protect the boy. And that, they had seen ample evidence, was not enough.

Twice already in Israel both Rahab and the child had been near death. There would be other times, too, for the powerful tribe of Judah and the family of Zerah would not soon forgive her—although the verdict of guilty had actually been Yahweh's according to the ordeal—for establishing the guilt of one of their members and bringing shame upon the tribe.

"You know yourself it cannot be," Rahab said gently.

"But I would treat the boy as if he were my own."

"I know that, but it would still not be the same. Today—

since what happened this morning—I have been thinking of a way out of all this. I think Joshua loved me once, at least for a little while. Caleb has told me how he was shamed before the men when I disappeared with the bride price."

"It was only his pride——"

"I know," she agreed. "Joshua's pride is very important to him, and, I know now that he will never accept me. But every man wants a son, Salmon, even Joshua. I think he would take Jaschar as his own if I were not involved, so the only thing for me to do is go away. Joshua can feel no shame then. The son of a concubine bought for a price often becomes the heir of his father and sometimes even a king."

"Who would look after the child?"

"Myrnah loves Jaschar and so does Senu. Joshua could take them as his slaves. And you would be here."

"What would you do?"

"The only thing I seem to know how to do, I suppose; the only way a woman alone can live."

"You never were a harlot," Salmon cried indignantly.

Rahab shrugged. "What difference does a word make? I could have let Kanofer kill Jaschar and me in Jericho—perhaps both of us would have been better off. But I preferred to live—even in the arms of a man I hated. That makes me a harlot."

"It was to save the baby," he protested.

"I may have used Jaschar as an excuse to save myself."

They had been sitting outside Rahab's tent, and now Salmon got to his feet. "I must go, else the tongues of Judah will be murmuring against you," he told her. "Promise me that you will do nothing until I have had time to think this out. Joshua may acknowledge the boy yet as his son. If he does, you and I will go to the Sea of Chinnereth together."

"You will only make Joshua angry," she warned. "Let me do this my way—by going away alone."

"They have named me more than once the cleverest man in Israel," he told her with a smile. "I will find an answer to this somehow."

308

Twelve

SALMON was passing Joshua's tent on the way to his own when he heard his name spoken. He looked up and saw the Israelite leader sitting on a cushion before the tent, with a bed of glowing coals before him.

"Come here a moment, Salmon," Joshua called. "I would talk to you."

The physician moved over to the tent and took a cushion beside Joshua. "What did you wish with me?" he asked.

"I want us to be comrades again as we were in the wilderness and in the battles east of the Jordan."

"Much has happened since then," Salmon said quickly. "Neither of us is the same."

"You and Caleb have turned against me. Why?"

"Perhaps we have all changed," Salmon admitted. "But you have become the mouthpiece of Yahweh."

Joshua smiled. "Once they only called me the Hornet of God. I think I was happier then."

"I am tired of bloodshed and burning and pillaging," Salmon cried, his anger breaking through now. "And you—sometimes I think you believe yourself to be a god or his avenging angel, Joshua."

For a long moment Joshua did not speak. "When I was merely a soldier, Salmon," he said finally, "I thought only of fighting and left other things to the priests. It must have been the will of Yahweh that I should lead his people, else I would have been struck down long ago."

"I think it *was* his will that you should lead Israel," Salmon agreed. "But not as you are doing."

"I must lead as Joshua would lead, not as Caleb or even Salmon. Our god directs his people through men; even Moses became angered and struck the rock, remember, and his anger brought hardships and suffering upon our people. When God raises up a man to a high place, he raises him with all his faults as well as his virtues. If his virtues exceed

309

his faults, he will succeed; if they do not, he will fail. But either way, he is doing the will of the Lord, for he cannot do otherwise."

"I never thought of it that way," Salmon admitted.

"Nor I, until tonight. You think we lost Ai because I wished to make a great show by conquering the city with a few men, don't you?"

"Yes. And so does Caleb."

"Had I been you, Salmon, or Caleb, I might have acted in some other way," Joshua admitted. "But being me, I could only act in the one way that I did—and we were defeated. Yet this morning God named Achan the traitor responsible for my defeat."

"God—or you, Joshua?"

"Then you know Rahab told me yesterday that Achan had stolen the devoted things?"

"Yes."

"And you believe I cast the lots to identify Achan?"

"What else would you expect me to believe?"

"Nothing, I suppose," Joshua admitted. "But I will swear to you upon the Ark of the Covenant that lies within the tent there that I did nothing to influence the fall of the Urim and Thummim this morning."

It was Salmon's turn to be startled. And when he looked into the other man's eyes by the faint light of the fire still glowing before the tent, he knew that Joshua was telling the truth.

"Would you have let them fall of their own accord on the last throw? The one between Rahab and Achan?"

Joshua looked down at the fire. "I don't know, Salmon," he admitted. "That is what I have been wrestling with here tonight."

"There is one way you can ease your conscience. By acknowledging the child as your own."

"Is it my own?" Joshua asked without raising his head.

"You need only to look to know that it is. In every way except the twisted foot Jaschar is a small image of you."

"Even a deformed foot would not keep Joshua's son from being respected in Israel."

"Rahab knows that," Salmon told him. "She asks only that you take Jaschar and rear him as your son."

"What of her?"

"She will come to you—as your slave if you want it that way—if only you will accept the child as your son." He was throwing away his own chances for happiness with the woman he loved, but he still must do it, if by any chance he could enable Rahab to remain with her baby.

Joshua studied Salmon for a long moment. "You ask me to do that? Even though you love her and want her for yourself?"

"I love Rahab enough to want what is best for her—and the boy," Salmon said simply.

Joshua drew a line in the dust with his finger. "I once heard Moses tell how the Lord commanded him, 'You shall not hate your brother in your heart, but you shall reason with your neighbor, lest you bear sin because of him. You shall not take vengeance or bear any grudge against the sons of your own people, but you shall love your neighbor as yourself.' I wear the mantle of Moses, Salmon, but your love goes even farther than the commandments of God. I wonder why this should be?"

"Once you would have risked your life to save mine——"

"I would do it still."

"Is that not the same thing? We were comrades then."

"Until love for a woman came between us."

"It will not any longer," Salmon said slowly. "If you take the child—and Rahab—as your own."

Joshua smiled wryly, and Salmon thought that he was handsomer and more godlike now than he had ever been before. "That is what I have been wrestling with here tonight," he admitted.

"And the outcome?"

"Were my name Salmon, my course would be clear. But I am Joshua. The girl shamed me before my comrades, and other men have lain with her since. I cannot take her as my wife—or even as a slave."

"Jaschar was conceived before Rahab shamed you. She will give him up and go away if you will take him as your son."

"Did she say that?" Joshua asked, startled.

"Just now," Salmon confirmed. "If you refuse to take her with the child, it is the next best thing."

Joshua took a deep breath. "I am slow in thought, Salmon,

311

not quick like you. Let me think of this for a while and give you my decision later, perhaps after our next battle."

"You are going against Ai then?"

"Tomorrow we start preparing. And this time I will follow your strategy, as I did when we were comrades in arms."

Salmon stood up. "Any plan of mine would fail without the arms of the son of Nun to carry it out."

Joshua, too, got to his feet and put his arm around the physician's shoulders. "Then my sword and your keen mind will fight together for the glory of Israel." With his hand on the flap of his tent he turned back to where Salmon stood. "I remember now that I stopped you tonight to ask you a question. Why did you have Rahab elect the ordeal by fire this morning?"

"Because I could not be sure whose hand was directing the throw of the Urim and Thummim."

Joshua nodded slowly. "You were afraid I might take that opportunity to get rid of Rahab and the child. I can see now how far apart we had drifted, my friend."

"Do you deny that the thought came to you?" Salmon asked.

"No," Joshua admitted frankly. "Nor do I deny that I was loath to anger the tribe of Judah. But I don't think I would have cast the lots against Rahab, even so. It was you who took a chance, Salmon—with her life and the boy's. The lot was falling true this morning; it would have gone in her favor because she was innocent."

"I took no chance," Salmon assured him with a smile.

"How can you say that when Rahab could have been stoned with her whole household?"

"I was watching Achan," Salmon explained. "He was continually swallowing because his mouth and his throat were dry, as well as his tongue. Guilt and fear have that effect upon a man."

"How could you be sure of Rahab?"

"She knows I love her and she trusts me. Being unafraid, the moisture on her tongue kept the heat of the arrow point from burning her flesh. But Achan, with no protection for his tongue because of its dryness, was burned."

Joshua looked at him for a moment, a strange light of

humility in his eyes. "Only the stiff-necked pride of the son of Nun would ever have made him believe he could conquer Canaan alone, Salmon," he said. "From now on your nimble mind and Caleb's strong arms will always march beside me into battle."

Book Five

THE VALLEY OF AJALON

*Sun, stand thou still upon Gibeon; and thou, Moon,
in the valley of Ajalon.*

JOSHUA 10:12

One

JOSHUA began preparing the next day for the attack upon the city of Ai, where he had met his first major setback in the campaign to conquer Canaan. He was anxious to launch the new campaign as soon as possible, while the King of Ai and his men were still jubilant over having outwitted the vaunted Israelites. Thus they would more easily fall victims to the stratagem Salmon had devised, involving an ambush when the defenders left the protection of the city's strong wall to destroy what seemed to be a helpless smaller body of Israelite warriors.

This time Joshua took no chances. In order to set up the ambush properly, it was necessary that the main body of men move by night and hide behind the hill separating Ai from Bethel, the next city to the west. There they could prepare a perfect ambush by screening themselves behind a ridge of broken rocks separated from Ai by a short slope.

Having been over the ground around the city twice, once when he had explored Canaan before the crossing of the Jord and the attack upon Jericho, and the other at the time of the recent defeat, Salmon was able to draw a map on a piece of papyrus to guide the troops in the forced march under cover of darkness to take up the position for the ambush.

The easier and more open route ran northwestward, skirting a range of hills around a narrow valley on fairly low ground, then turned westward for a steep ascent to the uplands and past the city of Ai on the north side of the valley it overlooked. But since that route brought them dangerously close to Bethel, from which a warning might be given, it could not be used.

A second main road entered the hills west of Jericho and followed the course of a steep-sided valley westward for about two hours' march, then bent northward around a high ridge. From there it approached Ai by way of a tortuous and rough track that would take them in sight of the wall. This was the route they had taken on the first attack. It, too, was obviously unsuited for a surprise attack since, if the King of Ai exerted even the ordinary military precautions of posting lookouts on the road, he would discover that a large body of troops had passed the city in the night and disappeared, followed by a smaller one which posted itself for the early-morning attack. From these facts it would have been immediately apparent that an ambush was planned.

With obvious disadvantages to both these approaches, Salmon chose a third route instead. And since it required the troops to pass in single file along a narrow ridge-topped path traversing the middle of the crest between the two longer valley routes, they left Gilgal as soon as twilight fell on the evening after the day in which the lots had been cast. Two hours of marching found them in the uplands with a clear path ahead, although still rocky and narrow.

The critical moment in this ascent came shortly before dawn, when a body of troops led by Caleb, with Salmon as usual among them, skirted the sleeping city of Ai through a narrow valley to the south in order to reach the road leading to Bethel, beside which they were planning to hide themselves. Holding their weapons tightly to prevent noise that might warn the defenders of the city, they negotiated the narrow path safely, however. Before the sun rose above the deep valley of the Jord to the east, the main body was securely hidden among the rocks beside the road just outside the city of Ai, but hidden from its defenders by the sharp upthrust of the ridge between it and Bethel.

As the sun rose, Caleb and Salmon with the other captains posted themselves upon the ridge overlooking the valley in which the city of Ai stood, in order to watch the initial moves in this tense game of war. Joshua and the other band of warriors, who were to make the direct attack against Ai in order to draw its defenders from within the walls, were to have left several hours after the main group. Traveling the main road and making no attempt to hide their presence from the enemy, they could achieve a much faster pace than the troops who had been forced to negotiate the high ridge during the darkness.

Salmon saw a file of armed men appear in the hills across the valley and knew that Joshua had executed his part of the preliminary movements exactly on schedule. Well behind him would be the main body of Israel itself, for Joshua had insisted that they should come up to witness the destruction of Ai.

Looking down into the city, Salmon was sure that the defenders were already warned—as he had planned they would be—that a body of Israelite troops was moving to attack them again. Few men showed on the wall, and not many people could be seen moving about inside the city itself. The King of Ai, it seemed, had a low opinion of his opponents' intelligence, for he was using the same stratagem that had been effective against them a few days before.

"I still wonder if they will be such fools as to chase Joshua when he runs away this time," Caleb said as he watched.

"They seem to be following the same tactics as before," Salmon pointed out.

"It will be a great day for the son of Nun if we destroy them. Nothing galls him so much as defeat."

"I had a long talk with Joshua the other night. We may have misjudged him, Caleb."

The old captain shot him a keen speculative glance. "Don't tell me he charmed you into taking his side."

"No. But I understand Joshua better now. If, as he believes, Yahweh has chosen him as his right hand in fulfilling his promise to Abram, he must do what he has to do in his own way."

"Joshua would never do otherwise."

"Would you act other than the way you do if you were chosen instead of Joshua to lead Israel?"

It was Caleb's turn to be thoughtful. "I suppose each of us

must follow his own way of doing things, even in the service of Yahweh," he admitted.

"Joshua says because he is Joshua—not Salmon or Caleb—he can only act as Joshua would act, not as you or I would."

"Must he act as if he is God?" Caleb snorted.

"Being Joshua, he can do nothing else."

"This is a strange sort of idea, Salmon, especially coming from one the son of Nun has wronged as he has you."

"If he has wronged me, it must have been for the good of Israel," Salmon pointed out. "And for that I could forgive him anything."

Caleb shook his grizzled head. "You are more tolerant than I."

"It could be you and I who are wrong, Caleb," Salmon said earnestly. "Remember the commandments Yahweh gave to Moses?"

"They are many," Caleb said, shrugging. "I leave it to the priests to tell me which one I have broken and what sacrifice I should make."

"This one is very simple," Salmon said with a smile. "*What does the Lord require of you, but to fear the Lord your God, to walk in all his ways, to love him, to serve the Lord your God with all your heart and with all your soul.'*"

"Don't tell me Joshua is doing that when he lords it over the rest of us?"

"Yahweh does favor Joshua. Why else would he have sent the earthquake to block the Jord and destroy the walls of Jericho?"

"Enough of this, Salmon," Caleb said irritably. "You are talking like a priest more than ever. Why would Joshua bring all the people to Ai, if not because he wants to play the Hornet of God again before them when the city is destroyed?"

"It could be to give them heart once more when they see how Yahweh gives us victory over the city."

"*If* they see Ai destroyed," Caleb corrected grimly. "I never count a military campaign won until the enemy is dead."

"I'll wager it all comes out as Joshua has planned," Salmon insisted.

"As *you* planned," Caleb corrected him. "If the Lord does

317

indeed fight beside Joshua, he also gave him his best weapon in your cunning mind, Salmon. Don't forget that."

And indeed, as he watched the battle develop, Salmon could not help a feeling of pride. Once the smallness of Joshua's forces was evident to the eager watchers within the city of Ai, they bit sharply upon the tempting bait of an opportunity to destroy another army of Israel. Hardly had the rising sun revealed the presence of the Israelites on the northern slopes when trumpets began to blow inside the city. Shortly, a large body of men marched from it, accompanied by a few chariots. They moved swiftly, obviously intending to take up a position toward the Jord Valley to the southeast and thus cut off any retreat by the Israelites in that direction. In keeping with the deception, Joshua sent a small force to harry their flanks. When these turned to fight, the Israelites retreated, pursued eagerly by the now confident enemy.

Watching from the hillside, Salmon felt a thrill of satisfaction when he saw the battle proceed exactly as he had drawn it for Joshua on a sheet of papyrus, like a game of senit played out on a giant board. When the guardians of the city had been lured beyond the safety of the walls by Joshua's small forces, the large body under Caleb's leadership began to move out of their hiding place, taking shelter where they could to hide their numbers somewhat. They had little need for deception, however; the city's gate stood open while everyone watched the beginning of the great victory they expected their warriors to win this day.

Caleb and his picked group were not more than a hundred paces from the gate of Ai when the first shout of recognition went up from the now doomed city. It was too late then to organize any effective defense. Breaking into a run, Caleb and his troops were inside before the defenders could close the massive wooden barrier. After them poured the full might of Israel, shouting the high-pitched keening cry that was by now their hallmark in battle.

In the valley, the main body of warriors from the city stopped in their pursuit of the fleeing Israelites when the sudden clash of arms came from the gate. While they watched, the Israelite forces split into two streams, one pouring through the gate to take the city, the other down to attack the warriors of Ai. At just this moment Joshua's great curved trumpet

318

of ram's horn sounded from the hillside, and the Israelites who had pretended to flee turned and fell upon the luckless warriors who had been pursuing them in full cry only a moment before.

Salmon shouldered his bag of supplies and made his way down the hillside toward the plain below, for his services would be needed soon, now that the fighting had really begun. Joshua would get the credit, he knew, but the satisfaction was his of knowing that he too had fought for Israel today. And that Yahweh had given him strength—even though of another kind than that which wielded spear and shield in battle.

The battle itself did not last long. With the major part of its defenders trapped on the plain, where they were methodically cut to pieces by the Israelites, and the gate opened for an invading horde, Ai was as defenseless as Jericho had been once its walls had been breached. Soon the roar of flames drowned out even the screams of the dying as the curse of Yahweh was executed upon the city, bringing it to complete destruction, save only for the booty which the Israelites carried from it before the flames devoured everything else.

Two

SALMON had been separated from Rahab during the attack upon Ai, having gone with the main body of men to set up the ambush, while she was with the people who had accompanied Joshua. But he joined her and her household—which now included Chazan in addition to Myrnah and Senu—on the way back to Gilgal.

The journey was a leisurely one, there being no reason for haste now. Besides, the people were heavily laden with loot from the sack of Ai. Myrnah and Senu alternately carried little Jaschar, who was growing stronger and more like Joshua each day, leaving Rahab to walk with Salmon as he led the ass bearing his own medical supplies.

"Caleb told me how your plan of battle made the victory possible," Rahab said. "Why don't you demand your rightful place in the councils of Israel, Salmon?"

"I serve others, not lead them. That is the task of soldiers like Joshua." He had postponed telling Rahab about his talk with her son's father, not wanting to hurt her with the knowledge that Joshua would never accept her and the child together. But now seemed a good time to bring it up.

"I spoke to Joshua about the boy," he said.

"When?" she asked quickly.

"The night after the ordeal. He saw me crossing the camp from your tent and called to me."

"What did he say?"

"He gave me no final answer—but he promised to think about taking Jaschar as his son."

"Without me?"

Salmon nodded. "Joshua still blames you for the embarrassment he felt after you went away."

"Then if he takes the child I must go away?"

"He will have it no other way, I think. It may be the best way, Rahab," he added. "Let Joshua take the boy. You and I can go to Chinnereth together."

She shook her head slowly. "Israel needs you, Salmon, as long as she is at war with the other cities. I realized that more than ever when I saw how easy it was to take Ai with your plan."

"But if I stay in Israel we cannot be together."

"It may be for only a few years," Rahab told him. "You can watch over Jaschar until he is a little older, and send me word how he grows and what he does."

"Where would you go?"

"Hazor had a kinsman in Gibeon, one of the elders who ruled the Hivites, a fine man named Jochab. They worked together trying to build an alliance between Jericho and the cities of Gibeon, Beeroth, Chephirah, and Kirjath-jearim, but the other elders of the Hivites would not agree. Jochab is an old man. If I went to him and asked for shelter, I am sure he would give it to me—for Hazor's sake. I would be safe there and"—she smiled—"not a harlot."

"The Hivite cities will be Joshua's next target after Ai," Salmon pointed out.

"Why? They live together in peace and trouble no one."

An idea had struck Salmon like a ray of light shining through darkness. "This man Jochab," he said quickly. "Would he talk to me about an alliance with Israel if you gave me a letter to him?"

"I am sure he would. Jochab wants peace. But Joshua would never make such an alliance."

"It is worth trying," he insisted. "If Joshua knew he had nothing to fear from the cities to the west, he would be free to move northward. Northern Canaan is large enough for all of Israel, so there would be no need to fight any more. Then we could be together in Chinnereth."

All of Israel was jubilant after the great victory at Ai. When Joshua led them in a great ceremony of thanksgiving, the feasting lasted until far into the night. The next day the council of the elders and the chief captains was called.

More affable than Salmon remembered seeing him in a long time—perhaps not since the attack on King Sihon over a year ago which had brought them their first victory in the land of their forefathers—Joshua opened the conference with an account of the conquests they had achieved in Canaan and a listing of the treasure that had accrued to the glory of Yahweh. His oration completed, they got down to the business at hand, the choice of the next phase of the campaign against Canaan.

"What say you?" he asked the priests. "Against whom will Yahweh lead us next?"

The priests could offer nothing, however, save the assurance that no doubt the voice of God would direct them, as it had in the past, through their great leader.

Joshua turned to Salmon then. "As the physician Samma, you have visited the cities to the west of us, Salmon," he said. "Tell us again what you found there."

Salmon rose to his feet at once, for this was an opportunity he had been hoping would come. He unrolled a large sheet of papyrus upon which he had drawn a rough map of the entire surrounding area. His friend Khalith held it up so that all could see.

"As you can see," Salmon pointed out, "Urusalim lies to the southeast here. The city of the Jebusites is the strongest center in Canaan. It is set upon a high, rolling hill, and the walls are very thick."

"The walls of Ai were thick too," Joshua reminded him genially, "but they have been destroyed."

"Urusalim is partially defended by Egyptian troops, too," one of the captains interposed. "I say choose a lesser target and avoid the wrath of Pharaoh."

"And I," echoed a dozen voices.

"What about the Hivite cities?" someone asked.

"The cities of the Hivites lie north of Urusalim." Salmon pointed them out on his map. "Gibeon and Beeroth are the largest and strongest, Chephirah and Kirjath-jearim smaller and weaker."

"Why not go against them?" one of the captains inquired.

"The Hivites govern themselves by a council as we do, and have no king," Salmon explained. "The four cities are bound by a tight alliance, and to attack one is to attack all. Besides"—he pointed out on the map—"to reach the smaller Hivite centers, we would have to pass the larger ones. They will certainly attack us on the flank as soon as our purpose is evident."

"Have they as many men as we have, taken together?" Joshua asked.

"I can judge only by the talk of the people I treated as a physician," Salmon told him. "But I would say they equal us in numbers at least, or perhaps exceed us. And they have the advantage of strong walls from which to fight off our attack."

"After Ai," Caleb observed, "I doubt if any of the Canaanites will leave their walls to fight against us again."

"What do you advise then?" Joshua asked.

"If we move against Urusalim," Salmon pointed out, "the Hivites will be upon our flank. If we attack one of their cities, the others will come to their defense, and Adoni-zedek, the King of Urusalim, could then attack us from the rear. He might even use troops from some of the cities to the south of him, such as Hebron, Jarmuth, Lachish, and Eglon. In Urusalim I was told that these cities are more directly under the control of Pharaoh than any others in Canaan, and the Egyptian officers in their garrisons might persuade them to make an alliance against us."

Joshua's laugh boomed out confidently. "To hear you tell

it, Salmon, we are bottled up here, with no place to go except back across the Jord."

There was general laughter at the sally, but Salmon did not let it disturb him. He knew that what he planned to propose must be approached in a roundabout fashion if it was to have any hope at all of success.

"The northern part of Canaan contains some of the best land for grazing and farming in the whole country and is poorly defended as well," he continued. "It may have been too risky, before we conquered Jericho, to move north upon Shechem and the towns beside the Sea of Chinnereth, as I once proposed. But with both Jericho and Ai destroyed, the route lies open to us. We could march through Ai, turn northward to Shechem, and be in the upland country given to our forefathers by Yahweh. Between Shechem and the north of Canaan there are no cities as large as Ai."

Joshua was studying the map, his lips pursed in thought. "That means leaving Bethel and the Hivite cities on our flank. What of them?"

"Bethel is of no importance," Salmon said. "It would fall to a siege in a week."

"And the Hivite cities?"

"I propose that we make a covenant with them, a covenant of peace. If they let us pass to seize the uplands of northern Canaan, where there are pastures for our flocks, fields for the planting of grain, and lakes teeming with fish, we will covenant not to attack them. With the four cities of the Hivites between us and Urusalim, King Adoni-zedek would hardly dare to trouble us."

For a moment there was silence, then everyone started talking at once. The idea of making an alliance with any of the peoples of Canaan had never come up before. And yet, to Salmon's surprise, Joshua did not lash out at him as Salmon had fully expected him to do.

"Silence!" Joshua's stern voice cut through the babble of voices, and a hush fell over the council as he turned back to the map. "Do you have any reason to believe the Hivite cities might seek an alliance with us, Salmon?"

"I have knowledge that King Hazor of Jericho was parleying with them before we attacked."

"Why did they not join him against us then?" Khalith asked.

"Jericho is on a plain and a whole day's march beyond Ai at the edge of the uplands. Would you commit yourself to defend such a city?"

"Salmon is right," Joshua said. "Only a fool would make such an alliance. But what makes you so sure the Hivites would join with us?"

"I have no assurance," Salmon admitted. "But they have no kings to be jealous of each other and they have joined together to keep peace and protect themselves. They would probably be even more anxious to make an alliance with us than we with them and could easily be convinced of the advantages it offers them."

"Convinced?" Joshua's voice hardened. "Then the proposal would have to come from us first?"

"How else could they know we would even consider such an alliance?"

Joshua pounded the table with his fist. "We are conquerors now, and all of Canaan fears us. I will beg no one to make a covenant with us."

"Suppose the proposal came from them?" Salmon suggested.

"We will consider that if it comes." Joshua's face was dark now with anger. "And mind you, Salmon," he warned, "I will have no going behind my back to other people. Do so and the wrath of Yahweh will be loosed upon you by my own hand."

Salmon said no more. He had failed, that was obvious, failed by stumbling over the one insuperable obstacle to any scheme involving overtures by Israel, Joshua's pride.

Three

CHAZAN had been ill for some time, but he had tried to keep going in order not to be a burden upon Rahab at a time when she had enough troubles herself. The trip to Ai, which he undertook without telling anyone how near his strength was to giving way, proved too much for him, however.

Upon his return to Gilgal, the old scribe had been forced to take to his couch. Salmon dosed him with medicines, but both of them knew it was only temporizing. A hardness that grew in size from day to day had seized the old man's belly. With such things a lingering and painful death was the only prospect.

There were only a few scribes in Israel. And since Rahab knew how to read and write, she voluntarily took her father's place, copying the records of each family's share in the loot from the captured cities and keeping a record of the increasing wealth that went to the priests in the name of Yahweh. She was working in the tent headquarters of the army of Israel about a week later, when a group of strangers entered the camp and asked to be taken to Joshua. From this vantage point she saw and heard all that transpired.

The four men seemed to be exhausted, for they staggered as they walked. One of them led a miserable-looking pack ass upon whose back were several bags of provisions and dirty wineskins, their surfaces cracked from the sun and heat. The robes of the travelers were dingy and torn, too, having been crudely patched here and there. Their sandals were worn through in spots, and bloodstains from blistered feet had soaked into the leather.

The sentries brought the newcomers to Joshua. They prostrated themselves in the dirt before him, but Joshua courteously bade them rise and ordered food and wine brought to refresh them.

"We have come from a far country," the oldest of the travelers said. "We beg you to make a covenant with us."

"How can we make a covenant with you?" Joshua demanded suspiciously. "Perhaps you live among us, in one of the nearby cities."

The old man bowed low. "We are your servants," he said. "Do with us as you will."

"Who are you?" Joshua asked. "And where do you come from?"

"Your servants have come from a very poor country," the spokesman assured him. "We have heard a report concerning Yahweh, your god, and all that he did in Egypt. We have heard also what he did to the two kings of the Amorites who were beyond the Jord—Sihon, the King of Heshbon, and Og, King of Bashan."

"Go on," Joshua told him. Some of the suspicion seemed to be leaving his voice.

"Our elders and all the inhabitants of our country said to us, 'Take provisions in your hand for the journey and go to meet them and say to them, *we are your servants; come now, make a covenant with us.*'"

The spokesman for the four took a dingy cloth bag from the back of the ass and dumped the bread it contained upon the ground. "Here is our bread. It was still warm when we took it from our homes as food for the journey. Behold how it is dry and moldy."

Turning to the pack animal once more, he lifted a flabby wineskin from it and traced the cracks in the dried outer surface with his fingernail. When he squeezed the skin it cracked open, spilling the wine into the dirt.

"These wineskins were new when we filled them before coming to you," he said. "Behold they have burst. And you have seen how these garments and shoes of ours are worn out from the very long journey."

It was a convincing story to everyone except Rahab. Without waiting to hear the rest of the account, she hurried off in search of Salmon. He was not in the camp, however, and when she saw Caleb at the edge of the camp, directing the training of some youths in the use of bow and spear, she called to him.

The sturdy old warrior looked up and smiled. "Were I twenty years younger, the sight of you coming toward me would set my heart to pounding, Rahab," he told her.

"I must tell you something," she said quickly. "Where no one else can hear."

"Off with you," Caleb told the men he had been drilling. Then he turned back to Rahab. "Now, what is troubling you, O beautiful one?"

Rahab told him quickly about the four ambassadors and how they had convinced Joshua and the others that they had come from a great distance.

"Why are you so disturbed then?" Caleb asked. "News of our strength is spreading abroad, and people will be coming in from small villages every day now, wanting to make covenants with us. It is a good thing; they can give us information about the larger cities."

"These men did not come from any villages, Caleb. I recognized one of them."

"So?" Caleb was alert now, for he knew Rahab was not one to be disturbed by happenings of no importance. "When did you see him before?"

"In Jericho, discussing an alliance with my master, the King. The men are from Gibeon."

"From Gibeon! Then Salmon was right."

"About what?"

"At the meeting of the council a week ago Salmon advocated making an alliance with the Hivite cities so we could advance into northern Canaan without having to conquer them. He said they were probably more anxious to join with us than we were with them. This proves it."

"Why do these men pretend to be from a far country then? If Israel sent ambassadors to them proposing an alliance, they must know that they would be well received."

"Joshua would not hear of Salmon's suggestion," Caleb explained, "so Israel sent no ambassadors. The son of Nun thinks such a thing could be interpreted as a sign of weakness on his part. He even warned Salmon against trying to arrange an alliance behind his back and threatened him with the wrath of Yahweh."

Rahab caught her breath. "Joshua couldn't blame Salmon because these men came of their own accord, could he?"

"No one can tell what the son of Nun will do any more." Caleb rubbed his chin. "I wonder if he could possibly have sent word to Gibeon himself, without letting anyone else know. It would solve his whole problem." Then he shook his head. "No, Joshua is not that clever."

"Shouldn't I tell Joshua who they are," Rahab asked, "before he makes any covenant with them?"

Caleb shook his head. "Let Joshua alone. It will be a good thing for Israel if he does give these men their covenant. And I want to see his face when I tell him how he let himself be cozened by them." His eyes suddenly brightened. "There is the physician now."

Salmon was returning to camp from one of his daily visits

327

to the small villages and herdsmen's houses in the neighborhood where he helped the sick. When Caleb called to him, he came over to them at once. He listened attentively while Rahab told about the emissaries and her discovery that they were not what they appeared to be. When she finished, he was smiling.

"Their coming is an answer to my prayers," he assured her. "Now Joshua will have no reason not to make the alliance, and Israel will be saved a long, terrible war."

"But if Joshua thinks you or I sent word to Gibeon——"

"How could he? You have been here all the time, and I have been no farther than the surrounding villages." He took her hands. "This is the best thing that could possibly happen, Rahab. If the Hivite cities fear us enough to want to make peace, others will do so too. Then we may be able to find homes in Canaan without any more fighting."

"I hope you are right," Rahab said dubiously. But in her heart she felt the heavy weight of fear hanging over her once more, the sense of impending disaster that had so often in the past warned her of trouble.

Joshua and the elders were eating the symbolic meal of the covenant with the Hivite ambassadors when Rahab returned to the center of the camp with Caleb and Salmon.

"These men are from a far country, Caleb," Joshua called. "They heard of our victories over King Og and King Sihon and came a long distance to make peace with us."

"Have you made the covenant?" Caleb asked.

"We are just now going to swear it. Come and join us."

Rahab looked quickly at Salmon. There was still time to reveal the identity of the strangers, since a covenant was not binding from the ceremonial meal alone. Only the swearing of an oath between the elders of Israel and the ambassadors would make it finally binding upon both parties. But Israel would then be committed to it once and for all, and to break such an oath meant invoking the wrath of Yahweh.

Salmon shook his head, however, and they watched in silence while the ceremonial oath was sworn, binding Israel to its first alliance in Canaan.

For three days Joshua feasted and honored the Hivite ambassadors, still not knowing whence they came. On the third day a caravan driver appeared on the road from Urusalim and stopped as usual to trade with the Israelites, who were now wealthy with booty taken from the cities they had sacked.

Joshua questioned the caravan driver closely about Urusalim and the cities to the west, but the man could give little information that Salmon had not already gained—except to confirm that King Adoni-zedek and the cities to the south of Urusalim were talking of an alliance against the Israelites.

As the caravan driver was leaving the camp, he met the Hivite ambassadors coming to Joshua's tent for another feast. "What are these men doing here?" he asked in amazement. "I thought you Habiru were at war with all of Canaan."

"These are ambassadors from a far country," Joshua explained. "We have made an alliance with them."

The caravan driver's eyebrows rose. "Adoni-zedek would give much to know Israel has joined forces with the Hivites. It is too bad I am traveling the other way."

Angrily Joshua seized the man by his robe. "Why do you lie?" he demanded. "These men came a long distance. We all saw their sandals, their moldy bread, and their cracked and dry wineskins."

"You have been taken in by an old trick," the driver assured him. "I will swear by the altar of Baal and the loins of Ashtarth that these are the leading men of Gibeon and Beeroth. All of them are merchants; I have bought and sold with them many times."

Joshua wheeled upon the ambassadors. "Did you hear what this man says? He claims you are from Gibeon and Beeroth."

"He speaks the truth," the oldest of the ambassadors admitted. "Two of us are from Gibeon and two from Beeroth. We speak for the four cities of the Hivite people."

Word had swept through the camp of the drama taking place before Joshua's tent, and people had already begun to converge upon it from all sides. Joshua paced up and down like a caged lion, but there was little else he could do.

"Be off with you," he shouted to the caravan driver finally, and turned savagely on the four Hivites. "How do I know you are telling the truth?" he demanded. "You lied about the location of your country, and you could be lying now."

"Send an emissary to our cities," the spokesman suggested. "I will give him a letter to the chief of our council. He will tell your representative that we speak for all the Hivites."

For a moment it seemed that Joshua would strike the old man, then he let his arm drop. "Where are Caleb and Khalith?" he demanded.

The two had been standing at the edge of the crowd; now they came forward.

"Take two chariots," Joshua ordered, "and ride to Gibeon with the letter this man will give you. If what he says is true, Khalith can come back at once with the message. Caleb will remain in Gibeon and find out whether the Hivite cities will fight with us against Urusalim and what strength they can muster."

Joshua's lips tightened to a thin line and his eyes swept the crowd. "Someone in Israel sent word to them to come here and trick us," he accused. "I will reward whoever brings proof of it with a hundred shekels of silver." Turning angrily, he entered his tent, leaving the four Hivite ambassadors standing outside.

That night and the following day the whole camp buzzed with this dramatic and exciting turn of events. Most of the people approved of the Hivite alliance, even though Joshua had been inveigled into it by deception. But the few who opposed Joshua—and particularly the families of Judah from which Achan had come—used the occurrence as an excuse to stir up resentment against him. By the middle of the next day a considerable party in opposition to Joshua had arisen, the first time there had been any serious division. They criticized him openly, saying that he had been made a fool of by the Hivite ambassadors and was no longer fit to lead Israel.

As the day wore on, Joshua's rage steadily mounted. He would see no one but remained in his tent, drinking wine and cursing anyone who came near. When Khalith returned in the late afternoon, Joshua summoned the four ambassadors again to his tent.

All the camp had been waiting for Khalith to arrive, and now they gathered to witness the next act in the strange drama. Rahab and Salmon stood together, and as Joshua faced the ambassadors, his face suffused with anger, she shivered and her fingers crept into Salmon's hand.

"I told you there would be trouble when he found he'd been deceived," she whispered. "I'm afraid, Salmon."

"He cannot get out of the alliance," Salmon assured her.

"In the end it will be the best thing that could happen for Israel."

"What do the Hivite leaders say?" Joshua asked Khalith as soon as he stepped down from the chariot. "Did they send these men to make an alliance with us?"

"They sent them," Khalith confirmed. "I bring a letter confirming the treaty of peace." He held out the papyrus roll to Joshua, but the Israelite leader struck it from his hand angrily.

"An alliance gained by stealth is void," he shouted. "Cut off the heads of these spies and send them back to their cities as a warning that Israel wants no help from anyone."

When no one moved to obey him, Joshua's face purpled. "Do I command here?" he demanded. "Or must I call down the wrath of Yahweh upon Israel?"

In the hush following his words, the voice of the high priest was loud and clear from where he stood before the tent housing the sacred Ark of the Covenant.

"You are our leader, Joshua," the old man said. "But we have sworn a covenant with these men in the name of the God of Israel, and now we may not touch them. Let them live, lest the wrath of Yahweh fall upon us because of the oath we swore to them."

One by one the elders spoke in agreement. "Achan's sin over the devoted things brought the wrath of God upon us before Ai," one of them added. "The son of Nun will not wish to bring down the anger of Yahweh upon us again for breaking a sacred oath."

For a moment Salmon was sure Joshua would defy them all, but finally his ingrained obedience to the will of Yahweh —taught to all Israelites as soon as they could listen to their mothers' words—won in the battle with his pride and his anger at having been thwarted by the Hivites.

"Let them live then," he agreed. "I will not let my anger bring a curse upon my people." He wheeled upon the Hivite ambassadors. "Why did you deceive us?" he demanded.

"Because we were told that the Lord your God commanded his servant Moses to give you all the land," said the spokesman. "And to destroy all the inhabitants." He bowed his head. "Behold, we are in your hands, do as it seems right and good in your sight to do to us."

"This is my decision," Joshua told him. "Go tell the men of

331

Gibeon and Beeroth that they shall become hewers of wood and drawers of water for the congregation of Israel and for the altar of the Lord." Turning on his heel, he strode into his tent, closing the flap behind him.

Four

SALMON was greatly elated by the alliance with Gibeon, but Rahab was still oppressed by the sense of foreboding that had troubled her since she had recognized the Hivite ambassadors.

"This is a time for celebration," Salmon chided her as they sat before her tent in the early evening. "We may not have to fight any more. Think what that means."

"Did you see Joshua's face when the high priest kept him from executing the Hivites?" she asked. "This thing is not settled yet, Salmon. Remember what happened to Achan when Joshua was defeated before Ai? Someone always suffers when he is forced to swallow his pride. Who knows that better than I?"

"It was the high priest who kept him from killing the Hivite ambassadors," Salmon reminded her. "Even Joshua can do nothing against him."

"I know." Rahab shivered. "That is why I am concerned."

Salmon squeezed her hand reassuringly. "Go on to bed now. Tomorrow things will look different."

Oddly enough, though, Salmon found that he could not take his own advice. Try as he might to sleep, the picture of Joshua's face in the moment just before he had given way to the high priest and the elders kept coming back to him. If ever he had seen hell pictured in anyone's eyes, it was then, as if Joshua's overweening pride could not let him yield, even to Yahweh himself.

The jingle of military harness brought Salmon's thoughts back to the present. He sat up as someone fumbled at the flap of his tent.

"Salmon." It was Khalith. "Are you asleep?"

"No." Salmon opened the flap and let his friend into the tent. "What is it?" he asked, for Khalith's face was grave. "Are you troubled because you brought news of the Hivite alliance?"

The tall captain shook his head. "Israel should thank you for getting word to them that we were willing to make an alliance if they made the first move."

"I sent no such word."

"Migda says he saw you riding toward Gibeon. He has denounced you to Joshua and claims the reward for evidence that the Hivites had been warned."

"How do you know this?" Salmon asked quickly.

"I just left Joshua's tent. He sent for me and gave me orders to arrest you and Rahab with all her household tomorrow morning. Migda has demanded that you both be brought before the council. He charges you both with seeking to bring Israel into an alliance with Gibeon against Joshua's orders!"

For a moment Salmon could hardly believe he had heard aright. Then a new thought struck him. "Why did Joshua send for you?"

"I don't know," Khalith admitted. "It will not be my turn to command the guard for another week."

Salmon nodded slowly, for the pattern had suddenly fallen into place. "Go to your couch and trouble yourself no more about this," he told Khalith.

"But in the morning——"

"In the morning—if we are here—you can arrest us as Joshua ordered. Do you understand?"

Khalith nodded slowly and turned away. "Go with God, my friend," he said. "May the Lord bless you and keep you."

For a long moment Salmon stood looking at the sleeping camp of Israel. Then he turned and crossed with a resolute stride to Joshua's tent.

"Joshua," he called in a low voice outside the tent. "Joshua! I would speak with you."

"What do you want, Salmon?" The words came from so close beside him that the physician jumped. He turned to see the Israelite leader sitting on a large boulder only a few paces away.

333

"Khalith told me of your plan to arrest Rahab and me in the morning—as you expected him to do."

Joshua did not bother to deny the charge. "I warned you that the wrath of God would fall upon you if you went behind my back to promote an alliance with the Hivites," he said calmly. "Migda has already denounced you."

"Migda is of the family of Zerah. He hates me because I was right about Ai and he was wrong. The Zerahites and all of Judah hate Rahab because she exposed the sin of Achan. Those would be reasons enough for him to lie about us, even if you had not offered a reward."

"It was Yahweh who exposed the sin of Achan," Joshua said heavily.

"Perhaps he did. But you would never have known where to place the blame for your defeat at Ai if Rahab had not told you he had stolen the gold and silver."

"Take care, Salmon," Joshua warned. "I was not to blame for the defeat at Ai. It was the wrath of Yahweh because Achan had taken the dedicated things. The harlot only helped me discover the reason."

"And what of the trumped-up charge that I sent word to the Hivite cities so they would send the ambassadors here?" Salmon demanded. "Don't tell me you believe that."

"If you are guilty, you and the harlot will be destroyed by the wrath of Yahweh," Joshua said calmly.

"With no chance to defend ourselves?"

"You will be heard by the council—if you are here tomorrow morning."

"The council will do as you say. What you are actually doing is destroying us to appease your own pride because of the shame you must feel at being taken in by the Hivites."

When Joshua did not reply at once, Salmon added, "Or were you taken in, Joshua? It could be that you were responsible for their coming here after all."

"You can accuse me before the council if you wish," Joshua said quietly.

"With what chance of success? Caleb could clear me of this charge, but he is in Gibeon. Will you wait until his return before accusing me?"

"You know the law." Joshua's voice was still patient. Not once during this interchange had he shown any sign of anger, which was a strange thing, for he was a man whose passions were never held very well in check. "A man accused of a crime must be brought before the council at once."

"Then why did you tell Khalith to wait until morning to arrest me and Rahab?"

"You have served Israel well, Salmon," Joshua said, still in that even, almost monotonous voice. "We were once comrades—until you sought to direct Israel according to your plans instead of according to the word of Yahweh as revealed to me. It would cause me pain to demand your death before the council. You should thank me for giving you an opportunity to leave before the sun rises."

There was the whole thing, Salmon realized now. From the beginning it had been inevitable that he and Joshua would come to the parting of the ways once he had saved Rahab and brought her into Israel with the boy Jaschar. The matter of the Hivite alliance had only brought matters to a head.

The words of the high priest forbidding him to break the covenant he had sworn must have come as a shock to Joshua. And having been wounded in his most vulnerable spot, he had willingly accepted Migda's accusations as true, for they gave him a scapegoat, as Achan had been. The difference was that Achan had been guilty of the crime of which he had been accused, while Salmon and Rahab were not. But here, too, Joshua's conscience would be clear, for it was Migda who had made the accusation. And it would be Migda's trumped-up charges upon which the council would declare them guilty tomorrow and execute them.

By Joshua's own standards he had done a magnanimous thing in summoning Khalith tonight and giving him the order for the arrest of Salmon and Rahab in the morning rather than immediately—knowing that Khalith was a friend of Salmon's and would tell him, giving them time to leave Israel.

"What of Rahab?" Salmon inquired.

"The anointed of God can have nothing to do with harlots."

"And your son?"

"I have no son."

"I will leave Israel tonight," Salmon told him, "and I will take Rahab and the child so they will trouble you no more.

335

But I suspect you will never know peace, Joshua. You are too much a man, with a man's weaknesses, ever to be the god you think yourself to be. And you are too near godhood ever to be satisfied as a man. I pity you, for I once loved you as a brother."

The still figure upon the boulder did not move as Salmon turned and walked back across the sleeping camp to his tent. Tomorrow—when it was announced in the camp that Salmon, the physician, and Rahab, the harlot, had fled before they could be arrested, thus establishing their guilt—Joshua would have his scapegoat. But Salmon could not help wondering whether someday the Israelite leader would suffer a failure for which there could be no cause save in himself. Then he would be forced to face the denunciation of his own conscience, a voice to which no man can ever shut his ears entirely.

Dawn found a weary caravan winding its way toward the springs beyond Jericho on the northern route to Ai. Salmon walked at the head of the little procession; Chazan, pale and drawn with pain, rode upon an ass beside him. Two more of the patient beasts carried their possessions; Rahab's belongings were strapped to the back of one of them and Salmon's medical supplies were on the other, with little Jaschar snugly nested in blankets on top of them. Rahab walked beside one of the asses, Myrnah beside the other. Senu brought up the rear of the procession, trotting nimbly along on his short, stubby legs and carrying a long-handled spear with great pride.

None of them had questioned Salmon's decision when he awakened them at midnight to announce that they must leave Israel at once. There had been little opportunity for talk on the road, save for a brief account of what Khalith had told him the night before. Perturbed as Rahab had been by the task of moving her household from the camp in the middle of the night, she could not fail to notice that none of the guards challenged them, proof in itself that Joshua had made no objection to their going.

In the late afternoon they made camp in a small glen where a spring gave an ample water supply, and they were protected against the storms that sometimes lashed this upland country with terrible fury. Everyone was busy setting up the two goatskin tents and staking out the asses to graze on the thick grass in the glen. Senu proved adept with the sling, and two fat birds were soon roasting on a spit over a bed of coals.

Altogether it was not an unhappy group who ate the evening meal around the campfire and settled down for the night. Salmon propped himself against a stump close to the fire for protection against the chill of the night, having given his blankets to Chazan, who had been taken with a chill. He was not surprised when Rahab came over and sat on a flat stone beside him.

"I looked back several times today," she said, "but saw no sign of pursuit."

"They will not come after us."

"For the same reason that the guards did not stop us last night?"

He nodded. "Joshua sent Khalith to warn me—we would have been arrested this morning if we had remained in the camp."

"Why would he order our arrest and still warn you so we could escape?"

"After yesterday, Joshua needed someone he could blame for the coming of the ambassadors from Gibeon and Beeroth."

"Do you think they really fooled him?"

"My guess would be that he believed they came from a distant country," he said. "But you heard the talk in the camp yesterday against him, especially from the tribe of Judah."

"Why wouldn't he just admit that he was deceived? That is what you would have done."

"To the people who follow Joshua in Israel, he is the anointed of Yahweh, sent to restore the land of Canaan to its rightful owners. But Joshua is also a man. If much of Israel should turn against him, his downfall could be just as swift as his rise. I think I understand him better now than I ever did before, Rahab."

"Don't you feel any bitterness at all toward him?" she asked in amazement.

"No. Joshua is—Joshua. He cannot act in any way except

337

the way he does act. So far it has been best for Israel; even you must admit that."

Rahab touched his hand, and when he took her fingers in his she let them lie warm and serene within his grasp. "What are we going to do now, Salmon?" she asked. "Father cannot go on much longer."

"I was hoping we could head north from Ai and strike the road leading to Shechem," he told her. "But Chazan could never last through the trip."

"Why don't you just leave us behind? We have been nothing but trouble for you since you found us in Jericho."

He lifted her hand to his lips and kissed her fingers gently. "You know the answer to that. I have loved you since the day I first saw you on Mount Nebo—with no eyes for anyone save Joshua."

"How could you love me when I've been such a fool?"

"You brought me the joy of knowing you needed me and that I was able to help you. If you truly love another person, Rahab, nothing brings more happiness than that."

She leaned over and kissed him on the lips for the first time. Her mouth was warm on his—and utterly trusting. "We are all in your hands now, dearest Salmon," she said softly. "What do we do next?"

"From Ai a road leads past Bethel to Beeroth and then to Gibeon," he told her. "In two days' journey we should be able to skirt around Beeroth and reach Gibeon safely. Do you think your friend Jochab would give us shelter there?"

"I know he will," Rahab said quickly. "Especially since there is peace between Israel and the Hivite cities."

"We will go that way then."

"And afterward?"

"Every man has his dream, Rahab. Mine is still of a house overlooking the Sea of Chinnereth, with you and little Jaschar there beside me."

For a long moment Rahab did not speak. When she did, her voice was soft and warm, with a new note in it he had not heard before. "I never saw that vision of yours very well before, Salmon," she admitted. "But it is much clearer now. Give me time, and someday I will see it as you do."

Two days later, when the sun hung low over the hills behind them, they looked down upon the city of Gibeon, be-

338

hind its thick walls, from a turn of the road that wound down the mountain ridge to the east of the city. And where they had expected to find refuge and an end, for a while, to their travels, they saw instead something that filled them once again with dread.

A great army was encamped around the Hivite capital, obviously holding it under siege. They needed only to see the flash of gold from the crested helmets of the captains commanding the mercenary bands that helped swell its numbers to know that Egypt had at last risen against Israel by attacking its newest allies, the Hivites. Adoni-zedek, the King of Urusalim, Salmon knew at once, had finally succeeded in allying the kings to the south in a massive attack upon the Hivite stronghold to punish Gibeon for its covenant with an enemy.

Five

LEAVING MYRNAH with the baby, Rahab hurried up to where Salmon stood beside the path, looking down at the spectacular scene below them.

"Those look like Egyptian troops," she said. "I can recognize the golden crests on the officers' helmets."

"They are only mercenaries with Egyptian officers," he explained. "Adoni-zedek and the kings near him are attacking Gibeon. No one else in this area has that many mercenaries."

"Because the Gibeonites made an alliance with Israel?"

"Yes. Together, the Hivites and our warriors would make an army larger than any in Canaan. Adoni-zedek has evidently decided to destroy the Hivites first and prevent the two forces from joining together."

"Shouldn't we go back then?"

He shook his head. "We were lucky to get this far. Evidently the siege has just begun, but they will have men posted along all the roads by now to give warning in case Israel tries to come to the rescue."

"Then we are trapped?"

Salmon looked around him speculatively. The narrow track they were following was not a main road but a hill path he had chosen because it led around Beeroth so they could approach Gibeon first from the northern slopes above the city. Only that had saved them, it was obvious now, for had they come by the main roads which entered Gibeon from the south, they would have walked into the very midst of the besieging army.

The hillside, like most in that region, was very rocky and pocked here and there by caves. Their best chance of keeping clear of the conflict below, Salmon saw at once, lay in using one of these as a hiding place from which to observe the coming battle. Until that was decided, they hardly dared move in any direction.

"We are not trapped—yet," he assured Rahab. "Stay here while I look for a cave large enough to hide us."

Luckily Salmon found one only a few hundred paces away from the path they were traveling and slightly above it. Its mouth was hidden by a heavy growth of trees, so they could safely light a cooking fire. They led the animals up the hillside and tethered them to trees where they could graze. Then Salmon lifted Chazan, pitifully thin now from his illness, and carried him into the cave to a bed of goatskins.

"We must get word to Israel of the attack on Gibeon," he told Rahab as they came out of the cave.

"Even after what Joshua did to us?"

"It is Israel that is important now, not Joshua. If Adonizedek is victorious here, he will move on against our own people. His army is already larger than ours."

"Will you have to go?" she asked quickly.

Salmon shook his head. "I will not leave you again. Senu can take one of the animals and ride to Gilgal over the back trails. There are papyrus rolls and ink in my medical supplies. I will send a letter to Joshua describing the situation here."

Salmon hurriedly wrote a brief account of what they had seen below them, with a rough estimate of the number of the besiegers and the fact that they included Egyptian mercenaries. By the time he had finished, the small black coachman was already astride one of the asses, with a hunk of bread in his hand and a small skin of wine slung over his shoulder. He put the small papyrus roll inside his robe and

340

listened with bright, intelligent eyes to Salmon's instructions. Then, nodding his understanding, he turned the animal down the hillside and went trotting eastward along the path.

Five hours at most would bring Senu to Gilgal, Salmon calculated, well before midnight. But it hardly seemed likely that Joshua could get his troops ready to march before morning, since he would need every man who could bear a weapon in this, the most important battle they would have to fight in Canaan.

Using only a small fire so the smoke would not attract attention to their presence, Myrnah cooked the evening meal. They ate it huddled at the mouth of the cave while below them the fires of the vast army winked into being one by one as darkness fell. In the besieged city of Gibeon, the lights of torches could be plainly seen as the defenders moved along the walls.

Nothing happened that night, except that Chazan was obviously weaker with the coming of morning, a weakness that could only mean impending death. Shortly after they had eaten a frugal meal of bread and cold meat, Chazan called to Rahab and she went into the cave. While she was gone Salmon led the remaining two asses down the hill to a small stream that leaped from rock to rock and watered them. Rahab was standing outside the cave when he returned, and he saw that she had been weeping.

"My father wishes to speak to us together," she told him.

Salmon took the hand she held out to him and they went inside the cave. It was cool here where the bright spring sun did not penetrate. Chazan lay propped up on a pile of dirt covered with goatskin. His face was like marble, and the light—what there was of it—seemed to pass through his skin, so thin and pale had he become.

"Salmon, my son," the old scribe said in a low voice, "I am dying."

Salmon did not try to keep the truth from him; there seemed to be no point in denying what they had all known for days now. "Yes, Chazan," he said. "Our god will soon take you to himself."

"I have tried to live by the principles and teachings of Yah," the old man said. "The pain grows worse each day, and death to such as me becomes a blessing."

341

"I have a little medicine left," Salmon offered. "It would ease the pain somewhat."

Chazan shook his head. "Later. A task must be done now, and nothing must cloud my senses. When it is finished I can die in peace." He paused a moment while his face was contorted by a spasm of pain. "Do you love my daughter Rahab?"

"You know the answer to that," Salmon said simply.

"Enough to cling only to her, for as long as you both shall live?"

"There has been no other since the day I first saw her."

Chazan turned to Rahab. "And you, Rahab? Will you cling only to Salmon from this day on?"

"I will, Father," she said softly, the tears rolling down her cheeks.

Chazan lay back on the improvised bed, obviously exhausted even by this small effort, but with a look of great happiness on his face. "I could not let myself die until I knew you two were wed and Rahab was safe with someone to care for her," he said in a whisper. "If—if you will give me the bride price now, Salmon, it will be finished."

Salmon detached the money pouch that hung at his belt. It was not very heavy. "All that I have I give thee, Chazan, as the bride price for your daughter Rahab." He spoke in the formal language of the marriage ceremony. Then he added, "Were this all the wealth of Egypt, it would still not be enough for her."

"No one can give more than all he possesses," Rahab said softly. "A love like yours, Salmon, is the greatest treasure any man could bring as the bride price."

"Take this gold, Rahab," Chazan whispered. "As you take the physician Salmon to be your husband."

"I take this gold," Rahab said quietly, and lifted the pouch from Chazan's fingers. "And I take the physician Salmon to be my husband, just as I give it with all I possess to him." She placed the purse in Salmon's hand and, taking him by the shoulders, leaned forward and kissed him on the lips, a gentle kiss, without passion, that told him nevertheless the fullness of her love and her trust in him.

"Now I can die in peace," Chazan said with a sigh. "If you have any poppy leaves, Salmon, I will swallow a dose, for the pain is hard to bear."

342

While Salmon mixed a draught and gave it to the old scribe, Rahab went out of the cave. When he came outside, Myrnah told him that she had gone down to the spring for water. Taking up an empty skin and a cup with which to fill it, he went down the hillside to where he could see Rahab kneeling beside the stream, with the sunlight glinting through the leaves and turning her hair into a crown of gold.

She looked up as he knelt beside her and he saw that she had been washing the tears from her cheeks in the cool running water. "They say all brides weep on their wedding day, Salmon," she said with a smile. "Perhaps that is a good omen for us."

With the loose fold of his sleeve he gently wiped the water from her cheeks. "We will be happy, my dear," he assured her. "Trust me in that, too, and I know it will come true."

She looked down at the running water, and her fingers tightened upon his. "I—I don't think it will be much longer until I can come to you as a wife should and share your couch, Salmon. Bear with me, please, until then."

Six

ON THE PLAIN outside the city of Gibeon below them, the siege continued without any let-up, but to Salmon's surprise, the Jebusites and their allies did not seem disposed to attack at once. The only explanation he could see was that they must be waiting for more troops to arrive. This was confirmed in the afternoon when a column of men approached from the south and marched into the camp below Gibeon.

It was a little over an hour before sunset when Rahab, who was at the stream with Myrnah washing clothes, reported the sound of hoofs on the path below them. Shortly, Khalith rode into view upon an ass, with Senu following. Salmon hurried to greet his friend and led him up the hillside to the cave.

From the vantage point of a craggy outcrop some distance from the cave, Khalith carefully studied the vast array of troops and equipment on the plain before Gibeon. When he turned back to where Rahab and Salmon waited before the cave, his face was grave. "They outnumber Israel," he said. "Gibeon will be lost without help."

"Is Joshua coming?" Rahab asked.

"He is marching with our whole army tonight." Khalith looked up at the sun. "They will already be on the road by now."

"I was sure Joshua would come to Gibeon's aid when he learned that it was being attacked," Salmon said.

"He had no choice," said Khalith. "An emissary arrived from Gibeon early this morning, demanding that we come to their aid. Joshua could not refuse because of the oath sworn by him and the elders to the ambassadors of the Hivites."

"But the enemy will be warned," Rahab said quickly. "They must have outposts along all the roads."

"Senu and I saw some, but he led me around them," said Khalith. "Joshua will be traveling by night, and I am going back to warn him where the outposts are located. Then we can slip upon them by stealth and kill them so the enemy will have no warning of our coming until we attack at dawn."

"It will be a great battle," Salmon said. "If Israel can destroy that army down there tomorrow, the whole of Canaan will lie open before them."

"Before us," Khalith corrected him. "You are still a part of Israel, Salmon."

"We fled the camp, remember? You had been ordered to arrest us the next morning."

"The order was never issued."

"But when Migda denounced us to the council for sending word to the Hivites——"

"Migda did not denounce you."

Salmon stared at him for a long moment. "Are you sure, Khalith?"

"Joshua sent word to me early in the morning to say nothing of the order. I spread word abroad in the camp that you had left in the night to take Chazan to a healing spring on the shores of the Sea of Chinnereth."

"What made Joshua change his mind?" Rahab asked.

Khalith shook his head. "Who knows what Joshua will do?"

Salmon thought he knew the answer. The Israelite leader's

344

dormant conscience must have finally been stirred by his words that night before they had left. At the same time, the fact that they could return to Israel now if they chose might make a difference in the relationship between him and Rahab, even though they were married.

Chazan slept through the day after the potion Salmon had given him. That night, however, he was delirious with the approach of death, and Rahab and Salmon took turns watching beside his couch. Salmon was asleep just outside the mouth of the cave in the early hours of the morning when Rahab awakened him.

"I heard men moving below us," she whispered. "One of them spoke just now and it sounded like our own tongue."

Salmon was instantly alert. "It must be our soldiers moving into position," he said. "Khalith was going to recommend to Joshua that the attack be launched from the slopes of this hill."

"Shouldn't we go down and find out?"

"If those are our own people, we are safe," he told her. "If not, they still may not know we are here."

"I'm afraid, Salmon." Rahab clung to him suddenly. "Something is wrong; I can feel such things."

"It is always like this before a battle," he assured her. "Everyone is afraid then. But once it begins, you forget fear, in the excitement."

"This is something else." She moved closer to him. "Hold me in your arms for a moment."

She was trembling when he took her in his arms and clung to him tightly with her face buried against his breast. Below them an occasional sound broke the silence, enough to tell Salmon that a body of men was moving into position under cover of darkness there on the hillside. He thought they were the troops of Israel, but he could not be certain until two men climbed the hillside from the path below. One was Joshua, in full military gear, the other a captain serving as his aide.

Rahab heard the jingle of harness and moved out of Salmon's arms. When the faint light from the coals of the cooking fire revealed Joshua's face to her, she gasped with surprise and put her hand on Salmon's sleeve as if for reassurance.

345

"You are welcome, Joshua," Salmon said quietly. "What brings you to our camp?"

The Israelite leader looked out across the black void hiding the great army of the Jebusite alliance and the besieged city of Gibeon, with the warriors of Israel facing them in the darkness. "When the sun rises," he said, "I must lead Israel in its greatest battle. It is not right that a man should go to what may be his death without seeing the face of his son."

"Then you have acknowledged him at last?" Rahab asked quickly.

"Bring the child," Joshua told her, "that I may look upon him."

Rahab hurried into the mouth of the cave and brought out a blanket-wrapped bundle. She stood before Joshua and laid aside the covers, revealing the baby's face.

"Stir up the fire there," Joshua commanded, "so I may have light."

Salmon threw some dry sticks on the coals of the cooking fire, making it blaze up, as Rahab knelt with Jaschar in her arms so the light would fall on his face. Standing beside her, Salmon looked down at the small, dark head and beautiful face of the sleeping baby, then up at the features of its father, and felt a chill settle upon his heart. Except for the difference in size, they were the same. No one, not even Joshua himself, could look upon the face of the baby and not know he was its father.

For a long moment Joshua studied the sleeping child with no change in his face, no sign of recognition. But when he spoke, his voice was strangely gentle. "Turn him over," he told Rahab. "Let me see the marks upon his shoulders."

Rahab did as she was bid, exposing Jaschar's sturdy shoulders and back with the small pits of the inherited marks over the shoulder blades. "See," she said then. "The marks are the same. You cannot doubt any longer that he is your son."

"Let me see the foot."

"No!" Rahab cried. Instinctively she held the baby close, as if to protect him from some unseen danger.

"Let me see it," Joshua repeated.

When she did not move, Salmon said quietly, "It is his right, Rahab. Let him see the foot."

346

She unwrapped the baby then but held him tightly to her with that odd protective gesture, as if Joshua's presence were a threat. The cool air on his skin awakened Jaschar and he started to cry. Salmon saw Joshua's hand clench suddenly at the sight of the pitifully twisted foot and felt a stab of pity for him. To Joshua, who was himself perfect physically, this deformity in the child who was otherwise a perfect copy of himself must have been a terrible blow.

"The Lord has punished me for my sins," Joshua said harshly. The pain in his voice was so great that Salmon knew anyone less strong than Joshua would have broken in a sob. "Cover the child," he ordered, and turned away.

"Do you acknowledge him as your son now?" Rahab asked a second time.

Joshua nodded. "When the battle is over, return the child to Gilgal. Henceforth he shall be known in Israel as Jaschar, the son of Joshua."

No one spoke until Salmon asked, "What of his mother?"

"She may come if she wishes and care for the child," Joshua said. "But no harlot shall dwell in my household." He turned to the captain. "Send soldiers to guard my son until the battle is over."

Rahab and Salmon watched while the tall, handsome figure was swallowed up in the night, then she turned wide-eyed to Salmon. "He almost wept when he saw the baby's twisted foot," she said in an awed voice. "I never knew Joshua could weep."

"Perhaps we saw the man Joshua for the first time tonight," Salmon said slowly. "A man who has finally realized he cannot be a god."

Half blinded by tears that he did not want Rahab to see, Salmon stumbled to where the pack containing his medicinal supplies had been placed under a tree. With fumbling fingers he began to knot the ropes again, preparatory to lashing the pack upon the back of an ass. Rahab had gone into the cave to put Jaschar back in his crib. She soon came out and he felt her hand on the ropes beside him. "What are you doing, Salmon?" she asked in a low voice.

"Israel is going into battle. She will need every man's skill today—even that of a physician."

Silently she helped him lash the pack and lift it to the

347

back of the pack ass. Only when he was leaving did she lift her lips to his. "God bless you and keep you, my husband," she said then, "until the time when I can come to you."

Both of them knew what she meant. By acknowledging Jaschar as his son at last, Joshua had bound Rahab to him once again with a tie that was stronger now than at any time since that day when she had come happily down the slopes of Mount Nebo bearing the bride price that would have made her his wife.

Seven

MINSTRELS and poets have sung of the day when the armies of Israel came to the aid of their sworn allies, the Hivites of Gibeon, besieged by the combined forces of five kings and an army whose like was never seen before or since in the land of Canaan. They tell how Joshua, the son of Nun, led his forces from the darkness of the hillside of Gibeon in the early dawn, led them in a great charge upon the only half-awakened camp of the Jebusites, spitting thousands of the enemy upon sharp spear points before they even had a chance to seize their weapons.

The poets sing, too, of the great storm that rose to the west when the forces of Adoni-zedek sought to escape the onslaught of a victorious Israel by way of Beth-horon and the Valley of Ajalon, only to be turned back by an avalanche of hailstones from the sky. Some even claim that more of the Jebusites died from the hail than from the spears, knives, arrows, and swords of Israel. All account it the great victory that it was on that day when the Lord God of Israel gave to the sword of Joshua a power never before seen, so that he fought as a hundred men and none could stand against him.

No minstrel sings of what happened on the hillside overlooking Gibeon, however. For that was a small affair, involving only the household of Rahab, the harlot of Jericho, the two soldiers of Israel sent by Joshua to guard his son, and a pair of Egyptian mercenaries bent on saving their own lives now that the battle on the plains below was already lost.

Salmon, his hands and arms red to the elbows with the blood of the wounded who poured to the spot beside a spring at the foot of the mountain where he had set up his equipment, heard of the trouble at the cave when Senu, with blood streaming down his face from a cut on his head and tears pouring from his eyes, brought the news that of those he had left on the hillside that morning only Rahab and the child were alive—and Jaschar so badly hurt that he must already be dead.

The story, as Salmon pieced it together from Senu's babbled account while he quickly wound a cloth around the dwarf's head to stop the bleeding, was simple. They had all been watching eagerly the great victory being written for Israel below them when two Egyptian mercenaries, fleeing from the battlefield, had burst upon the camp from behind the rocks. Myrnah had been bringing water up the hill from the stream below and was killed with a single spear thrust. Her dying scream had warned the others, or all of them would have been killed with no chance to defend themselves.

The two Israelite guards had fought bravely, killing one of the mercenaries but losing their own lives in the first encounter. Senu had bravely tried to stop the other mercenary, a giant Sherdan, but both he and Rahab had been knocked down by the slashing swing of a spear shaft that had also laid the dwarf's head open. Charging on into the cave, the mercenary had not deemed the child worthy of a spear thrust and had smashed its head with the butt of the handle before turning to stab Chazan, mercifully, with the point.

Only one thing had saved any of them in that brief orgy of bloodshed upon the mountainside, the fact that the murderous spear had stuck momentarily in Chazan's body, affording time for Rahab, bearing a spear she had wrested from the dying hands of the first mercenary, to plunge it into the second one's back. She had shouted to Senu to run for Salmon, while she gathered up the baby.

As to Jaschar's condition, Senu knew only that he had heard the child cry as he started down the mountainside and that it was therefore alive. But having witnessed the vicious bludgeoning the Sherdan had given the sleeping baby, Senu was sure that Jaschar must be gravely wounded or, more probably, already dead.

While Senu was finishing his account, Salmon had been tossing instruments, bandages, and medicines into a goatskin bag. As he swung this over his shoulder, he turned back to the black hunchback. "Go find Joshua," he directed. "Tell him his son is gravely wounded and to come as quickly as he can."

Salmon found Rahab sitting in the mouth of the cave, crooning to the child. She looked up at him with pain-dulled eyes when he stooped to take the baby, still wrapped in its blankets, from her arms.

"It is Salmon, Rahab," he said gently, knowing that she was in a state almost of trance from the shock of what she had experienced. "Let me see if I can help him."

"Jaschar is dead, Salmon," she repeated dully. "The soldier killed him."

"Let me look at him, please," he begged. "Perhaps I can do something."

She let him take the child from her and lay it on a folded goatskin where he could unwrap the coverings. The evidence of the brief moment of violence that had raged here was all around them. The bodies of the two Israelites and the Sherdan they had killed were sprawled at the edge of the open space before the cave. Farther down the slope, almost at the spring, Myrnah's body was stretched out on the ground. The cave itself reeked with the sticky sweet smell of blood and death from where the second mercenary lay across Chazan's body, with the point of the spear Rahab had used to kill him still embedded in his back.

Gently Salmon parted the blankets in which Jaschar was wrapped. They were stained with blood, and he saw a bloodstain on Rahab's breast where she had held the child against her. There was only one wound, however—a deep gash above the baby's left ear, from which blood was still oozing.

"Is he dead?" Rahab asked, and Salmon saw that she was already regaining control of herself.

"He still breathes, so it may be only a wound of the scalp." But he said that only to give her hope, for his trained senses had already noted several telltale signs indicating that this was far worse than a mere scalp wound.

The limpness of the child's body, even though the only injury seemed to be on his head; the shallow, sighing breath-

350

ing; the oddly slow pounding of Jaschar's heart when Salmon put his hand over the child's chest to feel it—all of these fitted a pattern Salmon had read about in the papyrus rolls he had studied in Egypt at the Temple of Thoth, god of healing.

The accounts dated back as much as a thousand years, it was said, and had been compiled by wise old physicians who had observed cases like this. Some had even dared to treat them, using the bronze knife to scrape an opening in the bone of the skull. But whatever the method, all agreed that nearly all the victims died.

Salmon had treated successfully a few wounds of this character, sustained in battle during the first disastrous sortie against Heshbon. But though none had been accounted more skillful in Tanis and in the Temple of Thoth at Thebes where he had studied than he, he knew that the chances for a baby with such an injury were very small indeed.

Gently the physician ran his fingers along the edge of the cut over Jaschar's temple, noting how the skull seemed depressed, just as he had expected it to be from the symptoms. Even from so brief an examination, there could be little question about what had happened. The butt end of the spear handle, driven directly down upon the helpless child's head, had burst the skin by pressure alone. Then it had gone on to break a circular piece of bone from the skull itself, driving it down upon the soft brain beneath.

Rahab reached down and took the tiny fingers of Jaschar's hand in hers. When they did not curl about her finger as they usually did, she lifted her eyes to Salmon's.

"Tell me the truth," she said. "It is worse than just a cut, isn't it?"

"The skull is broken," he admitted. "A piece of bone has been driven down upon the brain."

"Is that why he is so limp?"

"Yes. Egyptian physicians described the effects of such a wound many hundreds of years ago."

"I think I knew when Myrnah brought him to me the first time that Jaschar would never grow to be a man," she said quietly. "But I hoped that if Joshua acknowledged him as his son people would overlook his foot. Now I know that Jaschar

351

would always have been ashamed of not being perfect like his father."

"Joshua has accepted him as his son," Salmon reminded her.

"We cannot break the laws of Yah and not suffer, Salmon. Joshua and I sinned together; now Yah has taken the baby to punish us."

"Sometimes cases like this can be saved by cutting away the bone."

"Even as badly injured as he is?"

"It is a faint hope, but there is a chance. I wanted to wait until Joshua came before suggesting it. But time is more important than anything else now."

"I have no right to ask you to do it," she said. "If Jaschar lives, Joshua will take him and I must go wherever my child goes."

"Even if it meant losing my own life," he said quietly, "I would still do what I could as a physician to save the child."

She nodded slowly. "If only all men were like you, Salmon, there would be no such thing as unhappiness. I give Jaschar's life into your hands."

Quickly Salmon laid out his tools on a clean cloth, while Rahab placed Jaschar on a flat rock in the sunlight. Fortunately there was no need to cut the skin more than it was already cut. Separating the edges of the wound with a thumb and forefinger of his left hand, he cleaned away the blood from its depths. In the bone thus exposed the curved line of the break was easily visible.

On one side of the line marking the injured area the contours of the bone were normal. But on the other a section of the skull had been driven down for a depth equaling the width of his thumb, a severe wound indeed for a grown man —and almost certainly a fatal one for a mere baby. Blood was oozing from the jagged edge of the bone, but so slowly as not to obscure the field in which he planned to work, proof in itself that life was ebbing away.

Using the broad-bladed knife he had bought from the Babylonian caravan—the one he had first shown to Rahab in the Cave of Yah on Mount Nebo, Salmon began to shave away at the bone on the upper side of the crack. Although this part was not pressing upon the brain, he must first make

352

an opening here to insert the slender instrument of bronze he had used to pry the arrowhead from Joshua's back that afternoon in the Cave of Yah when he had first seen Rahab. Only when he had succeeded in doing this could he pry up the depressed section of bone.

Working slowly, intent upon the delicate task of scraping an opening in the injured baby's skull, Salmon did not even notice when a chariot stopped on the road just below the cave and Joshua came up the hillside, with little Senu following him. Only when Salmon put down the scraping tool used in trepanning—as this procedure was called—did he notice Joshua kneeling beside Rahab just across from him, watching as he worked.

"I am trying to raise a piece of bone pressing on the baby's brain," he explained to the Israelite captain.

"Is there any hope?" Joshua asked in a strangely gentle voice.

"Only a little. It is a very grave injury."

He was through the skull now. Taking up the slender tool, he gently levered the flattened end beneath the depressed side of the bone and applied pressure to it. At first nothing happened, then suddenly there was a cracking sound and the depressed section broke in two pieces. With his fingers Salmon gently worked one side of it loose and lifted it from the wound, then treated the other in the same way. There was hardly any bleeding now. Gently he placed a clean cloth over the wound and watched the tiny chest for a long moment: When there was no movement, he slowly shook his head.

"I'm sorry, Rahab," he said. "I did what I could."

"I know." The shocked look had gone out of her eyes. "Thank you for trying, Salmon."

From the roadway below came the sudden thud of horses' hoofs and the rumble of chariot wheels.

"Joshua!" Caleb's voice floated up to them. "The Jebusites are fleeing toward the Valley of Ajalon. I have led the soldiers of Gibeon from the city. If we strike now, we can destroy them."

"I am coming." Joshua got to his feet, but still looked down at the body of his son, making no immediate move to depart.

"Hurry!" Caleb called anxiously. "The sun is going down.

353

We will not have time to destroy them before darkness falls."

"We will have time," Joshua said, as if there were not the least doubt in his mind about it. He turned to Salmon and Rahab then. "Forgive me, please, Salmon," he said slowly. "And you, Rahab. I have sinned grievously against you both and against the Lord. It is meet that Yahweh should punish me, but not that I should bring sorrow upon you for my sins."

"The leader of Israel and the chosen of Yahweh needs no forgiveness from me," Salmon said simply. "You must do what you must do."

"Nor from me," Rahab added. "My sin was as great as yours."

"The record is made clean again then," Joshua said. "A man can give no greater offering in recompense for his sins than the life of his first-born son."

Standing close together, Rahab and Salmon watched Joshua stride down the hillside and leap into the chariot. The rumble of its wheels was like thunder on the mountainside as it rolled away. When they could hear it no longer, Salmon spoke gently.

"Come, Rahab," he said. "We must bury our dead and our sorrows. It is a long way to the lake called Chinnereth."

"Israel still needs you. And so does Joshua."

"After today's victory no one will be able to stand against Israel," he assured her. "Joshua needs only himself now—and Yahweh. Listen."

From somewhere below them a great but familiar voice rolled across the valley, drowning out even the noises of battle. Looking toward the now safe city of the Hivites, they saw Joshua standing, a majestic and godly figure, upon a rocky outcrop looming above the plain. His arms were uplifted to heaven and his words floated across the hot spring air to them:

"Sun, stand thou still upon Gibeon; and thou, Moon, in the valley of Ajalon."

And the sun stood still, and the moon stayed, until the people had avenged themselves upon their enemies.

JOSHUA 10:13

354

HAROLD ROBBINS
THE ADVENTURERS

78014/$1.25

Another engrossing chapter in the
continuing story of the town
made famous by the best-selling
novels of GRACE METALIOUS

Secrets
of
Peyton
Place

by ROGER FULLER

75285/75¢
Other titles:

PUBLISHED BY
POCKET BOOKS
A 9/0